THE SENTENCE

GAUTAM BHATIA

THE SENTENCE

Published by Westland Books, a division of Nasadiya Technologies Private Limited, in 2024

No. 269/2B, First Floor, 'Irai Arul', Vimalraj Street, Nethaji Nagar, Alapakkam Main Road, Maduravoyal, Chennai 600095

Westland and the Westland logo are the trademarks of Nasadiya Technologies Private Limited, or its affiliates.

ISBN: 9789360451523

10 9 8 7 6 5 4 3 2 1

This is a work of fiction. Names, characters, organisations, places, events and incidents are either products of the author's imagination or used fictitiously.

Typeset by Mukul

Printed at Thomson Press (India) Ltd

Aux morts de la Commune

Contents

Day Three
The Commune

Day Four
The Zone

Day Five
The Cryochamber

Day Six
The Archive

Day Seven
The Tribunal

Prologue
The Day of the Barricades

LONG AFTER THE REVOLUTION, WHEN RUST had tinted the faces of drowned statues, songs corroded into symbols and memory congealed into memorials, there were some who still came to ask Milana Maran about the day it all began.

Years had passed and the world changed, but they still came: from all over Peruma City, trudging through the rubble of the Bulwark Zone, to the last house on Vashi Street.

They came from the Right Bank, still called High Town, to ask about the chronicle of mistakes that had, on the Day of the Barricades, brought insurrection to their city and left it rent in two.

They came from the Commune, once called Low Town, to understand the facts unvarnished by song, to learn the story of their birth, and to know what really happened the day their revolution triumphed.

Sometimes they even came from elsewhere: from the country, or from the other cities of the subcontinent, where they had had (or hoped to have) their own Days of the Barricades, to ask about beginnings.

Whatever her audience, Milana's telling of it never changed, or so she believed.

It began on the morning that had dawned like any other: a mild sun straggling into the ashen autumn sky; grey clouds impaling themselves upon the tips of High Town's towers; weak rivulets of light streaming onto the manicured lawn centred within the many-pillared courtyard of the director's compound.

Amidst a row of parked skimmers, Milana Maran, secretary to the director, stood waiting. On either side, the Directorate's white sea-stone buildings rose into turrets that curved inwards, shredding the sky. Beneath her feet, the grass was springy. Autumn dew seeped into her sandals.

She heard his steps before she saw him emerge into the courtyard, dressed for the occasion: black achkan embellished with gold foil, complete with the gold tiger brooch of his office neatly affixed to his chest.

'You're alone,' she said.

Director Purul approached her, running his right hand through his jet-black hair, messing up the careful parting; a darting, scratchy movement she'd come to know well over the past two years. 'As we decided.' He gave her the ghost of a smile. 'How do I look?'

She glanced at him, mock-appraising. 'Imperial.'

'Not the style we should be invoking today, don't you think?'

'Just teasing,' she grinned. 'No, Director—you look ready.'

Purul nodded. 'Shall we?'

'Before that—there's something you need to know,' she said, sobering. 'I received a report from the switchback half an hour ago. One of the mandalium mines was flooded overnight.'

'Which one?'

'A-241.'

'*Bloody*—how bad is it?'

'They're pumping out the water, but ... it's bad, Director. By the time it's functional again—'

'Commission a report on the revenue loss, and—accident or sabotage?'

'The miners working the night shift just happened to be absent when the water came in. Wildcat strike, they claimed.'

Director Purul closed his eyes. When he opened them again, she saw his gaze turn to the transparent binder clutched in his left hand. Two pages lay within, filled with dense, hurried handwriting, words crossed out and rewritten—red-inked editorial corrections—and marked all over with smudgy fingerprints.

'We're still doing this?' Milana said.

After a moment, Purul nodded.

'The Council will accuse you of weakness, especially now.'

'They will do that anyway,' he said. 'Probably moving a resolution as we speak.'

But his eyes were unfocused, staring at something far away, beyond the courtyard, beyond the northern periphery of Peruma—at the slopes of the switchback, where the beating heart of the city's economy now lay submerged beneath brackish water and flotsam.

'Director, you haven't had breakfast, no? You—'

'I can't eat till this is done. You know that, Milana. Let's go.'

'Very well.' She gestured to the skimmers. 'Which one?'

'Anything. Just keep the top open.'

Milana caught his eye. 'You sure? There are whispers in the city—maybe a closed top with just the windows—?'

'No. Not today, Milana. Not today.'

She stared at the ground, biting her lip.

'I trust you.' Purul's eyes glinted. 'Come on. Let's mess with the Council a bit.'

In her telling of the story, Milana left out those last words.

She tapped her wristheld. A silver-grey, pearl-shaped skimmer detached itself from the parking row and floated up to them. She got in.

Purul climbed in beside her, the fluttering rhythm of his heartbeat like a hummingbird in a cage.

'Slowly,' said the director.

Milana guided the skimmer through the compound gates. As they passed into High Town, the director straightened beside her. He tucked the binder carefully under his arm.

Before them, the ground sloped gently towards the river. Clean-cut boulevards separated the skyscrapers of High Town into symmetrical blocks. The early morning sounds of the Tower City were muffled and distant, as though wrapped in gauze. Milana's gaze darted above, around, to the side. Victory Road was cordoned off, just as she'd arranged with the Intelligence Bureau the night before.

'Relax,' the director said. 'It's a beautiful day. Sculpted like a Sanya poem.' She heard the smile in his voice, and let her grip on the controls loosen.

'I hope she's watching, then,' Milana said. 'Because her words will frame Peruma's remembrance of today.'

'And may we be worthy of them,' said Purul.

A stiff breeze rustled the branches of the amaltas trees. A handful of flowers swirled around them, settling on the road in a carpet of gold and amber. In the years to come, the songs would write themselves, Milana thought.

They moved forward, suspended a couple of feet above the ground.

From the towers that lined Victory Road, eyes bored into them. People on balconies, crowding the arched bridges between the towers or lurking behind bare windows, watching them, curious, wondering. Because all anyone knew was that for the first time in post-Imperial Peruma, a director had announced that, instead of sending in the city guard to break up a general strike, he was going to cross the river, come down to the Maidan, and address the workers of Low Town face-to-face.

Unarmed. Unguarded. Unafraid.

Worker unrest from across Urai River, spilling into the precincts of High Town, was something they were all familiar with. Failed uprisings littered the pages of Peruman history, each suppressed revolt a harbinger of the next, entrenching Peruma's reputation across the subcontinent as a city living from tumult to tumult. But this—*this* was something new. And so, the rumours had done their work. Just as Purul had wanted.

Halfway to the Urai, Milana glimpsed, inscribed into the landscape, the first signs of a city divided. Rubbish lay by the roadside, trash bins overflowing after the tenth day of the cleaners' strike mixing with the fallen amaltas flowers—a scavengers' feast. Two lampposts were uprooted, laying sideways upon the ground. Shattered glass lay scattered around them, innumerable tiny crystals sandpapering the pavement. Just beyond, the warehouse of the recently formed

Peruma Mandalium Processing Company was a firebombed, hollow shell, its innards spilling out onto the road.

Milana shivered.

A sparkle in the distance grew into the shape and scent of water. Victory Road widened into a little circle with an obelisk, marking the end of High Town, just before the strip of land called the Bulwark Zone. Beyond it, the three-arched Unity Bridge curved over the river into Low Town, the workers' half of Peruma.

'Stop,' said the director.

She halted.

'On foot.'

Milana sucked in a breath. The door slid open. High Town's towers behind them, they trudged through the Bulwark Zone until they were standing side by side on the edge of the bridge. On the other side, a row of closely packed single-storey houses looked back at them. A thin mist hung over Low Town. Nothing moved.

Low Town was quiet. So quiet, Milana thought, that you could almost forget the last six months of protests, cordon searches, strikes, surveillance, summary trials, and now—sabotage. Almost.

The director looked up at the sky. 'Milana,' he whispered.

'Director?'

'Am I doing the right thing?'

'Are you having doubts?'

Purul stared at his papers. 'I don't—I—'

'We can—you can still turn back,' she said. 'If you need more time to think about this ...'

In her telling of the story, she would wonder aloud how different the future might have been had she spoken those last words with greater surety.

Purul screwed his eyes shut and clenched his teeth. A muscle worked at the base of his jaw. When he opened his eyes again, Milana saw that he had reasoned himself into conviction.

'I have to try.'

Milana took one last look behind, at High Town, at home, at safety. 'IB doesn't have control beyond the bridge. Let me go ahead.'

'No,' Purul said. 'We'll walk together.' He gripped the binder firmly.

They took a step upon the bridge.

The ground burst open.

The roar ripped through her eardrums. The blast flung her backwards, away from the river. Smoke blinded her and a sharp pain shot through her side. Milana brought her hand to her stomach. It was wet.

As the smoke thinned, she struggled to her knees. Through the ringing in her ears, she heard dim shouts and running steps. There was an acrid smell in the air.

Her clouded brain cleared just enough to notice that Purul was beside her. '*Director!*' she gasped. 'Are you—?'

Purul coughed. 'Missed me.' His voice was a croak. He struggled to one knee, supporting himself with the weight of his shoulder. 'I'm okay, Milana.'

'We have to get you out of here,' Milana said, as the noise in her ears rose to a crescendo. 'Can you stand? You—'

In that moment, the world around her slowed to a halt.

The air in front of them was clear again. Two feet away, blotting out the sun, stood a man.

She squinted at his face, a face she would be asked to describe to a summary judge before the day was done. Young, clean-shaven, hair carefully pulled back, dressed neatly, as if for a night at the theatre.

She saw it all in one unforgiving second because none of it mattered. All that mattered was the gun, its barrel towards the director.

Pounding feet and pounding voices, not too far, but a world away.

'Director Purul,' the man said. The gun clicked.

'No, wait,' Purul raised a hand. 'You don't know what you—'

'In the name of the Commune unborn,' the man spoke over him. 'Die.'

Milana's eyes closed.

A crack tore through the world.

A feeling of weight. She forced her eyes open. Purul was in her arms. Her gaze snagged upon his. His ragged, uneven breath passed over her face.

'Director! I—can you stand—' she said dumbly. 'Let me support you, I—'

'Ah, Milana,' Purul whispered. 'What a shame.'

That was when she saw the red that stained his black achkan, speckled his brooch and flowed in thin rivulets to the stone base of the bridge.

'Purul! *No*—you're not—'

Purul slumped.

'No!' Milana whispered over him, cradling his body, clutching it to herself. 'You can't—not now—'

She heard a splash and looked up. The man stood there still, unmoving, his face blank, as though he was just here to admire the view from the bridge. His hands were empty.

Twenty-two seconds later—twenty-two seconds too late—Intelligence Bureau reached the bridge.

That was the point at which Milana would stop speaking.

And to those who implored her with their eyes, to the few who asked her to go on, she would only say:

'And the rest, as you know, is history.'

Peruma, from Empire to Revolution: A Brief Timeline

Chronicler's Note: Historical opinion is divided as to the exact moment of the 'fall' of the Peruman empire, but for ease of reference, we date it to the one week in winter that saw the storming of the palace, the arrest and execution of the last emperor, the proclamation of the Independent Republican City of Peruma (swiftly followed by similar proclamations across the subcontinent) and the declaration of a new calendar.

Glossator's Note: The 'inflection points' marked in grey refer to a theory of history, popularised by Professor D.D. Mausambi, according to which the great class struggle of post-Imperial Peruma City—sometimes hidden, sometimes open—erupts every few generations into a violent and ruinous clash between the contending classes, the outcome of which fundamentally alters society. Followers of the Mausambi School tend to agree that post-Imperial Peruma has experienced four such points in its five centuries of existence.

Year 0: The fall of the Peruman empire [the Crumbling]; the breakdown of society across the subcontinent, rapid de-urbanisation and the loss of significant Imperial technology.

Year 1: Declaration of independence by the former Imperial capital, Peruma City, and the proclamation of a republic; similar proclamations by other Imperial cities before the end of the year. The enactment of the Peruman Constitution by popular acclamation; the abolition of all existing debts, expropriation of private property and a general amnesty.

Years 2–4: The Years of Blood and Lead; widespread riots throughout Peruma City, the proclamation of Emergency and the suspension of the Constitution in Year 4.

Year 5: The end of the Emergency, the establishment of the Council and the Directorate, and the election of Priya C. as head of the Council and the first director of Peruma.

Year 8: The enactment of the Constitution of Moderation [First Inflection Point].

Year 10: The reopening of the mandalium mines and the beginning of the Great Peruman Economic Miracle.

Years 10–17: The gradual stabilisation of the subcontinent into six independent republican cities as political and economic centres, each in a loose and interdependent relationship with a set of smaller semi-urban and rural settlements.

Year 18: The signing of a treaty of peace and friendship between the six cities; the treaty divides the subcontinent into six 'zones of influence,' one for each city.

Year 65: The first workers' revolt. The firebombing of the Directorate. Widespread reprisals following the suppression of the revolt, with families of alleged participants forced into a single, surveilled ghetto on the south side of the Urai River [Second Inflection Point].

Year 85: Director Praavita the Enlightened lifts the restrictions on movement in the ghetto. Rapid expansion and construction south of the Urai.

Years 140–160: The construction of the business and administrative districts—collectively referred to as the Tower City—on the north side of the Urai. Rapid gentrification of the northern side, leading to a clustering of workers south of the river. The building of the underground transport system to convey workers from the south to the mandalium mines.

Year 190: The second workers' revolt. Suppressed.

Year 211: The third workers' revolt. Suppressed.

Year 241: The fourth workers' revolt, and the two-day proclamation of independence. Suppressed [Third Inflection Point].

Years 241–262: The great reconstruction of Peruma. The expansion of the Tower City to the entire north bank, now known as High Town. The division of the south side into geometrical grids, known as Low Town. The construction of the Bulwark Zone. The resettling of workers in Low Town.

Year 249: The abolition of the death penalty.

Year 267: The invention of cryogenic preservation.

Year 274: The crash of the mandalium market and widespread riots in Peruma. The permanent abandonment of the construction of the 'grid city' in Low Town.

Year 275: The reinstatement of 'reversible death penalty', popularly known as the 'the sleep of death' or 'the sentence'.

Years 310–360: The Second Great Economic Miracle of Peruma; years of peace and prosperity.

Year 392: The accession of Director Purul.

Year 396: The second crash of the mandalium market.

Year 397: The year of the general strike.

Year 398: The assassination of Director Purul and the start of the revolution. The declaration of the Commune. The partition of Peruma. The signing of the Charter Of Peace And Unity. The abolition of the Bulwark Zone and the creation of the Confederation of the Guardians [Fourth Inflection Point].

Year 498: Present day.

Day One

The Chapterhouse

1

Today Will Give Everything Meaning

THE CHAPTERHOUSE OF THE FREE AND EQUAL Confederation of the Guardians of Peruma—otherwise known as Fortress Drab—was built in the image of the guild that called it home: pompously dour, pointedly melancholy and held together by quicklime, cement and sheer cantankerousness.

There were rumours that when the Chapterhouse was built after the revolution, its bricks were thrown into the Urai to age faster and look appropriately antique when dredged back up, and its brand-new windows were chipped to seem like they had withstood the passing of centuries. Inside, the corridors were narrower than they should have been, stairways spiralled more than architecturally necessary and the wind whistled through strategically placed cracks.

Through these halls the guardians stalked, their steps to the beat of a solemn dirge that only they could hear. After all, the Free and Equal Confederation had to look and feel the part before it got down to the real work.

Nila stood at her window high up in the pupils' wing, hands behind her back, looking down upon the grey river. Thin ribbons of smoke drifted over the water; a memory of fire. The banks were bare.

'So this morning comes at last,' she said, 'and it feels so ordinary.'

From the desk, behind his tabletop screen, Maru glanced up. 'The weather doesn't appreciate the stakes well enough for you?'

'It could do better,' said Nila.

The pale waters looked like soft ash underneath the shifting smoke. Wreathed in clouds, the morning sky was blurry, as if the world was struggling to come into focus.

'As Sanya wrote on the death of Director Purul,' Maru said, '*Far from the bullet/The birds flew in Peruma's sky/The everyday river—*'

'*—unmoved by human acts/Flowed on*. I know.' Nila exhaled. 'It's just—it's like today will give everything meaning. You know?'

'I do,' he said. 'But you'll be chosen, Nila. Just, hopefully ... not for the wrong side.'

'There's no wrong side, Maru,' she said quickly. 'There is only—'

'—equal justice under law, yeah, yeah. And will you still feel that way if the Executive Committee assigns you to the Council? Because aren't they packed with—what was it you said—*oily little frauds*?'

'Not here!' Nila hissed, darting a glance around their small round room as if she expected one to leap out from a non-existent corner.

Maru pushed his glasses a little further up his nose. He folded up his screen. 'Nila, they don't bug pupil chambers.'

'Just—don't jinx it. Not today.'

Nila walked back to the desk and sat across from him. She picked up her seagull plushy from the table and fiddled with his orange beak.

'No sleep last night?' said Maru.

'Urgh.'

'I guess not.'

'I went up to the terrace—around 2 a.m., I think?' Nila said. 'They were still going.' She pointed towards the river, where the last ribbons of smoke were dissolving into wisps of nothingness. 'High Town was out in force but the Commune—the Commune march was massive, Maru, like a sea of fireflies. They had those pattern flares—words burning in the night.'

'What were they saying?'

'*The Agreement must die.*'

Maru grinned. 'And you'll be the one to kill it.'

'Or save it.'

'Or that. Either way—hey!' he said, as Nila twisted the seagull's beak too hard. 'Don't take it out on Baili! Give him here.' He reached across the table and prised the seagull from her hands. 'Don't mind her,' he crooned. 'Your human has just lost her mind today.' He looked up at her. 'Breathe, Nila.'

'How?'

'Think of it as just another assignment.'

'Really, now? What's the news ticker saying this morning, Maru?'

'Ignore—'

'No, no. Let's have a look.' Nila flicked on her wristheld and looked at a moving news ticker at the bottom of her screen. Muttering under his breath, Maru peeked over her shoulder.

Anarchist March Turns Violent on Unity Bridge. Amidst This Sad and Shameful Intimidation, Will Guardians Stand Firm Today?

'That's the *High Town Herald*, I can tell,' said Maru. 'Absolute rag. Mouthpiece for the Council. My mom knows the editor, he has lunch at the Directorate every week.'

Smoke on the Water, War Cries in the Skies: As Fifth Inflection Point Nears, Confederation to Choose Teams Today in Case of the Century

'Fifth Inflection Point, is it? Pure clickbait. *The Peruman* has history, my mom knows—'

'—the editor, yes, he owns shares in the mandalium mines. You've told me. How about a Commune newspaper then, which your mom definitely doesn't know?

A Hundred Years of Injustice: An Interactive Timeline from Revolution to Case Of the Century

'That's *The Commune Tribune,*' said Nila. 'And here's *The Voice of the People.*'

It's Time to Destroy the Mandalium Agreement and Finish Our Unfinished Revolution

'You're just picking out the crazies—'

'—on both sides? Knew you'd say that. See this piece of ditch-water sobriety, *The Centre Ground.*

Council vs Commune to Get Underway Today, Confederation to Choose the Twelve

'Nila—'

'Oh look, even *The Peruman Glam* is in on it.'

I Don't Really Understand It but It Excites Me: Celebrities Weigh in on So-Called Case of the Centur—

'Give me that!' Maru made an unsuccessful grab for her wristheld.

'You know some people say that the guardians—that we were created for this day?'

'Some people love to believe they're the main character of a webnovel,' said Maru. 'Especially around these parts. You know what the Wits say about delusions of grandeur? In their newsletter today—'

'I've blocked their newsletter.'

'Fine, deprive yourself of the good stuff.'

'Hmph.' She held out a palm. 'Give me back my emotional support seagull.'

He handed Baili over. She cradled the seagull against her cheek.

Maru watched her. 'You can tell me, Nila,' he said after a while.

Nila stroked the seagull's beak, eyes unfocused, saying nothing.

'It *is* about sides, isn't it?' Maru prompted gently.

'No. Yes.' She said at last. 'I guess it is.'

'Nila. You're allowed to feel things despite the neutrality oath, you know?'

'Do you think, Maru, that if I end up on the other side ... the Commune will forgive me?'

'It's your literal job,' said Maru. '*If* the chips fall that way, the Commune—they'll understand that.'

'The Fifth Inflection Point—'

'Screw that. It doesn't change—' Maru suddenly broke off as he caught sight of something through the window. 'Nila—look!'

There was a flurry of activity in the sky. She jumped up. Together, they hurried out on to the balcony.

A rush of autumn breeze, heady and cool, met them. The clouds had parted; the Peruman morning glittered. Shards of sunlight scattered molten gold upon the river, setting the extravagance of bridges ablaze.

Beyond the Urai, to the south, the Commune was a forever-unfinished patchwork quilt: each district a wave of intense colour—blue, red, pink, gold—meshed with weaves of green, the famous hanging gardens. The terraces jumbled, sloped and arced into one another, in angles soft and sharp, resisting definition, forcing the eye to travel, to never settle.

To the north, facing the Commune across the river, High Town was diamond-hard and diamond-bright in its symmetry, the first row of monochrome towers yielding to the next—and the next, and the next—as the ground rose all the way up to the hill where the Directorate was perched. The Tower City rolled itself out as a sea of terraced slopes, a staircase for the gods to walk up to heaven.

Peruma, once the empire's capital, once—after the empire's fall—the greatest of the six independent cities of the subcontinent; now riven Peruma, the river a scar of permanent rupture between its two halves.

Dancing from south to north, Nila's gaze caught upon a rent in the fabric of stillness.

From the sky, a fleet of skimmers approached the Chapterhouse. Seven vehicles, sleek and silver-bright, cleaved unhurriedly through the air in the formation of a tiger's claw.

'They're here,' said Maru.

The array drew closer and passed over them, making for the landing pad on the Chapterhouse's upper terrace. As they soared past, Nila saw the man who rode at their head. He was clean-shaven, dark-haired, clad in white. He sat stiffly in the skimmer, his gaze fixed on something far away, his lips sewn together in a line so averse to a smile that it felt like the world would end if he ever gave free rein to the muscles of his jaw. A gold tiger's claw was emblazoned on the front of his cloak.

Just behind him flew a woman. She was older, salt-grey hair pulled back from a lined forehead. Her lips did smile, a smile that broadened as she looked down and noticed the two young guardian pupils gazing at her, wide-eyed. It was the kind of smile that made you think of loyalty pledges and of marching into battle. A slight nod of acknowledgement, and she too was past.

'They've both come,' Maru breathed. 'Director *and* deputy director. Wow.'

'*Just another assignment*, Maru?'

One by one, the rest of the fleet followed: skimmers of the most recent vintage, elegant and powerful, cutting through the air with the easy grace of a shark's fin slicing through water. The last one bore the Council flag: grey field, tiger with one raised paw, claws extended.

Nila's mind supplied the accompaniment: a quick-tempo percussive march, tabla in the background.

As the sky emptied and the music in her head faded, there was movement on the ground.

'Party's complete,' Maru said.

On the road that led to the Chapterhouse, seven people walked together in no obvious formation and with no visible leader. From the distance, the collective looked like the Commune's patchwork quilt in motion: kurtas dyed in turquoise and emerald, salwars sequined and embroidered in amber, a medley of motley colour and style. Only the seven black Commune sashes suggested that these people were more than just travelling companions thrown together by chance.

The group turned into the approach to the Chapterhouse and stopped by its wrought-iron gates. One of them glanced up towards their balcony.

Nila's heart bounced out of its ribcage and careened down into the pit of her stomach. She tore her eyes away.

'Maru—*she's* here!'

'Hey, hey,' Maru's arm was around her shoulder. 'It's alright.'

'It's not!' Nila swallowed, tasting something bitter at the back of her throat. Her voice sounded shrill in her own ears. 'I can't—I don't—I don't want all this playing out before *Ma* ...'

'She'll be proud of you, whatever happens. You know that, right?'

'Will she? Will she really, Maru? Even if—'

'Even if you have to argue for the Council. Yes. She will. She'll understand.' Maru looked down, his arm still around her. 'Relax. They've gone inside.'

'I need to sit,' Nila said. Blood was still rushing to her head, dizzying. She walked back into the room and collapsed on her chair. The pins and needles in her legs subsided slowly.

'Sorry, Maru,' she said after a while. 'I didn't mean to dump that on you. It's just that ... seeing her suddenly ... it's been ...'

'Three years. Yes.'

Nila stared at her fingers. *'I know you'll be brilliant. And I can't wait to see it.* The last thing she said to me, the day I walked away from the Commune. From her. That life. And all these years, I could almost believe that I had nothing to live up to and no one to let down. But now ...'

She tailed off, shaking her head. Maru reached into his pocket and pulled out the last two squares of a bar of dark chocolate. 'Sugar high?'

'Give.'

He tossed it to her. She munched, trying to still the clamour in her mind. Somewhere in the winding corridors of the Chapterhouse, she knew, Council and Commune were converging upon the president's chamber, lining up by the oakwood-panelled walls, beside silver candelabras and stained-glass windows, until they finally faced each other in the lamplight, intimate strangers, the two fragments of a sundered city that had once been whole.

She saw the Executive Committee arrayed in an arch, and in the middle, beneath the great chandelier ...

'Please let him not drag it out,' she said out loud, 'with his cabinet of clichés.'

'As if he's going to miss *this* chance—'

The crackling of the intercom cut Maru off. A reedy voice filled the room.

'Director Pulis; Deputy Director Maiyam A.; dignitaries of the Council. Administrator Vani; deputies of the Commune. I, Mehmandost Naram, welcome you to the Chapterhouse, and to the Free and Equal Confederation of the Guardians of Peruma.'

'Wow, he's broadcasting his own speech through the building,' Maru said. 'Talk about a damn captive audience!'

Nila grasped the underside of table with both hands.

'*You have come here today,*' the voice continued, '*to fulfil the pledge your ancestors made a century ago, amidst ash and ruin: to end the civil war, to staunch the blood that ran in the streets and to say "never again".*'

'*That is why you created us: the guardians. You chose judgement over violence, law over chaos, resolution over revolution. In a city divided, you could not trust each other but you chose to trust us. And every time in the last one hundred years, when you have brought your bitterest disputes to us and abided by our judgement, you have redeemed that pledge.*'

'He really fancies his alliterations,' Maru said, as the speaker gave a long beat. Nila's knuckles ached.

'*This week, your pledge will be tested like never before. The civil war—the Fourth Inflection Point—was brought to an end by the Charter of Peace And Unity. But our ancestors were wise. They knew that if they tried to solve everything, they would solve nothing. So they agreed to postpone their gravest disagreements to another day. They trusted their descendants to accomplish, in a quieter time, what their generation could not. And so they said: for a hundred years, this Charter cannot be altered. We—Council and Commune—will learn to live together in peace. And then, one day, there will be a time to disagree again.*

'*In a week, on Monday, those hundred years will run out. And then what? On the appointed day, will the clock reset to zero? Will we start all over again, as if it is merely the day after the civil war, as if the last hundred years had never been? A blank slate upon which to write the future of Peruma?*

'*This is what the Commune urges.*

'*Or—will elements of the old order remain? Are there parts of that order, such as the Mandalium Agreement, that were always meant to endure, to become ... permanent? Will they still bind us after Monday?*

'This is what the Council believes.

'When the day comes, do we tear it all up—the Charter, our institutions, our laws—and begin afresh? Or do we preserve … something? What, really, did our ancestors agree upon on Unity Bridge, a hundred years ago? And how do we honour their sacrifice today?

'A hundred years ago, you would have gone to war to settle this question. Today, instead, you have come to us to decide.'

'Way to up the stakes, idiot,' Maru said.

'Ugh,' said Nila.

'And so it begins. The Executive Committee has decided, on merit, the teams that will represent your positions before the tribunal. Given the magnitude of this dispute, we have assigned to each side three senior guardians and six final-year pupils to assist them in preparing the case. For the case of the century, we are giving to you our very best.

'And it is to you—the twelve pupils—that I now speak.'

Nila closed her eyes.

'Pupils: all your years in the Chapterhouse, you have prepared—been prepared—for this day. Some of you will find yourselves representing the side of your birth. Some of you will be for the other side. How that worked out has not been our decision. After we chose the twelve, assignation was by lottery, as always. But above all else, we—the Confederation of the Guardians—have faith that whatever side you're for, the only side you're on is equal justice under law. For a hundred years, that is what it has meant to be a guardian.

'Now, the names. I move—'

A siren call rent the air. Their eyes turned to the panel above the door. It had turned into a transparent screen, with a flashing cursive script.

Assignment: Case No. 491/8024—Council of Peruma vs Commune of Peruma
Subject: Regarding Certain Questions of Great Public Importance Concerning the Interpretation of the Charter of Peace and Unity

Nila leapt out of her chair and rushed towards the door, stopping right below the panel. The notification lingered on the screen, prolonging the moments like an elastic band stretched to its thinnest before it snaps.

'I bet they do this on purpose,' Maru said.

The announcement dissolved back into a blank panel. The moments ticked away, each one like a grain of sand slipping through her fingers.

On the tenth second, a name appeared on the panel in gold lettering accompanied by a flat monotone of a voice.

Noor (Commune)

'Of course,' said Nila. Her breath felt like it had lodged permanently at the back of her throat.

Noor's name stayed on the panel for five seconds before disappearing. Five more seconds passed. Then, once again, the words and the voice.

Raman (Council)

'Expected.' Nila swallowed hard.

'Good sign,' said Maru. 'They're picking the usual suspects, the top performers—there, see?'

Another name flashed on the panel.

Suneen (Commune)

Nila hopped from one foot to the other. Each name felt like a fist had squeezed itself around her heart, releasing her for a moment only to seize her again five seconds later.

The names continued to flash on the screen.

'Still nothing,' said Nila.

'Wait,' said Maru.

The eleventh name appeared.

Nimat (Council)

Nila jumped. Behind her, Maru groaned. 'I thought that was you. But that's six for the Council, Nila. One left, for the Commune. It has to be you—'

'There's still Velu—'

'That posturing muppet? They would never—'

Maru's voice died in the air as the twelfth name flashed on the panel.

Velu (Commune)

'Oh, you've got to be joking!' said Maru.

As if to drive the point home, the hateful flat voice pronounced the name.

'Velu.'

With the suddenness of a punctured balloon, the panel flashed out of existence. The wall returned to being a wall.

Nila stood there, staring at where the panel had been, willing a correction, a retraction, a rerun, anything.

The wall stared back.

She slumped then, one elbow against the door, supporting the weight of her head.

'It's done, isn't it?' she said. 'It's actually done?

'They really are oily little frauds,' Maru said.

'And here I was worrying about being on the *wrong* side,' Nila let out a long, juddering breath. 'Right in front of Ma, too. So it goes.' She shook herself, walked slowly back to the table and hugged the seagull to her face. 'At least you don't think I'm useless, Baili.'

'Nila, nobody thinks you're—'

'Whatever.' Nila rubbed her eyes and cast a dead look at her own tabletop screen. 'And I see I've been assigned a brief as well while all this was going on, just to rub it in. What's the bet it's a Vashi Street border dispute?'

'There'll be a waiting list,' Maru said tentatively. 'If someone drops out ...'

'Drops out?' Nila drew a finger across her screen, opening the new folder in her inbox. 'Wow, it *is* actually a fight over Vashi Street. Maru, dearest, loveliest Maru. You know you're not really the best at comfort, yeah?' Maru squirmed. 'No offence, but this isn't one of your beloved mining injury disputes where pupils keep dropping out.'

'I'd drop right out of any case that called itself *Certain Questions of Great Public Importance*,' Maru muttered.

Nila ran her hands through her hair. 'I thought I did everything right.' She tried to keep her voice even. 'Exam scores. Senior reports. Papers.'

'This isn't on you.'

'This is ...' she tailed off, feeling that hated catch forming at the edge of her throat.

Maru looked at her. 'Can I make you some cold coffee?'

She nodded, swallowing twice before the catch turned into something else.

Maru stood and busied himself by the refrigerator and kitchen. She watched him for a while, until her wristheld pinged. She glanced down at it.

'Oh, *screw* this!'

Maru jumped. 'What happened?'

Nila pointed.

And The Teams Are In! Meet The Six Pupil Guardians Who Will Be Fighting For High Town

Six familiar faces stared back at them from the screen, looking ready, looking glorious, looking ... happy.

'*High Town Herald*?' Maru asked.

'Who else?' She scrolled with her finger. '*Anarchist Daily's* on it too. Look.'

Our Revolution, In Your Hands: The Commune's Six

'Wow, they even have profiles done in advance.' She bit her lip. 'Maru, do you think they had mine written out as well? Until ...'

'What I think,' said Maru, 'is that you need to go offline for a bit.'

'Gah, you're right.' Nila pushed her wristheld away, and let her head sink down on the table. She heard the sloshing of milk, the familiar sound of the blender and then the tinkling of the spoon against the side of the glass.

When Maru spoke again, it was in a quiet voice.

'You know there's still time, don't you?'

Nila lifted her head, feeling a blurry wetness at the corner of her eyes. Maru dropped two ice cubes with a *clink* into the glass.

'You really think it's that?' she said, trying to blink it away.

Maru swirled the coffee around furiously with the spoon, making a tiny whirlpool in the glass. 'You can't prove that it is. But as I've said before, you can't prove that it isn't either.'

He brought the glass to her. Nila took a draught, still blinking fiercely. She unclasped the guardian's pendant at her neck and held it in her palm. The jade caught the light and glowed softly. At the centre, the sign of the Free and Equal Confederation of the Guardians of Peruma—a dragonfly with its 360-degree vision—was ringed by an engraving of text, calligraphed into the stone.

Let justice be done, though the world burn.

She remembered how that line had taken over her mind the first time she had come across it in *No More Regrets*, a chain-fantasy story, written in real time by an anonymous collective of authors, that had gone viral throughout the networks on both sides of the Urai, its quotes on everyone's lips, its characters in every head's canon. Childish though it felt now, it was *No More Regrets* that had fired her imagination and given a recognisable shape to her vague desire to feel a life outside of the Commune, outside of the way of being that her mother lived intensely, so intensely that, like a magnet, it had begun to repel her, driving her towards ... a different path, one that she hadn't understood yet.

But after *No More Regrets*, she had.

She had taken the guardian aptitude test. She had passed it. It had brought her to the gates of the Chapterhouse seven years ago, two weeks shy of her fifteenth birthday, a new life, with the words that had propelled her to this place ringing in her ears as those wrought-iron gates opened to let her into Fortress Drab.

She had come to the place that would do justice. No matter if the world burned.

The line had enraptured her long enough for her to take the unconventional step, after passing her pupil exam at the top of her class, of exercising her right to choose her own inscription instead of one of the five standard Chapterhouse options.

The Executive Committee had discouraged her in their glum, discouraging way. Never explicit rejection, just variants of '*you may, Pupil Nila, wish to take under advisement the advisability of the step that you are about to undertake*'. But she knew she had the right to choose, because she was, after all, free and equal, and most certainly in a confederation, where all that mattered was how you performed in the briefs assigned to you.

Maru had warned her. 'You're singling yourself out,' he'd said, just after they'd agreed to apply for a chamber together. 'Painting a target on your back. Giving a reason for someone on the committee to strike your name off a shortlist as *that troublemaker.* And for what? An engraving on a pendent?'

She'd laughed at him then.

She wasn't laughing now.

'You can't be saying—' she began.

'But I am saying it. *Again*. You didn't want to listen to me, so I stopped, but ... if the Executive Committee thinks that you really believe justice should be done even if the world is on fire, they're going to be damn careful not to let you anywhere near a lighter. Or a tinderbox. Or matches. Or wood. And this case, at *this* time, just when tensions are rising, when there's the first ever threat of a general strike since the revolution, when the Charter is really starting to *matter*—the city is like a whole forest that someone has drenched in oil, and now we guardians have to sit in the treetops and play frisbee with a lantern.'

Nila flinched. Beside her, the melting ice cubes had turned her untouched coffee watery.

Maru gestured at the window. 'Duelling marches, you said. Smoke on the river. Literal fires. And what do you think the Executive Committee would have felt when they woke up this morning and read those headlines? You think they wouldn't remember the time when the old court was firebombed? Your approach is all well and good, Nila, until the world *actually* starts to burn.'

'I don't know ...'

He leaned forward. 'You *can* still change it, you know?' he said. 'You can change your inscription.'

'It's a damn line from a book,' Nila protested weakly.

'Yeah, the oily frauds are known for their open-mindedness—*and* their sense of humour, right?' Maru said. 'Listen, Nila, you could be like me and just not care all that much. This brief I'm on right now—figuring out who's liable for the mining cancer cases? I don't need more. But since you do care, since you care so much, and since the power to give you what you want is with the committee—'

'Thanks Maru, which account do I send the money to for this therapy session?'

'You can be sarcastic with me later, Nila. *As I was saying* ...' He held up his own pendant to the light. 'How does "*Balance. Proportionality. Justice.*" sound?'

'*Proportionality?* Ew, wash your mouth out!' said Nila. 'That's what I'd say to warn you I'd been kidnapped.'

But the pit in the depths of her stomach had only grown heavier since she had first seen her mother walk up to the Chapterhouse, heavier than when the panel had gone blank and it grew heavier every time she caught sight of the unopened folder on her tabletop screen.

Maru sighed. 'Let it be. Tell you what. We'll go out to the Agora this evening. There's a troupe from Chemur performing Urumi sword forms at the amphitheatre. We can have a drink or two and make an evening of it.'

'Um—I don't know,' said Nila. 'I think I'd rather not.'

'Nila,' said Maru. 'I'm not going to let you sit here and mope the night away. We're going to—'

But his voice had begun to fade in her ears as her mind drifted. She looked down at the pendant nestled in her palm again, at the words that carried a weight they were never meant to bear. Maybe if she *did* replace it with ...

The jade lit up, a luminous green. The inscription glowed.

Incoming, said a disembodied voice.

'Huh? Who's calling me on my guardian key?' Nila said.

Maru's eyebrows shot up so high that they almost disappeared into his hair.

Nila looked at her pendant, then at Maru and then back again at the pendant. There was no pop-up screen with the caller's face. A masked ID.

'I think you should take that call,' Maru said.

'But—'

'*Take it*, Nila.'

Nila ran her index finger over the inscription and held it up to her face.

'I am speaking to Nila M., pupil of the Confederation of the Guardians.' A woman's voice crackled into her ear. The sentence was not a question.

'I—yes,' Nila said.

'I'm calling to make an appointment.'

'An appoint—' Nila scrabbled for firm ground, her responses slipping on the woman's words like feet on mossy stone. 'You need to speak to the Executive Committee—'

Oily, Maru mouthed across the table.

Shut up, she mouthed back, grinning in spite of herself.

The woman's next words wiped the grin off her face.

'If I wanted an assignment, I would have called the Executive Committee. This is a private brief.'

'*What!*' Nila almost choked into the pendant. *Fuck YES!* Maru mouthed.

'A private—how do you even know who I am?' she said, lowering her voice and bringing the pendant closer to her mouth, as if someone was eavesdropping.

'You are Nila M, the candidate who topped the last pupil examination?'

'Yes, but—'

'I'd like to meet you in the Well.'

'When?'

'Now, if you're so inclined.'

'But—'

The line went dead.

Nila stared at the pendant in her hand, which had stopped glowing.

Maru leapt to his feet with a whoop. 'Great public importance my foot! *That'll* show the oily little frauds!'

'I—'

'You, nothing. How many people get a private brief? Forget that, how many pupils in the history of the Chapterhouse, after poor old Naina L., have *ever* been offered a private brief?' He came over to her and pulled her to her feet. 'Go for it, Nila. And for Peruma's sake, *do not* overthink now. Just go.'

'I don't even know who—'

'Well, you're just going to find out, aren't you?'

'Maru—' Nila stammered. 'I can't deal with this. I didn't—I wanted—*Council vs Commune*—'

'Is the past. Dead. Buried. Go now. Just remember, you haven't signed anything yet. Nobody's forcing you into anything.'

Nila took a deep breath and wiped her eyes dry. 'You're right—sorry—this is a lot. But yes. Not going to overthink. Haven't signed anything yet. Going down to the Well for a meeting. That's all.'

She stood on unsteady feet, and moved towards the door.

'One thing, Nila,' Maru said, as she opened it.

'Yes.'

'It just occurred to me. Your would-be client knows your guardian key. And they know the rules of the Confederation well enough to ask you to meet them in the Well. They know exactly what they want. So—be alert.'

She gave him an uncertain smile. 'I guess.'

'Good luck. Should I finish the coffee?'

'Go wild.'

The door closed on him.

2

The Life That Was Stolen

THE FREE AND EQUAL CONFEDERATION OF THE Guardians of Peruma got rather prickly when, every so often, the Coalition of the Wits publicly jibed that it was neither free, nor equal and most certainly not a confederation. It sullenly maintained that, notwithstanding the hurtful barbs that came its way from Peruma's longest-standing and most annoying collective of anonymous online satirists, it was both free and equal, and beyond peradventure a confederation—and it was always more than eager to provide a history lesson to those who remained unconvinced.

It had all begun that morning a hundred years ago with the shot that had claimed Director Purul's life on Unity Bridge. By afternoon, Low Town—the Workers' Town—was bristling with barricades. By evening, the Council had lost all control beyond the river. The morning after, half the mandalium mines on the switchback were flooded, not a worker could be found on the slopes of the mountain and the Peruman economy had been brought to a shuddering halt.

By the end of that day, the city was in a state of emergency, and the military patrolled a curfewed night.

So, the loudspeakers boomed out from High Town. *Is this a revolt?*

No, came the answer from across the river. *This is a revolution.*

Under siege, the Council called for aid. *We be of one flesh*, it broadcast to the five other independent republican cities on the subcontinent. *Remember the past, Old Empire, when we were one. Consider the future, when we might be again. Help us.*

Far away in a white tower by the sea, in a hall of a hundred pillars, under a glowing chandelier of purest crystal, the ambassadors of the independent cities of Chemur, Monara, Lubini, Jharna and Sampi—long resentful of Peruma's preeminence in the post-Imperial subcontinent—inked their names upon a treaty of mutual non-interference and clinked glasses.

It was to be Peruma's war, and Peruma's war alone.

In the bloody week that followed, decades passed; until at last, with hollowed buildings, firebombed bridges and permanent economic ruin staring Peruma in the face, the Council and the (newly-born) Commune of Free Revolutionary Workers came to the table to negotiate, and hammered out the Charter of Peace and Unity: a compromise document full of vague phrases, escape clauses and sections that began with *notwithstanding that*, *provided that*, *except insofar as* and *nothing in this Charter shall*. So much so that the Wits—who suddenly had a wealth of fresh material to work with—immediately labelled it the Cop-Out Constitution, a name that unfortunately stuck through the years.

The Charter—a 'transitional' document—divided Peruma into the two autonomous halves: High Town and the Commune. It set out, in tedious legal detail, the unchangeable terms that would govern their relationship for a hundred years to come: from mandatory demilitarisation to joint administration, and—most importantly—a mandalium revenue-sharing formula (the Agreement) so complicated that everyone would spend those hundred years figuring out what it meant.

The Council lost over half of Peruma and its landlords went bankrupt overnight but it retained control over the all-important mandalium mines through the High Town corporations. Within High Town itself, nothing changed. Representatives of the corporations sat on the Council, and elected from among themselves the tenured executive officers of the Directorate. Of course, the loss of half its territory remained a source of lasting bitterness for the Council, and the fact that High Town could no longer set wage rates for labour but had to bargain for everything with the Commune—from mining to urban cleaning services—was a hard pill to swallow.

The Commune, on the other hand, gained its freedom and autonomy. South of the Urai River, in the former Low Town, it could—and did—experiment with the anarchist forms of living and organisation that it had been dreaming of and fighting for all these years. And in its economic relations with High Town, when it came to wages and labour conditions, it could—and did—bargain collectively, as one, through its unions. But its goal of bringing the entire Peruman economy under public control was stymied, and its dream of liberating its citizens from waged labour remained a dream.

The Charter made everyone unhappy in equal measure; the surest formula for immediate stability. And to entrench that stability, they appended to it a Pact of Forgetting: neither side would seek redress for the crimes inflicted upon it in the bloody week, or before. Indeed, nobody would ever publicly bring them up in the future that was to come.

But who would enforce the Cop-Out Constitution, precarious arbiter between mortal enemies too weary to return to battle? So was born the Confederation of the Guardians, a compromise body for a compromise document, its members drawn from both High Town and Commune but meant to belong to neither, trained in an obsessive curriculum of impartiality and of representing the 'wrong' side when needed. And defying everyone's expectations (including its own) the Confederation survived—to the special chagrin of the Wits, whose newsletter headline about how the compromisers had become compromised had to remain in drafts.

Council and Commune did bring their disputes to the Chapterhouse, and they abided by the Confederation's rulings.

Grudgingly at the best of times, and bitterly, with barely-veiled threats at the worst, but they abided.

Not that that stopped the Wits. So, to burnish its free, equal and confederational credentials, the Confederation insisted that Council/Commune disputes were assigned impartially on merit, and that a guardian could find themselves on either 'side' in any case.

The skimmer-for-hire rule, they called it, enforced on pain of ostracism.

With one exception. For anyone who *really* wanted a specific senior or pupil to represent them, they could ask directly through their guardian key—if they knew someone who knew someone.

Private requests were rare. Private requests for *pupils* were almost non-existent.

But when such requests were made, the Chapterhouse provided a chamber with absolute privacy for guardian and client, where none—not even the Executive Committee—could enter without consent.

The Well.

Thoughts chased and swirled around each other in Nila's head until her brain was batter as she hurried through the draughty, whispering passages, the giddying spiral stairways, into the bowels of the Chapterhouse. For once, the secret passages, the fake sliding bookshelves and the trapdoors felt like they actually meant something, appropriate vehicles to take her to a mysterious appointment. She may even have enjoyed the feeling, were it not for the tendrils of stress that brushed across the surface of her mind.

At first, she kept up a stream of voice messages with Maru, a welcome diversion. But when the elevator creaked down the final levels, the network flickered, sighed and then gave out altogether. Nila was left alone with her clamouring thoughts.

Minutes ago, it looked like history had passed her by. From the moment Velu's name had flashed on the screen, the remainder of her life in the Chapterhouse had begun to unspool before her: meaningless cartographic disputes, a road that led nowhere, a tedium in which all her yesterdays and all her tomorrows blurred into one meaningless coagulation.

But then ...

The thoughts in her mind plunged and rose like the loops of Unity Bridge, ache contending with anticipation. At last, she turned into a dim corridor and squinted at the door that pupils would sometimes pass by with a longing look.

THE WELL
Entry only for private conference

Drawing a breath for courage, Nila opened the door and stepped in.

Keeping with the Confederation's determination to present to the outside world the look and taste of milk curdled by vinegar, the Well was a bare, circular room, where congealed light leaked in through a high window, the wind made an annoyed rustling in the cracks, and there was precisely one piece of furniture: a wooden table. To cut short the length of the conversations—and to exact a price in pain from those who chose to ramble on anyway—there were no chairs.

A woman stood across from the table, clad in white, her face in shadow.

'Thank you for coming,' she said.

Nila stepped up to her, the table between them. 'How do you know my key?

'I was given it. The person was happy to, once they knew my cause.'

'Hm,' said Nila. Most people who needed private guardian services did not think of themselves as tangled up in causes. 'Why didn't you ask the Executive Committee?'

'Don't trust 'em.'

Can't argue with that.

'Nature of the case?'

'Murder.'

Nila stiffened. 'I'm sorry, I—I don't do crime—'

'*Nobody* does this crime, Nila.' A smile lurked at the edges of the voice. 'Allow me.'

The woman tapped her wristheld. A viewing screen sprang up between them. Upon it, with a clarity so sharp that it felt almost three-dimensional there was the image of a chamber, bathed in soft, cool blue light. Between two pillars lay a diamond-shaped sarcophagus with a transparent cover.

Within the sarcophagus lay a man. He was young and clean shaven, ashen hair pulled back neatly from a pale forehead, a flat nose and full lips that curved ever so slightly. He was dressed in a grey smock. His arms were folded carefully around his chest, long loose sleeves hiding all but the fingertips.

'Do you see?' said the woman.

Nila gulped. The things in her stomach were tangled up in the wrong order.

A scene played in her mind, long seared into the collective memory of divided Peruma.

A bright summer morning. Amaltas flowers lining Victory Road. Two figures step on to Unity Bridge. And the ground is torn apart.

'Director!' the woman shouts.

The smoke begins to clear. There is a third person. A man, young, beardless, ashen hair pulled back neatly from his forehead, dressed as if for a night at the theatre.

There are people rushing in on them from all sides but as everyone who has replayed this scene in their head for the last hundred years knows, they are already too late, and in every single iteration, every single replay, every single time loop, they will always be too late.

The gun, raised. The click.
The sentence. 'In the name of the Commune unborn, die.'
The shot that changes the world forever.

'You cannot,' said Nila, 'be asking me to do what I think you're asking me to do.'

Behind the screen, the woman looked back at her, unperturbed. When she spoke, it was as if she was reciting a litany.

'Guardian. One hundred years ago, this man—Jagat R.—was found guilty of shooting Director Purul dead on Unity Bridge. The court held that political assassination was a *rarest of rare case*, warranting the highest punishment.'

'The sleep of death,' Nila whispered, staring at the cryobox in the cryochamber.

The sleep of death—or, as it had simply come to be known, the sentence—the highest penalty in a society that had long been divided bitterly over capital punishment, and had claimed to abolish it in a bid to appear civilised but had never been *entirely* convinced. And so—as soon as the technology was invented—chosen that most bizarre of compromises: *reversible death penalty*. You would freeze the body of a convict and cast them in a cryobox. There they would remain unless one day someone could prove that there had been a miscarriage of justice, and they could be revived to live again.

Guilt-free capital punishment, the Wits mocked. You kept the essence of the punishment, but told yourself it could be undone. You had your cake and ate it too.

'Prove his innocence.' The woman's words sliced through Nila's galloping thoughts. 'So that he can live the life that was stolen from him.'

'Prove his—what? He all but confessed to—'

No. Nila stopped herself. Jagat had not denied shooting the director but nor had he confessed. In fact, as the popular legend went, he had said nothing at all after the one sentence he had spoken to Purul. From summary trial to sleep of death: only silence.

All but.

She looked down at her hands, cupped around the edges of the table. 'Who is he to you?'

'I am Ani. His great-granddaughter.'

'Now I understand,' said Nila, finding tether. 'Ani—I understand why you want to do this. And I sympathise. But you see, Director Purul was shot dead at point-blank range. Your great-grandfather was the only one with a weapon near him. He never denied it. They arrested him, tried him, sentenced him, froze him. And he said not a word.'

'I know. I also know he was innocent.'

'Then why didn't he say so?'

'Only he can tell us. I want you to give him back the voice that was taken from him. I want you to give him back the life he deserves.'

'But Ani, in the last hundred years, even the Commune has never tried to overturn the sentence. Even we—sorry, *they*—have never doubted his guilt.'

'That's because they've never known what I know.'

Ani tapped her wrist. Jagat disappeared. In his place there was a handwritten letter.

'You're probably aware,' said Ani, 'that at the time he was sentenced, Jagat had a teenage daughter. My grandmother. She died a long time ago but recently, with the hundredth anniversary of the revolution coming up, I decided to archive her effects. I found this.'

Nila read the words off the screen.

My love,

I almost don't know why I'm writing this to you. But I am bad with words, and it is easier to write than it is to speak.

There are not many things in this world that can break me, but one of them is if you would ever be disappointed in me. I would break at that, even from beyond the grave.

I want to tell you that if there are those who one day smear me when I can no longer defend myself, do not believe them. It is easier to accuse those who cannot answer back. If there is any offence I have committed, it is of loving you too dearly, and only wanting your happiness, to whatever end.

There are no other crimes on my conscience.

With love, always
Pa

'You see?' said Ani.

'I see,' said Nila slowly, 'a letter that a father wrote to his daughter, just before he was going to sacrifice his life for a cause. How does this help you?'

'No, no,' said Ani. 'He talks about being smeared, being accused. *Framed.*'

'So he wrote this letter and then walked onto that bridge, gun in hand, to be framed?' Nila shook her head. 'What's the date of this letter, Ani? Is it the day of the assassination?'

'It's undated. But what else could it be about?'

Nila tapped on the desk, letting herself think.

'Let's take a step back,' she said at last. 'Let's say you're right. Let's say Jagat was framed. Someone else shot the director all those years ago, and for some reason, Jagat couldn't—or wouldn't—defend himself at trial. How can we prove it a century later? How can we find out who really did it, when nearly everyone from the time of the revolution has been dead for generations—except him, and he can't speak?'

'Because nobody's ever tried. Because of the Pact of Forgetting, nobody's ever wanted to ask what truly happened that day. They'd rather we move on forever. You know this.' Ani shrugged. 'Besides, this is *your* job, isn't it? You don't even have to prove he was innocent. You just have to show that there's reasonable doubt whether he was guilty.'

Nila walked away from the table, towards the window. She stood in the refracted light, her hands behind her back.

She reached for her wristheld to call Maru, to talk to him—

There was no network in the Well.

Nila cursed.

She thought of walking away, out of the room, far from Ani and her strange request; away from this impossible case and her role, defence counsel for the damned.

Then she remembered the folder sitting in her inbox, yet another soul-wearying meaningless border dispute along the Bulwark Zone, Maru's sympathetic—yet helpless—look; the life that was waiting for her back in the chamber.

I know you'll be brilliant. And I can't wait to see it.

It *was* true that Jagat had never confessed his guilt.

It *was* true that Milana Maran had not seen Jagat shoot the director with her own eyes.

It *was* true that the trial was summary, the sentence rendered in a day, overtaken by a revolution that had cast a curtain over everything that had happened before. A curtain that both Council and Commune had reason not to tear away. A curtain that they soon drew permanently through the Pact of Forgetting.

And it *was* true that, read one way, the letter seemed a cry of innocence: a last attempt at retaining control over the story of his own life from a man who knew that his name would soon escape him.

So many disparate elements, innocuous when regarded separately, but when put together, maybe—just maybe—they could form the shape of *reasonable doubt.*

Maybe all that it needed was a pair of fresh eyes and the distance of a century, a stone to disturb the surface of a still pool.

Maybe.

Nila took a breath, and let it run through her body. She turned back to the table.

'I'll do it.'

Ani's only reaction was a slight nod of acknowledgement.

Nila's mind moved through the gears, creating categories for research, for investigation, for arguments. Her pulse quickened.

'However,' she said, 'before I can file an application for reopening, I will need to conduct a preliminary investigation for evidence, a process that—'

'We don't have time,' said Ani.

'Why not?'

'This has to be heard within seven days. Monday, at the latest.'

'Huh? Monday? The hundreth anniversary of the rev—*oh*!' Nila's hand flew to her mouth.

Nothing lasted forever. Cryogenic preservation was no exception. After a point, the sleep of death *became* death. In its frozen vault, the human body finally broke down, and revival was no longer possible.

According to the cutting-edge preservation science of the continent, this period took slightly over a hundred years.

Peruma claimed to acknowledge this reality in law. A century to the day after a person was sentenced to the sleep of death, they would be unplugged, removed from the cryochamber, and allowed to die. After all, if evidence for your innocence hadn't turned up in a hundred years, the chance that it would do so in the time to come was vanishingly small—wasn't it?

'So you're saying,' Nila said, 'that I have to solve a hundred-year-old case in *seven* days? You took your own sweet time digging up your grandmother's archive, didn't you?'

'There was never a reason to—until now.'

Nila puffed out her cheeks and let the air escape her in an anguished whistle. 'Okay. Well. I can *try*. But if I can't find anything by the weekend—'

'No, no, that won't do. I need you to put in the application for reopening the case today.'

'*Today?!*' Nila spluttered. 'Apply—before I begin investigating? Before I even know if there are any grounds? You want me to commit to you right now, and risk us going into a hearing on Monday having nothing to say?'

'Because I have one chance to save him.' Ani's face was grim but without artifice. 'One chance, and I'm coming to you. It's only fair to have some insurance that prevents you from backing out two days before his death-day, isn't it? If you say no right now, I can still go to someone else.'

Nila clenched the table again, staring down at the coarse wood.

'If it helps your decision,' said Ani, 'You'll be given every resource you need. A skimmer will be placed at your disposal. Anything else, just call me. I'll see it done.'

Nila narrowed her eyes. 'How?'

Ani smiled. 'Our family bounced back pretty quickly after the revolution. My grandmother was a genius with investments. By the end of her life, she and her wife had shifted to High Town, and we've never looked back. I know the burden I'm putting upon you, Nila. But you don't need to worry about resources.'

'Ah—hm.'

You haven't signed anything yet.

But a vision was dancing in front of her eyes. The Chapterhouse's grand tribunal chamber, the great closed amphitheatre, arched and pillared, black and gold. The twelve selected pupils, along with their seniors, arrayed in their gowns; the eyes of thousands upon them in the hall, and the eyes of countless more who watched the broadcast, from Council to Commune and beyond, in the cities of the subcontinent; ready to begin the case that had been a hundred years in the making, the case that Council and Commune had spent a century preparing for, the case for which a whole revolution had been just a curtain-raiser. The Fifth Inflection Point of Peruman history.

And meanwhile, in a smaller room down the corridor, built for an intimate audience of thirty, another case would be beginning, also a hundred years in the making.

The songs would write themselves, even if Sanya was no longer around to sing the great moments of Peruma into historical memory. No matter. Someone would.

Reasonable doubt. That's all. Reasonable doubt.

Nila took one more breath, and looked Ani in the eye.

'One question,' she said.

'Ask.'

'Why me?'

For a moment, Ani was silent. Then she spoke deliberately, as if she'd prepared every word.

'Guardian Nila. I've asked you to reopen a murder case. But I know—you know—this is not an ordinary murder. Because Jagat is no ordinary person. He is an assassin. He is a martyr. He is the Last Mutineer and the First Anarchist. The world we live in was born that morning with that gunshot on Unity Bridge. And you'll be asking whether everything it's built on is just an illusion. How do you think the people will see this? For them, it wouldn't just be reopening a murder case, it will be reopening history itself, and all its wounds. The moment the first newspaper reports this case, from Council to Commune, everyone will be looking at you, because with what you do this week, with what you'll say in the tribunal on Monday morning, that world could shatter.'

'I know all this,' Nila whispered. 'I know what this case means. Why are you telling me?'

The eyes that locked on hers were obsidian black with something ageless, immovable.

'Because I want you to know, Nila—*Guardian* Nila—that I don't care about what this case means. I don't care about the judgement of the past or the weight of the future. I don't care about the inflection points of history. I only care about one thing: justice. Justice for Jagat, justice for the life that he lost. And I want someone who thinks that way, with everything they have. Someone who will see justice done, though ...'

Ani's eyes travelled to the pendant at her throat. Nila followed her gaze to the jade, and to the words below it.

3
Moral Luck

THE CHAPTERHOUSE'S WEST GATE OPENED INTO the pupils' garden, a stylised mélange of moss, rock, sand and floral arrangements that reflected the ever-changing design choices of the more horticulturally-minded among the pupils. Nila picked her way around a gravel patch, the winding path taking her around a moss pond and a miniature bamboo grove, before ending in a black kissing gate.

Outside, the Peruman dusk enfolded her. A little way away, the Urai flowed into the sunset, the water daubed in streaks of crimson. To her right, beyond the Chapterhouse grounds, slanting sunbeams glanced off the first row of High Town's towers, encasing the sea-stone walls in a blood-red tint. On the other side of the river, the first sprinkling of the Commune's night lights glimmered faintly in the eventide. The scent of wet grass mingled with the flowers, a mildness that matched the time of day.

'You're late,' said Maru, sitting on a bench just off the path.

'I can't believe I let you bully me into this,' said Nila. 'I should be working.'

Maru stood. 'That's all you'll be doing this week, Nila. Think of this as the last meal of the condemned.'

'Couldn't find a better metaphor?'

'Sorry.' Maru grinned. 'Come.'

They walked down to the river and caught the path that snaked around from the Chapterhouse's main gate, and went westwards. Pupils and guardians jogged past them on either side, out on their evening runs. In the grounds, a few picnickers were in the final stages of packing up before nightfall.

'All set?' said Maru.

'Finished up the case paperwork, yeah,' said Nila. 'That's what delayed me—I was just filing a bunch of applications with the registry.'

'Starting work when?'

'Tonight. I've downloaded and bookmarked the witness testimonies from the day of the assassination, to begin with.'

Maru took a look at her. 'How're you feeling?'

'To be honest, I really don't know.' Nila drew a breath. 'I haven't had a moment. I think I'll go sit in the library later and start figuring out just what I've gotten myself into.'

'Anyone spoken to you?

'No—I don't think anyone knows. Other than you.' She shrugged. 'They will, soon enough.'

The lights came on, casting the path in silvery-white illumination. Dusk had begun to darken.

'Here we are,' said Maru.

The path curved downwards to the river, ending in a pier that jutted out into the water. Beside the pier there rested a gondola, decked out in red and black.

Maru checked his wristheld. 'Just in time for the next one.' They clambered into the boat, ensconcing themselves in the stern.

'Evening, Maru. Evening, Nila,' said the gondolier, a tall, wiry woman whose eyes were hidden in the shadows of a wide-brimmed hat.

'Evening, Ketani,' said Maru.

'You're off to watch the Urumi, then?'

'That's right,' Maru said. He nudged Nila. 'Guess how much persuasion it took to make this one agree to an evening out.'

'Yes, wasn't *Council vs Commune* announced today?' said Ketani. 'Nila, you must be in that, no? Which side?'

'Not that one,' said Maru. '*But*—oooffff!' he broke off as Nila nudged him back, far less gently. 'Ah, moving on—expecting a full boatload then, Ketani, or can we push off?'

'There are a bunch of reserved seats for this circuit—' Ketani looked towards the pier. 'Oh, there they are at last!'

A troupe of people were coming down the pier. Nila counted twelve as they entered the gondola, making it sway alarmingly. A gaggle of voices filled the air.

'All aboard?' the gondolier called.

There were murmurs of assent.

'Maru,' Nila murmured, as Ketani threw off the rope, and the gondola slid into open water.

'Mm?'

'Am I completely out of touch, or are many of these people not from the Chapterhouse?'

'Na, you're right,' Maru kept his voice low. 'Half these folks are two years below us but the others are not ours.'

'What are non-pupils doing on the Agora Shuttle?'

She scanned the unfamiliar faces around her with a smidgen of disquiet: young, all of them, pupil-age, but strangers; and yet, oddly comfortable, at ease in the gondola, their laughter rising up to the darkening skies, and one of them was holding hands with a pupil …

She realised it just as Maru exhaled beside her, and said: 'Of course—it's Farewell Day.'

Farewell Day. Her stomach wrenched as a new note within the laughter made itself known: an undercurrent of melancholy, layered with wistfulness and the sense of things breaking apart.

The Confederation's neutrality rules were strict, and enforced with obsessive rigour. For the seven years between joining the Confederation and the end of pupillage, you could not set foot in the half of Peruma that you came from, except on a work visit. In the first four years, your parents and one other person could see you in the Chapterhouse during visiting hours, once every two months. In the fifth year, you were sent to live with an adoptive family in the opposite half from which you came. And in the last two years, you were not permitted to speak to anyone from your side of the river outside of work, on the pain of expulsion. In seven years, during the most formative years of a person's life, the Confederation prided itself on creating guardians who might still love wherever they came from—High Town or the Commune—but above all, were committed to Confederation impartiality.

For the *most* part, everyone admitted (if somewhat grudgingly) that the system, based on just the right combination of coercion, persuasion and incentive, worked.

But it was hard.

And few things were harder than Farewell Day, when the two-year exile formally began. In acknowledgement of what it was going to put its pupils through that day, the Chapterhouse relaxed its rules, allowing the soon-to-be exiles to take anyone they wanted with them to any place in Confederation territory, even the out-of-bounds Agora Island.

She looked at those faces anew, at the shadows that overhung the happiness. There was sadness in some, the sadness of endings; resolve in others; and in yet more, only confusion. Across the bridge of time, she felt a sense of fellowship with the last.

'You're missing him, aren't you?' said Maru softly.

Nila smiled. 'Never more so than in moments like this.'

'You know,' said Maru, 'You'll be going back to the Commune now, for the investigation. The work exception applies while you're there. And that means—'

'The thought had occurred to me,' Nila said.

'And? We still have six months left in our exile period. But you—'

'I—I don't know,' said Nila. 'I'm on brief, I can't abuse it for personal -'

'Stupid rules deserve to be abused. Nila, are you really telling me that when you go to the Commune this week, you'll actively avoid seeing Anam because of "duty to the brief"?'

Nila grinned. 'Sometimes I think I envy you, who came to the Chapterhouse without leaving anyone behind.'

The fleetest of shadows passed across Maru's face—passed, and was gone. 'Nice try evading my question,' he said.

'Maru, you—'

'Agora approaches!' The gondolier's voice cut through their conversation, sparing Nila the embarrassment of an answer.

The lights of Agora Island glittered before them.

In the western half of Peruma City, there came a point when the Urai widened suddenly, curving sharply outwards on both banks. Here there was an island shaped like a ship, whose own contours followed the shorelines so closely that it looked like the last, detached piece of a jigsaw puzzle, ready to fit into the one remaining gap. In the days of Old Empire, it had been a pleasure retreat for the Imperial family; under undivided republican Peruma, an expensive water-sports park; and now, after the revolution, it had been given over to the Confederation, a place for pupils—barred from going back home—to come to before they went stir-crazy within the Chapterhouse walls.

Agora Island, they called it, the one-stop getaway when you needed an evening out. Here was the social life of the Confederation, the bars and the cafés, the amphitheatre and the arcade, sports pitches under floodlights: a mini-city, or the closest thing to it, all paid for jointly by Council and Commune, along with a generous—if not ostentatious—pupil allowance.

The gondola drew up to the pier. They leapt off it and onto the shore. 'Thanks, Ketani,' said Maru.

'Enjoy the Urumi,' the gondolier said. 'And good luck with—whatever it is you have this week, Nila.'

Nila nodded her thanks. The six couples fanned out, and were quickly lost in the milling crowd by the shoreline. For a brief moment, she wondered how many of them would still be together when morning came.

Agora Island filled her senses, as it always did, a stark difference from the curated minimalism of the Chapterhouse: the milling pupils by the open-air bars near the shore, a constant undertow of conversation; starlight dissolving into the rows of lamps that marked out the paths that led inland, towards the arcade and the other buildings of the Agora; the scent of water, mingling with—

Maru saw her expression and laughed. 'We'll keep our tradition, come. First stop, as always.'

They stepped off the pier and towards the line of food stalls. Maru pulled out two Agora vouchers from his pocket. 'You know what we want, Shama,' he said to the stall owner.

'On it.'

'That's *your* allowance—' Nila began as Shama ladled two bowls of mrigel fish soup from a cauldron beside him.

'On me today,' Maru said. 'You can compensate me with a full gourmet tour of the Agora on Monday, to celebrate victory.'

'Do *not* jinx—'

'Yes, yes. Now eat.'

The mild, juicy sweetness of Peruma's celebrated freshwater fish overtook her, momentarily blocking out the rest of the Agora. She finished quickly, smacking her lips. They washed up the bowls in the sink behind the stall and returned them to Shama.

'What exactly are we watching today then?' said Nila, as they stepped onto a cobbled path that sloped gently uphill, towards an area of woodland. Ahead of them, rising above the trees, they could see the fin-shaped structure of the arcade, built on the Agora's highest point.

Maru took out his wristheld and pinched out a screen. A colourful—almost gaudy—flyer appeared before them as they walked. One part of it was a looped video of two people wielding coiled swords in a complex interchange of parry and riposte.

The Urumi Collective comes to Peruma! Immerse yourself in an evening of reliving the grandeur of Old Empire, with a performance of its famous, courtly sword form, the Urumi. The Urumi Collective has spent two decades painstakingly reconstructing and perfecting this lost art. We guarantee you an experience as authentic as can be—Urumi in Old Empire was not merely a clash of blades but a philosophy and a way of life. The collective will perform at the Arena in High Town on 1 August, at 7.30 p.m.; at the Maidan in the Commune on 2 August, at 7.30 p.m.; and deliver a special performance at the Amphitheatre at Agora Island on 3 August, at 7.30 p.m. One show only, one chance for you to witness the great sword form of Old Empire.

The Urumi Collective is a part of the Sepia Order, dedicated to preserving and protecting our common heritage of Old Empire. To learn more about our work—and to support us—CLICK HERE.

'So kitsch,' said Nila, as Maru pinched shut the screen. They'd entered the woodland; the leaves rustled in the mild breeze, the sound reminiscent of a gentle drizzle.

'Whatever gets the eyeballs,' said Maru. 'But they're genuine, Nila. I checked out some videos before buying tickets. These people are actually in love with Imperial history. They take all this very seriously.'

'Hey, what's not to love about some good duelling,' said Nila. 'Let's just drop the Imperial nostalgia and the *way of life* stuff, though?'

'I don't think you get one without the other,' Maru laughed. The path curved to the right and then downwards. Now they began to see others moving in the same direction, familiar faces, pupils from their year and below, even the odd senior guardian. The path ended in a large glade, where there stood the Agora's amphitheatre, the rings of seats rising up to the trees. There was a perfunctory check at the entrance, and then they were in.

'I'm glad I booked these tickets while you were still refusing to come,' said Maru as they climbed up to their seats. 'No way we were getting this view otherwise.'

The seats around them had begun to fill. On the stage, the illumination came on, spotlighting a rectangular strip. A buzz of anticipation ran around the amphitheatre.

There was a rustle of cloth to their left. A man sat down on the step. He turned to acknowledge them. Wavy black hair framed an unlined forehead, a tuft falling untidily down to his eyes. He was smiling.

'Maru—and Nila.'

'Guardian Ghorge, hello!' said Maru.

'Talk about a coincidence,' said Ghorge. 'I was just vetting your heads of argument for the cancer compensation claim against Mandalium Corp, Maru. Excellent work.'

'Thank you, Guardian.'

'Good thing we're on the same side in this—wouldn't want to be opposing the Chapterhouse's specialist in mining-related diseases.' Ghorge's eyes twinkled. 'Not that one would think of such a morbid specialty, to look at you—pardon the pun!'

'Long-term occupational injury law is the technical term,' Maru said lightly. 'Cancer claims are just my niche within that. But yes, looks can be deceptive. And speaking of which, Guardian, talk about finding you at an Urumi performance. Wouldn't have taken you to be into Imperial nostalgia.'

'Back at you!' Ghorge laughed. He was one of the younger guardians—originally from the Commune—who'd briefly taught their batch of pupils the collective bargaining and strike provisions of the Charter. Nila hadn't yet worked with him on a case but she remembered him as someone the pupils had instinctively warmed to, establishing a reflexive complicity against the older, stiffer guardians and the Executive Committee. Ghorge had refused to take himself (or the Charter) any more seriously than necessary; a refreshing break from many of their other classes. She had seen him around after that, in the corridors, or in the hall during meals, and he always had a smile and nod of recognition.

'But it's good to see you here, taking a break—and especially you, Nila,' he turned to her. 'I know pity is the last thing you want, but ... I cannot comprehend *what* the committee was thinking this morning.'

'Ah ... thanks!' said Nila, uncertainly.

On the stage, the first two practitioners materialised, their whip-like swords in their hands. A smattering of applause rose into the sky.

'Are you doing okay?' said Ghorge, lowering his voice, as the crowd around them began to fall silent.

'Yes, quite,' Nila said. She looked at the guardian. Concern was etched into his features, but also—despite what he said—a hint of pity. She felt a sudden rush of blood to the head.

'More than okay, actually,' she went on. 'I got an interesting brief just moments after the committee's announcement.'

Beside her, Maru stiffened.

On the stage, the performance began. A voice-over from behind the stage informed the audience that they were starting with a straightforward demonstration of attack and defence, simple lunges telegraphed to meet the five basic parries, the movements slowed down for the benefit of the viewers who might not have seen this before. The performers looked like they were gliding through water, an easy unhurried motion that could be tracked by the untrained eye—just about.

Ghorge half-turned towards her, eyebrows raised. 'A fresh brief?'

'Yes.' Nila kept her eyes on the stage. 'To reverse the sentence of Jagat R.'

'The sentence of—*oh!*' Ghorge's momentary incomprehension, shifting into astonishment, gave her an odd—almost shameful—feeling of satisfaction.

'A … *private* brief, Nila?'

'Yes, Guardian.'

A low whistle escaped Ghorge. Heads turned towards them, shushes hissed out through clenched teeth. He threw up his hand in apology.

'That is the very last thing I'd have expected to hear,' Ghorge said softly. 'A private pupil brief—the first time in forty years, since Naina L.'

'I was a touch surprised myself,' Nila deadpanned.

Ghorge chuckled at that, his eyes twinkling. 'I'll bet. How everything changes in a moment at the Chapterhouse, huh? When this news comes out, Nila, you're going to be *the* person in Peruma until the hearing. In fact, I'd mute my inbox if I were you, to avoid both the questions and the well-intentioned terrible pieces of advice.'

Nila nodded tightly.

Below, the Urumi wielders had taken the complexity up a level, demonstrating ripostes and counter-parries, and second-intention attacks that fell purposefully short and then exploded again, while the opponent was lulled into the security of a failed advance. They were quicker now, the movements still clean but harder to track.

Ghorge leaned back. 'So they *did* want him back after all,' he said, more to himself than to Nila. 'And to do it this way. Classic anarchists ...'

'Guardian,' she interrupted.

'Yes?'

'The Commune hasn't engaged me.'

'*What*? Who is your client, then?'

'A descendent of Jagat's.'

'You know them?'

'Not until this morning.'

'Then why'd they come to you?'

'Ahm—' for the first time, Nila realised how implausible it sounded, when spoken aloud. 'She said she had no trust in the committee.'

'I ... see.'

Ghorge subsided, and said nothing more. Maru turned to Nila, eyebrows raised. She nodded. *Go ahead.*

'Do you have any thoughts, Guardian?' Maru said.

Ghorge shook his head. 'It's just … odd,' he said. 'Family or Commune, there's been a hundred years to get Jagat back. Nobody's tried. He's been consigned to the past, to the period of the revolution, buried by the Pact of Forgetting, like everything else that happened that week. But *now* someone takes up that option—the very day of *Council vs Commune*—and bypasses the Executive Committee to do it?'

'What do you think it means?' said Nila.

'I don't know,' said Ghorge. 'Don't get me wrong, Nila, this is a massive case for you. But I'm just going to say—there are times where you have to be as careful about your own client as you have to be about the other side.'

'Mm.' Ani's face appeared in her mind's, eyes without guile.

'I'm not going to flood you with unsolicited advice,' Ghorge continued. 'You'll be getting more than enough of it this coming week. I'd only advise you to be cautious when talking to anyone, and that includes me. When it comes to the revival of Jagat, mixed up with *Council vs Commune* this week, there's not a single soul in Peruma who wouldn't have a very direct interest in the outcome of this case.'

'Understood, Guardian,' said Nila. 'Thank you.'

'If you do need anything, Nila, come and find me anytime, of course.' Ghorge leaned back again. 'And that's enough shop talk; I think our colleagues are on the verge of murdering us for this chatter. Let's enjoy the show.'

By now, the Urumi performance had evolved into its fourth or fifth level of complexity, with added wrinkles in every round: a sequence entirely without blade contact, made up solely of feints and disengages, drew gasps from the watchers; a circular parry that deflected the blade, millimetres from the chest after another sequence of counter-attacks, brought people to the edge of their seats. From time to time, Ghorge interjected, telling them more than the voice-over's basic taxonomies, placing a move in the context of its historical evolution; clearly, he had been long fascinated by the art.

'I do see what the flyer meant about the *way of life*,' Maru said, as the performance reached a crescendo of pace and energy, and gradually began to tail off into an ending.

'It's not inaccurate,' said Ghorge, 'but as with everything the Sepia Order does, they don't tell you the half of it.'

'I was just thinking that,' said Nila. 'The aesthetics are great, yes, but something doesn't become *the* Imperial court art without there being more to it.'

'You'll get an inkling when you look at when it really became popular,' said Ghorge. 'It was towards the very tail end of the Empire, the last hundred years or so. The century of chaos.'

'So,' said Maru, 'aestheticised performances of violence as a form of meditative catharsis for the actual violence the Empire was committing in its death throes?'

'Kind of, but there's also a bit more,' said Ghorge. Beneath them, the cadence of the practitioners was once again fluid like water, their movements distinct. A section of the audience near the stage had begun clapping along to the rhythm.

'When they formalised the rules of Urumi,' Ghorge continued, 'it was crafted so that every permitted move had a counter, a counter-counter, and so on. A parry for a lunge, a disengage for a parry, a change of line for a disengage—all the way until all sets were exhausted. For the master practitioners, it was a mind game as much as anything else: which of you could predict the other's moves far enough into a sequence to come up with the first move that had no answer? But it also meant that once you had mastered the craft, you *could*, in theory, play the perfect game. And a game between two masters could only end in a draw. The art of Urumi means the art of perfect control, from opening to endgame.'

'Perfect control does not sound like a lot of fun,' said Nila.

'The fun was when it actually didn't work like that,' said Ghorge. 'Because of course it didn't. You could plan and execute the perfect sequence, but something might happen. A sweaty thumb that would make the pommel turn in your hand—enough. A slip of an inch—enough. For a while, the Urumi masters were obsessed with inventing *the* perfect sequence, but finally, they had to concede: you could do everything right, and still lose.'

'Right,' said Nila. 'They learned, like we all do. But how did that make it an emblem for Old Empire?'

'The philosophers of the dying empire saw in that a metaphor for life,' said Ghorge. 'They extended it to other domains.'

'Such as?'

'Well, ethics,' Ghorge smiled slightly. 'They postulated a moral framework where you could do everything right—every individual action could be the right step—and yet, circumstances could bring you to a point where all those actions culminated in a choice where the only options were wrong, incommensurably wrong. They called it moral luck. You had done something wrong not because *you* were a bad person, but because you were just … morally unlucky.'

'Uh huh,' said Maru. 'I see where this is going.'

'You do, don't you? Moral luck became the philosophy of a crumbling empire where every month there was a fresh uprising, and you needed some justification for the massacre you were about to commit on your own people. It was just bad luck that brought the empire to a point where there were no right choices, only the wrong choice of carrying out a massacre, or the wrong choice of doing nothing and letting itself disintegrate in equal violence. Nothing to do with the empire's own choices, of course.'

'Hey, nobody taught this in the ethics class in the Chapterhouse!' said Maru.

'The moral philosophies of crumbled empires tend to crumble with them,' Ghorge chuckled.

Below them, the Urumi performance ended in a final flourish, and they rose along with the rest of the audience to deliver a standing ovation. The lights dimmed, the stage emptied, and a low buzz of conversation swelled again as people began to walk towards the exit.

'Good luck with everything, Nila,' said Ghorge. 'I'll see you around.'

And then he was gone, another body in the crowd that was milling towards the exit.

'Well, that was a cheerful end!' said Maru.

'Wasn't it just!' said Nila. 'From Urumi swordplay to Imperial crimes. *Moral luck*, huh.'

They walked out of the amphitheatre. Outside, the crowd was dispersing in various directions. The two took the path back up into the woodland.

'What did you think of his warning about Ani?' said Maru.

'It's logical,' said Nila. 'I get it. But—I just—I just don't think that's Ani? I have no reason, but my instinct says that she was being genuine.'

'*She* could be the one being set up, you know,' Maru said. 'I mean, how difficult can it be to plant a letter from Jagat, if you really wanted to?'

'I guess?' Nila shook her head. Maru was saying something about turning right but her own mind was elsewhere, in the dance and the rhythm that she had just seen, dissolving into something more sinister: the bloody handprints of Old Empire planted across the map of the subcontinent, a confession of guilt—or a plea for absolution.

Moral luck.

'Wait—where are we?' she said suddenly, as a sharp burst of floodlight broke into her thoughts.

'OY!' came the shout, as she saw it from the corner of her eye: a ball arcing towards her. Instinctively, she swung out a foot and intercepted it. It bounced off her heel and stopped a foot away.

'Great touch, Nila!' a woman came running towards her, and Nila noticed that they had come to the floodlit sports pitches on the east side of the Agora. Mechanically, she passed the ball back with the side of her foot.

'Join in?' the woman said. 'We could do with two more.'

Nila's head swivelled to her left. 'Maru!'

'I told you we were coming here! You just said *mmm* and went back to thinking about whatever you were thinking.'

'I assumed we were going back to the pier.'

Maru shrugged. 'An hour left until the last shuttle leaves. Just enough time for a pick-up game. Thought you might like to get a last one in before the madness begins tonight.'

'I—my shoes—'

'Got you covered,' he grinned, slinging his backpack to the ground and fishing out two pairs of shoes.

'Come quick,' said the woman, before turning and dribbling back to the centre of the pitch.

Nila shook her head as she began to put on the shoes. 'Trip to Agora, mrigel fish soup, a performance at the amphitheatre, a pick-up game—it's like you planned to cram all my favourite things into one night. *Really* making this into the last meal of the condemned, aren't you?'

Maru laughed. 'Get the adrenaline rush now, it'll be useful for the long, long nights ahead.'

'Don't remind me,' Nila muttered. 'I wish we didn't have to go back.' She tied up her laces, tied back her hair and jogged on to the field. Maru followed, and soon, for just an hour, the Chapterhouse, Ghorge, Jagat and *Council vs Commune* were utterly forgotten.

Day Two

The Directorate

4

The Crown of Infallibility

TWENTY-FIVE YEARS AGO, THE DIRECTORATE Court abolished the death penalty.

Our decision was celebrated not only in this city, but across the subcontinent: 'What Peruma thinks today, the subcontinent thinks tomorrow.' In our wake, city after city removed this vestige of barbarism from their own laws.

Today, this court has decided to consign its own legacy to a sleep of death.

In a way, it was a chronicle foretold. This court's ruling from twenty-five years ago was based on a single premise: that the death penalty assumes infallibility—infallibility of knowledge, of truth, of judgement. We are human. We make mistakes. Yet the death penalty does not allow us to atone for error, because you cannot bring an innocent person back to life.

Writing separately, the wise Judge Ilarum warned against this reasoning. The claim to infallibility was just one of the many reasons why the death penalty had to go. But to base judgement only upon that was to build a castle upon a foundation of smoke.

Perhaps Judge Ilarum saw the future. In her time, there was no indication that cryogenic preservation research would advance so fast, so far, that within twenty-five years it would go from a futuristic dream to a workable technology. And unfortunately, it has also given this court a chance to resile from its historic decision.

Today's court appears to argue thus: cryogenic preservation has turned the death penalty from an irreversible punishment to a reversible one. This has dissolved the only distinction that existed between the death penalty and any other form of punishment. We can, at last, atone for human error. If we find out that we made a mistake, we can just wake the sleeper up.

Let me take this argument on its own terms. There may have been a case to answer had the sleep of death (ironically) itself been permanent. But it is not. Our science only allows for preservation up to a hundred years. After that, the body breaks down. Death must come.

The court attempts to escape this bind by seeking refuge in mathematics. It takes the mathematical concept of the limit: X can approach Y, such that X is never equal to Y, but the difference between them grows so vanishingly small that for certain purposes, you might as well take X to be Y. Then the court says that while the possibility of an error can never be zero, with time it grows smaller and smaller, towards zero. And when hundred years have passed, 'for all practical purposes' the probability of error has become zero.

The court uses these fictions to exempt itself from the burden of infallibility.

But life is not quite as symmetrical and elegant as mathematics. When the court says that the probability of error approaches zero with time, it performs a sleight of hand. What it is really saying is that the probability of discovering error approaches zero. Evidence erodes. Witnesses die. Memories senesce. The fault is not with the truth. It is with our ability to discover it, flawed from the first to the last.

That is why I believe that this new technology solves nothing. By allowing this so-called sleep of death, the court readmits brutality into our justice system, only this time cloaked in the language of reversibility.

And what reversibility? Let me part with this thought. Imagine that in the ninety-ninth year of a sentence, irrefutable evidence of innocence comes out. You awaken the sleeper—into an alien world. Their parents, lovers, friends, children—all dead for generations. Every anchor to their world—gone. But memories remain. The half-life they have lived remains. They cannot escape from that. They cannot start over. They will live as ghosts, a part of their lives in one century, and a part in another; two broken halves.

And this is not reversible.

What do you expect will happen, then, to the half-life that remains, other than decay?

If we denied ourselves the right to kill in the name of justice, what right do we have to snap and weld and solder broken bits of life in the name of justice?

I have attempted to persuade my colleagues to this point of view. I have failed. With due deference to the tradition of consensus at the court, I exercise my prerogative to dissent. I believe that today we have once again arrogated to ourselves the crown of infallibility that we had set aside twenty-five years ago.

It is a burden that will, one day, haunt us.

Judge H.R. Khana
13 May 275 A.E.

Nila closed the book and slumped back into her chair. She turned bleary eyes to the high, dark-gabled library roof.

The Chapterhouse library, spread over three floors, appeared to have been designed by an architect who had a personal grudge against light. Slit windows high up on the walls, angled and slanted in a quest to let in air but keep out the sun. The darkest possible shade of fumed oakwood had been used for the bookshelves, the long tables and the roof gables: a formidable tone of brown bleeding into black. The walls themselves had been carefully painted the colour of rusted iron. And to round things off, the lighting was always turned down to the pitch of an oil lamp.

She ran her finger down the spine of the book. *The crown of infallibility. It is a burden that will, one day, haunt us.*

Words from more than a century ago, of dissent and doubt, turning and turning over in her mind, associating and dissociating like a child playing with a combination cube, rooting her to her chair, a strange inertia, as if waiting for ...

... the inevitable sound of footsteps down the stairs.

'Nila!'

She screwed her eyes shut. When she opened them, Noor and Suneen were standing there.

'You're here,' said Noor.

'And with paper books!' Suneen added.

'Um—' Nila said, 'No screen, no distractions.'

Suneen peered over her shoulder. '*Pre-Charter* case law? Whatcha reading, Nila?'

'Just stuff,' she said, pushing the book away. 'You're here for—that?'

They fell silent, and she sensed them looking at each other over her head. When she glanced up, Noor was rubbing her nose, a familiar gesture of unease. 'Uhm yes,' she said at last, her voice dripping with embarrassment. 'We just thought we'd come down early and get a head start on research.'

'Makes sense.' Her own words seemed to come from very far away. 'Mad week ahead for you.'

'Listen, Nila—' Noor paused, before it came out in a rush. 'I am *so* sorry about what happened. We were talking about it last night. It's crazy they didn't pick you. For *this.*'

'Yeah,' said Suneen. 'It's—'

'I'm over it,' Nila waved a hand. 'It is what it is. And I'm happy for you. You should enjoy the week. You're getting to shape the Fifth Inflection Point.' She tried to smile but abandoned it as it started to come out all twisted. To still a heaving in her chest, she said: 'Which side are you for?'

'Commune,' said Suneen.

'Aha.' Nila leaned forward, in spite of herself. 'The more interesting side. So, you have to kill the Mandalium Agreement?'

'Pretty much,' said Noor.

'How're you pitching it?

'Uh, we're still thinking,' said Noor. 'Like, we know what Council will argue. They're going to say that even if we can finally amend the Charter, we can't alter its fundamentals. And that if *anything* is fundamental to the Charter, it's the Mandalium Agreement. It's like a—a—'

'—basic structure,' Nila completed.

'Yes, exactly. And you can't amend the basic structure, because that's like destroying the Charter itself. So we're bound by the Agree—'

'Yes, yes,' said Nila. 'That's the boring side. What are *you* going to say?'

'I—we are discussing it,' said Noor. 'Still early days, but we're thinking of saying that the Agreement is not a part of the—'

'—basic structure? But you're conceding the premise!' Nila said.

'I mean, we can hardly—'

'Why can't you?' She was hardly aware of her voice rising in excitement. 'Noor! Why so conservative? It's not like you.'

'We can't *say*—'

'You damn well can! What is it that those jokers—Wits—keep calling it—the *Cop-Out Constitution*, yeah? Our Charter is a compromise. It *has* no basic structure or identity. It's just the result of brinkmanship between Council and Commune, and some extra stuff that the drafting committee sneaked in on the side when no one was looking. Why concede any coherence or principle to a mess like that?'

'Nila!' said Suneen. 'Theoretically, yes—but how's this going to sound before the tribunal? Before the entire subcontinent on the live broadcast? Perumans argue that their own constitution is a cop-out with no identity? How do you think we'll look?'

'Obviously you won't put it that way,' Nila said impatiently. She reached for her wristheld. 'Look, if you want suggestions for structuring—'

'I—' began Suneen, but Noor held up a hand. 'Go on,' she said to Nila. 'Please.'

'Okay, let's break this down to the absolute basics, right. Why does the Charter exist?'

'To prevent civil war.'

'Yes, yes, of course—prevent civil war, resolve disputes, blah blah. And?'

'Go on, then,' said Noor.

'To freeze time! When our ancestors agreed that the Charter wouldn't be amended for a hundred years, they thought that the only way to have peace was to make time stop, to freeze things as they were on the day after the revolution. It's like—the Charter is a cryobox, and Peruma has been in a sleep of death within it.'

Noor narrowed her eyes. 'That's a weird analogy, Nila.'

'Haha, I know, it just ... popped into my head. Ahem. Moving on. So the Charter—the Charter tries to create this entire architecture of law that will replace Peruma's class conflict—you know, the provisions on demilitarisation, the joint ratification of treaties with the other cities—and at the centre of it all is the Mandalium Agreement, to divide the revenue from the mines between High Town and Commune. Seems fair to everyone when it's negotiated but over the years, as we all know, the Mandalium Agreement works out to the benefit of High Town, and begins to push the Commune towards economic ruin. But time has been frozen by law—the Commune *agreed* to it being frozen by law—so they can't do anything but wait. Until now. Until the hundred years are over.'

Noor nodded. 'So ...?'

'*So* ...' Nila pinched out a viewing screen, and began to trace boxes upon it. 'With this in mind, if you frame the Charter as a response to the revolution—to the trauma of the partition—then its identity was never meant to be locked into a specific set of provisions. Its identity was *meant to be* transitional, changing, and so, once the freeze is over—hang on. Is this argument consistent with your instructions from the Commune?'

'The only instruction is to win,' said Noor. 'I don't think anarchists care very much for constitutions.'

A horrible, sneaking suspicion sent tendrils snaking through Nila's mind. 'Who briefed you?' she said. 'Who, specifically?'

The single moment that Noor hesitated gave Nila her answer.

'It was Meera—Meera D.' Another pause. 'Your mother.'

Nila's fingers dropped, allowing the screen to collapse. Reality came rushing back, a needle pricking the balloon within which she had filled her temporary illusions.

'What am I doing?' she whispered. 'I'm not even in this.'

Suneen and Noor exchanged another uneasy glance. 'Listen, Nila,' said Noor, 'we know how much you wanted—and if you still want to be involved—you know—to discuss ideas, review a draft, maybe ... we'd love to ... just say the word.'

Nila swallowed. For a few seconds, she didn't answer. Then, her voice somehow level, she said: 'I appreciate it. But this week, it's a little busy.'

'You're on a brief too?' asked Suneen.

She almost blurted it out, but stopped herself at the last moment. 'Some research. Probably a dead end.'

Out of the corner of her eye, she saw Noor gesture to Suneen. *Don't push her*. 'Alright, then,' Noor said to her. 'See you around. And if you change your mind ...'

The choking feeling returned. Nila stood. 'I'll be getting along. I *hate* the light in this place.'

Which was true, as things went.

She went up the stairs, and at the top, turned around once. Suneen was leafing curiously through the books she had left on the table. Nila clenched her fists, forced herself to wait until she was out of the library, and then, in the corridor, she let herself cry.

'You look terrible,' said Maru.

Nila ran her fingers through her tangled hair, grimacing. 'The last two years, I never had reason for an all-nighter. And now my body has forgotten how to do it. Or I'm just getting old.'

'Yeah, you're *really* old, that must be it. And speaking of age and time—what's that?' He gestured to the end of the table, towards a black screen with a grey countdown clock.

122:46:32

'What do you think?' said Nila. 'I got the listing on my application last night. The registry has put Jagat's case down for hearing at 10.00 a.m. on Monday.'

'That's the day of—'

'The centenary of the revolution, yeah. The day of Director Purul's assassination. They sent him to the cryochamber that same night, so ...'

'You'll fray your nerves to shreds within forty-eight hours at this rate, let alone a hundred and twenty-two,' said Maru.

'At least I have a medical law man around. Hey, will this qualify as an occupational injury?'

Maru sighed. 'How're you feeling?'

'Not great.'

'Mm?'

'Now there's a date, Maru. It's a capital case, a man's life—and I have no time—'

'At least the pressure will be off you on Monday. Which senior have you asked to argue?'

'Ah, on that,' Nila shuffled her feet, staring at the floor. 'Hm—'

Maru's eyes widened. 'You're going to do this *yourself?*'

'I called Ani last night, after the listing. Gave her a shortlist of seniors. She just said, "If I wanted that I'd have cut out the middleperson and gone straight to the Executive Committee."'

'Are you serious!' Maru gave her the broadest of grins. 'Nila! This—this is even better than we hoped for!'

'I don't know, Maru—I—I don't know ...'

'Haven't you been dreaming about such a moment for the last seven years?'

'Some dreams need to remain dreams.'

'You're just—'

'No, seriously. I didn't tell you last evening, but I regretted it the moment I came out of the Well, Maru. It was just a damn perfect storm in there. I wasn't thinking straight. I was mad about being overlooked, mad about letting Ma down, mad about all my life choices, there was Ani with her *take it or leave it*, and suddenly I saw myself, a character in a Sanya poem—and ... and I took it for all the wrong reasons.'

'There's never a wrong reason to take a case,' Maru said.

'But now I have to do it all myself. Literally *do* it myself, no senior. A capital case. And I don't know where to start—I feel lost, Maru. The last few hours, I gave up. Just sat in the library and read old death penalty judgements.'

'The abolition challenges?'

'Yeah. Wow, that whole abolition history reads like an epic struggle with a shit ending. Not even a tragic ending that would justify it. Just shit. Great gobs of shit.'

'Most epic struggles end up like that, hey.'

'I guess. But there *was* this dissent—'

'Oh, you read Khana?' Maru's eyes lit up. 'You know he was from the old aristocracy, the ones who used to control the mandalium mines? But once he was appointed judge, it was like a switch flipped in his head, and he started writing all those ethically tortured dissents ...'

'Mm,' said Nila. There were times—not too often but there *were* times—when she was reminded that for all their friendship, Maru came from the upper reaches of High Town, great-grandson of councillors and judges, son and grandson of guardian arbitrators. Not that you could really tell, but sometimes, in a moment ...

Maru noticed, as he always did. He went red. 'Hehe. Coffee?'

She let him have the lifeline. 'Yes, please.'

'Knew it. I prepared the decoction while you were getting your adrenaline from doomed dissents.'

'Angelic.' She crossed the room and slumped in her chair.

Maru went over to the fridge. 'But listen,' he said, taking the glass out. 'You were there all night. You weren't just reading old death penalty judgments, were you?'

'Oh no,' Nila said, supporting her chin with her fists on the table. 'That was only after I gave up on the witness testimonies.'

'Yeah?' Maru walked across to her.

'Remember those locked room murder mysteries we used to love when we were trainee pupils?'

'I still do. Like solving equations: clean, elegant, symmetrical.'

'I feel like I'm in the opposite of a locked room mystery, if you know what I mean? It's not one hidden, logical solution, but an infinite range of possibilities. An open sky mystery, even.'

'Go on.'

'I'm not sure. The only thing is—I get the sense that the director was out to do something big the day he was assassinated. Really big. And maybe dangerous.' Nila closed her eyes as she spoke, reliving the scene through the witness testimonies.

That summer morning in High Town, in a city undivided.

'He rode a skimmer that floated in the air. Black achkan, gold dust, gold brooch.'

'I saw him pass. He looked ready.'

'The director looked quiet, calm, as always—but also, a little worried, you know? I can't quite place it, but it was a look I hadn't seen before on his face.'

'There was a strange sadness to him. He seemed like a man watching something break apart before his eyes.'

'I saw him, but what I remember more is Milana Maran. She looked nervous, so nervous, but also determined to see this through. The loyal secretary, to the end ...'

The amaltas flowers strewn along the path like a carpet, the slow transit along Victory Road.

'I remember thinking how much it felt like a scene from the epics. The hero riding into battle on a golden morning. And, like all the heroes, he never came back.'

'There was only one person—one person in Peruma—who would be director in the middle of a riot, and still take a single skimmer down Victory Road to talk to Low Town. Purul, the Douser of Fires.'

'Like he wanted to make a point. To us.'

'The amaltas flowers, a carpet of fire. That's what I remember. I'd come out to see the director, but all I thought of was how beautiful our city looked.'

The moment when the director's skimmer passed beyond the range of High Town's surveillance cameras. And the world sped up.

Step. Bridge. Explosion.

'It's when the bomb—it was a bomb, wasn't it?—went off. I couldn't see anything after that, the smoke was too thick, I was too far away. And then everyone was running to the bridge.'

'No. Nothing. Too far away. And the smoke.'

'I heard it. It was like the world coming apart. And then nothing.'

Death. Arrest. Trial. Sentence. Revolution.

When she opened her eyes, the cold coffee was in front of her. 'Enjoy the swill,' said Maru. 'And this time, finish it. I don't know how you abide this stuff but I'm not going to drink it for you two days in a row.'

'No fear.' She sipped her coffee, the coldness spreading down her throat, easing her throbbing headache by a smidgen. Maru resumed his place opposite her. She reached out for Baili the seagull and snuggled him in the crook of her arm.

'What's the general consensus?' Maru said. 'That he was going to make some concessions to the workers? Living wage or mining safety conditions?'

'Yeah, although there's a minority view that he was going to take a harder line, exert authority. All speculative, though.'

'You could look into his personal archive at the Directorate?' said Maru. 'They're obsessive about cataloguing every scrap of paper.'

'I'm going to apply.' Nila paused. 'But even otherwise, there are way too many random events which don't add up. It's just that—I don't know where to start.'

'Hmm, okay,' Maru said. 'Try this hook, Nila. Of all the things that happened that day, what makes you feel the uneasiest? The one thing that doesn't seem to *fit*?'

'Mm, good question.' Nila looked up at the low domed ceiling, letting her gaze unfocus. She clicked her teeth a few times. 'It's not anything that happened, you know? It's a silence.'

'Go on.'

'Maru, Peruma's had a fair few political trials, right?'

'Treason, rebellion, sedition, the works.'

'What's been the common thing?'

'The state always wins?'

'That, of course. But it's the set piece, isn't it? After the arguments are done, the verdict is in. The last speech. *I am willing to die*: Kiproki to the executive tribunal. *I will return, and I will be millions*: Labina to the emperor's court. *Your verdict will be as dust on the mountain*: Bariyar to the Directorate.'

'Nyawa reading out her whole manifesto,' Maru added.

'Exactly. But here? Nothing. The sentence is read. He doesn't say anything. Not then. Not when he's led from the court. Not when they put him in the cryobox.'

'Maybe he just didn't want to?'

'Come on, Maru. The man who wrote a letter asking his daughter not to think badly of him? This man *wanted* to explain himself to history.'

'You're right.' Maru crinkled his nose. 'And it's interesting you say that, actually. The Commune calls him Jagat the Martyr, no? Do you know the origins of the word?'

'Tell me?'

'It's from the language of Old Empire—it means *to give testimony*. To speak. Martyrs and silences don't go together.'

'Mm.' Nila rotated the glass and watched the coffee swirl. 'Okay, Maru, think through this with me. There is only one way to cast reasonable doubt upon Jagat's guilt, and that's to have an alternate theory of how Director Purul died that day.' She held up a finger. 'Possibility one: the director shot himself.' A second finger. 'Possibility two: Milana Maran shot him.' A third finger. 'Possibility three: Another person shot him, who then jumped into the river and swam away. That third possibility is our range of infinite solutions.'

'You don't really believe one or two,' said Maru.

'Unless I find a suicide note or a confession letter in the next one week, yeah, I don't.'

'So, another person?'

'Someone whom Jagat knowingly covered for at trial. Note that I say *knowingly*, not *willingly*.'

'Note that you're the only person I know who says *note that* in ordinary conversation,' said Maru, 'but yes, *noted*.'

'Shut up,' said Nila. 'Now, to narrow it down, if Jagat *was* covering for someone, it would have to be someone from Low Town, someone more important to the revolution. Maybe one of those underground groups—like the Levellers—who used to go around shooting people during that time?'

Maru made a face. 'We're going to spend this week trying to find evidence to reverse engineer from this conclusion, aren't we?'

Nila took a deep swig from her glass. The sugar high had dissolved very suddenly. Her head felt heavy again. 'I don't know,' she said. 'I don't even ...' She tailed off, her eyes shifting to her files. Maru followed her gaze.

'What's wrong?' he said. 'You've been off since you came in, Nila. And it's not just about this case being hard.'

'Well.' She tapped at the screen on her wrist. An image sprang up between them.

Beneath a wall of glass, a man lay sleeping.

'Last night when I crashed for a bit,' said Nila. 'I dreamed about him.'

'Jagat?'

She nodded. 'I dreamed that I won. He came back to life. He was standing before me. And I—I tried to go towards him, to hug him, to talk to him—I don't really know what I wanted, dream-me is a bit like real-me, but every time I moved, he moved away—receded, like—like the rainbows that we used to chase when we were children. And when I woke up, I thought ... Maru. Can you imagine being brought back into the world a century after you left it? This isn't reopening a case five, ten, fifteen years after.' She gestured at the image. 'It's not even the same world. So what are we ...'

'I know,' said Maru. 'I know what you're thinking. I've been thinking the same. So I did a quick network search this morning—'

'You don't have to do my research for me ...'

'Oh hush,' Maru tapped his wristheld. A screen came up, blue in colour. Seven faces appeared before her. They were all young, their faces set like statues.

```
Sevaka Perumal: Conspiracy to wage war against Peruma
Sentenced: 277 A.E.
Sentence reversed: 277 A.E.
Cause of reversal: Third-party confession

Dattatreya B.: Conspiracy to wage war against Peruma
Sentenced: 284 A.E.
Sentence reversed: 309 A.E.
Cause of reversal: Retrospective pardon

Sammath L.: Mandalium trafficking
Sentenced: 289 A.E.
Sentence reversed: 319 A.E.
```

Cause of reversal: Retrospective abolition of offence

Saibanna R.: Mandalium trafficking
Sentenced: 292 A.E.
Sentence reversed: 319 A.E.
Cause of reversal: Retrospective abolition of offence

Sumer A.: Murder while serving sentence for murder
Sentenced: 336 A.E.
Sentence reversed: 352 A.E.
Cause of reversal: Third-party conviction for same offence

Deena N.: Conspiracy to wage war against Peruma
Sentenced: 347 A.E.
Sentence reversed: 384 A.E.
Cause of reversal: Use of sealed cover evidence, vitiating fair trial

Bariyar S.: Terrorism, economic terrorism, destruction of public infrastructure with intent to spread terror in the general populace, funding of banned organisations with the intent of promoting terrorism, armed dacoity, arson, impersonation of public official with intent to overthrow the state, murder (several), conspiracy to wage war against Peruma, theft
Sentenced: 359 A.E.
Sentence reversed: 382 A.E.
Cause of reversal: Mistaken identity

'Is that—'

'The seven times in our history that a sleep of death sentence has been reversed,' Maru said. 'From five months to ...'

'Fuck,' said Nila. 'Thirty-seven years.'

'Yeah.' Maru pressed on one of the faces, expanding it. It was the face of a woman, looking back at them with quiet eyes, wisps of curly hair around the edges of her forehead.

'Deena N.,' said Maru. 'And look, here.' He drew up a document. 'A hospital record.' He took a stylus and highlighted a line in green, before expanding it with his fingers.

```
Psychological adjustment problems:
Severe

Recommended prescription:
[Redacted], 3x a day, lifelong.
[Redacted], 2x a day, lifelong.
[Redacted], 2x a day, until notice.

Side effects:
[Redacted]
```

'Every once in a while you remind me of why we nicknamed you *lemme-look-it-up-Maru*. How did you even find this online?'

'I have my ways.'

'Thankfully.' Nila chewed her lip. 'I almost don't want to know—but dammit, Maru, I do want to know. Deena N. How long did she live? After.'

'She was twenty-seven when she was sentenced, in 347. After her resurrection, she lived till 409. Died at the age of fifty-two.' Maru's voice softened. 'There's nothing on record to say that her death was caused by ... "psychological adjustment problems".'

'Fifty-two,' Nila whispered. 'That's no age.'

She reached out to the seeing screen, and flicked it back to the seven faces, seven names, seven awakenings.

'Lives,' she said. Khana's dissent floated in her mind. 'Snapped off, regrafted. But what happens when you uproot a half-life and plant it into the soil of another time? Will it live? Or have ... psychological adjustment problems?'

'Still better than being dead.'

'Is it?' Nila said. 'I guess.'

'I was also thinking—as in, I wonder if something like thirty-seven years is just the worst of all worlds,' said Maru. 'The world you knew is dying, but not yet dead. The people you knew are still there. They're just changed forever. You will outlive your friends, your lovers. You will bury your children. But Nila. Ninety-nine years. It *is* a whole new world. You can—maybe you *can* start over. You just need to ... keep some ghosts at bay.'

Nila laughed. 'Look at us, Maru. Playing the gods. Dispensing life. Withholding it.'

'No, *no*.' Maru leaned forward, his eyes on her, quiet, intense. 'I had this moment too, but no. *We* are not playing the gods. This isn't on us. We weren't the legislators who enacted the sleep of death. We weren't the judges who went back on their own word. We weren't the prosecutors who asked for this punishment. We weren't those other judges who passed the sentences. We didn't make this world, Nila, and we can't remake it, but what we *can* do is—' His eyes went to her pendant, to the words on it. 'Don't you think?'

Nila ran her hands through her hair again. 'Tell me,' she said. 'If *you* were placed in the sleep of death now, would you choose to come back a hundred years later? Would you want to?'

'I don't know,' said Maru. 'But I think—I think that's not a choice for us to make.' He swiped the seven faces away. Jagat appeared before them again.

'It's his.'

'Except that once he's brought back, we have made it for him,' Nila muttered. 'This is one of those times where the choice is *literally* irreversible.'

'Moral luck, huh?' said Maru.

'Just what I was thinking.' Nila tugged her hair with more violence. 'You don't even know if you've done the right thing until after you've done it, and it doesn't even depend on you. Consequential moral luck, as Ghorge would say.'

'Leave your hair alone,' said Maru.

'Yeah.' She dropped her hands. 'Maru—I should—I should keep doing this case, no? What *is* the right thing?'

'I don't know,' said Maru again. 'But I was thinking of Ghorge and moral luck, and all of this. Do you remember how you solved the peacemaker's dilemma?'

Nila stared at him for a moment, and then her face cleared. 'The peacemaker's—yes, yes, of course I do. But how—*oh!* I see what you're saying.'

'Radical uncertainty, remember?'

'Yes,' Nila nodded. 'Yes. I get it now.' She stood and walked to the window. 'I'll go ahead. Just—just remind me sometimes, if I flail.'

'I will.'

He joined her at the window. His eyes followed her gaze south, to the tumultuous weaves of the Commune's buildings, draped in the glow of morning sunlight.

'When are you going there?' he said.

'Tomorrow.'

'You feeling okay?'

'I don't have a choice,' she said. 'Just not going to think about it until I have to. And I can't afford to today, I have—'

A voice crackled over the internal intercom.

'Guardian Nila, please report to the president's chambers at your earliest convenience.'

'Well, well,' Maru said. 'Looks like the oily little frauds have finally gotten around to looking at the client contract you deposited with them yesterday.'

'Took them long enough,' Nila muttered. She stood up and tied her hair back, as if she was stepping on to the pitch again. 'Might as well get this over with.'

'Nila.'

'What?'

'*Try* not to get into a fight with them.

5

The Past is a Fragile Thing

BY THE TIME SHE GOT DOWN TO THE PRESIDENT'S chambers, the wind whistling through the curving corridors had brought back Nila's headache with a vengeance. She almost forgot to make the courtesy knock on the door before pushing it open.

Mehmandost Naram swivelled around in his chair to face her. A look at him suggested that Maru's critique was somewhat unfair, at least as far as the oily part of it went. In keeping with his second name, there was a soft, almost papyrus-like quality to the president's aged face and to the wispy white hair that crowned his head. But there was nothing soft about the look he turned upon Nila.

'Pupil Nila,' he said.

'President, good morning.'

The hologram of a contract sprung up to occupy the space between them.

'Is this true?' Naram asked, somewhat unnecessarily, given that it had Nila's digitally protected signature at the bottom.

'It is.'

'A *private* brief? To reopen the assassination of Director Purul?'

'That's correct.'

'As a *pupil* guardian,' Naram said, 'do you not think it would have been more appropriate to refer this case to the Executive Committee for allocation?'

Nila relaxed. *So they aren't actually upset about the case. They're upset about losing the glory.*

'As a matter of fact, President,' she said, 'I did suggest it. But—client's choice.'

'Hmph.' Mehmandost Naram sucked in his cheeks. 'You do not want the Executive Committee to allocate a senior to lead you on this case?'

'I would *love* that,' said Nila. 'But—client's choice.' She tried to keep the smugness out of her voice, but when she saw Naram's nostrils flare, she knew that she'd failed miserably.

'I see,' the president said. 'You've also moved an application for urgent hearing for this Monday, which has been allowed by the registry. Another application for exemption from filing a certified copy of the impugned judgement and sentence. An application to waive service. And finally, an application for bringing on record fresh evidence, which is entirely speculative, because you don't say what the fresh evidence is.

'Jagat R.'s cryobox is scheduled to be deactivated at midnight on Monday,' said Nila.

Naram narrowed his eyes. 'I assume you've moved these applications after finding tangible evidence towards a reasonable prospect of success?'

'Sorry, President Naram. Client confidentiality.'

He half-rose from his chair at that before controlling himself. *That's what you get for not even offering me a seat.*

'So is this what it's about?' the president said suddenly, abandoning civility, his voice dry as sandpaper. 'Going solo for the glory? Already seeing the headlines write themselves? *Guardian Nila: Defence counsel for the damned. Fighting the impossible fight. Righting the un-rightable wrong.*'

He stared at her pendant, the words hanging in the air, unsaid.

Nila bit her tongue. *Just ride it out. There's nothing he can do.*

'Are you aware that the eyes of the subcontinent are on us this week? From Lubini to Chemur, from Jharna to Sampi, they will all be watching.'

Nila caught sight of a crack running through the flagstone at her feet and focused her gaze on it.

Mehmandost Naram watched her in silence. 'Alright, Pupil Nila,' he said at last, his tone reverting to normal. 'Here are a couple of things that you need to understand, and I speak on behalf of the Executive Committee. The man you want to save is not only the most notorious political assassin in the history of Peruma—divided or undivided—but was also convicted after an open-and-shut trial.'

'President, I am aware that—'

'Don't interrupt. As such, Pupil, if you rock up to the tribunal next week with no evidence to speak of, the embarrassment is going to be as historical as the assassination itself. And it won't just be your embarrassment, but the Confederation's. An embarrassment compounded by the fact that you have chosen to schedule a hearing before you've even begun your investigation.'

'With respect, President,' Nila said, 'The client approached me just yesterday—'

'Not our problem,' Naram said, now smug in his turn. 'And perhaps if you'd *persuaded* your client to engage a senior—but be that as it may. The committee met this morning to discuss your case, and we've taken a decision. We can't prove that this is an ambush case, although some of us strongly believe that it is. That being so, you have the right to take this brief. We can't stop you. But be clear that it is *your* brief. Your investigation is your own, and if you wish to access Confederation resources—or invoke Confederation authority—at any point, you will do what seems to be your favourite thing: move an *application*, which will be considered on its own merits.'

Nila staggered a step back, her head pounding. 'The Confederation is hanging me out to dry?'

'The Confederation will not sink a century of hard-won public legitimacy into hopeless vanity projects,' Naram's voice hardened, 'instigated by pupils who get angry because they weren't picked for a case.'

Nila flushed. 'I did not instigate—'

'Pupil Nila,' Naram said, 'Thank you for your time.'

She should have left then. But the blood had rushed to her head, and there was a buzzing in her ears.

'President,' Nila said. 'You may choose not to support me. But let me tell you this: I intend to win. And I *will* win. With your help—or without.'

There was a long silence.

When Naram spoke again, his voice was like pieces of rock dropping onto the floor.

'Pupil Nila, if memory serves me right, you come from the Commune.'

'I do.'

'Born and brought up there until the age of fifteen, when you wrote the aptitude examination.'

'That's correct.'

'Your mother is an active Communard, a member of the Department of Historical Memory and a Commune deputy.'

Nila flared. 'My mother may be whatever. How's that relevant?'

'Did you not say on record, in your admission interview, that one of your dreams as a guardian was to make your mother proud?'

'*Again*, how is that—'

'Because here you are, handling a private brief, seeking to bring back to life the Commune's most venerated hero and martyr, at a time when the Commune is facing serious economic problems, the very week it is going to the tribunal to settle a century-old dispute with the Council. And you're talking about winning, as if it wasn't your case, but your *cause*.'

Nila went white. 'I—'

'Let me tell you, Pupil Nila,' Naram spoke over her. 'If I get one—just one—indication that you are handling this case in any manner that falls short of the Confederation's highest professional standards of impartiality, you *will* be stripped off this case, and you *will* be summarily expelled. Am I clear?'

Nila heard her voice tremble. 'You do not need to say this, President. I am aware of my oath.'

'Are you, really? Let's hear it. Recite the oath.'

She did not have to obey him. But it was all too far gone for anything else. Nila raised her head, looked Naram in the eye, and said the words.

'I am a guardian. This day, I renounce my bonds to the home I have come from. All other vows stand dissolved, save this: to the Charter, my loyalty, to the Confederation, my faith. This day on, I know neither Council nor Commune: only equal justice under law.'

She felt tears of rage and humiliation prick her eyelids. She blinked them back fiercely.

'Good,' said Mehmandost Naram. 'Do not force us to repeat the expulsion of Naina L.' And with that parting shot, the chair swivelled around, away from her, until she was only looking at the back of his head.

'Talk about not just being oily frauds ... but *sore* oily frauds!' She paced along the edge of the table, breathing hard. 'Just because *they* didn't get the case, they're now going to sabotage me ... Confederation ... more like the Cartel of Unfree and Unequal—'

'Nila—'

'Can you believe he brought up the expulsion of Naina L. ... the *audacity*. This is personal now.'

'Nila—'

'*Recite the oath.* Screw you Mehmandost Naram, you sack of hedgehog shit leading all the other sacks of—'

'NILA!'

'Yes?'

'Aren't you going to check your mail?' Maru said mildly.

'Mail—oh,' she paused. 'I'd written to the Directorate for an appointment. Guess *that* isn't happening now.'

'Well, in true Directorate style, they have solemnly replied by non-hackable written letter.' Maru pointed at the pidge by the wall. An envelope lay slantwise in the aperture. Nila walked over to it. She took out the letter first; it was sealed with the tiger claw emblem.

Nila sighed. 'Should I?'

'You might as well,' said Maru.

She tore open the seal and took out the letter.

To Nila M.
of the Free and Equal Confederation of the Guardians of Peruma

Kindly be informed that your urgent request for an audience is hereby
GRANTED.
Pursuant to this message, you are hereby
DIRECTED
to be present at the Directorate, on Wednesday, the 4th of August, at
TWELVE OF THE CLOCK.

'What!'

'Let me hereby guess,' said Maru. 'The Directorate hereby wants to see you.'

'Yes, but—oh damn!' she swore. 'Twelve o'clock'

'Twelve *of* the hereby clock.'

'That's in half an hour, how am I going to—' her wristheld beeped. Nila glanced at it idly—and then again as the name flashed up: *Ani L.*

The message on the screen was terse.

Nila,

As promised, I am placing at your disposal a skimmer for the period of one week. Its sensors are already adjusted to your finger patterns. You will find it on your balcony. Good luck.

—Ani

Her glance travelled to the balcony.

'Wow,' Nila whispered.

Hovering a foot above the balcony floor was Ani's skimmer, a one-seater, shark-shaped, all sleek curves and angles, the latest High Town model.

'Aren't we glad skimmer tech was one of those things that survived the Crumbling?' Maru said.

Nila's breath caught. 'I've never been in one of these things before.'

'Your adoptive period?'

'Grounded. Literally. That High Town family wasn't the skimmer-affording type.'

'Then it's a good thing that this model is almost entirely automated,' Maru grinned. 'And do you realise now, Nila, that the Executive Committee can only flail at trying to sabotage you? You're investigating the most famous assassination in our history. Everyone will want to talk to you. Directorate included.'

'Ah.' Nila stared at the skimmer, rapt.

'You're getting late,' said Maru gently.

'Oh—yes, yes, of course.' She hurried over to the balcony door and threw it open. A gust of warm summer breeze rushed in, fresh and heady.

'By the way,' said Maru, 'You may want to brush up a bit on High Town history on your way. The director, well ... don't go to this conversation unarmed.'

'Good thought,' said Nila, as she grasped at the side of the skimmer and clumsily hauled herself into the seat. 'I'll listen to that Ernika Hamza audio-reel I've been putting off for ages.' She was just about to press the start button, when she remembered something. 'Maru.'

'Yes?'

'Can you do me a favour? I was going to—I forgot—I was going to make an application to access the cryochamber to see Jagat's body. Can you draft and file it for me, please?'

'I'm not getting any of my own work done this week, am I?'

'Sorry, sorry—I totally get it if you—actually, forget it, Maru, I'll just come back and—'

'Oh, hush. I still haven't received Ghorge's mark-ups in my cancer claims case, so I'm free, and—no, don't you dare object. You need to learn how to accept help without trying to guilt yourself *and* me.'

Nila laughed in spite of herself, then placed a finger on the sensor. 'Destination: the Directorate' she said. A map opened before her. The skimmer responded to her touch like a dream, floating out of the window and soaring swiftly above the Chapterhouse. The ground dropped away, Peruma a toy city far below.

For the briefest of moments Nila felt vertigo, before her body oriented to flying. Then they were gliding through the air, the terraces of the Chapterhouse beneath them.

She flicked open her wristheld and started Enrika Hamza's audio-reel. A familiar voice filled her ears.

At its peak, Old Empire spanned the subcontinent. Its seat was the imperial city of Peruma (now High Town), between the mountains and the river. Peruma, the pearl of the north, city of ...

She took a last look south, at the Commune, and then plunged into the skylanes of High Town.

You could get around High Town well enough on foot, but taking a skimmer through the skylanes was a thrilling experience. Marvels of architectural engineering connected the different vertical levels of the Tower City to one another, a network of lanes bound together by mandalium filaments so thin so as to almost be invisible to the human eye, but entirely perceptible to the skimmers' sensors, which transmitted them to the navigation screen. One common trick Perumans used to impress visitors was to first show them High Town's skylanes with the naked eye. The visitors would see all the skimmers flying around seemingly at random, but never colliding and crashing; and then they would be shown a screen representation with the mandalium filaments coloured in: the sky turned into a labyrinthine filigree of aerial roads that directed traffic flawlessly.

> *... but every empire has an end,* Hamza's voice continued. *Old Empire fell. It fell to a republican revolution that originated in Peruma with the overthrow of the last emperor, setting off a chain of events known as the Crumbling. Much was lost, but as order returned, the remnants of the old regime coalesced around the former Imperial metropolises of Monara, Chemur, Lubini, Jharna and Sampi. Newly republican Peruma had neither the appetite, nor the will, to reimpose imperial control. Out of the ashes of the Old Empire were born the six independent cities, loosely connected to each other through the prior trade networks, but with different pathways into the future ...*

On either side of her, the sea-stone skyscrapers of Old Empire's capital glittered in the morning sunlight. Sunbeams—dancing and dispersing along the curved surfaces—made the shard, pearl and teardrop-shaped buildings glisten. The tops of the skyscrapers looked like little islands rising from the surface of a still, transparent lake. Her fear of dropping out of the air dissolved. The sky already felt like home.

The map indicated High Town's landmarks as she passed over and through them, names she vaguely remembered from her year north of the river. The Tower City was divided into sectors along axes both horizontal and vertical, each sector a self-defined unit named after—and under the control of—one of High Town's mega-corporations. In effect, it was an agglomeration of self-defined company towns, arranged in a spiralling hierarchy towards the centre, where the power and influence of your corporation was measured by your proximity to the Council and the Directorate on top of Dominion Hill.

> *... and so, post-Imperial Peruma was birthed in tumult. Once the capital, and site of the great mandalium mines, the city came into being with two contending classes: the captains of the mandalium industry in High Town, and the workers. Both had made common cause to overthrow Old Empire; but the moment that was done, the frayed threads that held them together were torn apart, especially as Peruma was forced to ramp up mandalium production and impose labour conscription in order to stave off the imminent economic collapse that accompanied its birth pangs. Exploitation was inevitable. Conflict, equally so. We have seen this story elsewhere. But here, we saw something new: the conflict persisted through the centuries, and after four failed revolts, at the fifth time of asking, the Commune was born—and it lived ...*

Her wristheld beeped.

'How's it going?' Maru's voice came through.

She paused the audio-reel, smiled and spoke into the screen. 'High Town looks so different from the sky. The towers are almost beautiful.'

'Where are you now?'

'I—' she looked out. Her skimmer was beginning to encircle two towers spiralling around each other in the shape of double helix. Beyond the glittering glass exterior, people were on the move, passing between floors, pacing the corridors, gathering in conference rooms. The skimmer map helpfully told her that she was crossing the headquarters of the Peruma Mandalium Processing Company. 'The double helix.'

'Oh yes, mandalium, the DNA of the city.'

'Not very subtle with symbolism, your lot.'

'Well, High Town's been accused of many things over the centuries but subtlety has not been one of them.'

Nila laughed as the double helix receded in the distance. Beneath her, the amaltas-lined avenues ascended the southern slope of Dominion Hill in a gentle incline: once the beating heart of the subcontinent, then the throbbing heart of Peruma, and now just the weary heart of old High Town.

Around a corner the towers ceased abruptly, yielding to a circular open space upon the hilltop, in the middle of which rose her destination: the Directorate, unchanged from the days of Purul, unchanged through the revolution and everything that had happened after. All angles and lines, rising towards the sky like a ring of canines, surrounding an open, grassy courtyard—a shape, it was said, that was specially designed to make a skimmer pilot feel that they were descending into the jaws of a tiger.

The last bit of the first section of Hamza's audio-reel played as she began her descent.

... the Commune was born at a time when the first tentative steps were being taken towards the reintegration of the independent cities into a league. But its birth put an end to

> *that. The other cities had always been somewhat ambivalent about being part of a league dominated by Peruma, and used the revolution to quickly ink a non-intervention pact amongst themselves. And so, in the last hundred years, Peruma has lived in stasis, a stalemate: an old world with its death aborted, and a new one that has been prevented from being born.*
>
> *Peruma, a battleground of dreams.* Hamza's voice began to fade. *High Town dreams of reunification as the first step towards the remaking of Empire, this time with capital as its guiding force. And the Commune dreams of taking its suspended revolution, at last, to its logical conclusion. So far, the balance of power has held this battleground petrified in place. But for how long? One cannot say ...*

The voice died. The shadows of the tooth-shaped building snaked around the skimmer as she descended. She made a soft landing in the courtyard, and hopped out on to firm ground. For a moment, she stood there. It was from here, a century ago, that Director Purul and Milana Maran had begun the journey to the Urai River, a journey that would end in a bullet, a trial, a sleep of death, revolution, partition, and eventually bring *her* here, into the jaw of the decaying tiger, on a clear summer morning.

'Guardian Nila,' said a young man in a faintly ridiculous lily-white uniform. 'We had word of your coming. Please follow me.'

She fell in behind him. Doors slid open for them. Nila found herself in a high-roofed hall, her feet tapping upon the sea-stone as she walked.

From the moment she had read the director's letter, everything had happened too fast, but now at last, she had a sliver of time to herself. She was truly in the Directorate—to be precise, the Hall of Remembrance, the first thing a visitor saw when they entered. Sculpted in the faux-classical style, statues littered the hall like the trees of the forest, looking down on her with identical, almost comically austere expressions. None of them were painted, their proportions were all larger than life, and disability, it seemed, was an unknown concept in Peruman history.

The Hall of Remembrance was where the Directorate narrated its interpretation of Peruman history to itself. Here were the half-historical, half-allegorical leaders of the early Peruman City-State; the legendary merchant princes from Peruma's glory days at the head of the Bathsea League; and the much-too-historical civilian—and then military—rulers who marked the rise, fall, rise and disintegration of Old Empire.

Just after the last emperor, with barely a gap, came the Directorate.

After the Crumbling, Peruma had moved to break with the Imperial past, from a new constitution to a new calendar; but before long, the republican revolution had turned upon itself, moving through the stages of terror, reaction and restoration. After the last drop of blood had been wiped off the last statue, the Council and the Directorate had taken over, on the slogan of revolutionary continuity. Thus the Hall of Remembrance, which would have astonished and dismayed the original republican revolutionaries: a space of unbroken time, where the directors of Peruma City acknowledged themselves the heirs of the buried emperors, princes and generals.

The last statue was of Director Purul.

She paused by his side. Sculpted out of marble—unpainted like the rest—and even accounting for artistic hagiography, the director had been a young man when he'd been shot. His forehead was only shallowly marked; the thinnest of lines in the sand. A full head of hair framed a beardless face.

'*You fell, as the amaltas falls*,' Sanya had written in her famous lament, '*Abloom/In the summer of your life/A memory of gold*.' Here, at last, Nila saw those lines made flesh—and stone.

She looked more closely. The director's face was upturned, his gaze fixed on something in the distance, away from Peruma and the city that had raised and cast him down.

There was a strange sadness to him. He seemed like a man watching something break apart before his eyes.

Not a man that seemed prime assassination material.

Beyond Purul, there was an empty space that spanned a century. As if continuity had been finally broken and history—the history that mattered—had died with the bullet on the bridge, the revolution, the division of Peruma and the birth of the Commune.

Or that history—the history which did not include the Commune—was only in a sleep of death, awaiting resurrection. Imperial dreams.

'Ahem.'

A very loud—and obvious—clearing of the throat snapped Nila out of her daydream. Her guide thumbed at the wall panel next to her. The doors of a glass elevator parted. Nila shook herself lightly and stepped inside. *Stop overthinking.*

With the gentlest of bumps, they ascended, climbing levels until Nila could make out the colourful frescoes on the ceiling. The elevator eventually opened on the other side, disgorging them into a curved, gently sloping passageway, leading up into one of the Directorate's towers. The passage moved beneath their feet in a gradual ascent that ended in front of an imposing door.

Her guide's touch opened the door. They entered a convex chamber with a transparent floor. Beneath their feet, far below, there was the courtyard, and the other towers that, from this angle, made her feel like they were at the centre of a crown.

Even with the glass between her and the drop, she felt a sudden surge of vertigo. She tore her gaze away, to take in the room.

And found herself hit by a different sense of disorientation.

Because in some strange way, the room reminded her of home—no, she corrected herself—of the home she had loved and left behind seven years ago, on the day she had entered the Chapterhouse, because there was a kind of love that left you with no choice but to let it go. The director's chamber looked less like the working office of the head of the Council and High Town's most powerful political functionary; instead, it had the carefully curated carelessness of an artist's studio. A violin hung from the wall. On the same wall, elegantly arranged, there was a set of five-dimensional holograms, windows into different parts of the subcontinent. Nila saw the seaside view from the white cliffs of Monara, with birds circling overhead; the sand dunes of Lubini, glittering like diamonds in the night; Chemur of the blue roofs, glimpsed from the balcony of its tallest temple; and in a nod to home, the cratered slopes of the Peruma switchback from the eagle-eye of a skimmer. The quality was good enough to set her heart racing, for her pulse to move with the threshing waves, for her nose to smell silver sands and for her skin to feel the deceptive softness of volcanic rock.

On the other wall, in a concession to two dimensions, paintings hung but here, there was no classical style of the Hall of Remembrance. Nila recognised the ordered lines and shapes of Symmetricism, the Commune's modern art form that had emerged as a rebellion against its own anarchic political structures. Her gaze travelled downwards, to the carved woodwork of—

—her mother.

She almost threw out a hand to steady herself, before remembering where she was. *Of course. He's clearly an art collector. Why wouldn't Ma's sculptures be here?*

But she looked away quickly from that achingly beautiful, subtly crafted, almost-too-lovingly-done wooden sculpture of High Town's tiger emblem, and let her eyes fix upon the bookshelf, with its real books, and then to the desk by the window, where a man was looking at her. 'Guardian Nila.'

He was approaching fifty. His hair and beard were black—as she had seen them from a distance the day before—but face-to-face, she noticed the flecks of silver. Around his neck, there was the familiar pendant of gold, in the shape of a tiger's claw.

'Good afternoon, Director Pulis.'

'And to you, Guardian. Make yourself at home.'

She suddenly had the feeling that this chamber had been curated specifically for her, that the next visitor would find a very different place to make themselves at *home*.

Overthinking again, Nila?

Not now. Shut up.

'Thank you for agreeing to see me,' she said, taking a seat.

Director Pulis steepled his fingers, and examined them carefully. 'As a guardian under formal engagement to investigate a sentence—but of course.'

A miracle! The smallest curl of the lips, the beginning of a shadow of a smile.

'But if I may say so,' he continued, 'I don't quite understand why the Confederation wants to reopen *this* case of all cases.'

'This is my brief, Director,' she said. 'I was approached by a descendant.'

'Sorry, just you then. And yes, I see why a descendant would want to give this a shot. But you, Guardian—surely, you've seen the trial transcripts. The assassination of Director Purul was clear-cut.'

'Was it really, though?'

He held her gaze. 'You're asking me?'

'I am.'

Director Pulis began ticking off numbers on his fingers, as if he'd prepared for this question. 'Two people in his vicinity, the secretary and the assassin. The secretary's account was verified by a truth serum at trial. The assassin never even bothered trying to defend himself. His comrades from the Low Town—sorry, the *Commune*, the mutineers, his own family—for all these years, nobody has contested his guilt. Even after the mutiny, after the civil war, the amnesty—when it would have been totally safe—nobody came forward and took credit for killing the director. I mean, the Commune calls him Jagat the Martyr and has a statue of him.' He leaned forward. 'What more do you want?'

'I know that,' Nila said. 'What I am unconvinced about, Director, is motive.'

His eyebrows shot up. 'Really?'

'Yes.'

He looked at her, his face still. Behind that fixed gaze, she sensed him thinking, weighing, calculating.

When he spoke again, it caught Nila off guard. His voice had altered, dissolving into something soft and rhythmic, almost a chant.

'"All history is a history of roads untaken. The path from the disintegration of the Old Empire to the birth of the Commune spans four hundred years and as many forks in the road. When the Old Empire fell and the independent republican city of Peruma was born, there was a brief window of time when the radicals prevailed over the restorationists. Had their vision of the social constitution triumphed, history would have taken a different road, and there would have been no gunshot on Unity Bridge that autumn morning, centuries later. Had Director Pari and Master Builder Bhushan—fresh from suppressing the June insurrection—not decided to segregate the workers beyond the Urai River, and thus create Low Town and High Town, there would have been no gunshot upon Unity Bridge that autumn morning. Had High Town not passed the anti-union laws and shed blood to break the general strike, there would have been no gunshot on Unity Bridge. Director Purul's death was not inevitable—right until the moment that it became so. And then, it was no longer relevant that the victim was Director Purul and the perpetrator was Jagat the assassin. It could have been anyone. Only in that moment, it happened to be a director named Purul and an assassin named Jagat."'

'Did you just quote the opening of the *Great Unravelling* at me?' Nila said, before silence could fill the space.

'You know it by memory?'

'Of course.' Of course she did. *The Great Unravelling*, by the Bulwark Collective, was a history of the revolution that was taught to every Commune child, and whose opening lines had become iconic. There was no way she would not have recognised them. And no way that Pulis would not have known that.

'A director of High Town, citing *The Great Unravelling*?' she said. 'You know what that book says about you all, don't you?'

'Obviously I don't agree with all of the analysis,' said Pulis. 'But Guardian, I am not a High Town bigot. I don't have to like it, but I *can* acknowledge that we made mistakes. And that's the thing, isn't it? If you go about looking for motive by analysing the personalities of Purul and Jagat—with respect, you're barking up the wrong tree. It wasn't just about the two of them.'

'With respect, Director, it was,' she replied. 'A man allegedly fired the shot that killed another man. Whether these two men represented the contending social classes of their time is neither here nor there, because crime and punishment are based on individual responsibility, not class conditions. What if there was the slightest chance that you got the wrong person all those years ago? Wouldn't it matter to you that you have a century-long ongoing miscarriage of justice, and you'd be making it permanent next week? Or would that be fine because, according to *The Great Unravelling*, the march of history determined that *someone* had to kill a director, so it's all okay as long as *someone* got punished for it?'

'No, no, of course not!' Pulis sounded mildly shocked. 'That wasn't what I meant at all. It's just that—please don't be offended, Guardian—when I heard you were coming, I went back and rechecked the facts, just to make sure we hadn't missed something these last hundred years. There was nothing. All this feels a little too much out of a chain fantasy webnovel. The eve of an inflection point, the last-minute questioning of known facts, the fight against all odds, the victory of justice—do you know what I mean? But history isn't quite as romantic. And I'm just wondering—I'm just wondering if maybe someone is playing you here, setting you up to fail.'

Nila breathed. *He's not making fun of you. It's a totally natural way to think about this case.*

She summoned up a confidence that she was not feeling. 'That's fair, Director. But think for a moment: what if you have got the wrong man lying there in that sleep of death? I don't need to understand from you *how* someone else might have done it—that's my job. But I would like to understand *why*.'

He spread out his hands. 'What do you think I can add?'

'Your predecessor,' she said, recalling the scant evidence she'd found in the online archives the evening before, and that strange, haunted look on the face of the last statue in the Hall of Remembrance. 'I know you think this is irrelevant, Director, but I do want to know—what kind of a man was he?'

'Director Purul?' Pulis was silent for a moment. Then, quietly, he began to recite again.

'You were afraid, like us/Your warmth survived it all/The whine of bullets, a shattered heart/Yourself. Peruma brought you into darkness/Now Peruma has her darkness and her splinters, still.'

'Sanya's lament,' said Nila softly.

'I wonder if he foresaw that he would be memorialised in a Sanya poem before day's end,' Pulis said, a faraway look in his eyes. 'Only, that it would be a dirge, not a song of triumph.' He shook himself. 'But I digress. So, you know the lament. Then you must also know what they used to call him?'

'The Douser of Fires.'

'That's right. Director Purul, he was—he was heaven-sent. One of the best we ever had. He understood the pulse of Peruma, and though he ascended to the Directorate in a time of conflict ... he knew how to heal, he knew how to put out the fires. That's why they killed him.'

'They?'

'The Commune. You know what the assassin said.'

'You seem very sure that it was the Commune. Jagat never—'

'Isn't history witness?' Bitterness crept into the director's voice. 'Just consider it. Director Purul was an astute leader, a compromiser, he was yielding when he needed to, and that was really taking the wind out of the sails of the rioters, the anarchists, those so-called Levellers. Low Town was coming over to the Council. And then he got shot. By a man from Low Town. And his blood hadn't yet run cold when the barricades were up everywhere. As if they were waiting for a signal. You wanted motive? *There's* your motive.'

She looked at him leaning towards her, fingers clasped together tightly, brows knitted.

Too eager? But nothing he's said so far is particularly unusual.

'In my line of work, Director,' she said, 'there is no such thing as a perfect alignment of circumstances and motive. Where there seems to be, we get a little suspicious.'

Pulis came as close as he would to rolling his eyes at her. *Anything would have been better than that cliché*, his face said. She grimaced. *Let's try a different approach.*

'Director Pulis,' she said, 'On the day he was killed, Purul was on his way to address Low Town in the Maidan. Do you know what he was going to say?

'That—nobody knows.'

'Exactly. And that's why I'd say that the question of motive hasn't quite been settled yet. I have a request: I would like to consult the Directorate's archives.'

Pulis leaned back in his chair. 'To open up Director Purul's personal papers to you, I'll need a formal letter of authorisation from the Confederation, Guardian.'

Nila cursed silently. 'I *am* investigating this crime at the behest of a descendant of the convicted.'

'I'm afraid that's not enough. I still require institutional authorisation.'

'I see,' said Nila. She nodded. 'Well, then. I'll continue with my investigation.' She began to rise.

'Guardian Nila,' said Pulis quietly. 'May I say something?'

'Of course.' She sat back down.

'The past is a fragile thing. Like a weave. You pull upon a strand, and you don't know what will unravel.'

She looked at him.

'Ever since the fall of Old Empire, Peruma has been riven by conflict. Every time we begin to limp towards an equilibrium, something comes along and tears our old wounds wide open.'

'The inflection points?'

'Yes. And now, this week, we might be heading into our fifth. I ask you to think once: reopening the assassination of Director Purul, turning the past upside down—is that really what Peruma needs right now? This week, of all weeks, when we have no choice but to reopen one huge wound, because the previous generation decided that they'd rather kick the can, borrow time at the expense of their great-grandchildren, and leave us to fight the fight they'd lost appetite for? Don't you think, Guardian—' his voice lowered, 'that some memories, at least, are better off turning into ghosts?'

'I thought you'd make this pitch, Director,' she said.

'And? You're an intelligent woman. You read the news.' He gestured to the window. 'You know what's happening out there. You can hear the whispers. Surely you see it? This city is kindling right now, it just needs a spark for fire. A fire that we saw a hundred years ago. And the return of the Martyr ...'

He let himself trail off, and looked at her. 'There may be a time, Guardian, when it doesn't matter whether our peace is founded on the truth or a lie. All that matters is that there be peace. Would you consider the possibility that that time is now?'

Imperial dreams.

'Speaking of peace, Director,' she said, 'Have you heard of the peacemaker's dilemma?'

'In the outline.'

'Well, I'll fill the rest in for you. The peacemaker's dilemma is the last test in our pupillage. Here's how the hypothetical is framed: after a long and bloody revolution—or mutiny, call it what you will—a city has arrived at a fragile peace. At the heart of this peace is a pact of amnesty, negotiated by the warring parties. It grants a one-time, absolute amnesty for all crimes that may have been committed during the violence so that the citizens can move on. Does that sound familiar? But before the pact can come into force, it must be ratified by a guardian—in this case, the test-taker—for compliance with the city's charter.'

'I recall.'

'Yes. But there's one problem. The charter makes clear that non-prosecution of a crime can only happen with the victim's *consent*. A simple principle of justice. Except that, here, the victims are dead. So if you apply the letter of the charter, the pact must fail.

'That's the problem you're given, Director. And baked into the hypothetical is a further twist. The hostile parties have made clear that if the pact falls, they will immediately recommence fighting, this time to the bitter end. It's in your hands. You *are* the one who has to decide. And just for verisimilitude, we don't take this test in an exam hall. We're all given A1-grade hypnosis before the test. We believe that the situation is entirely, physically, *real*. Do you know how most pupils decide?'

'I can guess,' said Pulis. 'Uphold the pact. Introduce a legal fiction of deemed consent. The standard kind of trick that you guardians are good at.'

'That's right.'

They held each other's gaze.

'But that's not how you decided,' said Pulis.

'No.'

'You struck down the pact? And they gave you the highest grade for plunging this hypothetical-slash-real city back into civil war?'

'They did, but not for that. The thing about the peacemaker's dilemma is that they don't judge you on what you decide. They judge you on how you defend your decision.'

'Oh?'

'Director, a hundred years ago, when Purul lay dying on the bridge, did anyone foresee that before the week was done, Peruma would be divided in two? It's a dangerous thing to predict the future. And it's far more dangerous when you're the tribunal, when lives—and deaths—will turn on what you decide. Say that in the peacemaker's dilemma, I uphold the pact of amnesty, because I think it's a better *outcome* than the resumption of civil war. Say that my decision permanently embitters the families, the loved ones and the friends of the dead, who feel they've been robbed of justice. Say their bitterness spreads, and a day comes when it bursts into violence. It's been known to happen before, Director, upon this continent. Who is to say it may not happen again? And if it does, in my quest for peace, by believing I know the future,. I've just done the city a far worse turn than I would have had I just applied the law.

'Because that's the point, Director. That's the point of having law. In a space of radical uncertainty, the law spares us from having to tell the future. It takes that entirely out of consideration. It's not relevant. In essence, it insulates us from what some call moral luck. Will you still say that it's a worse thing than having us play the gods?'

'That's what you wrote in your decision?' said Pulis.

'Yes.' She stared at her hands. The ground that had seemed like it was dissolving beneath her feet when Pulis had denied her access to the archives felt firm again.

'You said Peruma is like kindling that only needs a spark to catch fire,' she said. 'I understand that. And yet ...' she held the pendant at her throat, ran her fingers around the words. 'In a way, that's exactly why I was asked to take this case.' She raised her chin and looked him in the eye.

Director Pulis inclined his head. His eyes were expressionless. 'I wish you well in your investigation, Guardian.'

When construction on the Chapterhouse had started just after the revolution, its architects had vowed that it would be known throughout the subcontinent as the 'Fortress of Dreaming Spires'. But funding had dried up halfway through, and what they had built looked like a bedraggled hedgehog, with a few sad spikes still standing. Nila and Maru's allotted chamber was high up in one of those spikes, an eagle's nest with a panoramic view of both sides of the river.

As she approached the eagle's nest from the north, she saw what seemed to be a protruding dark sore clinging to the wall next to the window of her chamber.

Closer, and the sore resolved itself into its component parts: a fleet of skimmers hovering just outside her window, painted in bright press colours—crimson, saffron, vermillion—with large microphones hanging down the sides.

They began to blare at her as she drew up to her balcony.

'Guardian Nila—from the *High Town Herald*—is it true that you are fighting to bring the assassin Jagat R. back to life?'

'Guardian Nila—from the *Commune Guardian*—can you tell us why you think Jagat the Martyr was wrongly sentenced?

'Guardian Nila—do you feel confident about proving—'

'Guardian Nila—the Fifth Inflection—'

She flew over the balcony railing, alighted and turned around. They were crowding around the railings, the microphones extending towards her, cameras ready.

'Friends in the media,' she said, 'thank you for your questions. I am afraid that Confederation's regulations prohibit me from commenting on any pending cases that I may or may not be professionally involved in. Good evening.'

'Guardian Nila!' someone shouted from the back. 'From the *High Town Herald*—there are reports that the Commune is paying for your expenses in this case. Is that true?'

'Don't,' said Maru, from inside the room. 'Just don't.'

Nila looked, once, into the cameras, and squared her shoulders. 'I have just one thing to say, and after that, you will hear from me once this case is done. I am a Confederation guardian.' She held her pendant up, so that it caught the light. 'There is no Council. There is no Commune. My sole concern lies in seeing that justice is carried out, regardless of the consequences. *Goodly evening*.'

'Guardian, have you—'

She turned around and walked inside, closing the door behind her. The voice cut off abruptly. She drew the blinds around the window.

Maru shook his head. 'Just *couldn't* resist showing the committee the finger with that last bit, yeah?'

Nila looked at him, her face flushed, her eyes shining, breathing hard. 'I had to. Just this one time. And I was careful with my words.'

'You were,' said Maru, fiddling with his pen. 'But you know who else is going to be reading the papers, yeah, and seeing you deny the Commune in such an explicit way?'

'I do,' said Nila quietly. 'Ma will understand. She'll know why. She'll be proud of me. I hope.'

Day Three

The Commune

6

The Phoenix and the Salamander

THE ALARM PIERCED THROUGH TANGLED LAYERS of sleep, a hook dredging her up from the bottom of a marsh, into unwanted daylight.

'*Uuuurgh!*' Nila groped around until one finger landed on the snooze button. She let herself sink back into the oblivion that had finally found her an hour ago, and—

Bleep! Bleep! Bleep!

'*Bloody—*' Nila snaked her arm out from the sheets again. The hook released her once more, to float just below the skein of the world, shifting in and out of wakefulness, thoughts like wisps of smoke beginning to dissolve—

THE TWELVE ARE ALREADY WORKING.

The alarm's pre-set, human squawk, set to activate after the second snooze, jerked her bolt upright.

THE TWELVE ARE ALREADY—

'Shut up, I'm awake!' She punched the off button harder than necessary. Her head throbbed like someone had stuck a million tiny needles into it.

'Gnnnggggghhh.'

She sat up, hugging her knees. Silvery light wafted in through the window overlooking the Chapterhouse grounds. The other side of her bed was a mess. The covers were half-drawn. Her backpack, which she had dumped half-opened when she'd come back the night before, still lay there with its contents spilling out. The rest of the bed was a clutter of paper, prints she'd taken out of chambers, intending to read in bed, before her body sternly reminded her who was boss. All of it had a fragile quality in the half-light, the softness of dust.

She swung one leg over the side of the bed, forcing herself to her feet. For a while she stood by the window, running her hands through her hair, making little knots with her fingers, then undoing them. Wispy thoughts grew more solid, memories of the night's reading casting little tendrils towards each other, seeking patterns, grids, connections.

I've always had my most brilliant ideas in the shower, she'd once joked with Maru.

But when she stepped out of her room after a hot shower twenty minutes later, her ideas were still misty, resisting definition. Unity Bridge appeared in her mind's eye, its boundaries blurred and unfocused. Upon the bridge there were three figures, frozen in time: one on his knees, another cradling him, a third standing over them; and there, just beside them, a fourth in outlines of smoke and shadow: undefinable, impervious to her gaze.

She walked down the corridor, ignoring the dull aches that were engaged in voyages of exploration along her body.

Through slit windows on the walls, she glimpsed a leaden sky on the cusp of dawn. This early, the Chapterhouse was still abed, the corridors empty. Past the final year pupils' rooms, Nila descended a narrow stairway, into the junior pupils' wing. Cubicles and dormitories replaced individual rooms, and light laboured out from underneath the door. As she passed through, she heard the occasional movement, or a laugh. It reminded her, ever so fleetingly, of her own time in this wing as a junior pupil, where night and day were always in an identity crisis.

Around a turn, just as she was leaving the residential wing, she came upon two pupils, a couple of years below her. She raised a hand in half-greeting but they scurried away immediately, a look of awe in their eyes.

The morning news networks. Nila grimaced. The first thing she'd done after seeing the media scrum outside her balcony had been to follow Ghorge's advice and mute her own inbox.

The journey from the residential wing to her chamber took her through the Chapterhouse's Great Hall, pillared and floored in onyx. She crossed the open space, shivering in the draft. She was just about to exit for the passageway to the Hedgehog's Needle when her eyes snagged upon an arched doorway that bore the legend: TRIBUNAL CHAMBERS.

Nila walked through, into a winding passageway. At a fork, the sign on the left read: GRAND CHAMBER. On the right: CHAMBER II.

She turned left.

The passageway ended in a green baize door. She pushed it open and entered the roofed amphitheatre of the Grand Chamber.

She was at the top of a huge semi-circular chamber that dipped downwards, rows and rows of seats descending to the well and the rostrum, where the guardians stood and argued. At a slightly raised level—but still below the watchers—the arbitrators' bench faced her with its three high-backed chairs.

From the high vaulted ceiling, three banners dropped down behind the bench. The banner on the right featured a grey field with a tiger emblazoned, one paw raised: the sign of the Council. The banner on the left was a simple black cloth: the Commune. In the middle, there was the blue banner of the Confederation, with its annoying yellow dragonfly staring back at her, so infuriatingly lifelike that she heard its *bzzzzt bzzzzt bzzzzt* in her ears.

She leaned upon the bar and gave in to the temptation to imagine herself down there, in the well, before a packed chamber. Soft violin notes wafted into her mind, a soundtrack to the vision that she was composing. Only a slight ache in her heart reminded her that it wasn't real.

Behind her, high on the wall, were the Grand Chamber's giant screens that beamed out proceedings to Peruma and the rest of the continent. Both screens were black, save for two static lines of text:

Council vs Commune
Monday, 9 August, 10.00 A.M.

The violin died away just as footsteps sounded behind her.

'I thought I saw you come in here,' Noor said. She came up beside Nila, and for a while, they stood together in silence.

'I really wish you were with us, Phoenix,' Noor said then.

Nila stiffened.

Since the day they had entered the Chapterhouse seven years ago, she and Noor had been rivals, a rivalry sharpened to a knife's edge by how often they arrived at the solution together, but through radically different paths.

Noor was coolly rational and logical, a model of deductive reasoning. Nila walked the halls of induction, and rode upon intuition to vault the gaps between specifics. One of their classmates had finally named them the Phoenix and the Salamander when speaking of them together: Nila, all ash and resurrection; Noor, the slow burn, still and relentless. With Noor, she could never have the easy intimacy that she enjoyed with Maru, but there was something both more and less, wholly different and just as real.

The names had stuck, but Nila and Noor had never used them with each other. Until now.

'It would've been a thrill to go up against you on this case,' Noor continued, worrying the wood of the balustrade with her fingernail. 'But ten thousand times better to do it on the same side. The pressure, the adrenaline, the madness … without you, this just doesn't feel complete.'

Nila swallowed, throat dry. 'A bit more up your alley, this one, isn't it?' she said. Where's the scope for intuition in *Council vs Commune*? Just interpret the text.'

Noor turned searching eyes upon her. 'What have you turned your intuition to now?'

Was she pretending, or had she not seen the news yet?

'Nothing,' said Nila automatically, wondering why she was lying again.

'Ah.' Noor rested her chin upon her fists. 'We're still good, right? Terrace nights, smoking, arguing till dawn—we'll have that again after Monday?'

Nila caught a whiff of guilt. For an instant, she considered denying Noor reassurance, but immediately felt ashamed. She grinned. 'You're not getting rid of me that easily. Back to mock duels after the real one.

Noor closed her eyes, and nodded slightly.

'Good luck, Salamander,' Nila said at last, surprised by how easily it came. She walked away, without waiting for Noor's reaction, back to the Great Hall, through the corridor, up the ninety-five-year-old elevator, and to the pupils' chamber complex.

Her chamber was as she had left it last night. Maru wasn't in yet. Only the timer gave her company.

99:24:51

Nila looked around once, then guiltily hurried to the mini-kitchen.

Half an hour later, she heard humming outside the door. Maru walked in, saw her, and stopped. 'I see you've reached the ice-cream-with-cold-coffee-at-the-brink-of-dawn stage of the case,' he said.

'Cut me slack just this week, won't you?'

'Fine.' Maru moved to the table. 'How's it going? Slept last night?'

'Some. Not enough.'

'Made progress?'

'Some. Not enough.'

'And ...?'

'I have to ask the Commune a lot of questions today.' Nila stood and walked to the window. In the grey morning, the Commune's colourful weave was still, the shadow of a glimmer. 'You know something?' she said.

'Yes?'

'That place over there,' she nodded at the line of buildings beyond the river. 'Ever since I got this case, I've been thinking about my decision to leave.'

'Spontaneous, didn't you tell me?'

'I always thought I woke up one day and just *knew*, but—' Nila shook her head. 'Seven years is a lot of hindsight, especially when you've been repressing it.'

'What are you thinking?'

'You know that line the Commune has exported to the rest of the continent?'

'*Building the new in the ruins of the old*,' Maru quoted, '*every moment we exist, we remake the revolution*.'

'Yeah, and it's not just rhetoric, it's life. Growing up there, it felt like every single moment was charged with all the weight of history. Nothing existed between people that could exist on its own terms, independent of the revolution. It was … it was just too much pressure, that life.'

'Life in the Commune?' said Maru. 'Or as your mother lived it?'

Nila smiled wanly. 'In this case, the same thing.' The first sunbeam pierced through the clouds. 'I think I wanted a world more contained. A world I could cup in my hands, and know its limits. A world I thought this place offered: the law, with its lines, its borders, its boundaries. But now … I feel so untethered again.'

She walked back to the table, picked up her wristheld, and tapped a sequence of icons. A face appeared on the seeing screen before them. It was the face of a young woman with close-cropped hair, a tight mouth and a look of barely-contained anger.

'For example.'

'Who am I looking at?' said Maru.

'Varsha S.,' said Nila. 'From Low Town, before the revolution. A schoolteacher. A trade unionist. And for our purposes, a particularly notorious member of the Levellers.'

'I can totally believe that.'

'Reputed for being an excellent sniper. I found bundles of the Bureau's surveillance reports on her. Before Purul's death, she was directly involved in at least six High Town assassinations.'

'Nila,' said Maru. 'You don't really have to be a crack shot to put a bullet through someone at point-blank range.'

'I'm coming to it, Maru. I looked into her files more closely. And guess her other special skill?'

'Juggling frying pans?'

'Maru, she was a champion swimmer.'

Silence hung between them. Finally, Maru broke it. 'What happened to her?'

'Disappeared during the Levellers' siege of the Directorate on the second day of the revolution. Body never found.'

'How convenient.'

'There's motive. There's opportunity. There's ability. But no evidence. And that's just one of the many strange things about the Commune that came up when I was researching last night.'

'Hmm,' said Maru. He tapped his fingers on the table. 'I think—' he began, but at that moment Nila interrupted. 'Wait, what's this ticker on your screen? Maru—is that *me*?'

'I was waiting to tell you about this.' Maru reached for his wristheld and enlarged the screen.

Nila saw her own face superimposed against an animated background where flames licked the edges of a blood-red sky. Above her face, the headline shrieked:

THE COMMUNE'S MOST DANGEROUS HERO?

And below that, in slightly—but only slightly—smaller letters:

One week before the Fifth Inflection Point, as anarchist malcontents march in the streets, the addition of a new ingredient to this deadly cocktail should alarm us all: the return of Jagat R., the assassin of Director Purul and instigator of the civil war, fronted by this Confederation pupil, threatening to upend our hard-fought peace like nothing before.

'What the ...?' said Nila.

'*High Town Herald*,' said Maru. 'But the others are nicer, look. This is *The Centre Ground*.'

Defence Counsel for the Damned: Top Confederation Pupil 'Key Person' on Impossible Case

'Hey there, Key Person. Also, *The Commune Guardian* ...'

Martyr Returning? Yes! Says Confederation's Top Pupil

'Key person, huh,' Nila muttered. 'No pressure.'

'Well, at least you've totally upstaged *Council vs Commune* from the headlines. And ah yes, here, *The Daily Tide* has put it out there just like you wanted—'

Top Pupil to Argue for Retrial in Purul Assassination Case, Vows Justice Will Be Done No Matter What

'Eegh!' said Nila.

'Foreign media is on it too, by the way. We may end up having some correspondents from the independent cities by the window soon.'

'Double eegh. And what's the *Peruman Glam* saying?'

'Nothing, although I bet they're probably searching for a photo of you in full guardian attire, in appropriately dim light, standing before a Confederation banner, looking down at the viewer, arms folded.'

'Typical.'

'I mean, it would make the Executive Committee particularly mad.'

'And I would never be able to walk into breakfast again.' She paused. '*Anarchist malcontents*. Maru, was there another march last night?'

'They were going at it till three in the morning. The flares were out.'

'I must have slept right through it,' said Nila. She looked out of the window. A thin pall of smoke hung over the surface of the water. 'Good to know before I go there this morning, I guess.'

Her voice snagged. Maru caught it. 'What is it, Nila?'

Nila swallowed. 'I ... that morning, before I accepted the brief, I asked Ani: why *me*? She had her own answer, but these headlines now ... I remember why I asked. Maru. Jagat—he's the Commune's martyr. He's the Commune's history. I—' she stopped. 'Was this case mine to take in the first place?'

'Skimmer-for-hire rule—'

'No, no. You've said it yourself, our job doesn't spare us the responsibility for the consequences of our actions.'

'Yes, but—'

'What if the Commune thinks I'm a trespasser?'

'That would be ironic, no, given that they've abolished private landownership?'

'*Ugh* Maru, your stupid jokes! You know what I mean: an interloper, meddling in their history, meddling with their martyr. Because—be serious here for a moment—I became one, in a way, when I chose to leave. What if they hate me now for doing this?'

'In all seriousness?' Maru walked up to her. 'Jagat's story might be the Commune's story. But Jagat's life doesn't belong to them. If *anyone* has a claim there, it's Ani, and you're her choice. So if the Commune is that petty, it can, well, screw it.'

Nila laughed. 'Maru!'

'I said what I said. And now your overthinking quota for the day is done, so start moving. You should've been in the Commune yesterday already.

Nila saluted. 'Yessir. There was some more stuff I wanted to run by you, but we'll talk when I get back. Let me know if the oily frauds reply to my cryochamber application.'

'Oh wait, that reminds me,' Maru said. 'Did you say that Mehmandost Naram brought up the expulsion of Naina L. yesterday?'

'He did. Intimidation, I figured.'

'Do you remember the specific indictment against Naina?'

'Hm.' Nila rifled through the drawers of memory. The expulsion of Naina L.—now forty years in the past—was the Confederation's morality tale, the story that every trainee pupil was told soon after they passed through the Chapterhouse's gates, first in the unpassionate environment of ethics class, and then in more colourful strokes after lights-out in the dormitories and the corridors. Naina, hailing from the Commune, and acknowledged the most brilliant pupil in

Chapterhouse history; the only one to accomplish a perfect score on the guardian aptitude test. Naina, known to have searingly sharp memory combined with an inductive flair that made her a fearsome opponent and the first name among the pupils selected for any high-stakes case. Naina, who handled three private briefs while still a pupil, a feat unprecedented and never repeated. Naina, whose fall had been as meteoric as her rise—while representing the Commune in a bitter Council–Commune case about the legality of a wildcat strike (a case which had brought the two halves of the city closest to open conflict than they had ever been), she had tripped into the oldest of traps. A *High Town Herald* journalist, posing as a whistle-blower, had lured her into a meeting and filmed her in blatant breach of the impartiality oath. The resulting scandal had left the Confederation with no choice. Summary trial had been swift, expulsion swifter. Naina L. had walked out of the Chapterhouse, and out of Peruma, never to be heard from again.

Some said that she would never have made such a basic mistake if the Chapterhouse did not insist on driving its pupils to the absolute brink in any Council/Commune case. Others said that she had only done what guardians always did to win a case, just in the wrong place and at the wrong time. And the Wits—feeling more savage than usual—had maintained that the whole thing had been a set up by the Confederation itself, possibly due to the Executive Committee feeling deeply insecure about being repeatedly outshone by a pupil.

Whatever the truth, it was now buried deep beneath layers of meaning and symbolism in Confederation lore.

Nila shook her head. 'I can't recall the exact text.'

'It indicted her for being a *front* for the Commune,' said Maru. He pulled up his wristheld screen again, enlarging the *High Town Herald* sub-headline, and highlighting the words.

... instigator of the civil war, fronted by this confederation pupil, threatening to ...

'Mehmandost Naram was a contemporary of Naina's, a ringside spectator during the expulsion scandal,' said Maru. 'Mehmandost Naram is now the president of the Executive Committee. Mehmandost Naram also comes from the extended family that owns the *High Town Herald*.'

My family, he left the last words unsaid.

Nila stared at him.

'Maybe I'm being paranoid,' said Maru. 'Maybe it's nothing. But if I wanted to make you a second Naina, this is how I'd start building the case against you.'

Nila put both her palms down on the table, bent her head and closed her eyes. She breathed once, twice. 'There's no reason to—I'm not another Naina. I'm just a regular pupil trying to do my job.'

'Remember what Ghorge said? You stopped being *regular* the moment you signed the contract of engagement.'

Nila let the breath escape her in a long, slow whistle. She straightened. 'Okay. It is what it is. I just need to be hyper-aware of what I'm doing. Do this case like a guardian, that's all.'

'Just be really careful today, Nila,' said Maru. 'It's the Commune. Don't let your heart betray you.'

'I won't.' Nila drew her lips into a tight line. 'Because I know they won't.'

7

An Invented Tradition

THE THREE-ARCHED UNITY BRIDGE CURVED over the Urai. Standing on the northern bank, Nila saw words hewn into a sea-stone pillar—its careful polish belied its age:

Bridge of Tears

Beneath that was a memorial plaque to Director Purul.

She looked back. Beyond the patch of land that had once been the Bulwark Zone, where High Town proper began, two cops from the Council's Border Security Force stood facing the river, hands placed loosely on their holsters. Unease licked the edges of her throat. She could not remember ever seeing an armed guard by the bridge; this surely was testing the absolute limits of the Charter's mandatory demilitarisation provisions.

She turned to the river and watched the bridge undulate away from her, towards the glimmering cluster of buildings on the other side: light brown, like silk paper, interspersed with a haze of blossoming green. Whatever else had changed in Peruma in the course of the last century, this view had remained constant. The scene before her could be superimposed upon countless artistic renditions of that summer morning. Other than the memorial pillar, they would fit together like a tracing.

Nila closed her eyes and tried to recreate the scene in her head.

All that she felt was a chill in the small of her back, forcing her eyes open.

Nila swung around. The cops stood there, unmoving. Beyond them, Victory Road ascended up the hillside, an arrow-straight line up to the Directorate, the skyscrapers on either side quiet and watchful.

Turning again, Nila took a step upon the bridge.

She leaned over the side. Below her, the Urai gurgled onwards, all the way to the Western Sea.

She measured the drop with her eye. From the base of the bridge to the water, it was twelve feet, no more.

She eyeballed the current.

On this still autumn day, nothing a good swimmer wouldn't be able to handle. As for a champion swimmer ...

Nila strode forward, unable to shake off a vague sensation of being watched. At the end of the bridge, the Commune was here before her, very real. When she looked back, it was High Town that now seemed far away, the tops of the skyscrapers no longer quite so solid.

For the first time in seven years, Nila crossed the river.

On the other side, the Commune had its own words carved onto a slab.

Martyr's Bridge

Victory Road—the name that, in a move redolent with spite, the Commune had elected to retain even after the revolution—cut through a cluster of buildings. But nobody really called it that anymore.

The statues that once lined the side of road had been torn down soon after the revolution. By a unanimous resolution of the Commune, cleaning up the scree from the street was forbidden—and Victory Road had become a street utterly frozen in time, a calcified museum beneath the open sky; a memorial of broken stone.

Rubble Street, they called it instead, a name famous throughout the subcontinent, a defining image of post-revolution Peruma.

Nila picked her way through decades-old ruins strewn upon the ground, between a shattered pillar and a cracked marble thumb the size of her head.

A sedimented street for sedimented memories, including her own.

A little buzz on her wrist directed her left, into the heart of the Commune.

No, she corrected herself. There was no 'heart of the Commune', as the Commune itself kept insisting to anyone who would listen, only the ANCs (Autonomous Neighbourhood Councils), or whatever term they were using right now (it changed every few years). After all, the entire urban design of the Commune was meant to be a revolt against the authoritarian architecture of Master Builder Bhushan, and defined by the axioms of *The Formless Form*, a document with mysterious origins and (fittingly) unattributed authorship; but the first of whose axioms was 'no centre, no periphery'. Cue the popular joke, made by the Wits, about the bewildered foreigner (lost in the streets of the Commune) asking a local '*Hey, how do I get to the centre?*' only to be met with '*The centre of what, comrade?*'

Here was a city without a centre, without fixity, a city that moved like breeze upon the water. If you wanted to see the administration (as Nila did) you would find out that morning where they were meeting; if you wanted to visit the museum or the library, you would have to track their movement through the topography of the city, and visit them where they were—a specific skill that she knew had long atrophied for her.

So she stopped for a moment on the edge of Rubble Street, and consulted the map on her wristheld, because that was all she had. The street names were crowding each other off her screen. She had to turn into Invitation to a Voyage Street, which led into the Impossible Melodies Lane, which opened up into Crevasses of Flowers Square, which was connected to her final destination—Reunion Square—through Incandescent Atoms Street.

Nila puffed out her cheeks, and breathed. Her heart had begun to thump loudly against her chest.

She walked off Rubble Street, and into an explosion of colour.

There was no section of the walls that had not come under the brush of the graffiti artists. The murals welcomed her in, fantastical, weird, grotesque; scenes from popular fantasy chain-novels rubbed shoulders with caricatures of Commune figures (her mother was on there somewhere), signed by those notorious satirists, the anonymous Zutiste Collective; finished artwork jostled for space with thinly sketched line drawings; duelling slogans overlay the art, like layers of a palimpsest; the whole, as it had seemed from afar across the river, in ceaseless motion. Around her, a thousand different stories were being told, a colour for each story, and she was in the telling of them. And through it all, she saw one slogan repeated more than others, sprayed in jet-black ink over older designs, an overwriting for this week out of all weeks.

THE AGREEMENT MUST DIE

As she walked, the Commune began to come alive around her. Indoors and outdoors exchanged places. The interior became the street, and the street became the interior. Lanes opened up into courtyards populated by washing lines and transformed back into passages, opening in turn into outdoor cafés where people were clustered around tables with chessboards and coffee mugs, twisting and turning into patches of greenery that were either public gardens or attached to homes or both. And at all times, visible beneath her through platings of glass, were the maze of pipes that constituted the Commune's sewage system.

Nobody paid her any attention. Very soon, Nila was thoroughly disoriented, trusting only the little beeps at her wrist.

Such an interloper, the thought came to her, unbidden.

'Nila? Nila M.?'

Seated upon a three-legged stool on the edge of one of the canals, a steaming coffee mug in hand, a man about her age waved to her. Nila blinked.

'Ah—hello!' she said, hoping that memory would supply a name to the face. It did not.

'It *is* you! It's been years!'

'I was—'

'Confederation neutrality rules, I know. But you're back. And what a comeback! The networks have been wild this morning. *And* the same week as the case of the century. Imagine, if we killed the Agreement and got back our Martyr the same day? Biggest Commune win in a hundred years.'

'Ah, right …' Nila continued to search her mind for a name but it lingered just beyond her reach, mist in her hands.

The man seemed not to have noticed anything amiss. 'You're off to Reunion Square, yeah?'

'Yes.'

'Round the corner, past the ateliers—you'll remember, of course. Be prepared for a crowd. So lovely to see you again, Nila, after all these years.'

'*Lovely* to see you too!' she infused all the enthusiasm she could muster in her voice, and passed on quickly, blushing like a beetroot.

'You've given us hope,' he called after her. 'Your mother must be so proud.'

She didn't break stride, but shook her head violently, as if to physically expel the last words from her ears. Around the promised corner, and then—

—all thoughts of her mother flew from her mind, as Nila paused, and took the scene in.

Reunion Square was an open cobbled square surrounded by a maze of multicoloured octagonal buildings with sharp lines and jagged edges running into each other, interspersed with hanging gardens, climbing ivy and other varieties of vegetation that she had forgotten: one of the Commune's phalansteries, its experiments in communal living. But it was the centre of the square that caught her eye.

Looking like a leaf that had been plucked from its stem and placed upon the surface of a lake, the Commune's only statue rose up before her.

She had seen it many times before, but as a child, more fascinated by the form than by what it represented. Hand-hewn in marble, it was the statue of a man, down on one knee, his neck and face turned to the sky. His hands were behind his head, tightening a rag around his mouth, covering his lips. Only his eyes could speak, and there the sculptor, with cunning skill, had wrought a look of both despair and defiance.

He was clean-shaven. His hair was pulled back carefully. He was dressed as if for a night at the theatre.

'Admiring our Falling Star, Comrade-Guardian?'

A young woman stood before her, clipboard in hand and pen behind ear.

'It's … good,' said Nila, feeling a little silly. Her eyes travelled down, to the inscription underneath the statue's feet.

His silence let the revolution sing.

'I can't wait,' said the woman, 'for him to stroll up here and say, *that looks nothing like me!* Isn't that what you're going to do for us, Comrade-Guardian?'

'Name's Nila,' said Nila carefully. 'Nila M. And you are?'

'Irama. Comrade Irama G., second secretary to the administration.'

'Right. I had asked for—'

'An appointment, yes,' Irama withdrew the pen from her ear, sucked on it and then began to underline something on the clipboard. 'But I'm afraid your request has gotten a little stuck in a jurisdictional conflict between—ah, yes, the Department for the Preservation of Historical Memory, the Department of Relations with the Confederation of the Guardians and the Department of the Future.'

'*Huh?*'

'You see,' said Irama, who seemed to be enjoying herself, 'your request is so irregular, that it is precisely the shape of the crack between the three departments. To cut a long story short, Comrade-Guardian, we don't know where to send you.'

'What are you talking about? I'm investigating a murder. This should go to the Department of Law or whatever the equivalent–'

'We do not have a Department of *Law*, imagine such a thing!' Irama gave her what seemed a highly contrived shiver of distaste. 'Or have you forgotten already?'

Nila flinched. 'Okay, listen,' she said. 'I don't have time, and more importantly, *you* don't have time. Jagat R.'s cryobox is going to be deactivated on Monday, and then he's going to be Martyr Permanent instead of Martyr Contingent, so—'

'*Procedures*, Comrade-Guardian,' Irama interrupted. 'Just because we're anarchists, you think we can just do anything we want, but let me remind you—'

'Thank you, Comrade-Secretary, I'll take it from here.'

Irama swung around. A figure slipped into Nila's sight: a woman, grey-haired, grey-eyed, and with such a grey look that a portraitist would have given her a halo of ash.

'Administrator Vani,' said Irama, 'the jurisdictional conflict—'

'Has been overridden,' Vani completed. 'By me. Emergency powers. Approved by the autonomous Councils in a snap vote, *Comrade*, before you ask.'

Irama drooped noticeably. Nila felt a vicious surge of satisfaction. *Screw you and your pencil and clipboard.*

Irama backed away with a sweep of her arm, as if to say *the stage is yours*, although there was no stage. The administrator turned her gaze upon Nila. A light, searching, almost curious look came—and passed.

'Comrade-Guardian. The Commune has authorised me to speak with you.'

Nila suddenly noticed that they were surrounded by people. They had come and formed a wide circle around her so quietly that she hadn't even noticed, and were now listening intently.

'Ahem—a private discussion?' she said.

'Radical transparency, Comrade-Guardian,' said Vani. '*Any deliberation or decision that affects the Commune as a whole, may only be conducted or taken in a space that is open and accessible to the public.* Axiom Four of the Commune's charter.'

'Ah, right.'

'I've seen the news,' said Vani. 'Let's get straight to the point. You're going to bring back Jagat the Martyr?'

'If I succeed.'

'Is it your case that Jagat did not assassinate the director? That he was wrongly convicted?'

'Yes to the second,' Nila said carefully, 'No to the first. I am a guardian, not a historian. I can't say if Jagat did or did not assassinate Director Purul. What I can say is that if there is doubt about whether he did—reasonable doubt—then he will live again.'

'Thanks for the condescension, Guardian,' Vani said. 'We know how criminal convictions work. In this case you're hardly going to be able to establish reasonable doubt unless you have an alternate theory.'

'I'm working on that,' said Nila. 'I need your help.'

'Oh?' said Vani. A rustling of cloth in the circle, a movement of bodies. 'Go on, then.'

'Well, first up—Jagat. A citizen of Low Town, in the pre-revolutionary days. I looked him up in the public library database, in the genealogies, in school registers. And you know what I found?'

'Tell us.'

'Nothing. Or next to nothing. A birth record. A school enrolment certificate and a school graduation certificate, no particular distinction. And the next thing, Administrator? The gunshot on the bridge, the trial, the sentence, and suddenly, he is embedded in the pages of history. Jagat is like a breath on glass—and the glass shatters.

'So I checked the databases on the major leaders of the revolutions, the ones who were at the forefront on the Day of the Barricades: Bhumi. Almas. Mouli. Levellers like Varsha ... and so many more. There, the records spoke. Long before the revolution, they were *here*.' She indicated the Commune with a sweep of her arm. 'They edited radical newspapers. They composed viral pamphlets. They organised protests and strikes. They spoke at public meetings. They were union leaders. They were members of revolutionary cells. They were detained, beaten, tortured and jailed; some of them even got shot. At the very least, Administrator, *at the very least*, High Town's Intelligence Bureau had files on all of them. You know how extensive the Directorate's surveillance network was. The most inconsequential actors had a file, even if all it contained was a single line: *person of interest*.

'But for Jagat—nothing.'

The rustling around her had stopped.

'To understand what happened that day, Administrator,' Nila continued, her voice soft, 'I need to know who Jagat was. But history is silent—or has been silenced. And so I've come here to ask you: who was—*is*—Jagat R., the Commune's best-kept secret?'

'And why do you think,' said Vani, 'that after a hundred years, we will know what the databases don't—or, as you say, what the databases have chosen to forget?'

Nila gestured at the statue. 'This was the revolution, Administrator, *your* revolution. Your Commune was born with it. With him. Don't say that you know nothing, that the Department of Historical Memory *has* nothing. You don't need to worry about sifting legend from fact. That's my job. Just tell me the stories.'

Vani's nostrils flared. 'That's where you're wrong, Guardian. You think the revolution had leaders and followers. A vanguard, like every other failed revolution of the past. That's what you looked for in the databases. And because that's what you were looking for, you found it. But our revolution had no leaders, Guardian. Do you think that if it had, we'd have been able to build the Commune in its ruins and make it last for a hundred years? The Commune, where our first axiom is *no centre*, and our first slogan is *no such thing as harmless power*?'

Nila suddenly had a sense that Vani's words were not meant just for her.

'No wonder,' Vani continued, her voice gentling, 'you're so struck by something so ordinary. That Jagat might have been ordinary. That this was a revolution of ordinary people.'

'Ordinary?' said Nila. 'You have a statue of him. The only statue in the Commune. You don't call him Jagat, you call him the Martyr. The Falling Star.' She searched for memories of childhood. 'The moment of silence before every meal—doesn't it commemorate the Martyr's original silence? The silence with which he refused to condemn his comrades, the silence that let the revolution sing? And don't you say, after that moment is done: *to the Commune, born in the gift of silence*, before you eat? Isn't the first right in the Commune's charter the right not to speak, the right to silence? And then you tell me: *ordinary*?'

The grey look became black. 'Is it so hard to understand, Guardian, that an ordinary person could do an extraordinary thing?'

'Now you're just trading in clichés,' said Nila. 'Come on, Administrator.'

She realised that they were glaring at each other, their fists clenched at their sides.

'Listen,' Nila strove to keep her voice level. 'There is a historical narrative: that not only was Director Purul's assassination pre-planned, it was a signal for the revolution to begin in the chaos that followed his death. Jagat's responsibility for the assassination is embedded within this story. To cast reasonable doubt—to bring him back—I need to examine this. But for that, I need to know *who* Jagat was. If not for the record, then for myself.'

Vani smiled faintly. 'And I thought you just said you were a guardian, not a historian. But you know what they say: it could have been any director and any assassin. Only in that moment …'

'Don't quote *The Great Unravelling* to me,' Nila interrupted. 'Yes, I know it *could* have been anyone. I'm interested in who it *was*. The human being, not the bearer of social relations. Because that's what matters to me. To his life.'

Vani's smile faded. 'Guardian, I—we understand what you're saying. But you have to believe me when I say this: you're chasing shadows. It's not just that all this happened a hundred years ago, it's not just that all the documents were erased in the Pact of Forgetting. It's also that it happened in the most unusual of times. The old Low Town, the workers' town, it was a mad, mad place. There were secret societies. Undercover reading circles. Militant cells. Banned student groups. None of them agreed. All of them fought. But above all else, you will understand, Guardian, they *did not keep membership lists*. Jagat could have come out of literally any of these groups, and there were a hundred, a thousand, ten thousand like him. He just happened to be the one on the bridge that morning, but he was not *the* one. *The* one never existed. That's the meaning of those opening lines in *The Great Unravelling*, which High Town can never understand. This is why we always say heroes betray us, and we betray ourselves by having them. Our revolution was anarchist. It's what has let us be anarchist so long after the revolution.'

'The database—'

'Guardian,' Vani said quietly. 'You say that you saw the names of the leaders of the revolution in the database. But did you perhaps consider that you only think of those people as the leaders *because* you saw their names in the database?'

Nila chewed her lip. The faces around her were carefully arranged into expressions of neutrality, a polite interest that told her nothing.

'Alright,' Nila said, 'One more question, Administrator.'

'Yes?' A hint of weariness surfaced in Vani's tone.

'The last sentence Jagat spoke. *In the name of the Commune unborn, die.*'

A nod from Vani, nods all around. The words, etched in the collective memories of High Town and Low Town, Council and Commune.

'What about it?'

'You know what's interesting?' Her words were directed at the gathering, not just Vani. 'I looked up the database. In all the Low Town debates that led up to the revolution—in all the newspapers, the pamphlets, the online blogs, the forums—did you know that *nobody talked about the Commune?'*

Vani stiffened. 'What do you mean? The Commune has always—'

'No, that's what. A hundred years later you think the Commune has always been, but it was an invented tradition. The Commune was never a part of the vocabulary of your revolution, not until the day Purul was assassinated. Of course, there was talk of a unified city, true freedom, equal toil, workers' Councils—but you know what? I saw only two references to Commune, and both of them spoke about the fourth workers' revolt from a century before—about the two-day *failed* Commune. But the Commune as a revolutionary dream, as the organising principle of revolutionary life—it's not there, Administrator. It's not there until Jagat spoke it into existence. The Commune was born with him.'

In the silence that followed, Nila let her next words fall like stones into still water.

'Or, should we say, *allegedly* spoke it into existence. And because of that—because of the story about how it was spoken, it became the slogan of the revolution, a thing of flesh and blood.'

Vani opened her mouth, but Nila went on quickly. 'Do you still think I'm chasing shadows? An unknown man, speaking an unknown sentence, in just the wrong place, at just the wrong time. Let me grant you your anarchist revolution that had no leaders upon the barricades. Let me grant you that the revolution wasn't about your vanguardist Levellers. But it's just a bit too much, isn't it, when it's not just the assassin of Director Purul who seems to have no existence before the revolution, but his very words as well?'

Vani was no longer looking at her. Her face was turned up, her gaze unfocused and far away, towards the towers of the High Town; shimmering wraiths in the far distance.

At length, she nodded. 'I can't promise you anything, Guardian, but we will speak with the Department of Historical Memory, and see if there are any Jagat-shaped feathers still floating upon the long river of the past. No guarantees.'

'I understand,' said Nila, a thrill running down her spine, making her almost jump. *Finally, we move!*

'Was there anything else?'

'Not at the moment, but I may need to come back here as my investigation progresses.'

'My emergency powers extend to the duration of your investigation, so come straight here and ask for me.' Vani glanced around. 'Under conditions of radical transparency, of course.'

Murmurs broke out in the circle that surrounded them.

'Thank you,' said Nila.

8

Don't Let Him Die

CAFÉ SUBVERSION

THE SIGN BELOW THE WOODCARVERS' ATELIERS brought her up short. Nila felt the first taste of memory force its way to the tip of her tongue, mixed with the pangs of barely-suppressed hunger. She went up to the counter, where a youngish-looking man stood. His face lit up in in recognition—until she held out a Chapterhouse voucher, and then his smile became a smidgen less natural, a tiny bit more fixed. She requested lunch and went to the bench closest to the street, the one she used to sit on as a child.

From somewhere within the ateliers, the music of the harmonium wafted into the street. It took a while before the melody wound its way through the passages of her mind, and into awareness: 'Leave with the Dawn', a song about the parting of two lovers who'd grown up together in the Commune, one of whom had lost belief in the revolution and longed to leave. It had been written two generations ago, during a period of particular disillusionment in the history of the Commune. The disillusionment had passed but its anthem had never gone out of fashion, and had, for a time, been the soundtrack to her own life.

As she silently mouthed the words to the song, the dam broke at last. The memories she had been suppressing, so that she could face the day unencumbered by the past, overwhelmed her with their taste, their smell, their touch: walks by the canal, under the amaltas trees bowed down with the weight of the flowers; swims when the water grew warmer, the feel of shaking silver droplets off one's hair onto emerald grass; games of hide-and-seek within the indoor micro-forests of the arcologies and around the sharp corners and higgledy-piggledy levels of the communal phalansteries; the scents of sweat and grass after a summer pick-up game played barefoot on the maidan; celebrating a goal to the backdrop of an interdepartmental meeting that had elected to have their discussion on sewage maintenance beside the banyan tree that served as one of the goalposts; the coolness of coconut water immediately after a game, and the warmth of mrigel curry after the tramp home; learning to be on first-name terms with the clumsiness of one's own body through the craft sessions at the ateliers; the comforting hum of an all-Commune public meeting, falling asleep on a shoulder, and waking up to find that the same speaker was still going; stolen kisses at the back of the hall of the Department of Historical Memory while her mother spoke upon the stage about insurrections and inflection points; stolen kisses at the back of the amphitheatre during the autumn theatre festival; stolen kisses through the morning tediousness of the monthly garbage collection assignment after having arranged to be on the same rota; sitting by the river aflame with the sunset, staring across the water at the towers of High Town, wondering about a future—and Nila knew then that memory could not be erased simply through an act of will.

She'd planned to leave after lunch and be back in chambers by afternoon but her feet had other ideas. They took her elsewhere, away from the river, through the neighbourhoods without centre or periphery, past the thousand stories on the walls, and through the outdoor cafés where, by late afternoon, the pianos and violins had come out in force, and music was everywhere. It was something they said about the Commune, those who visited it for the first time: walking in the streets gave you a curious sensation that time had wrapped itself up in contradictions.

She walked through old haunts, little knowing why she was lingering so long in the streets, even as her own time trickled away; but something within her clamoured for understanding, a sense of the dreams and nightmares, no longer her own, trapped within these stones, which had created a man like Jagat, and sent him into the world.

It was early evening, when she'd stopped by a micro-park to rest her legs, that Nila began to notice the decay that had escaped her when she'd been on the move, decay that could not be papered over by whoever was on the weekly town-cleaning rota: chipping plaster, fading paint, a crack in the street, wooden benches that seemed to have been worried by many fingernails, cobbles strewn upon the street. It was as if the Commune was suddenly coming into focus in a different way.

The Mandalium Agreement. Economic ruin, slow but sure.

Spray-painted on the cobblestones was the ever-present slogan:

THE AGREEMENT MUST DIE

She stood and wandered again as the sun sank lower in the sky. In the slowly fading light, even the disrepair began to look beautiful.

Get out of here before you fall in love all over again, you idiot.

But she didn't get out. Instead she meandered on, until she found herself just outside a little round gate. Beyond the gate, a pebbled path led up to a doorway which was missing a door. A pair of lilac curtains signified the beginnings of a home.

As she stood outside the gate, hesitating, the curtains parted. A woman came out, grey-haired, and wearing a beige apron, to which a couple of wood shavings were still clinging. She walked down the pebbled path, until she was standing on the other side of the gate, her hands on her hips.

'You're late,' she said.

'Do you know of displaced muscle memory?' Nila replied.

'Is this something you invented on your way here?'

'No, it's actually a thing. When you return to a place after a long time, you *think* you know its geography, but it turns out that it's just slightly displaced in your head, so you always end up a couple of streets away from where you thought you would be.'

'Well, you came.'

'I did. And now I must be going—'

'Oh no, you don't,' the woman said, her hands still on her hips. 'I am, technically, a member of the Department of Historical Memory. Is there anything that forbids you from speaking to me *in the course of your investigation?*'

'Hmm. Well, no.'

'Do you have dinner plans?'

'No, but I have to file—'

'Stop talking like you're drafting an application, Nila. Such a *bloody* guardian. You'll work better with food inside you.' The woman pushed open the gate and gripped Nila's wrist, a familiar touch. 'In you come. You will eat dinner at home tonight, and not another word.'

Nila broke into a smile. 'Yes, Ma.'

Meera D., woodcarver for the Autonomous Neighbourhood Council of Fourth Cross Road, and many other things besides, brought her daughter into the spacious, circular drawing room, and to a table set for three.

'Pa?' said Nila.

'On deputation to Chemur. I told him I'd likely see you sometime this week—he sends his love.'

'Ah dammit, I was hoping he wouldn't be on deputation.' Nila looked at the table. 'For three?'

'Maybe.'

'You know you're still a terrible actor, right, Ma?' Nila said. 'But okay. I'll wait.'

They sat down at the table, next to each other. Nila leaned back in her chair. Glazed woodwork was scattered around her: two cushioned rocking chairs by the window, painted bright red; little horses and tigers on the carpet, playmates of a childhood past, but never discarded; a chest of drawers against the wall, knobs a bright turquoise; just above that, a double-levelled shelf soldered into the wall; upon the first level, there were jars with condiments that stirred up old memories; on the second level, there were two dragon-patterned lampshades that had never actually been lit as far as she could remember; and between them, a cactus plant looking satisfied and well-watered.

'Still delicious chaos, I see,' said Nila. 'No wonder we never grew up in a phalanstery. They'd have thrown you out in a week.'

'Have a woodworker and a painter by inclination live together, what do you expect?' Meera said. 'Wonder how *you* turned out the way you did.'

'To make things more interesting for you, of course,' Nila said. 'I've missed being here.'

'Tell me,' said her mother, the beginnings of a grin crinkling her lips, 'how does this compare to your sojourn on the other side?'

'There's only one right answer here, isn't it?' Nila let herself grin back. 'Well. That house was bigger, of course. All clean-cut lines and rectangular windows, scientifically designed for the greatest amount of light. Oh yeah, the garden was *outside* the house. Can you imagine?'

'Typical High Town barbarism. And your adoptive family?'

'They were kind. Very respectful. Funnily so, at times, almost like they didn't quite know how to be with me. But we were just getting to know each other, I think, when the adoptive period ended.'

'Did you like them, Nila?'

She stared at the grain of the table. 'I … think so? It was different, but it was nice enough. Well, while it lasted.' She let out a little laugh. 'You don't have to get competitive, Ma.'

'I heard that today, in Reunion Square, you said "*your* revolution" and "*your* Commune".'

The room felt two shades darker.

'Ma, you know how it needs to be,' said Nila.

'I know how it needs to be *in public*.' Meera looked into the space behind her shoulder. 'But what I need to know is whether you really feel that way.'

'What I feel is,' said Nila slowly, 'that this,' she gestured at the space around her, 'is home, and always will be.'

Her mother put both her hands on the table, and looked at her. 'You haven't answered the question.'

A tinkling, musical sound wafted through the air.

Meera laughed, her mood altered. 'Saved by the bell.'

Nila unclenched, and laughed with her. 'That's my surprise, isn't it?'

The thud of footsteps came through the passageway. A man walked into the room. He stopped dead on seeing Nila, his mouth open.

She'd guessed it the moment she'd seen the table set for three, and her mother's wretched attempt at deflecting, but even then, for a moment, the bottom plunged out of Nila's stomach.

Two nights ago, at the Agora, she'd told Maru that she would not seek out Anam in the Commune. Until this instant, she'd believed it; but now she knew that from the moment after her meeting with Vani, when she'd decided to linger in the Commune instead of going back home, every step she'd taken had been a step towards this.

She stood. The sound of her chair scraping the ground came from a long way away. He was just as she remembered when she'd seen him last, a year and a half ago, on their Farewell Day: a shock of dark hair falling untidily over his forehead, eyes ever so slightly quizzical, mouth turned just slightly, as if he'd just stepped into a room and wasn't quite sure he belonged.

'Hey, Anam. You look like you've seen a ghost.'

'Nila—' he began, before she crossed the floor and lost herself in his arms, silencing him. He smelled of mild cedar, from the woods beyond the Peruma switchback just after the rains, soft and comforting. She gripped him tighter, so tight that he gasped for a moment, and then she stepped back, cupping her hands around his cheeks.

'You haven't changed.'

'You, on the other hand ...'

'Oh?'

'It's—it's the guardian aura.'

She laughed, delighted. 'As terribly awkward with compliments as ever. Next thing you'll say I look very impartial.'

Behind them, plates clinked audibly on the table. 'Dinner's ready!' her mother called.

The three plates on the table were no longer empty. Mrigel fish curry waited for them, steaming hot, smelling like heaven.

'Oh, yum!' Nila exclaimed, disengaging from Anam. 'Come.' She took his hand and led him to the table. She dragged her chair next to his, ruining the symmetry of the dinner table.

'I'm going to allow this just this once,' said Meera.

'Wow, thanks so much, Ma,' said Nila, shifting the plates.

'Only because this one has literally never been able to stop talking about you, every week,' said Meera. '*Auntie Meera, what do you think Nila will be doing right now? Auntie Meera, does she still think about us?*'

'I'd be so lucky,' said Nila, as Anam slipped into the seat next to her. She reached out to him beneath the table, while extending her other hand towards the fish curry.

'Wait!' Meera said, before she could tear off the first portion. 'The moment of silence!'

'Oh dammit, I totally forgot!' Nila blushed. 'Sorry.'

Meera looked down at the table. 'I guess you really *have* become a guardian.'

'I remember the words—'

'But it isn't reflexive anymore.'

'Oh, Ma!' Nila held her mother's gaze, ignoring a dull ache at the base of her chest. She felt Anam squeeze her hand gently, fleetingly. 'Would you really want me to have a fragment of my heart here and a fragment there? Always drifting between two worlds? Wasn't it you who once told me, *no half-choices?*'

'You know,' Meera said, 'I do believe you've inherited my talent for sounding much more convinced about something than you really are.'

There was a moment when the tension stretched like a frayed thread, before Meera laughed freely. Nila hesitated, then joined in. Out of the corner of her eye, she saw Anam smiling uncertainly.

'Okay, now close your eyes,' Meera said.

Nila complied. Silence filled the room.

Visions of the statue drifted before her, a man tying a gag around his own mouth, to hold his peace when it mattered the most.

Her mother's voice cut through her thoughts. 'The gift of silence let our Commune be born. We will never forget.' She spread out her hands. 'Eat well.'

For a while, nobody spoke, as they tucked in. Then Nila said: 'This is *so* much better than the Agora stalls.'

'My reputation was on the line,' Meera said.

'Ahh,' Nila sighed. 'So good.'

'So now, tell me,' her mother said, 'what's all this about? I mean, I know what it's about, but tell me in your own words.'

'I'm on a brief,' said Nila, 'to argue that Jagat was wrongly convicted for the assassination of Director Purul.'

'Who's the brief for?' Anam asked.

'His great-granddaughter.'

'He has a great-granddaughter?' her mother said. 'That entire family just vanished after the revolution.'

'They moved to High Town,' Nila said. 'Made good on some investments. That's how Ani—who's the client, by the way—can finance this.'

Her mother nodded. 'Checks. Can't blame them. If any family deserved a break ...'

'But wait,' said Anam. 'So the networks are right? If you win this case, the Martyr will come back? In the flesh?'

'He'll be revived, yes,' said Nila. '*If* I win on Monday.'

Anam let go of her hand and turned entirely towards her eyes shining. 'How's it going?'

Nila grimaced. 'I don't know. There are a lot of little niggling inconsistencies about what happened that day, but I'm just not being able to find that connecting thread—you know, the one you pull on and then the whole fabric unravels.' She turned to her mother, mock-accusingly. '*Your* administrator wasn't very helpful either.'

'What did you ask her?'

'I wanted to know more about Jagat, who he was, where he came from. Because the records have nothing. But she just wouldn't say.'

'But isn't that right?' Anam cut in.

'How do you mean?'

'Our Commune histories pretty much agree on this.'

'Anam's correct, Nila,' Meera said.

'I mean,' said Nila, 'there's a difference between being a hidden, undercover agent whom no one knows about, and being a nobody.'

'Hm,' her mother said. She pushed her plate away and wiped her mouth. 'What kind of history do they teach in the Chapterhouse anyway?'

'The usual, I guess?' said Nila.

'About the revolution?'

'I think it's pretty comprehensive,' said Nila, feeling suddenly defensive. 'There are testimonies from both sides, a fairly impartial account of what happened and the aftermath. It's taught from the perspective of constitutional history, of course.'

'Of course.'

'Come on, Ma,' said Nila. 'You can't expect the Confederation to be partisan, no? Especially given the role that they—that *we* have to play.'

Her mother smiled. 'No, no, I get it. They don't really have much choice there. It's just that I think there's a perspective that those histories don't allow you to grasp completely.'

'What do you mean?'

'What do you remember learning about the Martyr before you left for the Chapterhouse seven years ago?'

Nila chewed the inside of her cheek, trying to recall. 'The moment of silence, of course. The statue. And the parts about how it was the shot that birthed the Commune. I don't know, ma, he's always been this figure, so …'

'Larger than life?' Anam said.

'More like in a whole different dimension,' said Nila. 'It's like when you looked at me just now, Anam, when I said that if I win, he'll be back. You looked like you were seeing a legend made flesh.'

'That's because his story is our story.' Meera said. 'It's why Vani wasn't really being hostile, Nila. When we say that the Martyr was nothing, it's actually true. Not only that, what he did went against the grain of common sense. If you read all the Low Town propaganda around the time of the revolution, nobody believed that an inflection point was around the corner. It was about using the general strike to extract some concessions from Purul, codify the minimum wage, et cetera, et cetera.'

'I know. I read.' Nila leaned forward. 'And that's been bothering me. Most historians agree that when Purul decided to come down into Low Town, it was to announce that he was giving in—at least to some of the demands. What was the point of shooting him before he could do that?'

'Because,' her mother said, 'one man's reading of the revolutionary situation was more accurate than all established wisdom. *And* he had the courage to act on it.'

'So you're saying,' said Nila, 'that he was the original anarchist.'

'I'm saying that in the history of our subcontinent, almost every revolution has congealed into a new, vertical order the moment that it succeeds, and that's because every revolution *has been led*. Look at the beginnings, Nila. When Peruma overthrew the emperor, there was a moment in time when any future was possible. You know when that moment died? It was when the so-called radicals created an "enforcement committee", and put themselves at the head. That was the real First Inflection point, that was what morphed into the bloody Council and Directorate. And every attempt after that has been led, and it has failed: not just here in Peruma, but everywhere in the continent. Remember the December Insurgency of Chemur? Or that tragic Uprising of the Blues in Lubini?'

'But the Blues won—'

'And then proceeded to do in Lubini just what the restorationists did here. And why? Because they couldn't imagine a body without a head; a brain; a centralised directing nervous system.'

'Until the Commune?'

'Until us. We've survived a hundred years as we are, *no centre, no periphery*, because we began like that. Our unplanned, undirected, formless revolution.' Meera shook her head. 'It couldn't have been any other way, Nila. You have to understand. If Jagat was acting under the instructions of some secret group—the Levellers, for instance—which had this much power, this much influence, to organise the assassination of the director and make a man die for them without a word, then you can be damn well sure that they would have been in charge after the revolution. And by now we'd just be a mirror of High Town, or a mirror of Lubini where they call themselves the party of the "institutional revolution". But we're not. We're *us*, with our ANCs that can never agree with each other, our departments that argue over everything and our administration where writing dissent notes is a daily sport. And that's your strongest proof for Jagat being what he was.'

'Heroes betray us, and we betray ourselves by having them?' said Nila.

'I see Vani managed to get her favourite line in.'

'Heh,' said Nila, picking at a piece of fish. 'I did think that he may have been a front for the Levellers—for someone like Varsha ...'

'Impossible,' said Meera decisively.

It had been seven years since she had seen her mother like this, felt her sense of absolute command over history, over facts, over intuition, from premise to conclusion in an irrefutable chain of logic—a sense of *control* that Nila had left home to find for herself in the Confederation.

'Well, he may still have chosen to do it,' she said after a while, hesitantly. 'There's no other way I can make sense of his silence.'

She looked at her mother. A sudden—and familiar—sense of fear coursed through her, the feeling that something she'd said, without thinking it through, was about to be destroyed by a remorseless exercise of logic and judgment.

But Meera only said, mildly: 'It's a possibility, consistent with the *The Great Unravelling* thesis. I grant you that the silence is strange. It's totally unlike us anarchists. We will speak until our breath gives out, then we will write until the networks are overloaded with our words and after all that we'll paint the walls until the walls run out.'

'Yeah, reticence has never been your style, has it?' Nila said, realising a moment after the word had left her mouth that she'd said *you* instead of *we*.

Meera noticed as quickly as she did. Something shifted behind her eyes, an imperceptible movement of muscles. Nila opened her mouth without knowing what she was going to say, to retract—or not—but then:

'Auntie Meera,' Anam's smiling voice cut in. 'You know the best way of answering this question, no? Bring him home—and ask him!'

Meera burst out laughing. The heaviness shattered. 'Now that would be one way,' she said, chuckling. 'Imagine he did come back and start telling us stories about the revolution! And that too right in the middle of *Council vs Commune*. It would turn Peruma upside-down.'

Nila played with the last piece of fish on her plate. 'Ma,' she said, 'can I ask you something?'

'Always.'

'Are we really on the eve of the Fifth Inflection Point?'

'Yes.' Meera's voice was utterly certain. 'One that's going to decide the true meaning of the last hundred years. If we win, if the Mandalium Agreement goes—we'll have some space to breathe, to fight; we'll have hope again. But if the Council triumphs, if the Agreement survives past this Monday—*we* won't survive too much longer.'

'Is there no other—'

'We're can't afford another war against High Town right now,' said Meera. 'So it'll either be a slow, crippling death under the Agreement—or swift ruin, if we're driven to go to war. And if our revolution ends, if Peruma is reunified under the Council, that will be the first step on the road back to the Old Empire. There will never be a Commune on the continent again. The dream will die. You know this.'

'I do,' Nila whispered.

Meera shook her head. 'The only inflection point that was planned a century in advance, when they signed that damned Charter and froze everything into law for a hundred years. They knew what they were doing, our ancestors, they knew this day would come, and we—we've all been living in the world they made, waiting for this day.'

'What other choice did they have?' said Nila.

'I don't know. Perhaps none. Perhaps they couldn't have done more. But it did ensure that for all that we call ourselves the Commune, all we really are is a glorified cooperative, still bargaining on the market with High Town, just trying to be fairer to each other within. And we can't move on from that as long as we're immobilised by the Charter. That's been the design of the document, as you probably understand better than me.' Her face broke into a sudden smile. 'But you know the one thing that was unplanned, the one thing *fully* outside the design?'

'What?'

'The return of the Martyr.' Was there a glimmer of … something that Nila saw in her mother's eyes? 'You might not be in *Council vs Commune*, Nila, but you're playing one hell of a role in how this inflection point will turn.'

'So … the Commune isn't mad at me?' Nila said. 'You all don't think I'm a meddlesome interloper messing up your history?'

'*I* think,' Meera said, 'that you're a very interesting variable, in this week of all weeks. And I can't wait to see what you do.'

Those last words made Nila suddenly, acutely aware of the passing of time. 'You know that's only going to happen if I get cracking on the case, no?'

Meera smiled with a hint of sadness. Something of the heaviness returned to hang between them. 'And I'm sure it will. It was nice seeing you again, my love. Even if just for an evening. If you need to investigate more this side of the river, come by again and eat.'

Nila walked over to her and gave her a fierce hug. 'Pupillage is getting over soon. And then all these stupid restrictions will end. Give Pa my love too, please.'

'I will.' Meera nodded at Anam. 'Walk her to the road, will you?'

Nila turned once, at the edge of the room. Her mother was looking back at her, and gave her the slightest of waves. '*You'll be brilliant*,' she mouthed.

Nila nodded. There were shards of glass in her throat. She turned again. In the passageway, her hands brushed against Anam. Their fingers entwined, fitting into each other as naturally as they had a year and a half ago.

They walked out on to the pebbled path, and to the gate. Night had fallen over Peruma. A crescent moon rode high in the clear sky.

'Come,' said Nila.

'Are you allowed?' said Anam.

'We'll take our secret path. And, anyway, I don't care.'

They took the pebbled pathway around the house, and through a warren of small streets. Perhaps it was the touch of Anam's fingers in hers, but her displaced muscle memory was now just a memory. She led him forward, sure-footed, on grass, on cobblestones, through a gap in a hedge, and then on grass once again, until they heard the sound of rushing water.

They sat together on the edge of the bank, feet dangling over the 9 August Canal, which gurgled on its way to join the Urai. Leaves rustled softly around them. Mynahs called to each other amidst the branches. In the sky, the moon danced in and out of the clouds, little silver beams glancing off the water.

Anam cuddled up against her. She put an arm around his shoulder, and nestled her cheek against the side of his head.

'What you thinking?' Anam said after a while.

She breathed. 'I'm not really sure. It's been like coming back to a world that isn't mine anymore.'

'Hey. We're here. Together. Just like it used to be.'

'I know.' She permitted herself a small smile and ran her fingers through Anam's hair. 'I know.'

'You're all clenched,' said Anam quietly.

She opened her mouth to protest, but then just nodded. 'Sorry. It's too much, all at once. The Commune, Vani, Jagat, this night, this spot, you. I feel …' An image popped into her head, unbidden: a man awakened from a sleep of death, stepping back into a familiar-unfamiliar world, a known-unknown love. She suppressed it.

'I'll be fully back, Anam, I promise. I just need a little time to … reorient. I guess it can't happen all in an evening.'

He brushed his forehead against her cheek. 'I get it. We'll start over if we need to. We'll be here; me, Auntie Meera—'

'Oh, *Ma* is wholly unchanged.' Nila chuckled. 'Knows exactly what the fight is about, who she's fighting with, what she's fighting against.' She drew Anam tighter to herself. 'I would die with so much certainty.'

She heard his quiet breathing for a while, before he moved slightly.

'You and her,' he said.

'Mm?' She felt her hair prickle.

'You know, I've never seen you two so natural together.'

'Oh.' A part of her relaxed. 'Yeah. I *felt* natural. Well, barring a couple of hairy moments, but yes. Like I was meeting her again in my own skin.'

'Can I be sappy, Nila?'

'Make it worthwhile.'

'Do you remember how you once told me that you felt invisible as your mother's daughter, because she was so much like the sun, and you were too close to the light?'

'Yes. The number of times I heard people tell me, *your Ma, she's so brilliant, you must be too*.'

'Yeah, so tonight I watched the two of you and I felt like now it was two stars with their own gravitational—*ow*!' He broke off theatrically after receiving a jab in his ribs. 'Don't hit me, I warned you!'

'You're saying I was anxious about being overshadowed, huh? That I was an insecure little twerp because of how much the whole Commune admires her?'

'I would never!'

'But I was. I mean, Ma is still Ma. And I've always really wanted to—I don't know, live up to—what? Her? Something she represents? A Commune ideal of the leader who isn't a leader, or something? I dunno, I've never really figured it out, but yeah, getting away for a bit from it all helped. You know what I said earlier about her certainty? I feel like I've come back to her with my own certainty—in my doubts.'

Anam nodded slowly. 'I remember the day you told me you were going to leave. When we were here … right here.'

Submerged memories, undisturbed for so long, came floating to the surface like sea-drift. They had not fought—they rarely did—but he had asked, and she had tried to explain, clumsily, her words sliding off the surface of his confusion, nothing sticking, until at last he'd only said *I don't get it, but I'll wait*, and she'd only said, at the end of all things, desperate to avoid confrontation, *thank you*, and walked away, expecting that they would be over within a month, but it was seven years and here they were again, as if she was the one who had awakened from a sleep of death and wandered back into a world that *had* waited.

She screwed her eyes shut now, wondering if the seven-year delayed confrontation was finally at hand. 'And?' she whispered.

'I didn't really understand then, but after tonight, I kind of think I do.'

Nila exhaled, feeling a tinge of embarrassed relief. 'Am I going to be forgiven so easily then?'

'You have some making up to do.'

'Be careful what you wish for.'

'Oh, should I be afraid of you? After all, you left us as Nila and have come back a hero—the Commune's *dangerous* hero!'

'Oh, shut up you!' She punched his shoulder.

'Anything you say, my Key Person.'

'Idiot!' She laughed out loud. 'Okay, Anam, that's enough fun at my expense for the evening. So … what have *you* been doing all this while?'

'Learning's done. I'm at—but wait. Guess. I know you won't be able to.'

She nudged him lightly. 'I hate guessing games. You know that. Tell me.'

'Just try.'

'Erm. Look, you either went into conservation, or you went into history. I'd say conservation, but the way you were talking about the Martyr, I'm going to guess you're in the Department of Historical Memory, with Ma.'

'Wrong!' he said triumphantly. 'Should've stuck with your first guess. What *do* they teach you at Fortress Drab?'

'Wait, so you're a card-carrying environmentalist now?'

'I'm in conservation. I study myco-remediation.'

'Myco—what?' she began, but then stopped. 'Oh wait, I know what that is. You work with fungi!'

'Thank you,' said Anam, 'for not subjecting me to the *oh, you took mushrooms a bit too seriously* joke for the five hundredth time.'

'It's why you love me.'

'Among other things. But yeah,' he said. 'You know, all our childhood hours by the canal, finding the best, the most secret places, like this one—it's what I do now. I'm working on myco-remediation in urban marine environments.'

'I *cannot* even.'

'You know how much your Ma loves it? Ever since we've been talking about fungi, she's been saying how perfect a metaphor it is for the Commune: autonomous mycelia with no centre, no defined boundaries. Now she's started a study group in the Department of Historical Memory to look into what non-human forms of life can teach us about political organisation.'

'Oh, she's moved on from *octopus vulgaris*, is it?' said Nila. 'I remember how she was obsessed with how the octopuses' decentralised nervous system is a metaphor for the Commune.'

'Yes, you could say she's evolved … sideways.'

They burst out laughing. 'Gods, Anam.' Nila placed a finger underneath his chin and gently turned his face around until they were looking at each other. 'I've *missed* you. I can't wait to discover you all over again. Six more months.'

'I'll wait.'

'Oh, *now* you'd better!' she laughed. 'I need to encounter the Commune all over again with you. And we will have nothing but time. Until then—'

She drew him close, kissed him. They swayed together. Nila kept her eyes closed, hearing the mild rustling of the breeze, all her other senses given over to the feel of Anam.

'Nila,' he whispered into her ear.

'Yes, love?'

'Don't let him die.'

For a moment, she was discomfited. Then context came rushing back into her brain, the Confederation, Ani and why she'd come to the Commune in the first place. She disengaged from him, looked him in the eye, and saw fear, uncertainty … and hope.

'I won't.'

9

You Were One of Us

AS SHE STEPPED OUT OF THE LAST LINE OF buildings, and into the stretch of the old Bulwark Zone, the skies opened up. Yet, for just a moment, Nila felt she was stepping back into a smaller, more constricted world. Her heart ached.

Upon Unity Bridge, Vani was standing, waiting for her.

'Hello, Administrator.'

'You aren't surprised to see me,' Vani said.

'I may be a rookie,' Nila said, 'but even I can tell when someone leaves a conversation unfinished.'

She stepped upon the bridge, ignoring a tingling at the base of her spine.

'No radical transparency anymore, am I right?'

Vani inclined her head. 'Perhaps I underestimated you.'

Nila tapped upon the balustrade. 'Back there, Administrator, you were hostile. Can I guess why? You suspect I'm a Council spy.'

Vani shook her head. 'No, Guardian, not quite. We're no great fans of the Free and Equal Whatever of Peruma, but we respect the role you play. You're flawed and you don't often get it, but you're independent.'

'Thanks, I guess?'

Vani ignored her. 'I'm not worried that you're a spy, Guardian. I'm worried that you're being played.'

'What do you mean?'

'Law, Guardian. The law you administer. It's a weapon given to your keeping. And there are always those who watch you, waiting for you to raise your arm, so that just as you do, they can grasp your wrist and turn your blow the way they would.'

'If you are talking about ambush cases—'

'You know the history of your Confederation,' Vani interrupted, 'and the history before your Confederation. You know what I'm talking about.'

Ambush cases. It was one of the terms most familiar to a student at the Chapterhouse: all those times where Council or Commune (responsibility was pretty much equally distributed here) had come to the guardians through fronts or proxy clients, *using* the guardians—and their reputation for impartiality—as weapons in their struggle against each other through strategically chosen cases. Everyone was trained to look out for an ambush, and the Executive Committee retained a permanent veto over any case precisely to guard against such a possibility. And yet …

'Let me be honest with you, Guardian, since you're now neck-deep into this,' said Vani, 'and you'll also understand why radical transparency wouldn't work here. The Commune is torn right now. Split.'

Nila remembered Irama, and her barely veiled look of hostility when Vani had taken over the conversation. 'Go on,' she said.

'It turned out that having no centre is a lovely theory, but it becomes damned hard when you try to implement it. The ideals of the revolution are a memory now, and what everyone sees is death by committee, discussions that never end, things that never get done, things made a thousand times worse by the fact that the Cop-Out Constitution brought us far less than our great-grandparents had bargained for. Accepting the Mandalium Agreement was our ancestors' historical error, and it's been steadily killing us ever since.' Vani smiled painfully. 'We've had to learn that basic lesson all over again: economic wounds make it so much harder to live your ideals.'

If the Confederation rules against us, if the Agreement survives past this Monday—we won't survive too much longer.

Pieces of the puzzle began to come together, the pieces that had long been invisible to her from the outside. Nila said nothing.

'Anyway,' said Vani. 'As I was saying, the emergency powers I invoked to bypass your jurisdictional conflict, Guardian, even fifteen years ago, I wouldn't have needed to. But now...'

'I read about something like this in the Chapterhouse classes,' Nila said, ignoring a pang at the thought that she was hearing this from Vani, instead of her mother, or Anam. 'The iron law of human institutions: the centralising drift.'

'High Town textbooks masquerading as neutral,' said Vani, dismissively. 'But yes. It's been harder and harder.' She lowered her voice. 'Every revolution in the history of this continent has failed, Guardian—either crushed, or became what it fought against, just to survive. Until now. Until us. We are a historical anomaly. An evolutionary accident. And that is why we cannot afford to fail. We dare not.'

'And, so …'

'And, so, the harder it gets to sustain ourselves as anarchists, the more we come into conflict with each other, the more important history becomes. If we can't find reasons in our present to go on the way we are, we look to the past.'

'To the revolution—?'

'To so much more,' Vani whispered. 'Don't you see, Guardian? The class struggle in Peruma began with the overthrow of the last emperor, and it never ended. We never stopped trying to liberate ourselves from wage slavery, from this life of labour, but until that morning on this very bridge, only one side had ever won. At every other inflection point, we lost. Again, and again, and again. Do you know what four hundred years of defeat does, Guardian? One forgets the word for victory. All you can think of is a little wage increase there, a little social insurance here, maybe a reduction in working hours. And then came that day, the day of the Martyr, the day of the revolution, *finally*, a fight that we won—or at least, didn't lose. Haven't lost … yet. Do you see, Guardian? You see what that day means to us? Jagat is *our* Martyr, whose memory is the glue that holds us together, even when other things fail. Guardian, you're now a historian, whether you like it or not.'

'I see,' said Nila. 'Administrator, can I ask you something? Why are you being so ambiguous?'

Vani stared at her for a moment, and then laughed freely. Somewhere, a spell broke. 'You know something your mother told me about you?'

'She speaks about me?'

'All the time. She *is* proud of you, you know?'

Nila stared down at the ground. 'What did she say?'

'She said that you're always going to be sceptical of something coming from any person claiming any authority, until you've worked it out in your own head, and given it your own words.'

Nila blushed furiously. 'She said that?'

'It is the highest compliment an anarchist can give. Was she wrong?'

'No, no.' Nila fell silent, thinking. 'Okay, then. In my own words?'

'In your own words, Guardian.'

'So … if things had continued as they were,' she said slowly, thinking as she went. 'When Jagat was to be put to death on Monday, his legend would have carried on, untainted. You'd have mourned your lost martyr, but he'd have remained undiminished. But now—now everything has changed. If I lose on Monday, people wouldn't think of it as Ani's failed attempt to save her great-grandfather. They'd say that in the last analysis, the Commune buckled, they cravenly tried to bring back the man they'd been tom-tomming as their Martyr for a century on some criminal law technicality, and they failed even at that. They weren't brave enough to let him die, and they weren't even competent enough to save him. They'd ask if you ever really believed in the revolution to begin with, if you were trying so hard to show that the man who began it might not have actually begun it—and *The Great Unravelling* wouldn't help you there.' Nila stopped, feeling her face flush. A terrible, gnawing suspicion was taking root in her mind. *Was it actually set up, as Pulis had hinted? Was it Ani, or someone else?* 'And if the case is actually impossible to defend, if it's a set-up, it's a set-up to make me think I have a chance, and then to watch me fail.' There was a rush of blood to her head, a dizziness, and she could hear her heartbeat. She moved forward and grasped Vani's arm.

'But if it is a set-up, Administrator,' she said, 'I can promise you this: they picked the wrong person to screw with. I'm not in this to resurrect the Martyr.' Suddenly, she remembered Ani's last words to her. 'I'm not in this for the judgement of the past or the weight of the future. I'm just—' she paused, considered. 'I'm just going to do my job.'

Even as the words came out, they sounded twisted, deformed and all wrong, and Nila wished she could take them back; but a small part of her felt a strange, nameless pride at having said them.

'Tell me something, Guardian,' Vani said, after a silence. 'You were one of us, no?'

Nila stiffened. Her brain sent immediate alarm signals down to her nerves. *Naina L.* 'I was born in the Commune, yes,' she said carefully. 'But I'm now of the guardians. And in this case, like all other cases, I am impartial between Council and Commune.'

Vani smiled, and said nothing. Her gaze travelled to Nila's neck, to the pendant that hung there, and the words etched into the gold. 'May I?' she said.

Nila nodded. Vani took the pendant in her hand, and traced the words with her fingers.

'I see,' Vani murmured.

The words lingered between them, the silence deafening.

In her chamber, there was a single lamp burning. On the table, a note:

Terrace, if you're still standing.

Nila exited the chamber, and made her way to the boxcar station at the end of the corridor. She got in, and pressed the lever. The boxcar ascended, taking her through the upper levels of the Chapterhouse, letting out what seemed like distinctly fake groans along the way. Lights flashed in and out around her, illumining sections of the track and the sediment-encrusted walls, before disgorging her onto a final flight of uneven stairs. Moonlight glimmered invitingly from beyond the doorway.

Nila emerged onto the Chapterhouse terrace, a wide-open space crenelated with faux battlements and turrets. Maru was at their familiar spot, looking out over the wall. She walked over and stood beside him.

He gestured towards the north with the glass that he held in his hand. Nila started.

High Town had gone dark. North of the Urai, it was pitch black: not even a firefly's glow interrupted the darkness.

'The week of mourning,' said Maru, quietly. 'Thursday night, they turn off all the lights. For the victims of the revolution. And for Director Purul.'

'You didn't say civil war, like the rest of them from over there,' said Nila.

'It was what it was,' said Maru. In the dark, she could not make out what his face was speaking. He handed her the glass of red. She took a sip, grimacing at the sourness.

He turned to her. 'How was the Commune?'

Nila let the wine run down her throat. 'Messy.'

'So, what's the verdict? Do they hate you?'

'If they did,' said Nila, 'they wouldn't tell me. I'm an outsider now, Maru. They were not … hostile, but they were wary. As if they didn't really trust me. And wouldn't open up until and unless they felt they could.'

'Even your mother?'

Nila exhaled forcibly. 'Yeah. Even her. Did her best to hide it, but I could tell.'

'Anam?'

'Oh my heavens, no, thank everything! I'd—I don't know what I would have done if he'd been like that too. But no, he was what he's always been—the still point. *I* was the one flailing.'

'I'm glad,' said Maru.

'But Ma, Vani, and the rest—what a mess. The way Vani spoke to me—as if I'd use every word she said in a trial. And the last thing she said—*you were one of us, no?* I never knew just how many barbs you could wrap around a word as simple as *were*.'

'And what did you say?'

'I told her I was impartial between Council and Commune. That was the end of the conversation.'

Maru chuckled. 'Class renegade, huh?'

Nila laughed at that. 'Look who's talking. You're not even on this brief, and you're helping me. If I'm a class renegade, what does that make you?'

'A class traitor, of course,' Maru laughed back softly. 'I accepted it a long time ago.'

'Oh, Maru.' She put the glass down on the battlements, and leaned her elbows upon the cool hard stone. 'I was hoping that returning home would help me shake off the feeling of being an interloper. But it's made everything worse. I wish I wasn't in control of shaping this case. I wish there was some way for the Commune to be.'

'Maybe there could,' said Maru.

'How do you mean?'

'Remember what they told us about criminal law? There's always a way to shift the frame of a case, always a procedural argument that will turn a case on its head. It's waiting to be made. The only question is whether we can find it in time.'

'I can't imagine what clever procedural argument there might be to bring about *this* outcome,' Nila said.

'You have time,' said Maru. 'All that needs to happen is for that famous Nila intuition to strike once.'

'But till then or otherwise, I have to keep going,' Nila whispered. 'Maru, all I wanted was to just do this case … do it well.'

'You will.'

'Is it messed up that I'm not sure I even know what that means anymore?'

'It's only this week,' said Maru. 'You know this. The week before is always hell, but the moment you step into the tribunal chamber, all this noise—it'll be gone. You'll know exactly what to do. We just have to get through this. Right?'

'Right,' Nila nodded. 'Yeah. I—'

At that moment, her pendant glowed. Nila stopped, and looked down. 'Huh? My guardian key. Ani again?'

'It's a written message,' said Maru.

Nila unclasped her pendant. Tongues of crimson leapt out at them, assembling into words at eye level, a little line of fire in the night.

Beware the Apoptosis Plan.

'What?' said Nila. 'The Apoptosis Plan?'

Maru narrowed his eyes. 'Apoptosis … programmable cell death?'

The words began to fade, and then dissolved into the night. A one-time, destructible message, now destroyed.

'Do you know what this is?' said Nila.

Maru shook his head. 'I've never heard of any Apoptosis Plan. Let me look it up tomorrow.'

They stared at the empty space where the words had been moments ago.

'Who wants me to beware?' Nila murmured. 'And of what?'

'Someone who has your guardian key?'

'After Ani, I don't know who else it's been given to.' Nila shook her head. 'I don't like this, Maru.'

'Put it out of your head,' said Maru. 'I'll see if I can find something—but you focus. It's the Zone tomorrow.'

Nila nodded. 'Yes. You're right. Four more days. I can't wait to be done.'

'When it's all over on Monday,' said Maru, 'let's go on that skylane trip we've been planning forever, huh? We'll get away from Peruma, away from, how did you put it, all this weight of history. Two weeks. We'll see all the great cities at last. We'll climb the Chemur temple spire and see what's so special about all those blue roofs.'

'Monara by the Western Sea,' said Nila, momentarily forgetting about the cryptic, anonymous message. 'I've never seen the sea, you know?'

'The horizon from the white cliffs,' said Maru. 'And then we'll take the north lanes right to Lubini and the Crystal Desert.'

'Yeah,' said Nila. 'Yeah, I think I'd like that.'

'And you know what?'

'What?'

'If he isn't too busy with having come back to life, we can take Jagat along to start a few more revolutions.'

Nila turned and punched him on the shoulder.

'Ouch!'

'Maru, you utter clown!'

Their laughter rose into the silent night.

Day Four

The Zone

10

Like the World Had Cracked Open

THE CHAPTERHOUSE REFECTORY WAS A LARGE, airy, high-roofed hall, bustling at breakfast. Curtains of light swaddled the long tables, which were arranged by seniority. The Executive Committee, seated at the high table, enjoyed most of the light, as well as the gold-brocaded napkins. There followed the senior guardians, who had to make do with silver brocades. The long tables, with their ordinary napkins, ran across the length of the hall. The first of them was reserved for the rest of the guardians, followed by a section for the final-year pupils, and finally, the junior pupils.

Nila entered the hall to the sound of the clinking of spoons and plates, and the crackle of conversation. She turned left into the kitchen, and promptly began salivating. The smell of freshly-made onion omelettes, cheese cutlets, smoked mrigel fish fry and sliced dragonfruit clamoured for first right to her nostrils. She had only come down to breakfast because Maru had threatened to withhold further supply of cold coffee if she skipped meals again.

She loaded her tray and took it into the hall, towards the senior pupils' section. As she approached, the chatter died around her as suddenly as the swirling of autumn leaves when the breeze ceases for a moment. Nila stopped. The fourteen faces at the table looked at her, inscrutable.

Noor stood up. Their eyes met. Noor put up both her hands and began to clap, deliberately, unhurriedly. One by one, the others at the table stood, and followed suit. The air filled with the sound of applause. The other tables stilled, and heads turned.

As the clapping died down, Noor gave her a big grin. 'Why didn't you tell us? We've been messaging you since yesterday afternoon!'

'I—' Nila gulped, and found she had nothing to say.

Noor turned to the table. 'This one,' she said, pointing back at Nila, 'has a private brief. And you know what? It's to bring back Jagat—THE Jagat—from the sleep of death. And she's too modest to tell us!'

'SHAME!' shouted four or five voices.

'And not just that—she's *arguing* it.' Theatrical gasps. 'No senior. One of us.'

'ONE OF US!' they shouted back.

Nila blushed, and placed her tray on the table. 'It's not that big a deal,' she muttered, sitting down.

'Oh really?' said Noor. 'Sole defence counsel in a capital case? Someone trusting you with saving a life? Not a big deal?'

'Don't remind me,' said Nila, staring at her plate.

'And not someone loved by just their great-granddaughter. You're defence counsel for half of Peruma, Nila,' said Suneen.

'The Commune didn't appoint me,' Nila cut in quickly.

'Have they gone to the committee and asked for a senior guardian to be added to the brief?'

'Well, no.'

'Which means *they* trust you. With the Martyr's life.'

'Ah,' Nila said, pushing at her cheese cutlet with her fork. There was a sinking feeling in the pit of her stomach. Her appetite was waning like water receding at low tide. 'I hadn't—I guess it is a reasonably big deal.'

'*Reasonably big deal*,' Noor mimicked her. 'Do you all know what the papers are calling our friend here?'

'What!' four or five voices—who knew perfectly well—shouted out again.

'She's the Commune's dangerous hero,' Noor said gleefully. 'And … a Key Person!'

Another round of claps, whistles and the stamping of feet.

'Hey, I wouldn't mind being someone's Key Person,' Noor gave her a grin. 'Want to swap places, Nila?'

Nila smiled back with an effort. 'You don't want that, Salamander.'

Noor's grin widened. 'No?'

'Give up *Council vs Commune*, with its defined questions, its certainty … for what? Right now, I don't know if I'm a guardian, an investigator, a historian or an archivist. It's been like walking up the switchback without even compass or map, looking for a way through.'

'Sounds just like your thing,' said Suneen.

'Wait a sec,' Areeb spoke from across her, cutting through chuckles of agreement. 'Investigator? Nila, you're not saying you filed the application for rehearing before finding threshold material?'

'I didn't have a choice.'

The chuckles died down around her.

'Oh yes, of course, isn't the cryobox getting deactivated Monday midnight?' Noor gave her shoulder a sympathetic squeeze, an uncharacteristic gesture almost making her jump. 'She'll obviously find material, Areeb. The guardian instinct, remember?'

'Yeah!' Suneen joined in. 'Also, forget all of that—can't you just see it now? Monday morning. Arguments are on in the Grand Chamber, *Council vs Commune*. *That* hall, *those* banners, five thousand in their seats, so many more watching across the continent.' Nila flinched. 'Senior Majeet is arguing vehemently, eloquently, there isn't a breath to be drawn, it's the moment of truth, and then, and *then*, the door opens—you know, like in those video-reels when the door is thrown open in the middle of a really important meeting by some legendary guy whom everyone thought is dead—except in this case, the door is actually thrown open by a legendary guy who was *indeed* dead, until he wasn't anymore. And then he's there. Jagat. The return of the anarchist. *What have I missed, comrades?* Can't you see it?'

'Nice fantasy,' said Nila, although she felt her own pulse quicken.

'I don't get why *you* aren't more excited,' said Suneen. 'I know we haven't been back in ages, but Nila, don't you remember growing up in the Commune, don't you remember how big a deal Jagat is?'

Don't let him die.

Nila closed her eyes. 'I remember.'

I don't care about the judgement of the past or the weight of the future.

'Yeah! It'll really be like bringing an icon back to life,' Suneen went on, his voice rising. 'Peruma's sake, he's the man that started the revolution. We're living in the world he made. And if you win on Monday, Nila, he'll come back to *see* it. The Falling Star, risen again—how's that for a story? The man who gave his life for a revolution, knowing he would never see it. And now, a hundred years on, you'll be the reason that he can.'

'It's a good story,' Nila said. 'And now that you put it that way, you know it's already been written, yeah?'

'Huh?'

Her mind reached out for the sanctuary of something known and familiar. She flicked her wristheld open and drew up the screen. A novel cover appeared; pulpy, featuring five people looking up at a disc-shaped spaceship in the sky. The title read *Waiting for the Witnesses*.

'Know this?'

Suneen stared. '*Waiting for the Witnesses?* Yeah, of course. We were all reading this, what, three years ago?'

'You remember it?'

'For sure. This is the webnovel in which there are these people who've built a perfect society, and then they send a few of their own into space, to travel at the speed of light?'

'Yeah,' said Nila, looking at the cover. Her mind was running on a track of its own. Her food lay congealing upon her plate. 'The idea being,' she continued, 'that these people will be in a kind of time stasis—a metaphorical sleep of death, even—while in the world, generations will pass. And then one day, after five hundred years, they'll come back to see how the world is getting along, and pass judgement on whether it's stayed true to the ideals of the founding.' She heard her voice rolling off her tongue, almost without thought. It was as if she was speaking an idea into existence. 'Original original intent, so to say.'

'We all remember,' said Areeb. 'So where's this going?'

'Do you also remember what happens? The society fails to evolve at all, because generation after generation, everyone is so terrified of what judgement the founders will pass when they return, that they just don't dare do anything different. Their origin story controls all their tomorrows.' She stopped suddenly, feeling the heat of her own cheeks, realising that they were all staring at her. She probably looked feverish.

'My *point* being,' she said, 'that Jagat may come back, look around and say, *what is this world that you've built in my name*? What then?'

'Oh,' said Suneen. He looked at her uncertainly.

It was Noor who finally broke the silence. 'She's just excited, Suneen.' She smiled at Nila mischievously. 'And she reads far too many of these pulp webnovels. What's really happening is that she's forcing herself to hold it all in, because as we know, Nila will die before she shows emotion about a case.' She turned to Nila. 'Isn't that right?'

Nila stabbed fiercely at her cutlet.

'Now they won't even let me resent them in peace,' said Nila.

'They're just happy for you,' said Maru.

'They're indulging me!'

'Why're you saying that? Was this some kind of 12-D chess move by Velu or something?'

'Velu wasn't even there. He's struggling with the case, apparently. Or so Noor said.'

'So then?'

'The rest of them. They can be nice because they have *Council vs Commune*. They can spare some happiness for me.

It's a luxury they have, but I don't, because I am living off applications and vibes.'

'I don't know, Nila, maybe they *are* actually happy for you,' said Maru, a twinkle in his eye.

'It's just their way of easing their own guilt,' said Nila. 'By telling me, who didn't make it, that we're still all in this together, maybe even convincing themselves of it.'

'You want them to *not* be happy for you?'

'Yeah, dammit! I want to feel robbed. Wronged, even. How else can I psych myself up for these last three days?'

'Okay. Are we quite done?' said Maru.

Nila took a deep breath. 'Yes,' she said. 'You know I didn't actually mean any of that, right?'

'You probably did,' Maru chuckled, 'until you got your chance to vent, and then you didn't mean it anymore. So, now what?'

Nila touched her wristheld. Jagat appeared between them.

'You know,' said Maru, 'I'm a little concerned that you're falling in love with him, the number of times you like to watch him sleeping.'

'Not my type.'

'I'm glad. He's literally old enough to be your great-grandfather.'

'He's *literally* not.'

'Well okay, but imagine bringing someone back from the dead and then asking them out? How would the power dynamics work there? Think of what the Wits—'

'You know, Maru, sometimes I think *you* are one of the Wits.'

'Me?!'

'They obviously have members in the Chapterhouse, and you tend to share the same wretched sense of humour.'

'I'm not mining you for material, Nila, excuse the pun—'

'See? That's exactly the kind of pun that would show up in the next newsletter.'

Maru threw up his hands. 'All right. No lightening of the mood in this house without being accused of all kinds of stuff. I take the hint.'

'Okay, okay, I believe you.' Nila laughed, in spite of herself. 'You're not one of the Wits, you're just a clown.'

'I don't know whether to be pleased or offended,' Maru raised his eyebrow in mock-exasperation. 'But now, Nila, in all seriousness, where do we stand after yesterday?'

'Yes.' Nila paused for a moment. 'I'm just not convinced by the explanations Vani and Ma gave me in the Commune.' She gestured towards the image of the sleeping man. 'Jagat, a man without a past, just *there*. He comes on the stage, one shot, then he walks off the stage, and the only sentence he ever speaks—*in the name of the Commune unborn, die*—make no sense.'

'We know it is exactly those words, yeah?'

'That's what I'm going to go to the Zone to confirm today,' said Nila.

The pidge squawked, flew open and a letter dropped on the floor.

'I'll get it,' said Maru. He picked up the letter. 'It's from the Executive Committee.'

'That'll be my application to access the cryochamber.'

Maru slit the envelope open and took out a paper. He squinted, and then frowned. 'They've rejected your application.'

'What?'

'There's a procedural objection.'

'What!'

'Yeah. It says that there's no rule that authorises a guardian to access the cryochamber.'

'Ugh. *I* am supposed to be the one who makes procedural objections, Maru. PO Nila, they call me.'

'Nobody calls you that.'

'I do. Who has made this objection?'

'Doesn't say, but we can guess. The cryochamber is under joint custody of Commune and Council, so it could be either of them, or—'

'Council. *Pulis*.' Nila breathed.

'*Or*,' repeated Maru, 'it could even be the Executive Committee, since they're the ones who screen these applications.'

'Those lumpy halfwits!'

'True and correct statement. But Nila, are you thinking of fighting this? Do you *really* need to go into the cryochamber? What good will looking at Jagat's face do you?'

'It's not that,' said Nila. 'It's just—I need to know I've covered all my bases. Even the most hopeless ones.'

'All right, then.' Maru's voice grew businesslike. 'As the PO is anonymous, we can just send in a written response for a ruling.'

'We'll tell them—' Nila closed her eyes. 'We'll tell them—*urgh*. Yes, I know. We'll claim the right of access.'

Maru raised an eyebrow. 'Jagat's asleep, Nila. He can't see, hear or talk to you.'

'Irrelevant. Technically, he has the right to meet his guardian.'

'Technically, he's not your client and you're not his guardian. You're representing Ani.'

Nila smiled. 'Isn't that why legal fictions are the most beautiful things? We're going to say that unless there's evidence otherwise, you can presume that a person in the sleep of death would want to be brought back to life. And so you must deem a standing permission to their next of kin to engage a guardian on their behalf. Through Ani, Jagat is deemed to be my client, and I his guardian. And he has the right of access. In whatever state he might be.'

'Nila ...' Maru said slowly.

'You don't think it'll work?'

'On the contrary, *PO* Nila, I think it's a great procedural argument. It's just that—'

'What?'

'Okay, this is going to sound really petty compared to the stakes here, but—it's just that yesterday, we were agonising about whether someone in the sleep of death *really* wants to be brought back, fifty, seventy, a hundred years after their world has passed on, and how we can ever dare to presume what they'd have wanted. But that's exactly what you're doing right now, making a whole set of assumptions about how Jagat would have been, what he would have thought and what he would have wanted. Sorry, I know, I just ...'

'Maru,' said Nila. 'I hear you. But this is just to access the damn cryochamber. We can suspend our beliefs for the moment. If it comes to that one day ...'

'I know, I know." Maru sighed. 'It just *feels* contradictory.'

'Isn't everything we do based on cognitive dissonance?'

'Ah, can't argue with that,' Maru grinned. 'Okay, then. As you say. You want me to draft this while you're in the Zone?'

She looked at him gratefully. 'Would you?'

'I've got this. Go forth and conquer.'

She caught sight of the timer on her way out.

70:39:26

The Bulwark Zone had been the brainchild of Master Builder Bhushan, in the aftermath of the fourth workers' revolt, two and a half centuries ago. It had been built around the same time that the workers were being forced into the grid city across the Urai River, and was designed to be a buffer between High Town and Low Town, in every sense of the word: a physical barrier that prevented the two sides from directly confronting each other—'cushioning' their encounters, in the notorious words of the then-Director Pari—and also an intellectual barrier, providing the unaligned, post-ideological class of bureaucrats that staffed the administration of undivided Peruma.

After the revolution, devastated by the fighting, and with the city divided, the Zone had lost both will and reason to exist, and had slowly been abandoned. All it housed now was the embassies of the other five cities, further away to the west.

Nila picked her way through the remnants of the Zone on the north bank, the line of towers in the distance looming above her. Once, the Zone had snaked through the heart of Peruma, following the line of the Urai River, the longest contiguous neighbourhood of the city. Now, as the Wits pointed out—somewhat cruelly—it was a state of mind: a stretch of no-person's land that even the shadows had abandoned but litigation had not. The unsettled border between High Town and (formerly) Low Town appeared differently on the city's maps that had been commissioned by Council and Commune immediately after the Revolution, with each side furiously accusing the other of 'cartographic aggression' and every cracked brick the subject of running legal disputes.

A monument of ruin—except for the last house on Vashi Street.

In a sequence of events that had passed into legend, Milana Maran, secretary to the slain Director Purul, after giving her testimony at the trial and sentencing of Jagat, had walked out of court, and out of the political life of Peruma. She had retired to her home on Vashi Street, staying indoors as the fiercest fighting took place in the Zone. She had stayed there long after it was all over, and as the Zone decayed around her.

And then, as the revolution passed into memory, it was to the last house on Vashi Street that they came, from both sides of the river, to hear the only remaining witness to the assassination. Milan eased into her role as Peruma's retrospective oracle, providing the scaffolding upon which her listeners built cathedrals of memory, within which they lost themselves.

So much so that when the time came to die, Milana Maran decided to turn her home into a museum and an archive. The entry fees—trading upon perpetual nostalgia and the most carefully curated of public images—kept up a steady stream of revenue for her grateful children and grandchildren, who had long ago moved out of the remnants of the Zone.

Nila passed through the foyer and into the two-room museum. Gentle sepia light washed over her for effect, and the chilling vents cooled her skin. A set of arrows on the wall directed her to the first of the museum's exhibits, a window into the day of the assassination.

There was a fine oakwood table, upon which a glass slab had been placed. In between the glass and the wood, a number of still images and portraits were artistically arranged. There were photographs of the old Directorate courthouse with its portico and its columns; one photograph of the guards marching Jagat through the courtroom's gate, surrounded by an indistinct mass of people; the courtroom artist's caricatures of the judges, of Jagat and, of course, of Milana Maran herself in the ceremonial act of lifting the vial of truth serum to her lips with both hands, head thrown back, followed by another of her speaking on the witness stand. They had all been decolourised, giving the assemblage a strange, ethereal quality, as if the scene had happened not just a hundred years ago but somewhere else altogether. On the wall by the desk, a plaque helpfully summarised the chronology of events.

Next to the table, there was a black reclining chair. Upon the glass slab and above the photographs, there was a single, unwieldy looking headset, the sort that had been in vogue around the time of the revolution. On the side of the table, a panel with five buttons—*play, pause, rewind, forward* and *stop*—was set into the wood.

During Milana's life, the events of the trial, which had been held behind closed doors, had seeped into popular memory through the secretary's retelling. Upon Milana's death, it also turned out that the she had privately recorded the proceedings through a body-cam that had escaped detection in the chaos after the assassination, and then bequeathed it to her own archive. A furious Council—the successor body of the pre-revolutionary version—had sued, claiming a right to property over the records of all trials before the revolution. To their even greater fury (and to the great amusement of the Commune and assorted Wits) a panel of the guardians dismissed the case without even hearing arguments, on the basis that the old Council had gone extinct with the division of Peruma. The recording of the trial belonged to … nobody.

So it stayed in the museum.

Nila sat upon the chair, which sank agreeably under her weight. She put the headset on and pressed play.

A rush of static.

There was a background murmur, swelling to a vague roar. Then a voice dropped like hammer on rock.

Prosecution Witness PW-1 will step forward.

Underneath the slab, the photographs came alive.

She didn't know if it was a trick of the light, a part of the exhibit, or her own brain setting them in motion. They came alive in a flickering, sputtering way, uncertain, as though she was seeing them beyond a frosted window.

Moments of silence, and then another, lighter voice.

Witness Milana Maran, in the name of Peruma, you will speak the truth.

Trapped in time, between the glass and the wood, she heard the witness's voice.

I will.

You were accompanying Director Purul—may his memory be a blessing—to the Maidan this morning?

I was.

You were with him when he stepped upon Unity Bridge at nine of the clock?

I was.

Can you describe to us precisely what happened then?

I … yes.

Nila frowned. Her hands sought the rewind button. She played back.

Can you describe to us precisely what happened then?

I … yes.

Please do.

We had come down from the director's residence, through Victory Road, in an open-topped skimmer. The skimmer was his choice—the open-top, I mean.

There was a hint of a quaver in the voice.

When we reached the Zone, he alighted. I did too. He stepped first upon Unity Bridge. And then … and then …

Go on. The prosecutor's voice was gentle, encouraging.

And then it was like the world had cracked open. A roaring blast of air threw me back. I fell. Everything went black …

The voice lowered to a whisper, and then a sudden silence; not the gradual sort that crept in when words ran dry, but the silence when someone clamps a fist around a throat or, Nila thought, when someone stops recording.

She heard the barely perceptible *click* release a moment before the voices resumed.

Take your time. Do you need a break?

No, I'll get this over with. The voice had settled into a permanent, low cadence, as if the speaker was holding themselves in check. The words now came quick and flat, the responses automatic.

When I opened my eyes, there was smoke. I knew it was a bomb. I looked for the director. He was there beside me, blood running down his side. And then …

Beyond frosted glass, one figure pointed to another.

You saw this man, with a gun? It was the prosecutor who completed her sentence, his voice quiet, insistent.

Yes.

You're sure it was this man?

Yes.

And then?

The voice rose, quickening in pace, in pitch. *I saw him raise his arm—*

Please specify who the word 'him' refers to here. The prosecutor's instinct, kicking in.

This man here, in the dock.

His name is Jagat.

Yes. I saw Jagat raise his arm. I saw the gun pointed at the director's head. I heard Jagat say, 'In the name of the Commune unborn, die.'

And then you saw Jagat shoot the director, yes?

No.

No?

I did not see him shoot.

Please explain, Secretary Maran.

I closed my eyes. I didn't see the shot. I heard it. When I opened my eyes again, the director was on the ground. And this man—Jagat—was standing there.

Did he say anything further?

He did not.

What happened then?

There was a lot of shouting. Intelligence Bureau arrived. I saw them dragging this man away—a cordon was formed around the bridge—and then they took me away …

The voice faded into ragged breathing, a struggle to hold back tears. The figures behind frosted glass grew fainter, more smoke than shadow, receding like breath.

That will be all. Thank you, Secretary Maran.

The transmission stopped. Underneath the glass slab, nothing moved.

She leaned back in the chair, eyes closed—leaned back too far. The chair teetered wildly, and almost toppled over before she threw out a hand to save herself, catching the edge of the table. The chair righted itself with a *thump*.

The prosecutor's final words were still bouncing off the walls of her mind. Nila took the headset off and stood.

There was another exhibit next to this one: a recording of the judges announcing their verdict. But Nila did not need to hear that, because those words were seared in memory. The judgement stated that Milana Maran's testimony, under the authorised truth serum, had established beyond reasonable doubt: *firstly*, that there were only three individuals present at the scene of the crime: Director Purul, Secretary Maran and Jagat; *secondly*, that Jagat had pointed a gun at the director and said, 'In the name of the Commune unborn, die'; *thirdly*, that the director's autopsy demonstrated the impact of a bullet through the heart, fired at close range; *fourthly*, and *therefore*, notwithstanding the fact that there was no visual witness to Jagat firing the shot that killed the director, the evidence established that conclusion *beyond any reasonable doubt*; and *finally*, that Jagat was guilty of the murder of Director Purul, a case that had shocked Peruma's collective conscience, a rare case, in fact, a *rarest of rare* case, which justified the most extreme punishment, to satisfy the aforesaid collective conscience: the sentence, or the sleep of death.

Nila leaned against the wall, letting Milana's voice wash over her with its rhythm and cadence, her mind picking at its bones, picking them apart. She cast a look around the chamber.

She first thought it was a vanity room dedicated to Milana's life, a life unmemorable but for the secretary's chance presence on the bridge that morning. But soon Nila realised that it was a memorial to the Zone, that little strip of land that had neither martyrs nor monuments, the place that slow decay rather than swift death had robbed of both mourners and memories, the space that revolution had passed through—and passed by. The Bulwark Zone had always just been that: a buffer, contingent upon things staying as they were; and there, in the video-reels of tentative, two-storey houses with their hesitant gardens, in the straight-lined streets the symmetries of which forestalled a spilling out into High Town or Low Town, Nila saw a quiet attempt to preserve a place and a people whose only legacy was that they had been here.

'Are you enjoying our archive?' The voice at her elbow made her jump. Nila turned, and found herself face to face with a person who seemed to have stepped out of the museum's section in a 'Ten Places to Visit on a Day Trip to Peruma' article: dim eyes that peered out at her from behind rimmed glasses, a bun of white hair so dour that it might have been doused in vinegar, and lips pursed in a line so thin that someone might have pencilled it on their face.

'Yes, very much,' said Nila, truthfully. 'It has been an … experience.'

'Good,' the person said. 'The next room has our most popular exhibit: the only surviving samples of Secretary Maran's correspondence. You may proceed to that room now, if you so wish.'

Nila nodded at them, and stepped into the second room of the museum.

The temperature cooled further. The room was empty and dark, save for a rectangular beam of light falling on a glass case in the centre. The plaque on the side of the case informed her that Secretary Maran had been a copious letter-writer during her time in this house, preferring the tactility of page over screen. However, regrettably, her interlocutors were insufficiently appreciative, and not only responded to her letters with e-messages, but didn't even bother keeping the letters after they had scanned them. The only exception had been Director Ilsa, Purul's successor (rather unkindly referred to by the Wits as Ilsa the Insignificant, Nila recalled), who had dutifully preserved the two letters that Maran had written to her: one on the day of the revolution, and the other near the end of her life.

Nila suddenly felt the person's presence at the threshold of the room, their gaze boring into the back of her neck like a jackhammer. She hurriedly moved to the edge of the glass box and pored over Secretary Maran's dense, neat handwriting on the clean-cut pages.

The first was a resignation letter, probably written the moment that Milana had reached home after the trial. In terse prose, it assured Director Ilsa that it was an honour to have served, that the secretary needed to relinquish her post for personal reasons, that she wished the director well in her role and that the handover documents were already in her inbox.

After forty years of silence, there was the second letter. Like the first one, it was short, but not quite so terse.

Dear Director,

You are probably surprised to receive this from me, and I do not expect you to reply. While I have not been involved with the Council since the day of the mutiny and the trial of the assassin, I have, needless to say, always followed the Council's affairs with affection and interest. Director, I have watched with some concern the influence of the Council dwindle with each passing year after the mutiny, watched it—pardon the pun—grow toothless. I believe we are now at crisis point, and I cannot in good conscience *stand by and watch without trying to help. Director, as you may remember, I was always against Operation Carbuncle,* which has brought us to where we are today. I think the years have proved me right. If you trust my judgement now, although you did not then, I can still help the Council, after all these years. I await your response.*

Faithfully,
Milana Maran

The response never came. A month later, Secretary Maran died.

Nila's eyes snagged upon the asterisk sign, and travelled down to where a footnote helpfully informed her that according to Professor Surma Katoch, High Town's foremost historian of the revolution/revolt/mutiny/troubles/civil war, Operation Carbuncle referred to a secret and controversial Council plan to sow discord and disruption in the ranks of the labour movement that had been roiling Low Town with its strikes and its sympathy strikes and its wildcat strikes and its pickets and its secondary pickets, by focusing, in particular, on the union's prominent journal, *The Carbuncle.*

A slight, impatient tap on the floor made her lift her head. But the threshold was empty.

Nila made her way back into the light. There was no sign of the person. She emerged from the museum, into evening sunlight and the rubble-lined former neighbourhoods of the Zone.

The door opened north. The towers of High Town loomed above her. Overnight, they had all been draped in black. It was as if she was standing on the edge of a forest of black pillars, shrouded, sepulchral, reaching into the sky.

Nila shivered. She turned her feet west, following the line of the river towards the Chapterhouse.

The sinking sun shed soft orange light upon the remnants of the Zone; a stark contrast to the blackness of High Town. At this hour of the evening, everything around her glimmered in the half-light of uncertainty, or possibility. She could almost believe that she was walking not in the aftermath of ruin, but in a city being born.

In the remains of the former square, her skimmer was waiting for her where she'd parked it.

Just as Nila got into it, she had the sense of being followed.

She had felt a glimmering of it earlier, when crossing the bridge into the Commune the day before; and again, when she had walked away from Vani. This time the feeling washed over her with a certainty that brooked no doubt: the odd clarity of knowing that she was under the sights of a hair trigger.

Nila glanced around. To her north, beyond the remnants of the Zone, High Town's black pillars rose into the sky, shadowing the roads of the Tower City. To her south was the river, with Unity Bridge away to the west, and nothing in between. Everything was silent.

She pressed the skimmer's controls, expecting at any moment to hear a rush of air, feel something at the base of her neck. The skimmer rose with her. Nila looked down at the Zone, peeling her eyes to see what she could amidst the ruins.

There was nothing.

11

Building the New in the Ruins of the Old

'HOW DID IT GO?' SAID MARU.

'I'll tell you,' Nila said. 'But first, you tell *me*. I know that look.'

'*Well.* Do you have plans for tomorrow, PO Nila?'

'Did it—?'

'You bet! You'll be going on your date with Jagat at the cryochamber after all. The Executive Committee came through on your procedural argument. The panel's order is still being processed, but it should arrive anytime now. They are annoying as hell but sometimes, they're fair. Most times, even.'

'Phew,' said Nila. 'I owe you, Maru. Lots.'

Maru waved a hand. 'This was one of the more entertaining applications I've done.'

'Oh, also, that reminds me—any luck on the Apoptosis Plan?'

'Absolutely nothing. I scoured the networks. I learned a lot about the mechanics of controlling cancer through the programmed killing of cells but nothing that explains last night's message.'

'Oh well.'

'Now you tell me. How was the museum?'

'I heard Milana Maran's testimony,' said Nila.

'And?'

'Um, I don't know how to explain it. It has this weird stop-start quality. Like it's been cut up and spliced and soldered back together.'

'Tampered?'

'No, no. I mean—how do I say this—it felt spliced at the origin.'

Maru raised an eyebrow.

'It, um … I can't put my finger on it. In the beginning, she's shocked and she's numb, she's stammering, and it's just what you'd expect. Then there's a shift. Her responses become … quicker, more automatic, but somehow it feels like every word has been chosen carefully, if you know what I mean. Like at the level of sentence structure, she's given a lot of thought to how exactly she'd put this—'

'What?' Maru broke in. 'Say that again, Nila? That last bit.'

'Hm? It's like she gave a lot of thought to how exactly she'd word her testimony—'

'That's *really* interesting. Because you know some people did that, right?'

'Did what?'

'Tried to dodge the truth serum.'

'*What*?'

'Well, not "dodge" exactly. It's like—I was looking this up today because I knew you were going to the museum—how did the truth serum work, Nila, before it got banned?

It just took the principles of the primitive narco-analysis test, refined to the highest degree of development, and put you in a psychological state where you said what you believed is true.'

'Yes.'

'So there's one way to get around that, which was believed to work—in theory. You trained yourself to speak in a way that what you actually meant was different from the meaning that others heard.'

'Huh?'

'How do I explain this … okay, take this really silly example. The sentence, "I picked up the doll in the box." What do you think it means?'

'*Huh*?'

'Arre, what do you think I have done?'

'Um, that there was a doll in the box? And that you picked it up?'

'That's what you'd think. But technically, *technically*, this sentence *could* mean that it was I who was in the box when I picked up the doll.'

She gave him a look. 'Maru, are you high?'

'No, Nila, I'm not messing with you. It's a bit like—think of it as a semi-private language. They'd train to think—and then speak—in a way that was technically correct, but not *conventionally* so. In my example, I have basically trained myself to speak in a way where, if I want to say that, "I was in a box and I picked up the doll" what I *will* say is that "I picked up the doll in the box." Now this won't work for you or me, because it's not how we normally speak. But if that has become how you naturally speak, the truth serum might not affect it. But still, what you *hear* is effectively a lie, because what you hear is that the doll was in the box—'

'Wait, wait, wait, Maru!' She ran her hands through her hair. 'You're hurting my head. First up, this sort of thing can only work with the simplest and stupidest of sentences. It wouldn't even work with basic compound sentences. And second of all, this would break down under any form of sustained questioning! Did it ever work in a trial? During a cross-examination?'

'Uh, no.'

'Did it ever work where anything was at stake?'

'Ahm—I couldn't find—but the theory—'

'There you go,' said Nila. 'And anyway, if you said it takes months to internalise speaking this way—'

'But,' said Maru, 'Wouldn't that fit with all this … splicing and soldering and sudden quickening of pace that you heard?'

'What are you suggesting?'

'Look,' Maru said, 'our working theory so far has been that Jagat was the fall guy for the actual assassin, who was probably a higher-ranking revolutionary, right? And that Milana Maran basically got duped? And we're tying ourselves up in knots trying to figure out how this fourth person showed up on the bridge, shot the director at close range, disappeared, and did it all so efficiently that Milana Maran saw nothing? Like, we're having to create this superhuman—Varsha or whoever—who's a rebel, a nerveless shot, a kind of spider-being who can hang on to the underside of the bridge and a champion swimmer. But you know the one assumption upon which all of this rests, right? That Milana Maran *was being honest*.'

'Maru, you can't be—'

'Think about it. You remember when everyone believed that the sun revolved around our planet, and they just couldn't figure out why their astronomical observations weren't fitting? And they kept inventing more and more complex theories about cycles and epicycles and epi-epicycles to make the data fit? Until one day, finally, they just ditched the premise, adopted its opposite—that we went around the sun—and suddenly there was no need of cycles and epicycles to explain the data. I'm just saying, *if* Milana Maran was lying, *if* Milana Maran was actually in on it all this while, then you don't need your spider-being champion swimmer assassin. All you need is a very normal assassin whom we never get to know of, because Milana Maran *lied in her testimony*.'

'Maru,' said Nila. 'Come on. Milana Maran, a traitor?'

'Is that so out there? Low Town, which pulled off a whole revolution, wouldn't also have been competent enough to stick a mole in the Directorate? Nila, what do we really know about Milana Maran?'

'It can't be,' said Nila. 'The museum has a letter she wrote to Director Ilsa soon before she died, where she offers her services again.'

Maru shrugged. 'Sounds like exactly the kind of letter you *would* write just before you died, if you feared for your legacy.'

'Heh, like Jagat's letter to his daughter?'

'You said it, not me.'

Nila chewed her lip. 'There's something off here, Maru.'

'Why are you so resistant to the idea?'

'I'm not *resistant*, for fuck's sake!'

'Wow—okay! Sorry!'

She sunk her head in her hands, cooling instantly. 'I'm sorry, I shouldn't have snapped. Ugh, it's just that—I was thinking I've *finally* gotten a handle on the narrative, and now you've just gone and given me a whole other story. It's like running up a slippery slide. My head is splitting.'

Maru raised a hand. 'I get it. Okay, listen, we won't talk more about this. I'll look at her witness transcript, see if something strikes me.'

'Argh, but now I can't stop thinking about it. It isn't your fault.' She pinched the bridge of her nose and exhaled, long and slow. 'You know what would *really* help with this?'

'What?'

'Those damn Purul Archives that Pulis won't let me see. Seeing how Milana worked so closely with Purul for years, we'd get a much clearer sense of what she was up to, even who she was. And if she was trained in some weird linguistic acrobatics to get around the truth serum, it would show up in some way, in file annotations, in something—especially if, as you said, the Directorate never discards a scrap of official paper. Bloody Pulis.'

'He may still change his mind,' said Maru. 'You have a fresh meeting with him tomorrow, right?'

'I do. But …' She shook her head violently. 'Can't think about it now. Can't think of anything anymore, actually. Distract me, Maru. Brain is mush. What are the papers saying?

'You really want to know?'

'Yeah, yeah, let me wallow. It helps.'

Maru tapped his wristheld and scrolled down the screen.

Desperation? With Three Days Left, Assassin's Counsel Seen in the Maran Museum

The Jagat Revival Case: Ten Facts That Will Shock You

'A Hopeless Vanity Project'—Former Tribunal President Dhan Chand Calls Probe into the Funding of the Jagat Revival Case, Suspects Anti-Peruma Elements

Nila snorted. 'They've already started turning against me?'

'Are you surprised?'

'No, I guess. And the Wits?'

'The Wits are silent. I think they're sitting this one out.'

Nila narrowed her eyes. 'Don't look at me!' Maru said. 'I told you, I'm not one of them.'

'I see.'

'Want to know something that will raise your spirits, though?' he said quickly. 'I was browsing the *Volcano of Peruma* forum today. Do you know they *already* have multiple metafictions about your case?'

'*What!*'

'Yes! Do you want to know the classifying tags?'

Nila laughed, unclenching. 'No, Maru. Please, no. I'd rather *not* know those tags. Just tell me, do they end well?'

'There were seventeen metafics when I checked this evening—fifteen of them have you winning and Jagat coming back.'

'At least somebody believes in me.'

'Many do, Nila.'

Don't let him die.

Nila closed her eyes. 'Yes. Yes.'

'Also, something else that may come in handy,' said Maru. 'There's apparently a kind of schism within the Directorate right now.'

'About?'

'Your case.'

Nila's eyes flew open. 'What!'

'Yeah, apparently there's a faction within the Directorate that's not happy with Pulis' stonewalling. They're saying that if there's any doubt about what happened with the assassination, it needs to be cleared up now, before the final death.'

'Really?'

'Yeah. Deputy Director Maiyam A. is quite vocal about this, seemingly. I don't know if we can use this information in any way, but for what it's worth …'

Nila cast her mind's eye back to the day of the assignment, that sharp clear morning when seven skimmers had cleaved the sky above them. She remembered the face of the woman who flew behind the director, her steel-grey hair; the way she'd caught their gaze and waved down at them …

'Nila!' Maru's voice cut through her thoughts. He was looking past her, at the window. 'What's happening by the river?'

She turned to the window.

The stars were out. The Urai was a dark ribbon running across the length of their vision. And just beyond, on the side of the Commune, there was a flashing pinprick of light. It blinked in, out, and then in again, a steady rhythm.

Nila watched for a while, her mind imposing a pattern upon the movement of the light, which resolved itself into something familiar.

'I know what it is,' she said.

'Oh?'

'Looks like I'll be going out again tonight.'

'Just wait one sec,' Maru said as she moved towards the window.

'Yes?'

'I was going to tell you this, before we got caught up. Commune sent a letter earlier today. They've authorised Vani as their sole representative for all dealings on the Jagat case.'

'Oh!'

'Yeah.' He nodded towards the light. 'By Chapterhouse law, you're still barred from the Commune, except on work. And now, if your only work liaison is Vani, then going to the Commune for any other purpose is a breach of your impartiality oath.'

Nila stood there for a few moments, twisting the ends of her hair. 'I'll take my chances. I think that light is within the Bulwark Zone.'

'Wherever it is, you can't talk to people from the Commune.'

'As long as nobody finds out. I'm pretty sure I know who this is, Maru. It's safe.'

'As you say.' Maru didn't argue further. 'Want me to tag along? Not that I'd be first choice for a bodyguard or anything, but I can cause a distraction.'

Nila grinned. 'Don't worry about it. But do you have a flashlight? Or anything stronger than a wristheld beam?'

'As a matter of fact, I do.' He turned and went to the chest of drawers, where she heard him fiddle around for a while. He came back to her with a bulky black flashlight. 'I'm just surprised you *don't*, given the lighting in this damn building.'

'Hey, *I've* never had reason to go sneaking around the Chapterhouse late at night,' she muttered, taking flashlight from him. 'Could you turn off the lights?'

She went to the window. Maru flicked the light switch off. Pointing the flashlight towards the Commune, Nila flicked it on and off, her fingers moving to the rhythm of an old memory.

Across the river, the light went out. Nila stopped. Then the light came on once again, a quick acknowledgement.

'I sure hope nobody caught that,' Maru muttered.

'None of the Executive Committee's rooms face the river,' Nila grinned. 'Don't you remember mapping all this out when we were planning that stink bomb prank? I'll see you in a bit.'

'Be back soon,' said Maru.

She squeezed his shoulder. 'Don't worry,' she said softly. 'I know what I'm doing.'

Reaching out of the window, she tapped the body of the skimmer. It eased itself back into the chamber, allowing her to board it. She checked once, just in case. There was no media machine parked nearby, although she wouldn't have put it past them to hover around all day and all night.

Nila flew out again, into the dark.

The cool breeze whipped her hair back. Behind her, the lights had come on, and High Town's towers were once again glittering carpets of dazzling light—yellow, white, red and blue. From the distance, she saw sleek silhouettes moving back and forth in the night sky, skimmer traffic along the skylanes that never ceased. In front of her, there was a gentler glimmering from the Commune, a web of pale-yellow light.

She descended. The riverbanks acquired clarity. She could see the undulating form of Unity Bridge in the near distance, two sets of lamps marking its boundaries.

Nila switched on her headlights. Pointing the skimmer's nose towards the opposite bank, she flashed them on and off in a remembered pattern. A swift response gave her a lock on the location.

Across the river, she landed in the wide-open space that used to be the Bulwark Zone on the Low Town side. The row of houses were dark asymmetric structures in the near distance, beyond an invisible border.

Before her were five shapes, hooded and cloaked in black. As she stepped out of the skimmer, they moved, surrounding her in a tight circle.

'Anam,' she said. 'Do you know that my career will be over if anyone finds out about this?'

One of the figures removed his hood. 'I know,' said Anam. 'Thanks for trusting me. And our code.' He gestured to one of his comrades, who unhooded in turn. It was a woman, around Nila's age, close-cut hair falling to her shoulders.

'I am Asana,' she said. "We are the SRVJM.'

'The what?'

'The Society for the Restoration of the Values of Jagat the Martyr.'

'Oh. A short and subtle name.'

'Indeed,' said Asana. 'I could give you our pitch, but we're here just as illegally as you, so let me cut to the chase: Administrator Vani presided over a meeting of the autonomous department heads earlier today. It was decided that the archives of the Department of Historical Memory would not be opened to you, and that the Commune would not extend you any further assistance in your investigations.'

'*What*!' Nila almost shouted, and then lowered her voice as she saw them flinch. 'Can she do that? I thought—anarchism—everyone has a say—'

'She can do it with the agreement of the chairs during an emergency,' said Asana. 'And she has. Much anarchism indeed.'

'But *why*!'

'I'll tell you,' said Asana. 'And it's for the same reason that our society exists. Over time, the Commune's administration has become more and more centralised. It's no longer an administration of things, it's halfway towards becoming a government of people. They've tried to justify it by saying that the Commune is in crisis with the Mandalium Agreement, that the only way we can survive this "transitional phase" is by establishing temporary hierarchies and power centres. They do this even as they continue to swear by anarchism in theory, to anyone on the outside, and that includes you, Guardian, pardon me.'

Nila flinched. 'That's okay. I know I'm an outsider now. It was my choice. Carry on.'

'Well, the one thing standing in the way of this faction is the memory of Jagat, and the fact that we owe our literal existence to an anarchist act. We are because Jagat was. Now imagine what will happen, just as they're trying carry out a power grab, if Jagat comes back? The man who was there at the beginning—heck, the man who *was* the beginning, and not just that, the only man from those times who is actually still alive, and who *can* return?'

I'm back. What is this world that you've built in my name?

'Vani's not having any of that, Guardian. So she's moved to block you.'

Nila closed her eyes. *What have I gotten myself into?*

'Vani wants me to fail? She doesn't want Jagat back?'

'She and her faction. That's what we believe.'

'And I take it,' she said carefully, 'that you don't agree with her.'

'We think that the return of our Martyr is the best thing that can happen right now.'

'So that he can vindicate your stand against the administration?'

'Well, yes, but not just that. We need the Martyr—'

'He won't be the Martyr if he comes back.'

'He'll be something even more.' In the darkness, Asana's eyes were glittering. 'He'll be a man who was not only willing to sacrifice his own life for the revolution, but sacrifice it for *another* person, so that they could take the revolution forward.'

'I—'

'Guardian, it takes courage to die for a dream, but can you imagine how much more courage it takes to die trusting someone else with your dream? That's what we need today.'

'Why now?'

'Guardian,' said Asana quietly, 'What do you know about the Apoptosis Plan?'

Nila strove to keep her voice level. 'It rings a bell, but I can't quite place it. What is it?'

'The Apoptosis Plan is a top-secret stratagem that was created in the Directorate four decades ago. It aims at the reconquest of the Commune as the first step towards the eventual reunification of the empire. Only the director of High Town knows the plan in all its detail, but what we've found out is that it's very specific, and sets a time limit of a quarter of a millennium for reunification.'

'How is this top secret?' said Nila. 'Everyone knows that High Town dreams of the Old Empire.'

'This is not a dream. This is a *blueprint*,' said Asana. 'With years and events. And you know the first event, Guardian? *Council vs Commune*. When they created the Apoptosis Plan, they viewed it as the case that would end us. The plan predicts that within twenty-five years—*if* we lose *Council vs Commune*—we will collapse entirely.'

'How?'

'The Plan models for two eventualities. One, that as our economic situation grows worse, we will turn on each other, fracture and eventually destroy ourselves. Two, that even if we stay together, driven to desperation, we will be eventually forced to launch another attack upon High Town, and the war that will follow will be the ruin of us. The Apoptosis Plan predicts a 98 per cent probability of at least one of these futures coming to pass, should we lose on Monday.'

'Removing cancerous cells, huh,' said Nila.

'Yes. *We* are the cancer, Guardian. And now you see why this is existential for us.'

It'll either be a slow, crippling death under the Agreement—or swift ruin. Her mother's words came back to her.

'But what if you win on Monday?' she said.

'You think we can leave that to chance? We need backup for the day after. If we lose, we need *something* to stave off the collapse. We need something to believe in. Or someone.'

'Whatever happened to *heroes betray us, and we betray ourselves by having them*?'

'Nice line. Nice book.' Asana shrugged. 'But needs must.'

'You really think a man of flesh and blood—especially resurrected flesh and blood—can bear the weight of all the ideals that you're going to put on him?'

'That's between him and us,' Asana said, her tone turning curt. 'After you do your job.'

The one thing fully outside the design.

'Well,' said Nila. 'I doubt that—'

'Guardian,' said Asana. 'In this hour, ethical doubt is a luxury only you have.'

Nila flinched. *Point taken.* She cast a glance at Anam.

Don't let him die.

'All right,' she said.

'And so,' said Asana, 'We wanted to tell you that *we* will help you. Whatever information you wanted from the department, or from the administration, we'll pull it out for you. In secret, if we need to.'

Nila narrowed her eyes. 'Is this *really* about Jagat?'

'Jagat. The Commune. The idea of the Commune. At this moment in time, they're all the same.'

'And you're willing to defy your administration to help me?'

Asana smiled. '*Building the new in the ruins of the old* includes ruins that are your own.'

'*Touché*,' said Nila. 'Okay. Since you've very kindly offered, I need two things.'

'Tell us.'

'First, I need every bit of information that you have about *The Carbuncle* newspaper, from the time of the revolution. Nothing is irrelevant. Get me all that you can.'

'Very well,' said Asana. 'And the second?'

'I need any information that the Commune may have on Milana Maran.'

'Huh? Milana Maran?'

'Yes.'

For a moment, Asana looked like she was going to press, but didn't. 'Understood. Anything else?'

'Not for the moment. If there is, I'll tell you.'

'Good. Comrade Anam will be your point of contact with us.'

Asana saluted her, and moved away with her companions. Anam lingered by her for a moment.

'Myco-remediation, huh? When what you've basically been doing is running around joining secret societies while I've been away?' She poked him in the ribs. 'We're going to have to talk about *that*.'

'You're literally in the biggest secret society of them all!'

'Fair point, I concede that.' She lowered her voice to a whisper. 'Listen, Anam. No more communication after today, okay? Executive Committee's just waiting for a chance to expel me. It's too risky.'

'I know, I know.' He bent his head towards hers. 'We just thought you should know what had happened with Vani. And see if we could help you.'

'I'm increasingly beginning to think that the answer to this puzzle is not in the Commune,' Nila said. 'It's somewhere else. Anam, just get me that information about *The Carbuncle*. And then radio silence. Okay?'

He nodded silently. They touched fingers, then Nila turned and got into her skimmer. It rose swiftly. The last thing she saw as she sped off was Anam, still standing on the shore, gazing up at her.

12

The Burden of Judgement

AS SHE ALIGHTED INTO HER CHAMBER, NILA realised that something was wrong.

Maru wasn't at his desk. Instead, he was pacing back and forth by the table, staring into his wristheld.

'Maru?' she said.

'We have a problem.'

'What happened?'

'Your cryochamber authorisation. It isn't here yet.'

'Huh? Didn't you tell me it was done?'

'It *is* done. The application was allowed by the ad hoc panel. I got the notification this evening from the registry. Which means that the order should have come by now.'

'So, then ...?'

'It's just that, it has to come via the president's office with his seal.' Maru tapped his wristheld screen. 'And the tracking status says that it has left the registry, but we don't have it yet.'

'Bloody Mehmandost Naram!' Nila swore. 'Is he trying to do a pocket veto?'

'Well, the only place the order can be right now is his office.'

Nila walked to the table and leaned over it, palms on the surface. 'How long can he hold onto the order?'

'The order left the registry after hours,' said Maru. 'If he wants to, he can count it as part of the next day's batch, and get around to signing it … by the end of tomorrow.'

Nila screwed her eyes shut. 'If we try asking—'

'I called the office extension. Not answering.'

'Maybe he's not seen it?'

'Impossible,' Maru said. 'I walked by the office earlier today, just to check. There was a light. The little reptile was inside. He's seen the file.'

Nila grasped the undersides of the table. She counted her breaths to five through clenched teeth. 'Maru,' she said quietly. 'Is there any other way to get the order before noon tomorrow?'

'Not until he gives it up himself.'

Nila paused for two seconds. Her face was set. 'Well, then,' she said, 'we take it from him.'

'Nila—'

'Do you remember,' she said, 'that time we planned to let off those stink bombs in the president's chamber?'

'Yes ...?'

'And you remember how we'd planned everything? Scoped the layout? Figured out the lock's mechanism? Acquired a duplicate key?'

'Nila!' Maru said. 'That was a prank. Which we aborted because Suneen got cold feet two hours before we were going to do it. *This* is not a prank. This is a break-in. If you're caught …'

'I won't get caught.'

'Okay, let's say you do it. And tomorrow, when Naram discovers the order is missing?'

'He won't be able to prove who took it. *Besides*, if he makes a fuss, it will come out that his negligence, at the very least, was going to sabotage an active case. He'll grind his teeth, that's all. We just need to seize the damn thing.'

'Okay. And who has that duplicate key, Nila?'

'I … we left it with Noor. The least likely among us all to ever face a "random" disciplinary raid. The understanding was that if anyone ever needed it—'

'You're going to give Noor that kind of power over you?' said Maru. 'Forever?'

'We all swore an oath of perpetual secrecy.'

'Oh, an *oath*, huh?'

'I trust her, Maru,' said Nila. 'You know her too. Am I wrong?'

Maru was silent for so long that she thought he wasn't going to answer.

'Noor is not the point here,' he said at last. 'You want to place your entire career on the line, Nila, just to look at Jagat's face for two minutes. Why?'

Nila held his gaze. 'Intuition,' she said. 'Will you help me, Maru?'

The office bell rang.

At his desk, Mehmandost Naram reached for the intercom.

'G. Maru.'

'Ah, yes,' the president said. 'Come through the antechamber. The door is open.'

After ten seconds of silence, Maru pushed open the door.

Mehmandost Naram half-rose. 'Pupil Maru,' he said, gesturing to the chair across from him. 'Sit, please.'

Maru padded across the carpeted floor. 'President, thank you for responding to my request for an appointment so promptly,' he said, settling into the chair. 'I didn't expect you to be in till tomorrow morning.'

'I don't work after hours as a rule,' Naram said, 'but when I saw your message, I knew some things can't wait.'

Was there the slightest hint of excitement in that dry, reedy voice?

'So,' said Naram. 'Pupil Maru, you've come to me to report a breach of the impartiality oath?'

Maru stared intently at the tiny grooves that were carved into the marble table between them.

'Yes, President.'

Nila sat alone in her chamber, sensing the seconds tick away. In the chamber, the very air seemed to have settled into an expectant silence.

She pulled up her wristheld and plucked out the seeing screen. 'Chapterhouse guardian archives,' she spoke to the screen. It altered into a screenpage that listed, alphabetically, the profile of every guardian to have passed through the gates of the Chapterhouse.

'Naina L.'

A single name appeared on the screen in blue hyperlinked format.

'Open.'

A guardian's profile page tended to be densely populated: links to all the cases they'd been in, as counsel or as arbitrators, to their theses and published papers, to public writing. In Naina L.'s case, however, the page was sparse. There were the three private briefs that she'd done as a pupil: complex disputes around the interpretation of flexible labour contracts between the Council and various workers' unions.

Then there was Naina's answer sheet to the peacemaker's dilemma. Nila's eyes snagged upon it. She tapped the link.

The future is another country.

The first line told her that Naina had resolved the dilemma in the same way that Nila had.

Nila made a mental note to come back to it when she had more time and returned to the main page. Just below the answer sheet, there were the records of Naina's summary trial: the chargesheet that Maru had read out to her the other day, Naina's written response, the oral records and the judgement of expulsion. Nila moved her finger over the file titled 'Statement of Defence'. She was just about to tap it when, out of the corner of her eye, she saw something else.

The trial folder was not the last set of documents on the page. Just below that, there was one final file. It simply read 'Open Letter'.

Nila narrowed her eyes. For a few seconds, her index finger hovered between 'Statement of Defence' and 'Open Letter.'

She tapped 'Open Letter.'

A page came up before her.

A letter to the pupils who will come after me

The first line was enough to snag her attention. Nila read on.

The Confederation has us believe that we are neutral and impartial arbiters between two equal contending forces: the Council and the Commune. That the Charter and the law create a balance that must be preserved, and that it is our task to preserve it.

The Confederation is persuasive because it truly believes this. But it believes a lie.

There can be no lasting balance between two forces, each of whose existence is a negation of the other.

The Council cannot tolerate the Commune because as long as the Commune exists, it is proof that another way of being is possible. The longer the Commune exists, the more powerful and undeniable this proof grows, not just in Peruma, but across all the cities of the subcontinent, where revolutions like ours have failed. The Commune must be crushed so that once again, it becomes impossible to imagine a future. The Commune must be crushed before the Old Empire can be reborn again.

And the Council knows it.

The Commune cannot tolerate the Council because as long as the Council exists, the revolution remains unfinished. No matter how far the Commune reorganises its internal structures to escape the mute compulsion of economic relations, in its external dealings with the Council, it is still bound by those, only somewhat softened by collective bargaining. As long as the Council exists, the Commune is nothing more than a glorified co-operative society, operating at a city-level scale, but that doesn't change the fact that it is partial, distorted, a shadow of the idea; a revolution half-born.

And the Commune knows it.

What the Charter, the law and the guardians preserve is an unstable equilibrium. It cannot last forever. There will come a time when, between equal right, force will decide.

We cannot understand our work as guardians in abstraction. Every time we wield the law, in one direction or another, we tip the balance of power. We may be neutral and impartial. But our work is not.

It is true not every case carries immense ethical weight. Petty border disputes have no real bearing in any of this, and there we can remain morally secure in our neutrality. But there are some cases that do. The case that I am now being expelled for—on the right to strike—does. And the case four decades from now—when the Charter runs out, when the Fifth Inflection Point arrives and we are asked to decide what law remains and what does not—will.

You may still believe, all things considered, that impartiality is the right path for the guardians. I can think of several arguments to support that, although none of them are very good. But be aware that you are still making a choice—a choice that history has every right to judge you for.

I know that today, disgraced and expelled as I am, these words will mean nothing. But my appeal is to the intelligence of a society in the future, when greater understanding might correct the error into which I believe we have all been betrayed.

I hope you remain free and equal, always.

Naina L.

'Phew.'

Nila leaned back and stared up at the ceiling. Her predecessor's words assembled and disassembled in her mind, embedding themselves within the network of thoughts that were her investigation into Jagat's case.

Her wristheld beeped. It was time.

Nila rose and left the chamber.

'I appreciate you coming to me,' said Mehmandost Naram. 'I understand that what you're doing is not easy.'

Maru continued to stare at the marble table. Somewhere in the depths of his mind, a clockwork mechanism had started, counting each second that dragged out between them.

'To be honest,' he said, 'I don't know if I'm doing the right thing.'

'Of that, you can rest assured,' said the president smoothly. 'All our bonds, our individual bonds, with our friends, our colleagues, even our … chambermates … all these bonds can—must dissolve before our bond with the Confederation.'

What a poor persuader, Maru thought. *How did you ever become president?*

'I don't doubt that,' he said, 'but I don't know—I'm not sure if—I'm not sure, President, why we're so obsessed with the impartiality oath.'

'Not every breach gets the harshest sanction. We always examine these complaints in a calibrated way—with proportionality, remember? But first, why don't you tell me what this is about?'

Not so fast, you greasy barnacle.

'I will, I will,' Maru said. 'I just want to be sure.'

'Yes, yes, no rush,' said Naram hurriedly. 'I don't want to pressurise you. If you need to clear any doubts, Pupil Maru, I'm here to answer them, as best as I can.'

Maru leaned back in his chair. It creaked comfortingly. If it were not for the clockwork inside his brain, he could almost have let himself enjoy this.

'I just need to understand for myself why the impartiality oath matters,' he said, 'so that I know I'm doing the right thing by coming to you, and breaking a very personal bond.'

I've never had to go sneaking around the Chapterhouse at night.

Nila grinned ruefully as she tiptoed through the darkened corridor, a slow descent down the Hedgehog's Needle. The light from her wristheld revealed outlines of chamber doors as she passed. They were all unlit and silent, but at the end of the corridor, a sliver of light struggled out from the crack under a door. She knocked softly.

Footsteps sounded across the chamber. The door creaked open. Noor was silhouetted in the frame.

'Nila?'

'I need the key,' said Nila.

For a moment, Noor stared at her. Then she nodded. 'Just a minute.'

She left the door ajar, giving Nila a glimpse of a tabletop widescreen computer that seemed to have fifty tabs open, papers scattered on the desk beside it, a bowl with what looked like the remnants of chocolate ice cream and Noor's own emotional support octopus looking quizzically back at her. An exercycle faced the window, a towel thrown carelessly over one handlebar. On a round table in the centre of the room, a ten-thousand-piece jigsaw puzzle of the Directorate and the Tiger's Jaw was in a state of partial completion.

There was a scrabbling noise from inside, and then Noor appeared again, holding a silver key in her hand.

'Thank you,' said Nila.

'For what?'

'For not asking me why I need it.'

Noor shook her head. 'Just—take care, Phoenix.'

Nila nodded towards her screen. 'How's it going?'

'Submissions drafting stage now.' Noor passed a hand over her brow. 'Working on the synopsis. Fuck my life. *There is just no time.*'

'Feeling's mutual.'

'Can imagine. Actually, I'd rather not. I'll get back to it, then.'

'Yeah, me too. See you tomorrow.'

The door closed on her. Nila turned and walked back up to the shaft, and got into the elevator. It took her down the Hedgehog's Needle. Squares of light and shadow passed over her. At ground level, the elevator's doors slid open.

Nila stepped out into the darkness.

'The oath,' said Mehmandost Naram, 'is the reason why we've survived a century.'

Maru searched his expression. *How much of this does he truly believe?*

'You have to remember,' the president continued, 'that we, the Confederation, exist on sufferance. We don't control an army. We can't raise taxes. I know you know all this, but I also know how easy it is to forget, because we're so used to our judgements being followed and enforced. We've become so used to Council and Commune obeying us, even when we rule against them, that we've forgotten what that obedience rests on and how quickly it could be lost.'

'I do know all this, President,' said Maru. 'But are you seriously suggesting that if a guardian oversteps from time to time, we can't excuse the odd transgression? Do we have to come down on them like a ton of bricks? Take the case of Naina L. for instance—'

'Naina, yes,' Mehmandost Naram leaned forward. 'I know it's fashionable these days to canonise her, but Pupil Maru, I was there—I was a pupil just as you are now when it happened. It was the highest-stakes fight between the Council and the Commune since—since the beginning, and there she was, collecting evidence illegally for the Commune. If we hadn't acted then, what confidence would the Council have had in the final judgement that we gave? What if they just refused to follow it? What would we have done then?'

'That's because it went public,' said Maru. 'I understand that there are times when we all have to perform for the world. But why have we elevated impartiality to a sacred law, President, a law over our human bonds here in the Confederation?'

'Because if we were to exercise judgement in every single case,' said Mehmandost Naram, 'if we were to start admitting exceptions and mitigating circumstances and loopholes, then we would soon perish. It's why we have rules, Pupil. It spares us the burden of judgement.'

Maru looked up from the table, into the president's eyes. *He really does believe it, the brainwashed ghoul.*

At ground level, the corridors were dimly lit and punctuated by arched alcoves. Nila tiptoed on the uneven stone floor, jumping at the slight noises that came from behind the walls. The network of disguised trapdoors and camouflaged inner passageways behind the alcoves—whose design nobody had ever quite figured out—made it impossible to tell just how close you were to another person in the Chapterhouse. Behind a wafer-thin wall that gave the impression of immense solidity, there might be someone's study, or a shortcut from the president's chamber to the Executive Committee's meeting room. Stories of private conversations that had been inconveniently overheard were their own genre in Chapterhouse lore.

She made it to the Great Hall without incident. Here, on the chequered onyx floor, designed to resemble a chessboard, her feet sounded disconcertingly loud in her ears. From their mock-braziers high up on the wall, the lamps cast strange patterns on the dark green and white floor. Nila stepped among the pillars as the shadows danced around her.

In the Great Hall, there was silence. The Chapterhouse slept.

She crossed the Great Hall and opened the door that led into the Executive Committee's office quarters.

The President's wristheld beeped. He looked down.

'I just need to take this for a moment, if you don't mind.'

'Of course, President.'

'Yes?' Mehmandost Naram spoke into the wristheld.

There was an inarticulate buzz from the other side.

'Ah,' said the president. 'I see. Well, thanks for informing me. I'll deal with it.' He cut the call. 'Sorry about that.'

'Not at all.' The clockwork had started to wind down.

'Now, where were we? Oh, yes.' Mehmandost Naram looked pensive, almost sad. 'Do you remember the story of the Kinnaras, Pupil Maru? From High Town childhood days?'

'Of course, President. The beings whose singing was irresistible to mortal ears.'

'Did you know, by the way, that they don't teach the story in the Commune? Indefensible imposition of a moral code, apparently. But that's not relevant. Do you recall the crux? The ship captain knows that when the Kinnaras sing, none will be unable to resist their call. The ship will be wrecked. So what does he do? He ties himself to the mast. He takes the choice away from his future self. It's the only way, he knows, to save himself, to save everyone. And that's the impartiality oath, Pupil. It survives—and *we* survive—because if we were to exercise the burden of judgement every time a friend, a comrade erred, we would be tempted to show mercy every time, and then—and *then,* Pupil—the Confederation would fall, and Peruma would return to its time of blood and fire.'

'Ah,' said Maru. 'Right.'

Okay. He's insane.

'Spare yourself the burden of judgement, Pupil,' Mehmandost Naram said gently, almost plausibly. 'Tell me what you've come to tell me. Even if it involves the dearest of friends and comrades. And trust your president to handle it.'

The clockwork ticked away into silence. *Time's up.*

'All right,' said Maru. 'All right.'

He sensed the president lean forward imperceptibly. Maru leaned back, revulsed, before he forced himself to sit up straight.

'It's just that ... I hope you don't think I've wasted your time on a triviality, President,' he said. 'But it struck me today, while I was working on a brief, that for all our medical law cases, we use and cite Mody's *Medical Jurisprudence and Toxicology*. But Mody was a doctor from High Town, President, from the pre-revolutionary era. Isn't it a breach of the oath to rely upon only one author from one side of the divide for all our medico-legal propositions?'

There was a long silence. Mehmandost Naram had gone white.

Maru nearly cracked a rib trying to keep a straight face.

After an eternity passed, the president said: 'You think you're very clever, don't you, *Pupil* Maru?'

'It was a genuine question, President.'

'Still keeping up the farce, are we?'

Maru stared back at him. Something snapped at last. 'The only farce I see here,' he said, 'is a president banging on and on about impartiality and rules and the burden of judgement, while actively sabotaging a critical investigation, and a pupil's future.'

'And what,' said Mehmandost Naram, 'would you understand about the impartiality oath—you're—you're an *abettor*!'

'I don't know what you're talking about,' Maru stood, abandoning all pretence. 'I am so glad I don't have to engage with you any longer, you oily little ... man.'

The shrill whine of an alarm pierced the air like a knife.

Maru stood, rooted to the spot.

It was all around, the noise, reminding him of dentists' chairs and drills in the back of his jaw. He screwed his eyes shut.

'Oh dear me,' said Mehmandost Naram, through a gap in the alarm. 'It looks as if someone's tried to break into my drawer, Pupil, while we were busy talking here.'

The alarm rang again, forcing Maru to cover his ears. When it died away, they were still throbbing.

'Shall we go take a look, Pupil Maru,' the president said, politely. 'The outer door locks automatically if someone trips the alarm, and I'm afraid old keys won't open it.'

'You wretched schemer,' Maru said.

'Just keeping the Chapterhouse honest,' said Mehmandost Naram. 'It's such a pity that every second generation throws up a Naina—but we have to do what we must.' He moved around the table and gripped Maru's arm. 'Come now.'

Maru slumped and let himself be pulled forward. Mehmandost Naram opened the door, and they stepped into—

—an empty room.

The president's jaw dropped. '*What?*'

'Oh dear *me*,' Maru said. 'It looks like no one's here anymore, President. Dear oh dear.'

'Impossible!' Mehmandost Naram scurried across the floor faster than Maru had expected a man of his age to be capable of. He tapped a code onto a keypad set into the second drawer of the desk in the antechamber and fished around inside. A look of bafflement crossed his face as he withdrew a piece of official-looking paper.

Maru had quickly crossed the floor after him, and now he looked over his shoulder.

'Oh dear me, President,' he repeated pleasantly. 'What have we here? An order allowing the application by Nila M. to access Jagat R.'s cryochamber tomorrow at noon, the existence of which you are *evidently* aware of, and have had occasion to read—ah look, there's your seal as well. How fortunate that I happened to be here—I can just take this back for my chambermate.' He held out his hand.

'I—you—'

'Yes?'

'Can you *imagine* how much the other cities will be laughing at us on Monday?'

'Oh, that's your worry, is it?' said Maru. 'Well, I hate to break it to you, but they laugh at us anyway. Peruma, once the pearl of the north, now Peruma the ruptured city that's been muddling through the last hundred years in suspended animation. But anyway, will you hand over the order, please? Unless—' his voice hardened, 'you want to be known as a president who was deliberately and intentionally attempting to scuttle an investigation. What if this were to go … public?'

Footsteps outside the chamber.

Nila lifted her head.

The door opened. Maru stood at the threshold. With a grin, he held up her cryochamber authorisation order.

'Maru!' She bounded across the chamber and caught him in a fierce hug. 'You fucking *genius*.'

'Uff!' Maru protested, the wind knocked out of him. 'This is a child-friendly chamber, please.'

Nila released him and shook her head. '*How*?'

Maru made his way inside and sank into a chair, his adrenaline beginning to peter out. 'Phew. There were a couple of hairy moments, but the moment his wristheld rang, I knew all our hunches had been right.'

'That call—it was someone ratting me out?'

'Had to be.'

'*Noor*?'

'I don't—but wait.' An expression that Nila had never seen before passed over his face. 'You *did* do what I said, Nila?'

'Yep. Walked in the general direction of his office, but turned back after the Great Hall.'

The expression passed, and Maru was Maru again. 'Yes, not Noor then—he must have set someone on you, and they called him from the Great Hall. The man was so obsessed with catching you that he walked into his own trap.'

She gave him a mock-glare. 'Fill in the gaps now, at least?'

'I suspected the only reason he was withholding the order was to trap you. He'd expect you to try and break in. And *that's* where, Nila,' he gave her a sly look, 'it helped that the president and I come from the same High Town extended family of … *aristocrats.* Generations of us have played these games. There is a very standard electric security alarm that my family prefers to use. And *that's* also why,' he reached into his pocket, and pulled out a small black box, 'there exists a very standard way of tripping it. So when I was getting up to leave, I tripped it for him. In five seconds, the order was out of the drawer.'

Nila looked at him, open-mouthed. 'Maru,' she said after a while, 'maybe you want to take over this case from me?'

'Ah, don't be an idiot,' Maru blushed. 'I'll play the games with the Executive Committee. You get the real work done.'

'I don't understand, though,' Nila said. 'Why is he *so* keen that I fail? Residual High Town loyalties?'

'I don't know,' said Maru. 'First he mentioned something about the other cities laughing at us, and when I was leaving, he insisted that he was going to send the order tomorrow morning, and that this was just to test if you were true to the impartiality oath. Pointed to the fact that he'd already signed it as evidence.'

'You mean there's no deeper game here? He's just basically a neutrality code zealot, seeing a Naina in every shadow?'

'I can't say,' said Maru. 'And now, I don't think we'll ever know. But what we do know,' he chuckled, 'is that we have one hopping mad president right now.'

'Oh dammit,' Nila said, 'You've made an enemy for life out of *the* Mehmandost Naram, Maru. I'm sorry, I didn't know—'

'See, this is why I didn't tell you in advance,' Maru said, laughing. 'You'd have gotten ethical cold feet and forbidden me.'

'I should think so! He'll hate you forever now.'

Maru smiled, his eyes crinkling. 'Listen. Make him hate me even more. Win.'

Day Five

The Cryochamber

13

Do It Like a Communard

THE WINDOW RATTLED.

Nila lifted her head from the table. She was alone. Maru had retired to bed a long time ago.

Just when she was putting her head back down, the rattling came again.

Her eyes flew open. Beyond the glass, there was a shifting figure.

The tip of a finger moved.

Tap, tap, tap.

She stood, walked to the window and pulled it open.

Balanced on the ledge beside the balcony, his toes on the stone, the rest of his feet in the air, was Anam.

Nila snatched her hand back from the window. 'Wha—*what?*' She stared at him, and then beneath him. The wall of the Hedgehog's Needle, steep, sheer and bare, slid all the way down to the river. There was no means of support.

'Anam!' she whispered fiercely. 'Didn't I tell you we couldn't—'

'Hey, Nila,' he whispered back at her. 'I found out about *The Carbuncle.*'

'Oh!' She leaned forward and seized his shoulder, forgetting that he was perched precariously on the ledge. 'Tell me. Quickly!'

The edges of Anam's face began to melt like wax from a long-burning candle, dripping molten, his features distorting as if someone was moulding him like soft clay. Suddenly, there was Jagat's face instead, a minute after being awakened from the sleep of death.

'*What is this world that you've built in my name?*' said the man.

Nila jerked back—

—and woke up screaming.

'Nila!' Noor whispered.

'Huh—wha—'

She was in the library. The candlelight of her dreams dissolved into the lamplight streaming from the library walls. Her wristheld was face-down on the table, with Baili the seagull lying next to it, one wing around its base. As she lifted her head, she saw a thin line of drool running along the line of the wood.

'You okay?' Noor said. 'You did not look like you were having a good time in that dream.'

'I'm fine, I'm fine,' she said, embarrassed. She fished in her pocket for a tissue, and quickly wiped the table. Her head felt as if someone was pounding it with a rock.

The lamplight throbbed and pulsed on the edge of her vision. 'What time is it?'

'6.00 a.m.'

'Here so early?'

Noor drew up a chair. 'Just thought I'd come down before the others and get some solo research done.'

Nila blinked. Anam's melting face had receded, but still sent tiny cold shivers down her spine. As the world slowly came into focus, she noticed that Noor had not switched on her own wristheld. Instead, she was sitting there, her hands propping up her chin, staring into the distance.

'Hey,' Nila said. 'Everything alright?'

'Yeah,' said Noor. 'I guess.'

'Or, not really?'

Noor shook her head. 'It's a mood.'

'What mood?'

Noor hesitated a moment, looking at Nila, sizing her up. Then she shrugged. 'There are just mornings when I feel like I'm on the wrong side,' she said.

'*Wrong* side?' Nila echoed. 'But there's no—'

'Hey,' said Noor, 'Imagine that you were on this case, for the Council. Cross your heart and tell me honestly, Nila, would you have been happy?'

'I try not to think about any hypothetical situations involving me being in this case.'

'Gods! Okay,' said Noor. 'Take your case. Imagine it was the prosecution who'd approached you. To argue against retrial, to send Jagat to a permanent death. Now?'

Coloured bits and pieces of the Commune floated like clouds in her mind, the colour and movement that lived on the walls, music from the ateliers by evening, a pebbled path, little remembered toys upon a carpet, the smell of mrigel curry, her mother's voice, Anam's feel under moonlight on the grass, Asana looking at her, *don't let him die*.

Noor grinned tiredly. 'You remember, Nila. But I remember too.'

'What do you remember, Salamander?' Nila whispered.

'My mornings refracted through cut glass, my wine-dark evenings breaking upon the sea-stone,' Noor's voice floated in the air. 'I remember the rajnigandha's scent around Purul's samadhi in summer, and Amaltas Avenue in the fall. I remember discovering a city through its skylanes, the feeling of flight, as if the sky were the sea and every tower an island rising in the mist. I remember school amidst the clouds, and late-night skimmer darts with friends for ice cream, when the night swirled with every colour, and dawn hikes camping upon the switchback, watching the sunrise upon a moonscape, your hand in another's, fitting like a glove. And I remember leaving, remember it most of all.'

Nila spoke to fill in the silence that rushed in upon them. 'So it's not just sea-stone and steel and chiselled avenues and polyhedral grids, then.'

'If only home were just that,' Noor smiled. 'But it never is. And that's why, Nila, neutrality curriculum's all good, but there are cases when we're not just guardians anymore, because all of us came to the Chapterhouse with fragments of our hearts left at home. The other day you said I wouldn't want to swap places with you. But at least you get to be on your side, Nila. You got to be on your side the one time in history when the sides really matter.'

'My side?' said Nila, trying to keep her voice level. 'Noor, we're not on any side, we're—'

'On the side of equal justice under law, yes, yes, I know,' said Noor. 'We both passed the neutrality test, Nila, that's why we're here. I didn't say I wouldn't do my duty. I don't have to enjoy it, though.'

'In our careers,' said Nila, 'there are going to be many times when we'll be up against the side where we were born. Already have.'

'But there'll never be a case like mine again. Or yours.'

'Can't tell the future, can we?'

'Will you just *try* and be human for once, damn the world!'

Nila fell silent, shocked.

For a moment, Noor looked equally shocked at herself, but then, as if realising that she'd come too far to stop, she said: 'Listen, Phoenix. Can I say something? You won't take offence?'

'Go on.'

Noor's words spilled into each other.

'I feel you're blocking yourself from *really* doing this case because you've psyched yourself into this constant fear of breaking impartiality. Nila, we've been trained in taking ourselves out of the context, and yes, we need to do that because we're playing a role, because everything depends on the Confederation being seen as impartial, and it's hard to keep up a mask all the time unless you really believe in it, our brains tells us that, and we do believe in it, and we'll believe in it with every case we do, but Nila, how many times in your life will you get a chance to do this kind of a case *and* be on the side where your heart really is? How many times will you get a case where if you win, you'd be changing the fate of the place you were born, the place that made you? I didn't get the rub of the green, but you did. So, screw it all, don't waste it. Just for these last three days, don't do this case like a guardian. Do it *like a Communard*.'

'But,' said Nila, 'that's not your side. I'm not on your side. If Jagat comes back—'

'I don't care. This is criminal defence, Nila. If you win, you'll be showing the finger to the criminal law, to this stupid sentence and this whole sleep of death business, and that's something I can get behind, whatever Jagat is or whatever he might do.'

We may be neutral and impartial. But our work is not.

Naina's open letter danced in her head. Nila looked at Noor. For a moment, a horrible suspicion came into her mind: *a trap. Do it like a Communard,* so that she'd drop her guard, overstep, give Mehmandost Naram that chance that he was so eagerly waiting for, and on Monday, for the second time, there would be no one to speak for Jagat.

The one time in history when sides really matter.

All those thoughts passed through her mind in an instant, before her gaze caught Noor's. Something of her own suspicion must have showed on her face, because she saw Noor's eyes widen, first in surprise, and then in hurt.

Nila felt herself go red to the tips of her ears with embarrassment. 'Noor, I—'

Noor waved her quiet, and smiled wearily, her eyes half-closed.

'I don't know what—,' Nila stammered. 'I've just become so paranoid these last two days, with everything going on.'

'Don't worry about it,' said Noor. 'It's a bad week and we're all a bunch of frayed nerve endings right now. Can't wait to get done, to be honest.'

'Yeah, me too,' said Nila. She swallowed, twice. Then she said: 'Noor—it's just—I've been dying inside ever since they rejected me for *Council vs Commune*. I—when I got Jagat's case—it's like this one thing I'm holding on to, that makes me believe I'm not worthless, that I'm part of history just like you, and that we're still in some way—' she choked over the word '*—equal*, so, it's not an excuse, but it is what it is. I'm sorry.'

Noor put both her hands on Nila's shoulders.

'One day,' she said, '*we'll* be on the Executive Committee. We'll remember how they made us feel. And we won't torment our pupils by having them fight a never-ending war for the highest-stakes cases.'

'Yeah.' Nila swallowed again. 'Yeah. Thank you, Salamander.'

Noor smiled. 'Maybe your anarchist Commune does have some good ideas about doing away with status, prestige, all that sort of stuff.'

'What, you think the anarchists have eliminated status and prestige?' Nila laughed. 'Have you met my mother?'

Noor laughed back, and the last of the barriers between them dissolved. 'Maybe after this is all over, you'll introduce me to her outside of an instructing table.'

'I will, and you'll see.' Nila paused, smiling. 'Actually, the only person I know who's done away with status and prestige—at least in his own head—isn't even a Communard, but one of yours.'

'Mm?'

'Maru?'

She heard a sharp intake of breath, saw something pass across Noor's face. 'Your chambermate?'

'And lifesaver now. It's funny how you can know someone so well and for so long,' Nila went on, 'and still have them surprise you. I thought that all he'd ever get up for was occupational injury law and bad puns, but he's been a brilliant help on this case, like having a second, complementary mind.' She laughed. 'Almost like having *you*.'

When she paused for a breath, she noticed that Noor looked stricken.

'Noor—what's wrong?'

A long time seemed to pass before Noor said: 'He's never told you?'

'Told me what?'

Noor didn't respond, staring past Nila, into the space beyond her shoulder.

'Told me *what*, Noor?'

Noor shook herself. 'I was wondering if I should—but no, you of all people should know.'

'Want to be a *little* less cryptic?'

'Yes, yes, sorry,' said Noor. 'You know Maru's family, yeah? The House of Balot?'

'Prominent High Town aristocrats and corporate heads. Blue blood,' said Nila. 'Mehmandost Naram also belongs to them.'

'About as aristocratic as it gets, just below the director,' Noor said. 'One of the great ancient families, tracing their lineage to the time of Old Empire. Held the balance of power in High Town for as far back as anyone can remember.'

'Yeah.'

'And also: ever since the civil war, every generation, they send one of their brightest and most ambitious to the Chapterhouse, where they're expected to be—and are—brilliant.'

'Such as Mehmandost Naram?'

'Exactly. It's a family tradition.'

'But,' said Nila, confused. 'Maru isn't anything like Mehmandost—'

'Yes,' said Noor quietly. 'Because Maru is the representative of the generation that would come of age in the Chapterhouse just as the Fifth Inflection Point came around. Now think of what would happen to the reputation of this family if, by some twist of fate, their son was picked on the Commune's side in *Council vs Commune*.'

'But assignment is arbitrary—'

'Try telling that to the *High Town Herald*, and imagine the headline. When it came time for Maru to join the Chapterhouse, the family did imagine it, and they did not like what they imagined.'

'But like it or not, how can you control the assignment?'

'You can't. But what you can do,' said Noor, 'is ensure you're never in the running.'

'How …' Nila broke off, as a terrible understanding made itself known. 'So you're telling me,' she said slowly, 'that this has all been an act? That Maru's been performing mediocrity all this while to ensure he'd never be one of the twelve because his family couldn't abide the thought that one of their own might represent the Commune in this case?'

I don't need more.

Maru's voice echoed in the halls of memory, its playfulness now revealing in ways that it hadn't been before.

'And if you knew him from before the Chapterhouse,' Noor smiled ruefully, 'you'd know how much of an effort *that* takes.'

'Why in the name of sanity did he ever agree to this?'

'Oh, he wasn't going to,' said Noor. 'Until they made him promise it to his grandmother, the family matriarch, whom he loved more than anyone else, and who was dying of cancer. Her last wish.'

'That's blackmail!'

'Welcome to High Town's aristocratic politics,' said Noor. 'And by the way, if you were wondering why he focuses so much on cancer compensation claims and occupational injuries law—that's his own, Maru-esque way of saying *fuck you* to his family: to become the best in dealing with the very thing that they leveraged against him.'

Class traitor. I accepted that a long time ago.

'Oh, Maru,' she whispered out loud, before noticing that Noor had turned, and was already on her way out.

'Noor,' she called after her. 'How do *you* know this? It's surely that family's best-kept secret.'

A final ghost of a smile, and Noor let her have it, without prelude.

'We were together. I saw it all. We ended things just before we entered the Chapterhouse that year.'

And then Noor was really gone, before Nila could ask her anything more.

The cold coffee sent a welcoming chill through her veins. Nila put the glass down and smacked her lips. 'More ice!'

Maru squeezed out a couple of cubes from the ice tray, picked them up with the tongs and dropped them into the glass. Nila reached for it and nursed the drink, taking slow sips.

Be normal, a voice in her head cautioned. *Don't let him know you know*.

'You need sleep,' said Maru.

'I'll sleep for a week after Monday.'

'You're going to make mistakes before that.'

'No bigger mistake than our entire history.'

'Wow, staying up half the night to read Surma Katoch on the revolution *really* got you down, I see.'

'Ugh,' said Nila. 'Whoever thought it was a good idea to make a confirmed misanthrope High Town's historian of revolution? Bleakness everywhere. *And* it gave me nightmares about some ghastly cross between Anam and Jagat showing up at my window. Got woken up just before I would have given myself a heart attack.'

'I think—' began Maru, but Nila never found out what he thought, because at that moment, her pidge squawked. A bulky envelope slid through and fell to the floor with a thump.

'Now what's so important and private that it can't be sent online?' said Nila. 'Directorate? Or Commune?'

Maru walked to the pidge and picked it up. 'No sender,' he said. 'Paper, by the looks of it. A lot of it.' He brought the envelope over to her. She took one of his cutters and slit open the top. It was paper. A lot of it.

At the top, there was a typed cover letter.

To

Guardian Nila
Confederation of the Free and Equal Guardians of Peruma
Chapterhouse

Dear Guardian Nila,

We are the Peruma Coalition for the Abolition of the Sleep of Death. We write to urge you that, when you argue for the revival of Jagat R. before the tribunal this Monday, to also raise the issue of the compliance of the sleep of death with the Charter of Peace and Unity, and request the tribunal to reconsider, revisit and overrule the shameful judgement that was Directorate vs Raila, and adopt the dissenting judgement of Judge H.R. Khana.

We think that, with the city-wide interest in the fate of Jagat R., there is no better time than now to make this case to the tribunal, and rid our society of this long-standing stain.

To aid in your efforts, we are enclosing our coalition's research on the sleep of death, including signed affidavits by expert psychologists who testify to the adaptive risks of revival after the passage of a generation. We believe that there is a strong case to be made that the so-called 'sentence' violates the right to life guaranteed by the Charter.

We think that such an opportunity will not come again for many years, and we therefore beseech you to press this argument before the tribunal. Should you need any assistance from us, please contact us directly using the code enclosed with this letter.

With best regards,
Noop Z.
Executive Director
Peruma Coalition for the Abolition of the Sleep of Death
Formerly Peruma Coalition for the Abolition of the Death Penalty

Nila started laughing.

She handed the letter over to Maru and continued to laugh, her chin on the table.

'Well,' said Maru, when he finished reading. 'This could have been a wristheld message, only it'd have gone to spam.'

'The abolitionist cranks have logged in, like clockwork' said Nila. 'Exactly what I needed now, isn't it, Maru? They want me to stand up there and say, *but ACTUALLY, Arbitrators, the sentence is anti-Charter and you should abolish it right here, right now.*'

'If only you could, heh.'

'On three days' prep, in an application for a criminal retrial, without instructions, at my own behest, *and* with the consequence of creating bad precedent and screwing up any chance for abolition for the next hundred years if I lose, which I will. Yes, Maru, I am totally going to stand up and challenge the sentence itself. What could possibly go wrong?'

'Why are they so convinced it's the best time?'

'They're always convinced it's the best time. Our whole history is overenthusiastic idiots jumping the gun and pushing everything further away rather than bringing it closer. And right now, what with the Charter itself up for renegotiation …' she tailed off suddenly.

'What?' said Maru.

She was looking past him, her gaze unfocused, staring at something in the distance.

'What, Nila?'

'Maru, wait, *wait*!' She leapt up from her chair and began to pace the room, her right hand gesturing at something, her lips moving. A couple of times he heard her say '*Yes!*' in almost an undertone, and then, 'No, *no,* not *that*.'

'Got it!' She was back at the table, her eyes shining.

'What?'

'Remember how you told me that there's always that one argument that shifts the frame of a case?'

'Yeah?'

'I think I've found it.'

'You're actually going to challenge the sleep of death?'

'No, but what I will do, Maru, what I *will* do is ask for it to be suspended.'

'What!'

'The Charter is up for renegotiation, right? And how much of it can be renegotiated, which bits of it, that's all going to be decided by the tribunal during *Certain Questions of Great Public Importance*, right?'

'Right.'

'And let's say the Commune wins, the tribunal holds that there's no such thing as a basic structure, then everything is going to be up for change, right? *Including* the clause on the continuation of the existing criminal code, *right*?'

'But—'

'So, potentially, the sleep of death may be abolished right after this. In days or weeks. What better reason to grant a stay on your *one* pending execution, when the punishment itself could go?'

'They are never going to agree with this,' said Maru. 'The renegotiation of the Charter is hypothetical, and they may not even do anything about the sleep of death. They didn't the last time, remember? Why would they stop the automatic operation of existing criminal law for what *might* happen in the future?'

'*Because it's irreversible!* That's the whole damn thing about death, remember?' Nila thumped the table with her fist. 'Maru, Maru, Maru! Basic rules for an injunction! What loss is there to anyone if Jagat is kept in cryosleep for a few weeks more? On the other hand, if they unplug him, that's it, he's dead, punished under a law that might be repudiated immediately after.'

'But even if they abolish it, it will be prospective—'

'Not necessarily. Maru! Have you forgotten your own research? Were there not two people who were revived from the sleep of death because the offences they were convicted under were retrospectively abolished? It's happened before. Why can't it happen again?' She looked at her seagull. 'Baili, what do you think?' She put a thumb and forefinger around his beak, and moved it vigorously forwards and backwards. 'Look, he agrees that it's a good idea.'

Maru laughed, then sobered. 'Nila, what you're basically arguing is something like: if we're writing a new charter or constitution, then release all convicts from jail because in that new constitution they might abolish punishment.'

'I could get behind that, but no, Maru, that's not what I'm arguing. To use your example, I'm saying that if we're writing a new constitution, just suspend executions until it's done, because there's a chance that the death penalty might itself go, and then you can't bring back the people you executed. And Maru, don't you see—what this does is it puts the decision in the hands of the Commune. If they want Jagat back, if they really want him back, they can just negotiate that into the Charter by retrospectively abolishing the sleep of death. I'm taking the decision out of the hands of the tribunal, out of the hands of the Confederation, *out of my own hands*. I'm giving the choice to the Commune!'

Don't do this case like a Guardian. Do it like a Communard.

'Hm,' said Maru.

'What are you hmming about?'

'About the last thing you said. This choice you're going to give to the Commune. Didn't they have exactly this choice a hundred years ago? And they chose not to exercise it? Don't you think that's a little weird?'

'How do you mean?'

'I'm thinking of the amnesty that was negotiated into the Charter. It was an amnesty for all crimes committed *after* the assassination of Director Purul, until the signing of the Charter. In fact, they made it explicit. The amnesty clock began ticking from noon on 9 August. That excludes exactly one person from the scope of the amnesty: Jagat, who assassinated the director that morning. Why didn't the Commune try to bring him back, in the one moment where it would have been easier to do so than at any point in the last hundred years?'

'The negotiation documents—'

'Were all permanently erased from the databases after the Charter was signed as part of the Pact of Forgetting.'

Nila shifted. 'I don't know. It may have been a red line for the Council. You can see it, no? You can agree to a lot of things, but can you really agree to amnesty for the man who assassinated your own director?'

'If Jagat really meant all that to the Commune ...' Maru shook his head. 'I don't know. There's something off.'

'Bracket it for a while?' Nila said. 'We'll come back to it later. Tell me what you think of my argument.'

'Well,' said Maru, chewing his lip. 'I guess it's worth a shot. And it gets you—and more importantly, *him*—a reprieve, if it works. But you do know what this means, right?'

'I do,' said Nila. 'This argument depends on the Commune winning. If Noor and Co. lose, then we're lost as well.'

'You wanted to be a part of *Certain Questions of Great Public Importance*,' Maru grinned. 'Well, you got your wish, in a way.'

'I'm going to draft the application now,' said Nila.

'Nila,' said Maru. 'It's still a long shot, you know? I can see a thousand objections a tribunal might raise.'

Nila nodded. 'You're right. I hope this works, but we need to have our main arguments ready.'

'Using clever little procedural objections to get a stay of execution and take the issue outside the Confederation,' said Maru admiringly. 'You sure you don't want to do criminal defence full time, Nila?'

'Oh, shut up!' said Nila. 'It's just this once. But one moment …' Her face fell. 'Maru, we forgot one detail. That hundred-year time period, it's biology, not law. What's the point of getting a stay if his body will break down?'

'You don't need to worry about that. The actual time period is closer to a hundred and seven years or so. Hundred years is just a convenient legal fiction. Which reminds me—cryochamber when?'

'Afternoon. I have another meeting with the director first. But Maru, I need to ask you something.'

'Yes?'

'I want to tell you if I'm being crazy.'

Quickly, she told him of what had happened the evening in the Zone, the continued sense that she was being followed through the city. 'I don't know. I … I *am* tired, I guess.'

Maru hesitated. 'It's not impossible, you know? There are a whole lot of people who were probably looking forward to the day that Jagat would finally be gone, buried forever. And then you come along, and in the same week as *Council vs Commune*, which is going to change everything … people are going to want to know what's happening. In particular, people with the means and the ability to surveil you.'

'That reminds me—Maru, I found out about the Apoptosis Plan.'

'Yeah?'

She filled him in.

'I've never heard of this,' said Maru. 'But Nila, it wouldn't surprise me if something like this did exist, deep in the bowels of the Directorate. It has all the imprints of the kind of stuff they do. I'm *very* impressed with your friends' espionage network for digging it up, though.'

'It would explain some things, wouldn't it?'

'Yes—if there is such a detailed strategy, then those behind it would absolutely not want to see an unexpected variable as large as Jagat enter the stage,' said Maru. 'And they'd want to stop you by any means necessary. But Nila, I wonder how deep it goes. Remember that internal dispute I was telling you about, within the Directorate?'

'Yeah?'

'It seems to have gotten worse. Borderline mutiny from the deputy director, I'm hearing. I don't know if even the Directorate is unified on this case, so this surveillance business ... it could really be anyone. And from what you've told me, it could even be the Commune—or its factions.'

They looked at each other.

'So Naina was right.,' said Nila.

'Eh?'

'Our role. The things we can't help.'

'Huh, Nila?'

'Oh, sorry!' Nila shook her head. 'I thought you knew?'

'Knew what?'

She reached for her wristheld, and went back into the guardian archives, until she got to Naina L.'s profile page. She expanded the screen and brought up the open letter. 'I thought you must have already read this.'

Maru mouthed the words of the opening paragraph to himself. His brow furrowed. 'Huh.'

'What?'

'I could have sworn I didn't see this when I logged into her profile two days ago.'

'How's that possible?'

'Hang on.' Maru turned to his own wristheld, and got busy with something. Nila waited, shifting from one foot to the other.

'Ha!' Maru said, suddenly. 'Knew it!'

'What, what?'

'The good old metadata check,' he grinned. 'Nila, this file was added to Naina's profile late Wednesday afternoon.'

'What the ...'

'Yep. Fake, through and through.'

'You mean to say …'

'Someone added this to Naina's profile page in the … well-founded expectation that at some point, the parallels between your situations would become so stark that you'd come looking. And you did.'

Nila felt a stab of disappointment that Naina's voice had not been her own, before it was quickly replaced by irritation. 'Ugh. Am I that easy to read?'

'I guess we all react predictably under extreme stress,' said Maru.

'It was a *rhetorical* question. Didn't deserve your serious answer.' Nila took a deep breath. 'But why though? Is this Mehmandost Naram or someone trying yet again to, I dunno, put some subliminal thoughts in my head about breaching impartiality to solve this problem?'

'Someone's probably trying to influence you, although this sort of stuff really isn't the president's style, no?' Maru chewed the edge of his pencil. 'But then again … if these people were good enough to get through the security protocol to make changes … why would they leave such an obvious metadata trail? Almost like they *wanted* you to find out this was fake.'

'And *then* what?' Nila groaned. 'What is this 12-D chess?'

Maru stood decisively. 'I don't know who's playing it, but very well. If you're going to High Town today, you're not going to go alone.'

14
He Will Live

AS SOON AS THE SKIMMER PASSED WITHIN THE long shadows of High Town's towers, she heard Maru's voice in her earpiece.

'You know this was less about your safety, and more about me getting to see Peruma from the sky after three years, no?'

Nila laughed, feeling the breeze in her hair. Having Maru with her, if only as a spectator looking out from her eyes, was oddly soothing, although they both knew that if anything happened, the most he could do was raise the alarm.

'Now that I *am* giving you this privilege,' she said 'why don't you take us through a scenic route and let me enjoy the view?'

Before Maru could speak, the skimmer came to a juddering halt, as if a fist had clamped around it.

'What the—'

'Wait—don't—' said Maru, as Nila pressed the power button. The skimmer revved, but didn't move. A shadow passed. Nila felt as if she'd been scanned to her bones.

The fist released her. The skimmer moved.

'*What* was that?'

'They've activated their Code Black security system,' Maru sounded almost shaken. 'Highest level of alert. You see the buildings?' High Town's skyscrapers were still draped in black, although it was translucent in the daylight. 'From those windows,' said Maru, his voice low, 'there are at least five guns trained on you—and on every other skimmer in the skylanes.'

'Are you serious!'

'Welcome to paranoid High Town on the hundredth anniversary of the revolution, heh. Still want that guided tour?'

Nila shook herself. 'Actually, I do.'

Maru murmured directions, guiding the skimmer along a winding route up the east side of Dominion Hill. Nila tried to put the guns out of her mind as they passed beneath high, arched bridges that connected one tower to another, through transparent glass tunnels between skimmer hangars and above hanging sky-gardens …

… until something caught her eye: far below, a mesh of intricate canals divided the ground into sections of glistening whiteness centred around a small circular island with a black stone. Something about the arrangement caught her gaze, and held it.

'What's that?'

Maru looked through her eyes. 'That's Purul's samadhi.'

The director's resting place.

'Can we go down there, or will someone shoot me out of the sky?'

'Should be safe as long as we don't make any sudden movements.'

Nila checked the time. She was early.

'I want to see it.' She nudged the skimmer downwards. It descended along a curved mandalium pathway, circling the samadhi from different angles. Further down, the white sheets resolved themselves into bowers of rajnigandha flowers, shimmering in the breeze.

The scent flooded her senses as she drew level with the ground. The heady, enveloping sweetness of the rajnigandha blended with dew and fresh water, a concoction you could get drunk on.

'Every director,' Maru said in her ear, 'would design their own future samadhi.'

Nila alighted. There was a narrow path that wound its way by the side of the canals and amidst the flowers, to the central island. Guns quite forgotten, she walked, letting her hand trail among the rajnigandha flowers, feeling petal, stem and fern slip through her fingers.

The pathways curved into little bridges over the canals, criss-crossing and turning back upon each other, heading slowly towards the centre. 'It's called *Forever Undecided*,' Maru said. 'The structure symbolises the impossibility of ever really knowing that you've done the right thing.'

'A little on the nose, no?'

'What did I tell you about High Town's torrid affair with subtlety?'

The last of the bridges circled around the island, arching down into a scattering of rajnigandhas. The black stone that she had seen from above revealed itself as a statue. Upon a plinth, marble-wrought Purul sat on a tree trunk, his chin cupped in his right palm, his face turned towards a book that he held in his left hand. It was the Purul of the Hall of

Remembrance: never entirely at ease in his power, a restless search for the shadow of peace.

You fell/As the amaltas falls, abloom/In the summer of your life/A memory of gold.

Her gaze ascended over the samadhi, and arrowed southwards: above the Tower City, above the ruins of the Bulwark Zone and the Hedgehog's Needle, above the glistening stone of Unity Bridge and the glinting silver of the river, down to the flowing weave of the Commune, until it came to rest in the centre of Reunion Square.

Across the sundered halves of Peruma they met each other's gaze, Purul and Jagat. The fallen amaltas, in full bloom. The falling star, whose descent had birthed a new world. Two men, entangled in sleep and death, unwitting architects of an origin story that had lasted a hundred years—and which she had forty-eight hours to unravel.

Her eyes travelled to the plinth below Purul's statue, which bore the epitaph:

What I shall leave will not be worth a tragedy.

She did not know how long she stood there, looking at the words, then up at Purul's head, bent over his book, and then back to his epitaph once again; until, at last, there was Maru's voice, gentle, insistent: 'It's time to go, Nila.'

'Ah, yes. Right.' Nila turned and slowly retraced her steps, away from the island and the centre, back to her waiting skimmer, back in the air. As the scent of rajnigandha dissolved into memory, she saw a line of people trooping into the samadhi, little stick-like figures that grew tinier as she rose.

She and Maru did not speak again until she saw the familiar shape of the Tiger's Jaw upon the peak of Dominion Hill.

'Just so you know,' said Maru, as the skimmer began to descend, 'they have jammers all over the Directorate, so I'm going to get cut off very soon. Not that anyone will try to do anything to you *in* the Directorate, but—'

His voice was lost in a rush of static.

Famous last words, thought Nila.

The office, she noted, was un-curated, other than the holograms on the wall. *No effort for you this time.*

'We'll have to make this a little quick, Guardian,' said Pulis. 'I'm quite tied up with preparations for Monday's case.'

'I know,' she said. 'Thank you for agreeing to see me again.'

The director leaned forward, one hand beneath his chin. 'I figured that you wouldn't have asked for another meeting unless you had something substantive to share.'

'Yes.'

'And? Like us, you're less than forty-eight hours away from arguments, aren't you, Guardian?'

'My investigations are ongoing,' said Nila, 'I have good reason to believe that what I told you last time was true. Jagat R. was not the man who shot Director Purul. A hundred years ago, the Directorate committed the greatest injustice it could have. On Monday, if the sentence isn't overturned, that injustice will be made permanent.'

Pulis pursed his lips. 'What have you found in four days, Guardian, that nobody else found in a hundred years?'

'Nobody looked, Director.' She took a deep breath. 'The silence of Jagat, which the Directorate judges took as the silence of guilt, was actually the silence of sacrifice. Jagat was innocent of murder. What he was guilty of—if guilt is the right word—was going to the sleep of death in someone else's stead.'

'And the *real* guilty party, then?'

'I have an idea. And I'm halfway there. But to get all the way there, Director, I need access to the Purul archives.'

'How will the archives help?'

'Director, I've told you as much as I can without laying out the particulars of my case.'

'I appreciate that,' said Pulis. 'Just as I'm sure you appreciate the fact that you've told me nothing that materially changes the situation from last time.'

'I've made actual progress.'

'In no way that I can see, and in no way that you say you can reveal to me.'

'Fair enough,' said Nila, casting around for more words, better words. 'What I am asking you to do is to take a chance on me.'

'But *why* would I do that, Guardian Nila?'

It was the sound of a door closing, once and for all. Nila sighed.

'Convince me.' Pulis said.

The door opened, the tiniest of cracks.

'Director,' she said, 'the last time we met, you said that some memories are better off turning into ghosts.'

'Yes.'

'The thing about ghosts is that they never really go away. You've seen what my pendant says. Do you know where that line is from?'

'From *No More Regrets.*' Pulis inclined his head. 'As a matter of fact, I am a great reader of fantasy webnovels.' He gave her a sudden and very uncharacteristically impish grin. 'And because you're never going to find out, I don't mind telling you that I also write metafictions on the *Volcano of Peruma* forum, obviously under a different name. As they say, I know my stuff.'

She smiled, refraining from telling him that the more enterprising members of the forum—including herself—had long ago deduced the identity behind the username *DarkTiger757*. 'And do you remember, Director, the story of *No More Regrets*?'

'In the outline. It came out a few years ago.'

'May I?'

'Go on.'

'There is a city. A happy city, unified and harmonious. The only problem is that its inhabitants are plagued by recurring nightmares that tear them from their sleep, screaming. Nightmares they forget the moment they wake. Nightmares that are passed down generations.

'One day, the wise women and men of the city come together to seek a solution. A decree is passed, ordering all citizens to remember anything they could when they wake up. A glimpse, a vision, a thought, a sense. Soon, the central square is filled with pages and pages of recollection seen through a clouded mirror. But still, they are none the wiser.

'After much reflection and debate, they come to the conclusion that in a time out of mind, their city was cursed to endure this fate. So the task shifts from the interpreters of dreams to the historians and the mythopoets. What did their ancestors do that brought to the city—this happy city—an eternity of nightmares and forgetting?

'I won't trouble you with a chapter-by-chapter account of how it unravels. But here is the explanation. Long ago, all the cities upon the continent were given a choice by the gods—they could pick *one* event, and have it erased from collective memory for five hundred years. This could be a humiliating defeat in war. It could be a famine or a plague. Or it could be a terrible crime.

'All the cities rejected this offer, because they knew it was a trap. Except one. You see, this city was unable to live with itself because it had committed nameless horrors against a section of its own people. And even as it denied it all to the world, it would give *anything* to not have to stay with the memory of what it had done. To just be able to forget. And so, it accepted the offer. To become a happy society, untroubled by its crimes, except for the nightmares.

'Except the price could not remain unpaid forever. Five hundred years passed. And just as the historians and the mythopoets were reaching the truth of what their ancestors had done, the dam broke and all the memories came flooding back. Without warning or preparation, without time to adapt or to rationalise, or create new myths and justifications, this society was forced to look at itself in an unclouded mirror.

'Not to give you any spoilers, Director, because the last chapter's really great, but it didn't go well for them.'

'I remember now,' said Pulis. 'Great story. No wonder it went viral.'

'And so, Director, the point is this: you can turn your memories into ghosts, and they will still haunt you. Last time we met, you said this city needs to heal. Why not let it heal with the truth? So what if the truth needs a ghost to be made flesh once more?'

'Have you been conspiring with my deputy director?' said Pulis lightly.

'I've never met her in my life.'

'Remarkably similar thought process. And one that I might be persuaded by,' said Pulis, 'if I had reason to think that you were after the truth, that you were actually getting there like you say, and that you were not a useful—if unintentional—tool for the Commune, muddying clear waters with some … reasonable doubt. But—' he raised a hand. 'I'll think about it.'

'Mhm. One final question, Director Pulis. Can you tell me about Operation Carbuncle?'

Pulis raised an eyebrow. 'What about Operation Carbuncle?'

'The one that Secretary Maran believed was the greatest mistake the Council ever made?' She watched the director closely for a reaction.

Pulis' face remained neutral, unaffected. 'Did she, now? I presume you got that out of the memorial museum?'

'You've never been?'

Pulis shrugged. 'This obsession with Secretary Maran is something I've never really understood. Or rather, I do understand it, but it doesn't interest me, personally.'

'But you *do* know about Operation Carbuncle.'

A tinge of impatience entered Pulis' voice. 'I am the Director of Peruma. It's my job to know Council history, especially around the time of the mutiny. And if you want to read up, there's Professor Surma Katoch—'

'Well, it's interesting you say that to a guardian,' said Nila, 'because the first thing we're taught is to go to the source. Last night, I *did* read Professor Surma Katoch, and I read about how Operation Carbuncle was named after Union journal *The Carbuncle*. And you know what else they teach us in the Chapterhouse, Director? Always double-check the footnotes. So I did. And here's where it gets interesting. In *A Comprehensive History of the Peruman Civil War*, Professor Surma Katoch's citation for Operation Carbuncle is an article in the *Annals and Events* journal, titled 'Some Thoughts on the Material Formation of Public Opinion', authored by a certain Professor Surma Katoch. When you go to the 'Some Thoughts' article, and look for Operation Carbuncle, you get a reference to a chapter called 'The Barricade', authored by Professor Surma Katoch, in a collection of essays called *A Modern History of Peruma in 100 Objects*, also edited by Professor Surma Katoch. And when you go to *that* article, you get a reference back to *A Comprehensive History of the Peruman Civil War*, by … well, you know who. In short, Operation Carbuncle seems to only exist in a self-referential perpetual loop of footnotes in the collected writings of Professor Surma Katoch.'

'History is an inexact science,' said Pulis.

'But the archives aren't.'

'Are you really suggesting that Milana Maran was—'

'I am suggesting nothing at the moment,' she held his gaze. 'I'm not interested in Milana Maran for her own sake, but I *am* interested in the death of Purul, and whether Operation Carbuncle had anything to do with that. His documents—'

Something passed across Pulis' face. 'I can assure you,' he said, 'that Director Purul's documents do not mention any Operation Carbuncle.'

'Why not just let me see for myself, Director? If you want me out of your hair, if you don't want me snooping around stumbling upon … other inconvenient things, just authorise my access to the archives. Two hours. No recording equipment. How does that sound?'

'It sounds,' said Pulis, 'like a very crude bluff from someone who has no cards left.'

Nila laughed, trying to still the rising feverishness that she felt. 'You just have to ask yourself, Director, about what it might cost you if you decided to call the bluff, and turned out to be wrong.' She stood. 'And just so you know, I have a parallel investigation about this ongoing in the Commune, so, like any good guardian, I'll be cross-checking information. You have some time to consider it. I'm visiting the cryochamber today, so I won't need to go to the archives until tomorrow.'

She watched his face again, but it did not change. 'I already told you I'll consider it. I take it that there's nothing more,' he said.

'You'll hear from me when there is.'

Pulis allowed his upper lip to curl ever so slightly. 'Good luck for your investigation, Guardian. Whatever's left of it.'

'How did that go?' Maru's voice returned to her very suddenly as the Tiger's Jaw fell away beneath the skimmer.

'As well as it could, given that he has three decades of experience in both persuasion and bluffing, and I just started this week.'

'Agh. I'm sorry. No archives trip, then?'

'I doubt it. Our Milana Maran angle got a lot tougher. But I do think—' Nila paused. 'Or rather, I don't think he was lying when he said that Purul's archives have nothing on Operation Carbuncle. I don't think Pulis himself knows much about Operation Carbuncle.'

'Well—oh look, there's the cryochamber already, to your south.'

The skimmer banked, and Nila saw it.

The cryochamber was located within a complex of buildings close to the Directorate, which had been the site of old Peruma's justice-dispensing machinery. The other buildings had been decommissioned, with most of their functions shifting to the Confederation. But the cryochamber building, being far too expensive to move, had been the subject of a grudging and ill-tempered compromise between Council and Commune, according to which the cryochamber would continue to be located where it was, but under the physical control of the Commune (the only permanent Commune presence in old High Town).

It took shape as she descended, a distinctive tear-shaped building that had gotten its architect roundly pilloried by the Wits, although he had maintained until his dying day that it was meant to resemble the shape of dreams; a century of dreaming.

That's not really the defence you think it is, the Wits had hooted.

Nila alighted on a skimmer pad just outside the building and stepped out to meet a bored-looking Commune man standing patrol by a large glass door. She transmitted her credentials to his pendant, and watched his face snap into sudden alertness.

'Guardian … Nila?'

'That's right. Is there a problem?'

'Not at all. Go in.'

'Thank you.'

Just as she moved past him, there was a pressure on her arm. The patrolman's voice was in her ear, soft and low.

'From the SRVJM, a message: *no information exists*.'

'Oh!' Nila's breath caught.

The union journal. Milana Maran. No information.

As quickly, her arm was free again and the patrolman had snapped back to attention. She forced herself not to look back at him.

The doors slid open into a white, sterilised passageway with a low, sloping roof. At the end of the passage, there was another set of opaque doors.

'That was … something,' Maru commented, as she crossed the passage.

'I feel like the Commune might be teetering on the edge of full-scale civil war if the SRVJM has factional allies to this extent,' Nila said. 'And at the worst possible time.' *The Apoptosis Plan.* She paused by the door. 'But let's focus. You ready?'

'Let's go.'

Nila stepped forward. The doors of the cryochamber opened. She walked into pale blue light and a wave of cold air hit her. Her teeth chattered.

'Can you cool it with the shivering,' Maru's voice complained into her earpiece. 'My whole world is shaking.'

'Even the Wits would disown you for that pun,' said Nila. Hugging herself to preserve some body heat, she walked deeper into the chamber.

She was in a round room with a domed roof supported by a row of pillars. A thin pall of mist meandered through the air, grey and ghostly in the blue light.

'Very afterlife-y,' Maru muttered in her ear, articulating her thoughts. 'Do you think they do it for show?'

'Show whom?' she muttered back. 'It's not like this place gets a lot of visitors.'

In the spaces between the pillars, eight cryoboxes filled the room. Diamond-shaped and resin-grey, they rested heavily upon the floor, giving the appearance of immense fixity. The tops were transparent, letting Nila look upon the features of the eight women and men who, in the last hundred years, had been sentenced to the sleep of death.

Their faces were at rest, calm and untroubled. After all, the cryogenic process was commenced only after the convicts had been lulled into a gradual sleep through an incremental dose of sedatives. The official version held that this was to reduce the trauma of the sleep of death. The Wits maintained that it was to ease the collective conscience of the city. Looking at the faces in the cryoboxes, it was easy to tell yourself that they were only sleeping.

Jagat's box was at the far end. Nila approached it, quietening her tread, even though she was the only person in the room and *he* couldn't hear her.

Over the edge of the box, she looked at last into the face that had upended her life.

The familiar youthful features, the hair neatly drawn back, the slightly parted lips with a purple tinge around the edges and the white smock of the convict, plain and without a wrinkle. She had seen it all before.

But here, with just a glass partition before them, there was something more.

'Ernian,' said Nila softly.

'Just what I was thinking,' Maru murmured.

Ernian was a distinctively Peruman word for a distinctively Peruman feeling. It was difficult to explain, because it was a composite of so many unknowable things. In the course of a lifetime, where countless possible futures winked in and out of existence with every breath you took, *ernian* was that moment when you first grew aware of all the lives you had not lived—and never would. In the brief, incandescent moments after the revolution, when everything had seemed possible, it had been the poets' favourite word. Years of overuse turned it into a cliché, and now it lived on as an archaism, a memory of unease, a name for a feeling that nobody wished any longer to name.

She saw *ernian* sketched into the creases and contours of Jagat's sleeping face, with a softness that would have done an artist proud.

She pressed her nose against the glass. There was a long-running debate about whether you dreamed in a sleep of death, unsettled because none of the seven people who had been resurrected could definitively remember either way.

But looking at Jagat, it was hard to believe that he wasn't dreaming.

He was so very different from his statue in the Commune, which claimed to capture the moment of trial: there, the kneeling, the gag, the determined look of a man who was utterly fortified in his faith, crenelated in his convictions.

But here was another man, a man wreathed in *ernian*, who did not seem quite so sure of himself.

'Do you think that in the last moment before he lost consciousness,' Nila murmured, 'he wondered if his life would mean anything?'

'Nila!'

Maru's voice, sharp and urgent, splintered the mood, jerking her back into the world. 'What?'

'What's that?'

She looked up.

'No, no, look down again so I can see—look at his face—not the eyes, come down—*there!*'

'What is it?' She was looking once again at the partly open lips and a hint of the teeth that they concealed.

'The edge of the lips—that purple colour—that's not the lighting, is it?'

Nila focused her gaze. Maru was right. What she had taken earlier to be a play of the ambient light upon Jagat's face was an odd, purplish tinge that discoloured the corners of the lips, and beyond. Once noticed, it was impossible to unsee.

'There's a pattern—can you see—look more closely?' Maru said.

Nila screwed her eyes, gluing her face to the glass. The purple colour resolved itself into filament-like criss-crossing lines; a grid of sorts.

Maru's breathing grew ragged in her ears.

'Hang on for a moment,' he said. 'Let me look it up. Don't go anywhere. Don't look away!'

She maintained her position, ignoring her aching neck and struggling not to lose focus. After what seemed an eternity, Maru spoke again.

'It can't—but it is …'

'What is it?' she repeated.

'Nila, the purple discolouration … it's a symptom of last-stage mandilicosis II-A.'

Memory kicked in, a dim recollection of basic medical history lessons from student days.

'Cancer?'

'The most virulent of all the mandalium-related cancers, yes—and the one they finally found a cure for just—yes, just a year after the revolution.'

'Wait,' said Nila. 'When you say advanced, *how* advanced, Maru?'

'By the time it's visible on the lips, it's more or less the end. Nila. At the time of his sentencing, he'd have had a few more months to live, tops. Give or take a few weeks.'

'*What!*' She swallowed. 'And he knew?'

'Of course! They were obsessed with mandilicosis because you didn't even have to go down into the mines to have it. He was a walking corpse that day upon Unity Bridge. And he knew it.'

Nila stumbled back from the sarcophagus. Her brain rebelled, refusing to factor in this new information into the neatly-patterned case diary that she had assembled in her head. Of all the questions that she could have asked then, the first one that found its way to her lips was not the one she expected.

'And if he was to be resurrected now—now that we've found the cure—he'd live?'

Maru's answer came after a very long time.

'Yes. He will live.'

15
I Need a Miracle

'ALRIGHT, THAT'S QUITE ENOUGH COLD COFFEE for the day.' Maru reached around and gently pressed down on her hand until the half-full glass was back on the table.

'Just when I was fuelling myself into a sugar high,' grumbled Nila.

'Nila, you need to think clearly—'

'*Well*, I've found that I think *most* clearly immediately after cold coffee—'

'No, you're not having any more of that.' Maru took the glass, stood, and, ignoring Nila's squawk of protest, carried it to the sink and poured the remaining liquid down the drain.

'Now,' he resumed, walking back to the table, 'let's get into it.'

'Hmph.'

'Tell me. What do we—*you*—know so far?'

'Well.' With an effort, Nila straightened, blinking. 'Before that, did you ever think your obsession with cancers and occupational injuries would end up helping you be a class traitor?'

'Are you complaining?'

'Never been more grateful. Now let's see.' She started to tick things off her fingers. *One,* Director Purul was a unifier, well-liked in High Town and Low Town. *Two*, on the day of his death, he was going to address the Maidan, but we don't know what he was going to say. *Three,* his secretary, Milana Maran, was there when the bomb exploded, and saw Jagat appear with a gun, but closed her eyes at the last moment, which indicates that she only heard the shot from close range. *Four,* Milana Maran also heard Jagat say, 'In the name of the Commune unborn, die'. *Five*, nobody used the word "commune" in the run-up to Purul's assassination. *Six*, at the end of her life, Milana Maran wrote a letter to the director expressing that Operation Carbuncle had been a mistake. But we don't know what that means, because the only reference for Operation Carbuncle is Surma Katoch's fever dream footnotes and, according to the SRVJM, there's no information on *The Carbuncle*—it's like it never actually existed. Nor does the Commune seem to have any data or information on Milana Maran herself, which either means that our theory about her involvement is bunk, or that she was a super-super-secret Commune spy before the Commune even officially existed. *Seven*, Jagat did not defend himself at his trial. *Eight*, on the day of his conviction and sentence, Jagat was suffering from advanced cancer and had only a few more months to live. *Nine*, on a scale of mild flu to mandilicosis, how screwed are we?'

'Right,' said Maru. 'And the obvious solution—'

'The mandilicosis really puts a seal on it,' said Nila glumly. 'The motive has strengthened a hundredfold. He knew he was going to die. What better way to go than in a blaze of glory? We'll probably never know if he was acting alone, but that doesn't matter.'

'And yet,' said Maru, 'something still doesn't add up.'

Nila shook her head. 'There's too much unexplained. The unborn Commune. Operation Carbuncle. And then ...'

She let the words trail off, but they both knew what was unsaid, lingering in the air between them.

Ernian.

Because the look on Jagat's face was not the look of a man who made his last sacrifice in service of a coming revolution. There was little there of the convinced rebel who would take this way out over lingering decay in a hospital bed. What they had seen, instead, was half-confusion and half-regret, a welter of dimly expressed feeling.

'Our problem is that we still don't have an alternate theory,' said Maru. 'If there was a fourth person, then either Milana Maran didn't see them, or both she *and* Jagat were covering for them. That still doesn't give us any clue about who this person was.'

'Yeah, and on Milana Maran being a Commune agent,' said Nila, 'any luck finding linguistic tricks in her testimony?'

'I reread the records twice,' said Maru. 'Nothing stood out.'

'*That's* not very helpful, Maru!' she snapped.

'I know,' said Maru. His quiet tone calmed her almost immediately.

'But I did look her up a bit,' said Maru, after a while. 'Milana Maran.'

'And?'

'Typical bureaucrat trajectory. Came from the Zone, brilliant results in school and college, rose through the ranks, the usual. Except one thing stood out, Nila ... it seems that she absolutely *hated* Low Town.'

'Shamming, most likely.'

'No, no, not during her years as secretary. There she was obviously barred from political writing. But you know, the networks never forget—there are some essays of hers floating around online from her college days. Referred to striking miners as "termites" who need to be tackled with a firm hand. Wanted to send in the BSF to break up strikes. One of those familiar stories of an economic libertarian turning very quickly to violence.'

'What in …!'

'Yeah, you can chalk some of it down to undergrad over-enthusiasm, and maybe she mellowed with the years, but—she sounded venomous, Nila.'

'There goes the spy theory, then,' said Nila.

They were silent again.

'We have one day more,' Maru said at last.

She nodded, glancing at the timer.

37:25:51

'What do we do now?' said Maru.

Nila closed her eyes. Once, in the years long gone by, her mother had taught her a way of quietening her mind, of reaching deep into its recesses, to seek out and weave frayed threads of thought, like putting broken crystal back together.

She tried that now, and found there was nothing to reassemble.

She opened her eyes. 'I don't know,' she whispered. 'I need a miracle, Maru.'

There was a knock on the door.

Maru raised an eyebrow. 'Come in,' he called.

The door opened. Five pupils walked in.

Noor. Suneen. Raman. Raisa. Raghul.

Five of the pupils who'd been assigned to *Council vs Commune.* All five, on the Commune side.

They all looked exhausted, running on fumes and adrenaline, their hair messy, eyes swollen, clothes rumpled. They probably felt as dead as she did, Nila thought.

'Hello?' said Maru, uncertainly. 'Can I make you some coffee?'

'No, no,' rasped Noor, avoiding Maru's eyes. 'This will be quick. Nila. We have some news.'

Nila forced herself to not look from Noor to Maru. 'Tell me.'

Noor gestured at the group wearily. 'You see we're five. This evening, Velu invoked one of his three prerogative options, and quit.'

'What!' She had no time to feel schadenfreude, vindication, or anything at all. 'Why?'

'He's not obliged to give a reason if it's prerogative. But you can guess. He's from High Town. In the last analysis, he couldn't bring himself to be for this side.'

'Ah,' said Nila carefully. 'I see.'

'So we're one short. And because the hearing is in two days, we immediately applied to the Executive Committee to choose our own replacement instead of accepting an automatic assignment from the waitlist. We were just told that the committee has granted our request. It's a no-brainer, Nila. We want you.'

Nila sat back down, her legs jelly.

'You know this case as well as any of us,' Noor continued. 'You've thought about this as obsessively as any of us. You can literally walk into our briefing with Senior Majeet and be right at home. So … Nila?'

'Wait, wait, one minute. *Council vs Commune* clashes with the Jagat trial,' said Nila. 'How am I going to be in two places at the same time?'

'We asked President Naram about this,' Suneen spoke for the first time. 'He said that if there's a direct conflict then, given the special circumstances, he's willing to exercise his discretion and schedule Jagat's trial to after hours on Monday. So you can finish up with us at four o'clock, and then proceed to the Jagat case.'

'How generous of him,' Maru snarked.

'And the next two days?' said Nila.

Noor and Suneen exchanged glances. 'We're in briefings with Senior Majeet today evening, and through tomorrow.'

'So between now and Monday, I won't be able to do any more work on Jagat's trial?'

'Ahm, yes,' said Noor. 'But Nila, you've been working on it all week. By now you know what you're going to argue on Monday, right?'

'Hah. I think I know what I'm *not* going to argue. But for the rest … '

'If you have specific research tasks for the trial,' said Suneen, 'we'll put two of our juniors on them. Is there anything there that needs your personal attention?'

'I mean,' said Nila. 'I have some stuff to figure out still.'

'Come on, Nila,' Noor looked at her intently. 'If anyone can shift gears over forty-eight hours, it's you. Haven't you always told us how easy it is for you to compartmentalise?'

Nila looked at Maru, who suddenly got very busy studying the grain of the wood upon the table.

'How much time do I have to decide?' she said.

'We need an answer now,' said Noor. 'I know this is a lot, Nila, and I'm sorry we're overwhelming you without any warning—but the meeting with Senior Majeet is scheduled directly after this, and you know the moment he starts giving us references to look up, it's going to be backs to the wall till Monday.'

'Yeah, fair enough, I get that,' said Nila. She stood. 'Give me a minute?' She walked to the window.

From the Hedgehog's Needle she saw the glittering lights of High Town, an almost vertical conglomeration rising up into the sky, the dark waters of the Urai, and then the dimmer glimmerings of the Commune, a softer light, more uncertain, more precarious, more … fragile.

There was a heaving in her chest, and her breath came in ragged gasps, almost as if she was coming up for air, throwing her hand out for …

… a lifeline.

Nila closed her eyes and took one long, shuddering breath, willing herself into composure. One more time, she ran over Jagat's case in her head: facts, evidence, testimonies, silences, inferences, deductions, one story, two stories, three stories, a self-contained narrative, a narrative with jagged edges waiting to be made whole, evidence that might or might not exist, which she might or might not find with only a day to go …

She opened her eyes. The Commune was before her, the most fragile of weaves. She willed those lights to come together, to conceive intelligibility, anything to make a miracle unnecessary.

Nothing did.

Nila turned. 'Alright. I'll do it.'

There was an audible release of breath. Noor's face broke into a smile. 'Welcome to the team, Guardian Nila.'

Something in her chest unclenched, but what came rushing in to fill the space was not relief, but the strange emptiness at the moment of a wish's fulfilment. 'What now?'

'I'll get the clerks to draw up your appearance memo and inbox it to you,' said Noor. 'It should reach you for your signature by the time we get to Majeet's chambers. I'll fill you in on case status on the way?'

'Yes. Let's go,' Nila muttered. She crossed the room almost in a rush, taking Noor by surprise, and forcing the rest to follow her out. Their steps echoed in the corridor, where the lamps seemed to be casting a light that swirled and whirled around them.

'Run it down for me, please,' she said. 'Text, structure, history—in that order.'

'On text,' said Noor, taking the lead for the group, 'the word "amend" is ambiguous—nothing to suggest that it limits the nature of the changes you can make to the Charter—'

'But cuts both ways,' said Nila. 'Implied limitations exist, as the tribunal has said a few times.'

They filed into the elevator.

'Yes, hence structure, to inform text,' said Noor, as they lurched down. 'The Charter's preamble says that it is meant to be *temporary*. Hence—'

'But *temporary* can mean temporary *in time*, or temporary *until* a defined event,' said Nila. 'There's the tribunal's secondary picketing judgement on that—'

'Yes, so here we have to argue that both are the same—temporary, meant to last for a hundred years, both a time period and the event—'

'The event being?'

'The event being the end of the freeze on Charter change.'

'That's circular.'

'But not viciously so, and that's where the historical argument—your point about the very identity of the Charter being transitional—comes in, Nila. The decision in—'

Noor's voice was in her ear, dissolving into the rhythm and movement of their steps as they passed into the chamber complex of the Confederation's seniors. Nila heard a week's worth of sleepless nights compressed into crystalline sentences, her mind taking in the information, tallying and cross-referencing it with her own knowledge of the Charter, moulding the two together into understanding, into interpretation, into argument; this, here, at last, was *life*.

They were now walking on plush, carpeted floors, their feet sinking into softness, through a lush corridor adorned with chandeliers and lamps. Heavy brass doors lined the walls, with the names of the Confederation's seniors blazoned on the side. Noor finally stopped before a door labelled 'J. MAJEET'. Through the crack underneath the door, Nila saw a chink of light.

Her wristheld pinged. The memo was in her email. Nila drew up the document on a viewing screen, and detached the stylus from her wristheld.

Noor nodded.

There it was, the appearance memo between them, carrying the electronic signature of President Mehmandost Naram certifying that Nila was now formally engaged, in her capacity as a guardian pupil, in the case of *Council vs Commune: Regarding Certain Questions of Great Public Importance Concerning the Interpretation of the Charter of Peace and Unity,* appearing on behalf of the Commune, on the terms and conditions set out hereinafter. A space at the bottom for her signature.

It was all she'd ever wanted.

She let the stylus drop from her fingers, watched it float, in slow motion, back into its holder.

'I'm sorry,' Nila whispered. 'I can't.'

'What?' said Noor.

Nila turned and ran. She ran back through the carpeted corridor, through the chamber complex, back across the stone floor of the Great Hall, up into the Needle. She leaned against the side of the elevator as it took her up, winded, a stitch in her side, and stumbled back into her chamber where Maru was sitting exactly where she'd left him.

'At last,' he said. 'I was starting to get worried.'

'I couldn't do it,' said Nila, her voice a half-sob 'I just couldn't, Maru.'

'Of course you couldn't,' Maru said.

She squinted at him. 'And how were *you* so sure?'

'As if you were going to give up on Jagat,' said Maru. 'Forget the principles, your pride wouldn't allow you to let this go. You and I both know if you didn't spend every waking minute between now and Monday morning working to save Jagat—and I'm *not* referring to a procedural objection on a wing and a prayer—you wouldn't be able to live with yourself, ever.'

Takes one to know one, Nila almost said, before checking herself. 'It was feeling suffocating,' she said instead. 'Just, in some way I couldn't define. Felt *off*.' She steadied herself. 'But Maru … Noor wasn't wrong, honestly. What am I going to do on Jagat's case between now and tomorrow anyway? I could've as well spent that time on *Council vs Commune*. And it's not just that. With our procedural objection, we've linked Jagat's fate to *Council vs Commune*. If I'd taken the case, that would have been in my hands, at least a little bit. But now I've given up control, I have to trust Noor and the rest to win this.' She looked at him. 'Do you think I made the right choice?'

Maru only shook his head. 'Sorry, but as Ghorge would tell us if he were here, this is literally one of those situations where you'll be right if you win and wrong if you lose. Consequential moral luck, remember?'

'Thanks for the ice-cold comfort, friend.'

'You know it too.'

'Yeah, I just didn't need to *hear* it. Dammit all! Imagine that I gave up *Council vs Commune*, and then I lose this too. What will I have left then?'

'Your principles?'

'Don't want them.'

'Well, then,' said Maru. 'We just have to make tomorrow count.' He offered Nila a letter. 'By the way, this just arrived in your pidge.'

She took it from him. The seal was of the Directorate's. With a quickening of the pulse, she broke the seal, opened it and read it aloud.

To Nila M.
The Free and Equal Confederation of the Guardians of Peruma

Kindly be informed that your urgent request to access the personal archives of Director Purul is hereby
GRANTED.
Pursuant to this message, you are hereby
DIRECTED
to be present at the Directorate, on Sunday, the 8th of August,
at
TWELVE OF THE CLOCK.

She whistled. 'How about that? The bluff worked.'

But Maru was staring at the letter, chewing his lip, saying nothing.

'Maru?' she said.

'I don't like it,' he said slowly. 'I know something of Pulis. He's not the kind to get swayed by a speech—sorry, Nila—no matter how eloquent it is. There's something—something off about this.'

'Oh,' said Nila. 'What should I do then?'

'I mean, go of course. It's not like you have something else lined up for tomorrow now that you've turned down *Commune vs Council*, heh. Just—I don't know—just be careful?'

'Careful about what?'

Maru shook his head in frustration. 'I don't know. Just—careful in general, I guess? Sorry, I know that's not very helpful.'

Nila let out a long breath. 'Well, then. It's on. We've all drank in the last-chance saloon, but now I guess we're going to be hunting in the archive of last chances.'

'Oh, *draaama!*' said Maru. 'But I'll grant you, it's earned this time.

Day Six

The Archive

16

Their Origin Myth

THE CREDITS ROLLED, TO THE SCORE OF A SOFT threnody and its melancholy refrain.

'Whew,' said Maru, leaning back in his chair. '*That* was intense.'

'Did you know,' said Nila, 'that there are twenty-seven video-reels about Jagat the Martyr? He's been mythologised. Memorialised. Dramatised. So much for anarchists rejecting heroes.'

'Any insights, though?'

'Nothing. They all start from the moment on the bridge. He walks on to the stage, hurls a lightning bolt upon history and vanishes, as if he wants to stay in the world as briefly as possible. In the empty space where he would have been, they fill in the story. And yet …' Nila tapped her fingernails on the table, and exhaled. 'And yet … the Jagat of the stories is *so* different from the man we saw sleeping in the cryobox. This is not even a man, he's …'

'He's their origin myth,' Maru finished.

'That's exactly it. He's the Commune's origin myth. The ordinary man, without a past or a future. Just like *The Great*

Unravelling says, *anybody* could have been Jagat. And everybody can convince themselves that they *could* be Jagat. Shoot the director. Refuse to give up your comrades. And then go silently to an ever-longer silence. The first Communard, before the Commune. The first and best anarchist.'

'Almost *too* ideal?' said Maru.

'You would think so, no?' said Nila. 'And yet, if you think about it … it wasn't *all* that extraordinary. People have done that—and more—during revolutions.'

'It wasn't a revolution when he did it. He couldn't have known the barricades would be up that night.'

'Mm, that's true.'

They looked at each other. Mandilicosis II-A hung between them, a tacit thought.

Nila's wristheld pinged. She looked down. '*WHAT?*'

Maru jumped. 'What happened?'

'It looks like the *High Town Herald* has done a profile on me!'

'What!'

'Yeah.' She pinched her fingers together on the wristheld, and drew up the viewing screen. The glossy pages of the *High Town Herald* appeared. There was a photograph of Nila, on the day two years ago when the results of the pupillage exam had been declared. A headline screamed the words:

WHO SPEAKS FOR THE ASSASSIN? MEET THE DEFENCE COUNSEL FOR THE DAMNED, THE KEY PERSON BRINGING CHAOS TO PERUMA (PART I)

'Wow!' said Maru.

She ran her eyes down the print.

> **With all of Peruma buzzing about the retrial of the assassin Jagat R. tomorrow, we bring you this EXCLUSIVE two-part series about the hidden hands behind this attempt to resurrect the dreaded terrorist. Working through the week, our investigative team found a well-oiled syndicate behind this so-called effort for justice, one with concealed links to the Commune, and an organised funding network, fronted—knowingly or unknowingly—by top pupil of the Confederation, Nila M. In Part I, we bring you the antecedents of Nila M. In Part II—which will be available in our afternoon edition online, at 1.30 p.m.—we will reveal who is funding and coordinating this attempt.**

'Funding?' said Maru. 'Like Ani paying from her own pocket?'

'Guess we'll find out this afternoon,' said Nila. She skimmed the piece, pausing at the third column, where her mother's name leaped out at her.

> **Nila M. comes from a family of leading Communards. She is the daughter of Meera D., whose woodworks adorn the rooms of many Peruman families, from Council to Commune, but who is also a prominent member of the Commune's Department for the Preservation of Historical Memory, has directed the premiere production in the Commune's annual theatre festival six times and is known for anti-High Town views. In one of her plays, the *Herald* has learned, a city of skyscrapers is set on fire by alien spaceships, while a man, watching from a distance, turns to his partner and says, 'What a pretty fire.' It is believed**

> **that this is a reference to High Town (click to read more).**

'I'd suggest not clicking to read more,' said Maru. 'I'd suggest not reading further at all, in fact.'

'No, wait,' said Nila. She traced her fingers down the screen. 'See this.'

> **Scepticism about Nila M.'s impartiality in this case is shared at the highest levels of the Confederation, as the *Herald* has learned. A source who declined to be named said, 'Yes, it's something that concerns us. The Confederation holds itself to the strictest standards of neutrality and impartiality.'**

'Maru, WHAT? Who has been briefing against me from inside the Chapterhouse?'

'It could be literally anyone in the Executive Committee, Mehmandost Naram down.'

'Those oily little frauds!'

'The same. And look at this.'

> **There is also substantial anger within the Confederation about the potential embarrassment that Nila M's antics might bring. 'It was an open-and-shut case,' another source who also declined to be named told the *Herald*. 'There's nothing to retry. We're risking turning ourselves into a joke on Monday before all of Peruma, in fact, before all of the subcontinent, because you know these proceedings are broadcast live everywhere. It will be a big hit to our reputation.' When pressed on whether the Confederation would consider action**

> **against Nila M., the source refused to comment. 'I don't want to speculate, let's see what happens on Monday. But we're keeping our options open, the Confederation Code has a provision for action in case of frivolous or malicious litigation—so we're going to see what happens on Monday—'**

Maru reached out and pinched the screen close. 'That's enough, Nila.'

'Maru—they're going to go after me even if I play by the book and lose!'

'Nobody is going to go after you. This is the damn *Herald*. Even in High Town it's our favourite choice of toilet paper.'

'They won't make up quotes.'

'Oh, they will *definitely* make up quotes if they think it will mess with someone's head. In this case, yours. *Besides!* We *are* going to win tomorrow, remember? The only action they will be taking is signing the order for waking Jagat up.'

Nila bit her lip. She opened up the seeing screen again, pulling up the Confederation Code. 'The highest penalty for proven malicious litigation by a guardian is expulsion from the Confederation,' she read.

Maru came around to her side and shook her. 'Nila, listen to me. You're *not* getting expelled. Now—'

The pidge squawked.

'I'll get it.' Nila stood, walked to the pidge and picked up a single sheet of paper.

'Maru!'

'What is it?'

'It's from Anam. He says they've found some information. He needs me to come see him so he can explain.'

'Why didn't he inbox the information to you? Or just directly pidge it if he's afraid of being hacked?'

'Ah, I asked him for something that he might not have used entirely legal means to get.'

Maru walked over. 'Let me see that.' He took the paper from her hand. 'Typed. Printed. No signature.'

'All right, so?'

'Isn't it interesting,' said Maru, 'that literally ten minutes after *The Herald's* hit piece on you goes online, you get an unsigned *and untrackable* message from Anam—the person you trust most in this world—to come and be party to an illegality?'

'You're saying—'

'I'm saying, Nila, that if I wanted to engineer your downfall for breaching the oath, I would definitely draw you into a trap the exact moment after you'd read a piece curated to mess with your head and make you feel desperate. Didn't you tell Anam that you'd have no direct contact until after the case?'

'Yes, but—'

'And would he ever put you into danger?'

'Never. But what if it's something really critical?'

'Then they'd find another way to get it to you, like they did yesterday. Nila, I'd bet everything that this message hasn't come from Anam, that Anam doesn't even know about it. You know what will happen if you go? A secret video recording, another piece in the *Herald,* and then a second Naina L.'

'But Maru! There's only one day left. Look at that damn timer. Twenty-three hours. What if Anam doesn't actually have another way to get to me? His faction has some pull, but they're not masters of Peruma.'

To her surprise, Maru put his hands upon her temples—something he'd never done before—and looked at her intently. 'Nila. Don't go. I do not want to watch you walk out of this chamber forever.'

She stared back at him for a while, then nodded. 'Okay.'

'Phew,' he said, dropping his hands. 'Just trust me on this. My instinct spends most of its time sleeping, but there are moments when it wakes up, and right now it's flashing vermillion.'

'What else is asleep?'

'What?'

'Oh—nothing!' *Just forget what Noor told you, or it'll come out.* She laughed. 'Looks like it's not just me who will need the verdict of history to tell them if they did the right thing. Consequential moral luck, huh.'

Maru narrowed his eyes at her for a moment, but only said: 'I'll take my chances.' Then his voice softened. 'Listen, if it really is Anam, as I said, he *will* find a way. You just focus on the archives.'

'Yeah, I guess.' She slumped, feeling the adrenaline recede.

'In fact, shouldn't you be on your way to them now?'

'Yeah. You're right.'

'You'll be able to navigate?'

'I mean, it doesn't take much,' Nila said. 'But you can help me again, yes. Just. One. More. Day. Maru. Then I can pass out.'

Maru sighed. 'Come on, time for you to go.'

Nila nodded. She stood, and they walked out to the balcony, where the skimmer floated, waiting. She almost stumbled as she climbed into it. Maru caught her and helped her up. 'You *really* need sleep.'

'You're telling me,' she muttered.

'Remember how we used to do exam prep together, and you insisted on not sleeping and cramming till the literal ringing of the exam bell? And I had to impose an embargo on studying after 10.00 p.m. the night before, and physically stand over you until you fell asleep?'

'I remember too well.'

'We're going to go back to that today. It doesn't matter what you find or don't find in the archives. We're setting a hard deadline of 10.00 p.m. tonight, and then you go right to bed. I'm not having you collapsing in the tribunal tomorrow.'

'Can I just say,' said Nila, 'that I'd wake after *you* had gone to sleep, and study till dawn anyway?'

'I did actually know about that, but at least you got four hours of rest. And this time, *I'll* stay up all night if needed. Okay, go.'

She typed instructions into the interface.

'Oh, by the way,' said Maru.

'Mm?'

'How did that article pop up on your wristheld, Nila? Have you set an alert for your own name?'

'Shut up, Maru!' She thumped the start button with unnecessary force. The skimmer flew out over the balcony. Maru's laughter sang in her ears.

The cold morning wind forced her drooping eyes open as she entered the now-familiar skylanes of High Town.

'No random stops today?' said Nila.

'They've probably secured all the skylanes, so it's a bit relaxed now.'

'Good to know.'

The skimmer turned towards the hill and the Directorate. 'Do we know what we're looking for?' Maru said.

'I checked the online catalogue last night,' said Nila. 'We'll focus on Purul's correspondence. I really want to know what he was planning to say that morning to Low Town.'

'Assuming there's something he left on record.'

'This would actually be much easier if the Directorate allowed us to scan through the digitised documents. Instead, I have to go sift through reams of paper.'

'There's a Council law on this, actually,' said Maru, a shrug in his voice. 'The Directorate archives cannot be put online. Security reasons, they say. It's for the same reason that intra-Council communication is still carried out through paper.'

'Makes no sense.'

'As is the case with most laws.'

The skimmer moved through the sparse weekend traffic, towards the Directorate, into the heart of old High Town, passing between the long shadows of the towers. As Nila flew, bits and pieces of the video-reels she had watched all night passed through her mind like little shards floating through sludge; and at the centre of it all, that man again, Jagat the Martyr, and all the worlds of silence she was trying to decode. The shot that nobody had seen fired, the shot that had killed Director Purul, barrelled and ricocheted off the walls of her mind, echoing through the halls of the old courtroom where the last great trial of the age had been held.

'Say something,' she murmured. 'Speak to me.'

'What?' said Maru.

'Nothing, nothing.'

Now she could see the courtroom, a young Milana Maran giving her witness testimony, damning Jagat by necessary implication. There was Jagat himself, never clearly in focus no matter how much she squinted, so she couldn't make out whether his face was the face of the statue in the Commune, or the face of Jagat in the cryochamber, and now there was a skimmer entering the courtroom, sleek and black and—

A skimmer?!

Nila's half-closed eyes jerked open. She was in a small skylane that branched out from the main thoroughfare, one of the many little capillaries snaking its way directly through the upper reaches of the towers. Around the bend, from the other side, a skimmer was coming directly towards her, veering alarmingly off course.

'Wait, what's that—' she began, just as Maru's voice cut in. 'Nila, this is a one-way. The skimmer is flying on the *wrong side*.'

She reached for the controls to reverse, to give the approaching skimmer a path to the main thoroughfare that she had just left behind; but just then, the skimmer sped up, almost careening forward.

'*What* the …!' The shout ripped itself from Nila's throat. 'Right—RIGHT, Nila!' Maru yelled. She slammed her hand down on the controls. Her skimmer jerked away, into a narrow alley between two towers.

Her hands were trembling. 'Good thing you saw that turn. What were they thinking—' but Maru cut in once more: 'Nila. Look *ahead*.'

Directly in front of her, the alley ended in another tower. From the awning, a second skimmer emerged, bearing down on them.

'This isn't an alley, it's a dead end,' said Nila. 'I don't have space—'

'Nila, right again!'

There was an opening, a wide circular hole carved out within one of the towers.

'That goes into a hangar!'

'It's not like we have a choice right now!'

She swerved the skimmer around, a second before the collision. They entered the tunnel, a rush of air bursting into her eardrums. Almost immediately, the tunnel widened, and they floated into a large, circular hangar. Behind her, she saw several parked skimmers.

It had all happened in under two minutes.

'What the hell happened to all that skylane surveillance, Maru?' she said. 'Shouldn't they have blown those skimmers out of the sky?'

'I don't know. This should not be happening.' Maru's voice sounded shaky in her ear. 'Turn around, let's get out of here.'

Nila let her hands fall from the controls. 'No point. It was an ambush. I'll bet the entrance has closed behind us.'

Her skimmer hummed, suspended in the air.

'Should I raise the alarm?' said Maru.

'Yeah—no, actually, wait,' said Nila. 'This is the heart of High Town, I'm hardly going to be abducted here. Let's find out what this is about.'

'Famous last words,' Maru muttered as she brought the skimmer down into the hangar and alighted into a huge domed chamber. Spot beams from a high, vaulted roof draped the chamber in afterlight. There was nobody else in sight.

'Hello? Nila called.

A door at the far end swung open.

'Well.'

'You sure about this?' Maru said.

'When have I ever been sure about anything?' She walked across the hangar, leaving the parked skimmers behind. Closer to the door, she saw that it opened into a plush, carpeted corridor, which reminded her of the seniors' chamber complex. Nila stepped inside, and immediately felt temperature control kick in: a mild coolness, sterilised air. Behind her, the door closed.

Fifty metres further, another set of doors slid open at her approach. Nila walked into an oval room with wall-to-wall glass windows granted her a panoramic view of rows upon rows of towers descending gradually towards the river.

Standing by the window, a woman turned to face her as she entered. Salt-grey hair receded tightly from a high forehead. Darting black eyes came and settled upon Nila appraisingly. Upon her neck, Nila saw a pendant in the shape of a tiger, wrought all in silver.

A face she had seen in the sky, a week—an eternity ago.

'Welcome to Haffen House,' said Deputy Director Maiyam A., her voice crisp. Her eyes narrowed. 'To you *and* your colleague.'

Maru made an inarticulate noise in her earpiece, but Maiyam was already speaking. 'I've been following your investigation into the Jagat affair. I was waiting for you to come and meet me. But since you didn't, I decided to bring you here.'

'I have an appointment at—'

'The Directorate, for the Purul archives. I know,' said Maiyam easily. 'At twelve of the clock hereby, isn't it? I won't make you late for it. Unless you're in so much of a hurry that you'd like to leave without hearing what I have to say.'

'You forced my skimmer here,' said Nila. 'Do I have a choice?'

'I did,' Maiyam allowed. 'But inviting you would have meant comms, and comms are a little less secure than a good old ambush. Now this room, on the other hand, the director has tried to bug no less than twenty-seven times, to no effect.'

'The director doesn't know I'm here?'

'Clever.' Maiyam gave her a brilliant smile. 'Sit, won't you?'

Nila perched gingerly on the edge of a chair to her side. There was a whirring from below. A tile in the ground opened up, and a small table rose into the room just ahead of her, making her jump. It came to a stop at waist height. On the table was a crystal glass filled with cold coffee just the right shade of brown.

'Help yourself,' said Maiyam.

Nila glared at her, and sipped delicately from the glass.

'We'll be done by the time you're done with your drink,' said Maiyam. 'So, how's the investigation going, Guardian?'

'I feel like you know exactly how it's going,' said Nila. 'Or not going.'

'Struggling with a lot of little bits and pieces that aren't coming together? As if someone emptied three different jigsaw puzzle boxes before you and asked you to make sense of it? Not quite sure *what* you're going to argue tomorrow, Guardian?'

'Did you call me here to gloat?' said Nila.

'On the contrary. I want to give you another piece of the puzzle.'

'*What*?' Nila started.

'Indeed. I don't know quite how you're going to put it all together. But I do know you can't do without this one.'

Nila stared at her, slowing down her drinking.

'What do you mean?'

Maiyam clasped her hands. 'I understand that the director has not been exactly … cooperative with your investigation.'

'He's not been the most eager,' said Nila. 'Nor has he been hostile. He's given me time when I've asked for it. And he authorised my request to access the archives.'

'He's given you time to try and figure out how you're doing,' said Maiyam. 'And he's given you access because he's confident you won't find anything useful in the archives.'

'Maybe. He could have been worse, though.'

'No doubt,' said Maiyam. 'Tell me, Guardian. Do you think that Pulis wants you to find out the truth behind Director Purul's assassination? Or do you think he fears the possibility that you might?'

'He hasn't seemed very enthusiastic about my brief,' said Nila carefully.

'He hates it,' said Maiyam. 'Oh no, don't get me wrong. Pulis isn't actively trying to cover something up. He's honest. But he's also an institutionalist to the core, and it has been the position of successive directors to maintain the Pact of Forgetting. Pulis isn't going to be the one who changes that tradition. Or even think about whether it makes sense.'

'And you disagree?' said Nila.

'Let's just say,' said Maiyam, 'that we'd benefit from some closure—either way. It's what you told him. Some ghosts will never stop haunting you.'

Nila held her gaze, and then turned her attention to her glass, swirling the coffee gently.

'Deputy Director,' she said at last, looking at the older woman again. 'Who really killed Director Purul?'

Maiyam's expression seemed earnest. 'I don't know. And to be honest with you, Pulis doesn't either. Nobody knows.'

'Right,' said Nila. She took a swig from the glass. 'Well?'

Maiyam nodded. 'In the archives, there is a shelf that holds Director Purul's published decrees from the last year of his tenure. It has a false bottom.'

'I see,' said Nila. 'And I assume you're telling me this because you'd like me to have all the information I need for my investigation? And this has nothing to do with using me as bait for a power struggle between you and the director?'

Maiyam arched an eyebrow. 'Who knows. But does a drowning person start questioning who is throwing them a lifeline—and why?'

Nila took her last swig and stood as well.

'And what of the Apoptosis Plan, then?' she said.

She waited for a reaction, a movement, a stiffening—anything.

The deputy director's face never changed. 'What?'

'Never mind.'

Maiyam turned away from Nila, back to the window, looking out over High Town. 'Last chance, Guardian,' she said softly. 'Make it count.'

Nila did not reply. She turned, and left.

17

The Archive of Last Chances

THEY MADE THE JOURNEY TO THE TIGER'S JAW in silence, with only the sound of Maru's quiet breathing giving her company. They were still five minutes away from the Directorate when her wristheld pinged.

'That would be Part II,' said Nila.

'No, Nila,' said Maru. 'Don't open it. *Don't* look down—oh dammit!'

She'd already put the skimmer on autopilot and tapped the wristheld. The article popped up on a screen before her.

HIDDEN HAND: WHO IS FUNDING THE EFFORT TO RESURRECT THE ASSASSIN? (PART II)

Thanks to the indefatigable efforts of our investigative journalists, the *Herald* can now reveal that the Guardian Nila M.—who has strong ties with the Commune—is receiving funding for prosecuting this case from one Ani L., a reclusive citizen of High Town. the *Herald* has accessed tax filings which reveal that Ani L. is a majority shareholder in the Peruma Mandalium Processing Company, which readers will know is Peruma's largest, most lucrative mandalium corporation. the *Herald* can confirm that Ani L.'s family holdings in Peruma mandalium go back more than a hundred years, to the company's first IPO.

That's right, folks: money earned from Peruma's most precious resource is being pumped into resurrecting the man who would burn it all down.

The *Herald* can further reveal that for her investigation, Ani L. has provided to Nila M. the latest Garud skimmer, a model that costs upward of twenty thousand nadirs. Once again, this is money from our city's resources being deployed to destabilise us. Which makes us ask: why? Why is Ani L. willing to throw her money at such a cause?

The *Herald* can now EXCLUSIVELY reveal to our readers that, having accessed birth records, Ani L. is the great-grand daughter of the assassin HIMSELF. Her ancestral family moved to High Town after the mutiny, and has lived among us ever since.

Which makes us ask once again: why? Having gained wealth, security and safety in High Town, why is this family now trying to tear down their adopted home?

Have they always been secretly loyal to the Commune?

Have they been planning this for the last hundred years?

Is Nila M.'s mother, Meera D., involved?

Are we, High Town, harbouring our own destroyers?

'Gods,' said Maru. 'How low.'

'The bar is in the basement,' said Nila through gritted teeth. 'Maru, I want to win this for no other reason than to make the *Herald* cry.'

'Careful, Nila,' Maru warned. 'This whole thing is designed to get a rise out of you, make you make mistakes.'

'Maru,' she snapped, 'when will you understand that there's a time to offer advice, and a time to just make bloody sympathy noises?'

'I—'

Mercifully, that was the moment when the skimmer began its descent into the Tiger's Jaw, and the jammers cut him off before he could say anything more.

When she alighted, still breathing hard, molten anger coursing through her veins, a Directorate official was already there, his face tight with distaste.

'I am to escort you to the archives,' he said shortly.

'How nice of you.'

He opened his mouth, but thought better of it. Nila was taken through a different wing of the Directorate, an older section where the stairs spiralled more steeply, and the corridors were studded with arched doors in a fashion long outworn. Everything here had the sense of stasis, of taking the past and quickly freezing it in place before it had the chance to turn into contested history.

Around halfway up, her guide stopped outside an opaque glass door of a more contemporary vintage. With one palm covering the other, he punched in a number into the keypad. The doors slid open.

'You have two hours.'

She stepped in. The door closed behind her, shutting off her escort and the corridor. Nila paused, stood still, and cast a look around the room. There was no obvious camera, but if she'd ever bet on something …

In the cool, sterilised atmosphere of the room, her mind quieted by slow degrees.

The Council's passion for cataloguing made the archive easy to navigate. A small screen on the left allowed her to access an index of documents. Nila moved smoothly through them. The archive began with Purul's election to directorship and was arranged year-by-year, through the eight years of his lopped-off tenure. She skimmed the documents, pausing occasionally when something caught her eye. Through the director's decrees, correspondence and speeches in the Council, she began to glimpse the vision of a city on the eve of insurrection: reactive decrees increasing the minimum wage—once, twice, a third time; letters to the food ministry enquiring about contingency stockpiles; to the public works ministry for strengthening the bridges and making them—oh, the irony—*bomb-proof*; letters to the other independent cities on the subcontinent to diversify Peruma's trade. But it was the Council speeches that were the most telling of them all, filled with colour and movement at first, but gradually becoming, over the course of eight years, sober, pessimistic and, at last, bleak.

And through those documents, she began to glimpse the man that the director had been: for and of his age, as Pulis had said. A reconciler in a fraught time, more yielding than yielded to. Purul, the Douser of Fires; Purul, the fallen amaltas.

The kind of man it was in nobody's interest to kill.

Unless, perhaps, you *wanted* an escalation.

With a start, she realised that there were only ten minutes left. Nila moved quickly to the last shelf, trying to use her body as an ineffective shield between her hands and whatever cameras there might have been in the room. The false bottom came away easily, yielding to a deeper shelf. It housed two pages. There were singe marks around the edges, the paper ending in dark curlicues, but the sheets were intact.

Before she even picked them up, Nila knew what they were. The papers that Director Purul had carried with him the morning of his death. The words he had meant to speak to Low Town at the Maidan, but never had.

With trembling hands, she picked them up and read:

Fellow Citizens of Peruma,

I come to you not as your director, because true it is that I am not, in any sense, yours, nor as a negotiator, because trust must be earned before you will negotiate with us, nor as a peacemaker, because there can be no peace before a just settlement. ???

I come to you as a penitent, for the wrongs that were done in the past—and also as a supplicant, praying for your generosity, so that we can set the future to rights.

There were marginalia. Someone had underlined the word 'penitent', and, with a red pen, slashed a '???' at the side of the page. Purul, editing himself?

Or someone else, editing him?

I will not waste time on words. As Director of Peruma and Head of the Council, I have authority to make regulations for the peace, order and good governance of this city, which will hold the field until the Council elects to make them permanent—or vetoes them. In that

bit too dry and technical?

capacity, I say to you that I have read your charter of demands, and that I agree. I have drafted the first of the regulations in response to your charter. Our primary regulation—which I submit for your consideration—will state that:

give a beat after demands

On the sixth month of the coming into force of this regulation, all land in Peruma—including the mandalium mines—shall be taken into the ownership of a public trust, to be composed of equal representation from High Town and Low Town. Land shall henceforth only be administered by this trust, which will take its decisions democratically, and in accordance with the principles of common good, equal distribution and reparations for past wrongs.

MANY beats here

If you approve of this regulation, I shall enact it this moment under my hand and seal, take it to the Council this afternoon, and I promise you, they will not veto it, not if I have anything to do with it. And then, we can all sit down and talk.

But before that, I appeal to you—if this is a sign, a sign of my good faith, then before we go any further ... let us douse the fires.

Nila let the papers fall from her numbed fingers and float back into the cavity.

Ever since the day of his death, people had speculated endlessly about what Director Purul had been going to say to the workers amidst the violence; whether he would have taken a hard and uncompromising line, or a softer one, promising concessions. But nobody had ever suspected that Purul had intended to go as far as to propose overhauling Peruma's entire property-owning structure for the sake of peace.

And yet, he had.

To go so far that even the revolution, which was inaugurated over his corpse, had not gone far enough.

It was the last throw of the dice, she understood, the last attempt to bring a negotiated peace to Peruma, a peace without violence. Purul's death had ensured that would never come to pass.

What came to pass was a city divided in blood.

And then she noticed the last annotation. Just after the word 'fires', on the side of the page:

> *Simply brilliant. They will love you. This is a speech for all ages. -M.M.*

M.M.

Milana Maran.

The eyewitness who had somehow forgotten to mention, in every story she had told of that day, what was written in the papers that Director Purul was carrying with him.

A soft footfall outside the door jerked her back to life. She had thirty seconds left. Nila scrabbled hurriedly, putting the false bottom back in place, snatching up one of Purul's last published decrees—on a water reclamation plant by the head of the river—and engrossed herself in it just as the door behind her opened again.

'Time.'

'Wow,' said Maru.

'Yes,' said Nila.

'How in the world did nobody think of destroying this document in the last hundred years?'

'I don't know,' said Nila. 'But I'd guess it's that institutional obsession with cataloguing and archiving everything for posterity, even when it would make sense to disappear a few pages? Either way, I'm not complaining.'

Her sleepiness had vanished, replaced by a curious, eerie alertness.

The skimmer lifted above the Tiger's Jaw one final time. In the west, beyond Dominion Hill, the sun was going down in a blaze of fire. Shards of crimson light sheared the clouds like ribbons.

'Wow,' said Maru again.

'What a different history we might have had, eh?' said Nila.

Maru chuckled in her ears. 'Well, the guardians wouldn't have existed had there been no revolution and no Cop-Out Constitution. We are the cop-out, after all.'

'Jury's out on whether that would have been good or bad.'

They laughed together, their previous tension about the *Herald's* piece dissolved. The air felt lighter. The skimmer turned south, towards the Urai and the Chapterhouse.

'Nila,' said Maru, jerking her out of her reverie.

'Mm?'

'Why are the skylanes empty?'

'Huh? Wait, oh—you're right—' she said, stupidly, as the world came back into focus. To her left, to her right and ahead of her, there wasn't a single skimmer in High Town's skylanes. She was flying alone.

'This is odd,' said Maru.

Nila blinked once, and then again, before a thought struck her. 'Um … maybe it's a curfew before tomorrow morning's *Council vs Commune* case? To avoid any escalation?'

'Perhaps.'

'You don't sound convinced.'

'I don't—ah, forget it,' said Maru. 'Your findings—tell me. What does it all mean … for tomorrow?'

'I have no idea,' she said. 'It's like, you know, it's like so many different people telling you a side of the story. You think that will help you put together what really happened. But instead you end up with seven different stories.'

'Great if you're a novelist, not so hot if you're before a tribunal.'

'Ugh!' Nila punched the side of the skimmer, and squealed as the sensitive machine careened before righting itself. She breathed. 'You know,' she said, 'I don't actually need seven stories. I just need *one* coherent, complete alternative story to the official one, and—'

'Nila!' Maru's shout shredded the rest of her thoughts. She jerked into focus. In the half-light, three skimmers were converging upon her, from the left, the right and in front of her. She cast a quick look around. The skylanes were still empty.

As if it had been planned.

'Oh, *that's* why,' She slammed into reverse gear, away from the skimmers. 'What do I do?'

'Nila,' Maru's voice was quick and urgent. 'Speed up.'

'I don't know the skylanes, I can't—'

'I've already downloaded the map, I'll give you instructions. Just drive—turn, NOW!'

She spun the skimmer around and pressed the accelerator. Immediately, the others gave chase.

'*Again.* Where are all those security guns when you really need them,' she muttered. The wind roared in her ears. She almost couldn't hear Maru barking orders into the earpiece. The world was a blur around her, the skyscrapers looming hulks in the gloaming, the headlights of the skimmers acting out a wild dance on the walls of sea-stone and glass. At first, she tried to keep track of where they were going, but soon she lost all sense of direction, with everything blurring into a succession of commands: *right, right—straight ahead—up a level—faster—Nila, down—right—*

A niggling feeling from the back of her mind forced its way to the front. At last, Nila focused on where she was. High Town's towers still loomed around her, with their bridges and skylanes, but now there was a darker set of shadows ahead, merging with the night, a doubtful distance away, but unmistakable.

The Peruma switchback, the old volcanic massif that rose in a sheer chain beyond Dominion Hill, home of the mandalium mines.

She had flown to the northernmost edge of the city, her pursuers content to hold off and drive her from where there was no turning back.

'Maru …' she whispered.

'Dammit.' His voice was angry, but defeated. 'It was a trap. They know these skylanes so much better, and—'

'We can't fly into the switchback,' she said. 'The fuel—'

'What else can we do? Nila,' Maru spoke with urgency. 'We have to carry on. I'll come for you, I'll find you on the switchback, but you can't be caught by these guys.'

'If I'm on the switchback,' said Nila, 'without a skimmer, there's no chance in hell I'm getting back home for the hearing tomorrow.'

'I'll get a skimmer, I'll come for you—'

'You're literally barred from stepping into High Town, you'll have to tell—'

A bolt of lightning cracked open the sky.

For one moment, suspended in an eternity, everything came alight. The switchback appeared before her in all its dubious glory, the side of a former volcano, now cratered and pockmarked with the mining, almost like—

An abscess.

A pustule.

A … carbuncle.

'Oh …' whispered Nila. Strands and filaments in her mind were weaving and waving at each other, moving and curling, shaping themselves into—

'*Nila!*' Maru shouted. 'You've stopped!'

She jerked to life. The skimmers were approaching her now, closer and closer, still three, sleek and glowing, and there, in the hands of one of the pilots, she saw—

'Oh, shit,' said Nila.

A flare lit up the sky in bright crimson, blinding her. She covered her face with an elbow, her eyes screwing shut. A screeching noise rent the air. Nila opened her eyes.

And then things happened very quickly. Four skimmers dropped from the sky, spitting bolts from their sides. For the quickest of instants, as one of them passed her, Nila caught sight of salt-grey hair beneath a helmet, the glimpse of a face that she had seen just hours ago, and a clenched fist salute directed at her. Then the skimmer was weaving around her pursuers, who were taking evasive action, but the newcomers were dancing around them, pushing them further down, away from the sky and towards the plateau of Dominion Hill. In moments they were far below, only pinpricks of light whirling and swirling around each other.

The sky was quiet again.

'*Nila!*' Maru's voice again.

'Mm,' she said, almost dreamily.

'Turn, turn. We have to move. We have all of High Town to cross before we're safe.'

'Oh … oh, yes.' She turned the skimmer around, and set a course due south once again.

As the skimmer moved, she looked back once. The lightning had stopped. The switchback was visible only as a dim, curving outline against the darker night. But in her mind, the sight was imprinted like one of those black-and-white photographs in the museum on Vashi Street: the mountainside in the starkest of white, its face turned to her with its grid of scars.

The skimmer re-entered the skylanes amidst the glittering lights of the towers. The night was calm now, almost unbearably peaceful, as if the chase and the fight had been a dream. They moved smoothly through the lanes, in between the skyscrapers and the bridges, navigating by the map.

'Well, well,' Maru muttered. 'Looks like the traffic is back out.'

And indeed, the lanes were normal again, skimmers moving back and forth upon the main arteries, blinking in and out through the capillaries, a choreographed dance of fireflies.

'I guess you're safe now,' said Maru. 'Just get back and stay in tonight.'

Nobody interrupted them as they flew south. Nila felt her breathing return to normal.

'Maru?' She spoke for the first time, as the rows of towers began to thin, and she caught the first glimpse of the Chapterhouse.

'Mm?'

'You still online?'

'How could I not be, until you're back?' She caught the smile in his voice. She smiled back into the night.

'Listen. Do you know commercial law?'

'Hm. A little bit?'

'Company ownership and shareholding structures? The regulatory landscape? Insider trading? You should, Maru, given all those cases you do about occupational injuries against these mandalium companies.'

'I let someone else on the team handle that aspect.'

'Want to learn something about it tonight?'

'Um, yeah, sure? Nila—what's this about?'

She gazed forward, her jaw set.

The mountain, abscessed. Abscesses and pockmarks. Like a cancer on the skin. A carbuncle. Operation Carbuncle.

'I think I've found my story.'

'What did I say about 10.00 p.m.?' said Maru, just as the clock chimed.

'*Aaaand* done!' said Nila. She closed her wristheld's screen. At one end of the room, next to the mini-fridge, a printer began to spit out sheets of paper.

'There we go,' said Nila. 'Heads of argument are ready. I'll print out my case pin cites tomorrow morning.'

'Headlined, indexed, bookmarked, arranged by A, A(1), A(1)(a), and A(1)(a)(i), I see,' said Maru. 'You intending to go into any deeper levels of argument in the heads, Nila?'

'That will do for now, thanks, Mr Sarcasm.'

'And you have the full texts of the judgements with you?' Maru counted them off his fingers. 'On burden of proof, circumstantial evidence, the last seen doctrine, the beyond reasonable doubt standard and, of course, the threshold for reopening a conviction.'

Nila tapped her wristheld. 'All here. Flagged, colour-coded and highlighted. I'll have the copies sent to the arbitrators once they announce their names tonight.'

'Right, then,' said Maru. 'Now, as per our agreement …'

'Please, sir,' said Nila, 'just a two-hour extension, sir. May I?'

'*Two* hours?' said Maru.

'I just need to go out and come back. I won't be long. And I'll get enough sleep, I promise.'

'You're going to the Commune, aren't you?' said Maru.

Nila was quiet.

'Nila, this is an insane risk. The hearing is tomorrow, the *Herald* has just today published—'

'I know, but I'm legally in the clear, Maru. It's the last twelve hours before the hearing—the grace period when all restrictions are lifted for *arguing* counsel, remember?'

'Oh? Never had a reason to look *that* rule up,' Maru chuckled. 'But still—you sure? We just saw how unsafe it is.'

'I need to do this.'

Maru sighed. 'I suppose you must. And I suppose you'd like your privacy as well. Go, then. I'll wait up for you.'

She squeezed his arm gratefully. 'Thank you, Maru,' she whispered.

One final time, the skimmer. She set a course south and across the river, never looking back towards the towers of High Town.

From the sky, she saw clusters of flickering lights on the southern bank. It wasn't the houses, or the streets; it was the people, gathered in little groups in the squares, moving, shifting, their assemblies dissolving and reconstituting, giving the Commune the appearance of a band of dancing fireflies, but chaotic and disordered, unlike the traffic in the skies of High Town.

Just beyond Unity Bridge, and at the edge of Rubble Street, she alighted.

From Rubble Street, she plunged into the Commune.

It was a night when nobody deigned to go to bed. The fireflies she had seen from the sky resolved themselves into wristheld torches that cast the squares in unsettled, floating light. Nila moved at the edges of the squares, staying in the shadows, watching. Most of the gatherings seemed to be impromptu political education classes, where three people sat on a slightly elevated dais and, before a transitory audience, debated intensely about the significance and the potential outcome of the Fifth Inflection Point of Peruman history. In other places, having debated to exhaustion, the sitars were out. There was singing, the harmonium played 'Leave with the Dawn' and elsewhere there was qawwali, with the Commune songs that she remembered from her own childhood, and which she too had once hummed in the squares. The tune she heard most was, of course, about Jagat, with its quick refrain: *silence has a sound*.

Speaking of …

'Tomorrow we may have the Martyr back among us. And he will take this frozen revolution in his hands, and he will say, *rise and be born again with me.*'

Nila stopped at the edge of the square, listening. The voice had come from the audience, tightly knit around the dais.

'Yes, we may,' one of the speakers—a young man who couldn't have been much older than her—said. 'Yes, we may. But, Bakasur, I wouldn't count on it.'

'You also think she has no chance?'

'You have to be realistic,' the man replied. 'Look, I'm no expert in the Peruma criminal code, but how's she going to prove, a century later, that the Martyr didn't do what we all know he did?'

'I heard she has a plan—she's going to challenge the sleep of death itself.'

'Impossible. Like I said, I'm no expert in the Peruma criminal code, but even I can tell you that there are some rules of procedure that they have to follow. You can't just stand up and challenge something like that.'

'I heard something else,' another voice piped up. 'I heard that she's got together a case to show that with all the evidence in play, you can't prove that the Martyr shot the director, *or* that he didn't, and if you can't prove it either way, they will have to revive him.'

'Look,' said the young man, 'As I said, I'm no—'

'Yes, yes,' the crowd hooted, 'we know you're no expert in the Peruma criminal code, so just stop guessing, and we'll all see what happens tomorrow.'

'Okay, STRAW POLL!' one of the people on the dais shouted. 'How many of us here are going to watch *Council vs Commune* tomorrow?'

Five hands shot up.

'Martyr's resurrection?'

She counted twenty-five glimmering pinpricks of wristheld light, held high above the heads of the people.

Nila gulped and moved away.

She passed bodies in the night, people moving this way and that in the darkness, going from one square to another, one assembly to the other, but she kept her head down and walked on. Nobody recognised her, or if they did, they did not challenge her. In other squares, she came upon more conversations about *Directorate vs Jagat R.*, but in time, the buzz in the air began to subside, and in more and more squares, outside the late-night cafés and amidst the inside-out gardens, music began to take its place.

She reached a gate with a pebbled path that led up to a pair of curtains swaying in the breeze.

Nila pushed open the gate. She walked up the pebbled path. She drew open the curtains, stepped through the passageway, and into the darkling room, with its table set for none, its woodwork, its paintings, its colours and its memories.

'Ma?' she said.

The house did not answer.

Navigating through muscle memory in the darkness, she found her way to the carpet where her old toys still were and let herself sink into that remembered softness.

'You should meet Baili,' she told them.

Nila leaned back, closed her eyes, and let memories wash over her. She didn't know how long she sat there in the silence, until the call of an owl from somewhere outside the window brought her back to reality, and she realised that her mother would not be coming home tonight.

From her back pocket, Nila pulled out her heads of argument, the three sheets of paper that she had sneaked out of the chamber when Maru's back had been turned.

Don't do this case like a Guardian. Do it like a Communard.

She placed the heads of argument on the table.

'Be proud of me, Ma,' she whispered.

Nila turned, and walked out of the room, the passageway, and the house, up the pebbled path, and—

—into the figure that stood waiting just beyond the gate.

She stopped, heart in mouth.

Asana unhooded herself.

'Guardian.'

Relief flooded through Nila.

'Are you going to do it?' Asana said.

Nila lifted her head and looked Asana in the eye. 'Yes. I'm going to do it.'

'Truly?'

'Yes.'

Asana looked at her for a long while, saying nothing. Then she spoke: 'You know you were followed here, yes?'

'I—' Nila stammered, 'I—I didn't—'

'You are rash. You take risks as if you're immortal. Just when you should be most keenly aware of your mortality.'

Nila looked down at the ground, feeling herself going red.

'Go back,' said Asana. 'We're watching. It'll be fine.'

'Thank you,' said Nila. She paused, remembering something. 'Just one question. Was it you who sent a message to my guardian key three nights ago, telling me to beware the Apoptosis Plan?'

Asana stared. 'No. We don't have your guardian key.'

'I see,' said Nila. 'Well, thanks anyway.' She turned to go, but just then Asana grasped Nila's wrist, and suddenly she was very close, so close that Nila could feel her dry, ragged breath upon her skin.

'Just don't let him die.'

'I won't.'

Asana let go of her. Nila walked away, not looking back. Two turns later, she was on Rubble Street, away from the moving lights, the conversation and the music, suddenly alone, suddenly lonelier. She retraced her steps hurriedly, picking her way through the scree, moving north, until she saw the familiar shape of Ani's skimmer.

Ani.

As the skimmer rose above the river and she left the Commune below, Nila flicked on her pendant, typing in the code that Ani had given her.

I cannot take your call at the moment. Please leave your message, and I will get back to you as soon as I can.

Nila frowned. She tried again. Once, twice.

Voicemail.

On the fourth attempt, she gave up.

'Ani,' she spoke into her pendant. 'It's me, Nila. I believe I've found the answer you were looking for. Tomorrow, I'll prove that Jagat was wrongly convicted. I'll bring him back for you. I don't know who is listening in here, so—come tomorrow. To the tribunal. It begins at 10.00 a.m.'

She switched the pendant off, and took a breath, a long one that escaped her body in a shudder, and climbed onto the skimmer.

Ahead of her, the Chapterhouse appeared in the darkness.

Day Seven

The Tribunal

18

Our Human Need

ON THE LONG TABLE THERE WERE FIVE SETS OF papers of varying thickness, stacked together neatly. Little flags—red, green and yellow—peeked out between the layers of documents, covered with tiny, curlicued handwriting.

'Check,' said Maru.

Nila placed her finger on the sets, one by one. 'My heads of argument. Three copies. The original judgement in *Directorate vs Jagat R*. Three copies. Excerpts from all the criminal law cases. Three copies, and the full judgements have been dispatched to the prosecutor and the tribunal this morning. The Peruma criminal code and the Charter of Peace and Unity. One copy. And my notes—'

'Let me guess,' said Maru. 'One copy.'

'Genius.' Nila paused at the end of the table, and looked around. 'Why do I get the feeling that I'm forgetting something?'

'You filed the application to bring fresh documents on record? And the application for exemption from proving those documents as they're public records?'

'Both filed last night, copies sent to the prosecutor and the tribunal, to be taken up alongside the main case today.'

'Then you're set.'

'I still feel I'm forgetting something.'

'You always feel that. Trust me, you've got this.'

Nila took a deep breath, and puffed out her cheeks. 'Is my hair settled? Nothing that will annoy a particularly cantankerous guardian, like Manyu?'

'Your hair's fine, but your sash *is* a little askew. May I?'

'Go for it.'

'Can you stop fidgeting?' said Maru, as he fiddled with the pins on the sash.

'I'm a little worried. About Ani's silence. How can she be *not reachable* today of all days?'

'Well, maybe that's how she copes,' said Maru. 'Ah, there we go.' A *snap*, as a pin slid into place. 'Now you look serious.'

Nila adjusted the blue guardian sash around her neck, and pulled the white scarf tighter. 'Remember what they always said? The more hopeless the cause, the more you should dress like you're sure of victory.'

'Aren't you?'

'Hah, we'll see,' she said. 'You'll be there?'

'Of course.'

Nila looked at him. 'The next time, we're going to do all this with the roles reversed.'

'Next time?' Maru smiled; a quiet smile. 'There will be no other cases quite like these.'

'You think? After the Commune wins today *and* Jagat comes back, and the world starts over tomorrow, can you begin to imagine the fights that will break out when they begin rewriting the Charter from scratch? And when those fights come here, I want you to—'

There was a knock on the door.

'Come in,' said Maru, sounding very relieved.

The door opened, and Noor entered, dressed, like Nila, in the blue sash and white scarf of the guardian-in-tribunal.

'Don't think this conversation is over,' Nila said to Maru. She turned to Noor. 'Oh my—you look ready.'

'So do you,' said Noor. She crossed around the table, and gave Nila a tight hug. 'I wish you hadn't left us high and dry like you did, but I understand. Good luck, Phoenix. I'm going to accept nothing less than seeing Jagat walk right into the Grand Chamber and disrupt our hearing, okay?'

'And to you, Salamander,' Nila whispered. 'I'm rooting for you,' she said, as they disengaged. 'Actually, you have no idea how much I'm rooting for *you*.'

'Thinking like a Communard?' said Noor.

'No, actually,' Nila laughed. 'Thinking *very much* like a guardian.'

Noor narrowed her eyes. 'Nila. Please don't tell me you've come up with one of your notorious procedural objections.' She turned to Maru. 'Maru, don't tell me *you've* encouraged this!'

'Ahm, I—' said Maru.

'Just wait, just wait and see,' Nila said. 'And please win!'

'And you,' said Noor. 'For you. See you after, well, whatever happens? We'll celebrate or cry on the terrace tonight.'

The door closed behind her.

'Look,' said Maru suddenly. 'They're coming.' He gestured at the window.

Nila leaned out. The sun was up. Beneath a clear sky, with High Town's towers to her north, and the Commune's sprawl on the other side of the water, Peruma seemed strangely beautiful. In the bright clear morning, Unity Bridge was glimmering in the sunlight. A procession was coming in from the Commune. Directly beneath her, on the ground, there was a flurry of activity. The Council had already begun to converge upon the Chapterhouse. Director Pulis and Deputy Director Maiyam were visible at the front.

She turned around, away from the window.

'Nila,' Maru said. 'How're you feeling?'

Nila closed her eyes. She exhaled.

'Fine,' she said. 'I feel fine. I know what I'm going to say.' She opened her eyes. 'Screw it, Maru, I really am ready. I can't wait.' She felt a rush of blood, a surge of something in her chest that threatened to explode through her ribcage. She sat down.

Maru checked his wristheld. 'An hour more,' he said. 'Want to do a practice run?'

Nila nodded. 'Yes. Yes, please.'

Maru settled himself in his chair, opposite her. 'Ready when you are.'

'Without papers, okay? I just want to get into my flow, so don't quiz me on pin cites and page numbers.'

'Got you.'

Nila stood again. She shifted a little until she was facing Maru across the table. He turned a neutral, cool gaze upon her.

Nila put her hands upon the table.

'Members of the tribunal.'

From the moment the first words left her mouth, she knew she was in the zone. Her brain was coolly directing the show, supplying her with words, with tones and inflections, pauses and stresses and the accompanying hand gestures.

'Members of the tribunal, I am Nila M., representing the applicant, Jagat R., through his great-granddaughter, Ani L., in *Jagat R. vs Directorate*, criminal review application no. 14/598, being an application to review and set aside the sentence of conviction and cryogenic sleep dated 9 August 398, in *Directorate vs Jagat R.*

'Members of the tribunal, a century ago, Director Purul was shot dead on Unity Bridge. That is not in dispute. In summary trial, the Directorate court found the applicant, Jagat R., guilty of the crime. The court based its findings on circumstantial evidence: the presence of Jagat at the scene of the crime and inferences from the truth serum-compliant testimony of the sole eyewitness, Milana Maran.

'For this application to succeed, I need to show to you that the Directorate court did not correctly appreciate the evidence when it found that there was no *reasonable doubt* that the applicant killed Director Purul with a shot to the heart. But I'm going to do something more. I'm not only going to show you that, on the basis of available evidence, there *is* reasonable doubt about the petitioner's guilt but also that the same evidence, accompanied with fresh material that is all a matter of public record, points even more strongly to *another* person's guilt. And for this other person, I'm going to show you motive. I'm going to show you opportunity. I'm going to show you execution. After I have done that, you will have two stories about what happened that morning on the bridge. The fate of the applicant will then be in your hands, under law—'

'Guardian Nila,' said Maru. 'This other person you speak of is presumably long dead. Can we call them to the stand? Put them on trial? Have them defend themselves?'

'You do not need to do any of those things,' said Nila. 'I am not asking you to convict someone else for the murder of Director Purul. What I am saying is that once you appreciate the evidence—*all* material evidence—as the Directorate Court ought to have done, you will find two equally plausible candidates for the murder of Director Purul. At that point, our laws compel only one decision: review and acquittal.'

'Proceed,' said Maru.

'What, then, is the first story, which we've all believed to be the only story, for a hundred years? Come back with me to an autumn morning in—'

A squawk from the end of the room. Nila stopped mid-sentence, and saw the pidge's mouth open. Three familiar papers floated to the ground.

'Oh, dammit, I was going so well.'

'Carry on, carry on,' said Maru. 'You can see what it is later.'

'No, wait,' said Nila, as she recognised the pages. She walked to the pidge and picked up the papers. 'Ah,' she said, embarrassed. 'It's my heads of argument.'

Maru shook his head. 'Let me guess. You went out last night to show them to your mother. Nila. How do you somehow manage to both be obsessive about your career, and also intent on setting fire to it every chance you get?'

'Hey, nobody found out.'

'The non-existent gods must be specially watching over fools. Why has the maternal unit sent it back?'

Nila was looking at the papers, her eyes alight. 'Maru, would you believe it,' she said, laughing. 'Ma's *annotated* it. She's sent back proofreading errors, broken up run-on sentences, and replaced passive with active voice. Typical.'

Maru shook his head again. 'What a family.' He came over and looked over her shoulder. 'Yeah, okay, these are good suggestions.'

'I'll just quickly rewrite these.'

'You sure you don't want to continue?'

'I think I'm good. I just needed to practice that start once.'

'Okay. Hey, what's that comment at the bottom?' said Maru, his eyes travelling down.

Nila followed his pointing finger. 'She's written—*unclean hands*?'

'Yup. Looks like it.'

'Huh? Is it the old equity maxim? *If you seek justice, come with clean hands*?'

'Except that that's *clean* hands.'

'Clean, unclean, potaato, potahyto.'

'Oh, come on, Nila. You're saying the person who just spotted and corrected nine proofing errors in a three-page document would just casually write the wrong maxim at the end?'

'It's not relevant to my case anyway,' said Nila. 'Equity doctrines have nothing to do with a criminal retrial.'

'Let me look it up.'

'You do that. I'll just get to making these corrections.'

She sat down at the table, pulled up her screen from her wristheld and, setting out the annotated draft before her, began to type.

She'd just about finished corrections when Maru spoke again. 'Oh, I think I got it.'

She looked up with a smidgen of irritation. '*What*, Maru?'

'*Unclean Hands* is a play by the famous Karantha V., the one that was written just after the revolution. It still gets an airing sometimes.'

Nila stared at him for a few moments, uncomprehending. Then she slapped her thigh.

'*Unclean Hands!* Of course! Oh gosh, legal language really fries your brain. Of course I know *Unclean Hands*, I acted in it as a child—it was a neighbourhood Council play directed by Ma.'

'What, really?'

'Yeah, how did it go? It's been such a while … hmm … there's a city, and it's soon after a revolution … except that this one went full vanguard, and it's now ruled by a single party—kind of an anti-Commune. Then a party functionary is ordered to kill a senior leader who's been deemed to be a traitor by the party executive—*typical* vanguardists. He finally succeeds, except that many years later …'

'… the man he kills is rehabilitated by the party, and the functionary's act, which was celebrated by the party for so many years, has now retrospectively become an act of villainy instead of an act of heroism. Everyone must condemn it—*even* its author,' Maru finished, looking down at his screen.

'Where are you reading that from? The Peruman encyclopaedia?'

Maru looked up and gave her a broad grin. 'You will not *believe* where I'm reading this from.'

'Tell me!'

'It turns out that the third hit on the network when you search *Unclean Hands Karantha V.* is a Rangashankara forum discussion thread about the play from around seven years ago where the top comment is a remarkably detailed summary of the plot by one *Nila_Dark_Angel*.'

'OH MY GOD! Maru! Stop reading that! I forbid you!'

She scrambled over the table and jumped at him. Laughing, Maru snatched his wristheld away just as she barrelled into him. His chair tipped over, and they went down in a tangle of arms and legs.

'Give me that!'

'Never!'

She prised his fingers open, and forced the wristheld out of his hands. 'You know I've already emailed it to myself, Nila_Dark_Angel?' Maru said, still laughing.

'I hate you, Maru.' She rolled off him, and sat down on her haunches.

Maru sat up cross-legged as well, wheezing. 'Props to your mother for devising the perfect stress-buster this morning.'

'Oh, shut up,' said Nila, laughing as well. 'What was teenage me even thinking?'

'Wouldn't we all like to know?' Maru said. 'Come on, Nila. You're dying to know yourself. Let's have that close literary analysis.'

'Maru, I will kill you.' She looked at his wristheld, enlarged the screen, and began to read.

> *In my opinion, Unclean Hands is a brilliant exploration of our human need for meaning. In the fictional city of Remala, meaning is under the absolute control of the party. They create the master narrative within which individual acts attain their meaning.*

She stopped. '*Wow*, I was a pretentious little twerp.'

'Go on, go on,' said Maru. 'I'm loving this.'

'Oh, might as well.'

In that context, killing a traitor to the revolution, on the command of the party, is the one, overarching act that gives meaning to the life of Juna. His entire sense of self, his idea of who he is, is bound up with that act, and what that act signifies within the totalising universe of the party. It's his own—if we can say—origin myth, the starting point for him to understand who he is, and what meaning his life has.

And that's why, when the party reverses stance two decades later, when the party now says that Heera was not a traitor but a patriot, a loyal son of the revolution, Juna's entire universe disintegrates. It is as if for the last twenty years, he has been living a lie—no, that he has been the author of the lie. Everything crumbles—who he is, why he has lived, what he has lived for.

Juma's death by suicide in the final scene is Karantha V.'s reminder to us all that individually or collectively, we cannot live without meaning.

I think he does a great job of it.

Nila's voice tailed off.

'That wasn't bad analysis, you know?' Maru said.

He received no answer. Maru looked up.

Nila's gaze had gone vacant. She was looking beyond his shoulder, at something in the distance.

'Nila?' he said.

She blinked once, but did not answer.

'Nila? What's wrong?'

'Maru,' she said. 'What have I done?'

19

Though the World Burn

A KNOCK ON THE CHAPTERHOUSE CHAMBER door.

Director Pulis turned from the mirror. 'Come in,' he said.

The door swung open. Nila stood on the threshold.

'Guardian,' Pulis said, frowning. 'Is this urgent? Less than two hours—'

'I'm aware,' said Nila. 'And it is.'

'Very well,' Pulis gestured to a chair, and took up one himself.

'Your deputy isn't here?'

'Not at the moment, no. She's briefing our assigned guardians. Why?'

'No reason.'

Sweat glistened on Nila's brow. Her hair was unkempt. When she spoke, her breath was short.

'Director Pulis. I've completed my investigation into the Jagat affair.'

He raised an eyebrow. 'Yes?'

'It's a little complicated, you see. I'd like to go through this with you. You are, of course, the director, and this is something—something from the past—that concerns you.'

'I'm listening.'

'Then walk back in time with me,' said Nila. 'It is a hundred years ago. A cool autumn morning in Peruma. Director Purul leaves the Directorate with his trusted secretary, Milana Maran. His destination: the Maidan. His plan: to address the citizens of Low Town. What he intends to speak of? Nobody knows. But people suspect. And talk. As the skimmer moves down Victory Road, they watch, from the balconies and rooftops of High Town. Now he's at the riverfront. He gets down with Milana, and they step into that borderland, the Bulwark Zone, out of sight of the cameras.

'And then the road is torn up. The impact doesn't kill the director, but it wounds him. Long before Intelligence Bureau—forbidden to travel this day with him—can reach him, before the smoke has cleared, there is a man. A young man, hair drawn back, a tint of purple around his lips. his name is Jagat. He draws his gun. The director starts to say something. Before he can finish, Jagat speaks. 'In the name of the Commune unborn, die.' He shoots. So ends the life of Director Purul. So changes the future of Peruma.'

'Why are you reciting history, Guardian?'

'This is one story, Director. Now I want you to hear another.' Nila paused, and then went on.

'How do we know this story, Director, in all its details? Who was travelling with Director Purul that day? Who was at his side when the bomb went off, and when the bullet struck?'

'Milana Maran's testimony was taken under voluntary consumption of a truth serum,' said Pulis.

'It was, yes. And what is that testimony, Director? It's funny how very different a written transcript is from hearing the real thing; the pauses, the inflections, the words that have been spliced together—something you wouldn't know, since you haven't been to the museum. Do you remember the prosecutor's exact question, Director? *You saw this man, with a gun? You* saw this man, *with* a gun. Who had the gun, Director? This man? Or the "you" that the sentence refers to?'

'What—'

'Let me finish. And now you will say, if it wasn't Jagat who held the gun, if it wasn't Jagat who shot the director, why was he even there on the bridge that morning, just when the director was busy getting shot? And after that, why did he go quietly to a sleep of death, with never a word in his defence? What kind of a man would do this? What kind of a man just accepts their own death in silence?

'A man, perhaps, who was due to die anyway. A man who was in the final stages of a cancer that was eating away his life. If you offered that man a deal, one that would cut short his doomed life by a few months but provide for his family for generations to come, wouldn't he take it? Wouldn't you?'

This time, as she paused, Pulis said nothing.

'And then you will ask, Director, if not Jagat, then who? One of those rebels, who used him as a cover? The Levellers? But why would the rebels want to murder the Douser of Fires, Director, the man with whom they had the greatest hope of a fair hearing, as opposed to whatever hardliner that would replace him were he to get killed? There was no revolution yet. There was no inflection point. In fact, they were all going to the Maidan that day to hear what Purul had to say.

'And what *did* Purul have to say? It's been there all these years in the Purul archives. You can't destroy it once it's been catalogued, so you've hidden it away from pesky interlopers, because you know that if Purul's promises come to light, even from a hundred years ago, it will tear open the borders of what is possible, what the Commune believes is possible. It will strengthen their hand. Because you know what he promised. And there's one constituency—*one* alone—that was going to be hurt by that promise. Hurt badly enough to eliminate him before he could speak a word of it in the Maidan. And it wasn't the Commune.

'So now walk back with me once again, Director. It is still a hundred years ago. A cool autumn morning in Peruma. Director Purul leaves the Directorate in an open-top skimmer, along with his trusted secretary, Milana Maran. His destination: the Maidan. His plan: to address the citizens of Low Town. What does he intend to speak about? It is all written in a decree that he has folded into a binder, tucked underneath his right arm. Property reforms on a scale never seen before in Peruma. Progressive, pragmatic Director Purul believes that this is the only way for the city to draw back from the knife's edge, to forestall revolution. It would mean great sacrifices from High Town, and that is why he has kept it secret from the Council.

'Purul has drafted the decree with the help of that same trusted secretary, Milana Maran. He has ensured the highest levels of secrecy. He has no reason to fear the Council, who do not have a clue about what he's going to do. And he has no reason to fear Low Town, because they will want to hear him. So he chooses to travel open-top, and keep all his security away.

'Little does he know. When he and Milana step into no-person's land, out of reach of the cameras, a bomb—sophisticated enough to be far beyond the reach of the technological capabilities available to Low Town—rips open the street, wounding him. As the smoke begins to clear, and Director Purul struggles to his feet, a figure stands over him. A figure with a gun in its hand.' Nila paused to draw a much-needed breath, and something fleeting flashed in her mind's eye.

'Traitor to High Town,' said Milana Maran. 'Die.'
'No,' said Purul. 'You don't know what you—'

'She shoots him. He falls. And then the last act of the drama, the act that has been planned ever since Purul first told Milana about his plans and she betrayed him to the Council. Upon the bridge, witnessing it all is Jagat, an inoffensive and apolitical young man from Low Town. He is unarmed, of course, as the Council was never going to trust a Low Towner with this task. There's only one thing about Jagat: the purple tint on the edge of his lips, the only outward signs of the cancer that has left him with only a few more months to live.

'To him, the Council had offered a simple deal: stand on the bridge, say the words that we will tell you to say, and then say nothing at all. You will be sent into the sleep of death, but your daughter, your children's children, for a hundred years, they will want for nothing.

'As deals go, it's a no-brainer. He takes it.

'For the corporation leaders on the Council, it's a no-brainer. Get rid of an overly progressive director. Blame it on Low Town, on those pesky revolutionaries, setting up an excuse for reprisals. Jagat will never talk. And Milana, in her testimony, under the truth serum, will scramble the sequence of events, so that every individual statement is true, and put together a tragic mosaic where the imagination of the listeners—and then the passage of time—pieces the story together. *You saw this man, with a gun*, the prosecutor says. *I saw this man, with a gun*, Milana replies. Everyone always thought that what she was saying was that she saw Jagat, and Jagat had a gun. But that isn't the only thing it can mean, can it, Director? *I saw Jagat, with a gun. I saw Jagat, I, with a gun.*' Both meanings. Trained for months to think in doublespeak that way, to speak in that way, and so, pass the truth serum. But you see, Director Pulis, she *never* says, "I saw Jagat kill Purul with a gun." Because he didn't.

'Except that the Council screwed up—*badly*,' Nila was breathing quickly now. 'They didn't know how far gone the revolution was, how Jagat's summary trial—it had to be done as quickly as possible, so he could be put away before he changed his mind—would have quite the opposite effect: Jagat the Martyr, Jagat the Falling Star, Jagat the symbol of the revolution. And so—and so, *Director*, the Council sacrificed an innocent man, and lost Peruma in the bargain. Talk about an own goal of historical significance.'

Now, as she paused, Pulis finally spoke. 'This is an impressive reconstruction. But it is all *very* hypothetical, Guardian, if you'll excuse me saying so.'

'Well, Director,' said Milana. 'Can you tell me why and how, one month before the assassination, stocks in the newly formed Peruma Mandalium Processing Company were registered in the name of Rimi, Jagat's daughter? And then this same Peruma Mandalium Processing Company was given an extremely lucrative mining contract one month *after* the revolution, sending its share price rocketing up twenty-fold? And why Rimi used that money to quietly move out of Low Town and buy a penthouse in the poshest part of the new north bank, where that family has lived ever since?'

'I—'

'Can you tell me why Jagat used the word "commune", which no revolutionary in Low Town had ever used for their own movement? Can you tell me why Milana Maran never revealed what Director Purul was going to speak about that day at the Maidan, but her annotations are on the document? Can you tell me why nobody appeared to ever notice the purple on Jagat's face, given how terrifying a thing mandilicosis cancer was a hundred years ago? And speaking of cancer, can you tell me what Operation Carbuncle—*your* Operation Carbuncle—might have been referring to, other than a very crass allusion to mandilicosis II-A, which was consuming Jagat's face?'

There was a long silence. Finally, Pulis leaned back in his chair, his fingers steepled. 'I see.'

'Do you, Director? What *do* you see?'

'I believe in the Pact of Forgetting,' said Pulis. 'I believe in moving on from what happened a century ago. But leaving that to one side, for my own part, Guardian, something never seemed quite right about the story of Unity Bridge. Because you're correct. Director Purul *was* progressive. He *was* a bridge-builder. The Douser of Fires. And your first instinct that day in the Directorate was right: we'd all convinced ourselves of the motive, reading *The Great Unravelling*, but it never really fit.' He paused for a moment. 'But Guardian, I presume you have some clinching evidence to back up some of these claims, other than the whole chain of circumstantial stuff that you've just told me?'

'I don't need to, Director,' Nila said. '*Beyond reasonable doubt*, remember? I have given you two versions of what happened that day, two equally plausible ones. That should be enough for a tribunal to review and acquit. Especially when the alternative is death.'

Pulis' face paled. 'Guardian,' he said, 'I don't know which way the tribunal will go on this. But before you make this case, I'd just ask you to think about the city, the Pact of Forgetting, and the possible consequences of—'

'—of bringing a long-dead martyr back to life on the eve of the Fifth Inflection Point, and what will happen the day after.' She finished for him. 'I know, Director. I remember. *If peace is based on a lie, what price will you pay to maintain that lie*, didn't you once say? And that's why I haven't finished yet.'

He raised an eyebrow.

'Martyr,' Nila said. '*To give testimony*. All these days I was trying to decode the meaning of his silence, little knowing that it was a fool's errand, because the silence actually meant nothing at all. Because, you know, Director, the Martyr was never a martyr to start with. But then, if he wasn't … what follows?'

'I—'

She held up a hand. 'One second, Director, before you start. Come with me, this time to the present day. Decades after the revolution, there is an uneasy equilibrium between what was once High Town and Low Town. They have their own autonomous governments, divided by the river. They live in their own way. When they engage for work, they engage on equal terms, through negotiation. High Town can no longer impose conditions of work on any sector of the economy. Just what the revolution wanted, just what the Charter envisioned. And yet, in some way or the other, the conflict continues. The Commune is in a bad way. The Charter of Peace and Unity has turned out to give them a worse deal than they thought. A lot depends on a forthcoming big case: *Council vs Commune*. But in the meantime, the Commune is split internally, cracked and splintered, coughing up structures of authority and hierarchy that they always claimed the revolution had destroyed. They are divided between an old guard and a younger group that believes they are straying from the true values of Jagat the Martyr. But in all that, there is one thing that unites them, one thing that they can rally around, one thing that prevents schism: the Martyr himself, and his legend.

'Jagat, the first anarchist. Their origin myth. In his name they united, in his name they continue to oppose you. His is the only statue in the Commune. His is the moment of silence before every meal. His is the lay and the litany. His is the name that they invoke when they challenge each other and when they challenge you. He gives them something to live for and something to die for: the Falling Star who sacrificed his life for an idea, the man who met his fate with silent acceptance rather than betray his comrades.

'Now what if it were to turn out, Director, that Jagat was no anarchist, no hero? What would happen if that legend were to die? If that legend were to die, if its meaning was to die, would the Commune have anything to live for?'

Director Pulis was staring intently at his fingers. Nila stood and looked down at him.

'How do you kill a legend, Director? Why, you bring it back to life. You destroy a martyr by taking away his martyrdom. Bring Jagat back to life, and Jagat the Martyr will die. Tell everyone that he sacrificed himself not out of loyalty to the unborn Commune—not even out of a desire to protect someone else—but for that most personal, most selfish of human reasons—to benefit his family. And then the Commune's origin myth is gone. Tell everyone that not only did he act selfishly, but that for generations after, his family have been benefiting from the mandalium mines, from the very arrangement that has kept the Commune impoverished under the Charter, and they won't just stop loving him, they will start to hate him. Tell them that the silence they celebrate is not a martyr's silence that speaks and bears witness, but the silence of cowardice—and their entire founding story will crumble. And with its origin myth gone, with the meaning of its birth is gone, with the hero a traitor, soon the Commune will be gone, destroying itself from the inside. Or at least, that's what you hope, isn't it?'

'Guardian—Nila—'

'And that's how you planned it,' she went on over him. 'You couldn't do it yourself because you have no legitimacy in the Commune's eyes. It would have to be a relative of Jagat's who would need to reopen the case, someone to whom you'd drop a hint of Jagat's innocence. And it would have to be through the guardians, with our reputation for obsessive impartiality.

'But if you went through the Executive Committee, they'd laugh at you. So you'd nudge Ani to go to the Well. You'd drop the name of a young, desperate junior, looking to make a name for themselves, to whom this case would seem like a gift from heaven. And *then* you'd leave a breadcrumb trail, subtle enough to make her believe that this was *her* doing, that she was finding out things on her own. And you'd pretend to be standing in her way, resisting her attempts, but never enough to really stop her, pretending to threaten her but never enough so that she'd really be in danger, just so that all the while she'd think she was fighting you and winning—down to this last moment where you pretended to be concerned about stability and peace. But what you *really* want is for me to march into the tribunal right now, for Jagat to be revived this evening … and for the legend to die before the day is done.'

She sank back into her seat.

'It was you, wasn't it? It was you who pretended to be hostile towards me, so I thought that I was fighting you. You arranged for me to know about the false bottom in the archives through your deputy, who *also* pretended to be fighting you. You planted that story in the *High Town Herald* about Ani's hereditary shares in the Mandalium Processing Company, knowing that I would read it. You even orchestrated that chase-and-rescue last night, making me think that the Directorate had its factions, so that when I "discovered" the truth, I'd never once suspect that all along, you *wanted* me to discover the truth. That you were leading me by the nose towards it, and making me think I was finding the path on my own.

'Bloody gods, Director. You even picked me not because you thought I was some genius pupil, but because you knew my chamber partner is obsessive about the history of cancers, didn't you? So that our discovery of mandilicosis II-A would just seem … natural. Oh, and speaking of cancer, was there ever an Apoptosis Plan, Director, or was that just something you fed the Commune rebels, knowing that they would feed it to me and make me believe even more that the Directorate needed Jagat to die? I'm betting on the latter.'

Pulis had not moved.

'And now we know all that, Director,' Nila continued, 'Now we know what this case is really about—not the truth, not justice, not Jagat's life, but about your desire to smash the Commune once and for all, finish the job your ancestors couldn't finish a hundred years ago; finally win the war that they lost—now that we know all that, I'd like you to give me one, *one* good reason why I should not go into that tribunal right now, tell them that my investigations have yielded nothing new and that there is no reason to reopen this century-old case.'

There was another silence between them. Aeons passed.

Finally, Pulis stirred.

'Is that what you're thinking of doing?'

'Do you think I wouldn't, Director? Do you think I'll stop out of fear for my career, fear of whatever action the Executive Committee might take against me if they decide I've embarrassed the Confederation before the world? Do you think I'm afraid of being a second Naina? Can you look me in the eye and say you believe I'm such a coward?'

'I have never believed you're a coward,' said Pulis. 'Anything but.' He lowered his gaze. 'What you choose to tell them, of course, is yours to decide. But since you began this with two plausible stories about what happened this day, a century ago, let's walk down that road a little more. Let's take two stories about today.

'One is the story you told me. Of a cynical director and a cynical Council trying to destroy a myth by reviving a man, playing their own factional game against the Commune. It's a good story, I'll admit. Strong. Convincing. I'm not going to persuade you to disbelieve it.

'But I will give you an alternative, just like you gave me an alternative. Let's start where you broke off the first time. Almost a hundred years have passed since the day that Director Purul was shot. A curious individual—let's call him P—is also a dabbler in history. His position allows him access to all the archives. P is particularly curious about that point in history when the fate of Peruma changed forever, and intrigued by the mysterious silence that a certain man maintained through his trial. P goes digging, much like you, and then it all unravels, as it has for you. P realises that the man was innocent. He did not deserve to die.

'But above all else, because it is still possible to change the past, he deserves to live.

'P knows that there is only one way to achieve this: a retrial through the guardians, who didn't even exist when the man was sentenced to the sleep of death. But he also knows that if the process is initiated by himself or anyone close to him, it will become an immediate political football between Council and Commune. That leaves him with just one choice: that it be done through kin of the accused, and through the guardians, known, as you so rightly observe, for their obsessive impartiality. But it can only work if everyone involved genuinely *believes* they are acting independently, until the very end.

'So you see, Guardian? Needs, must. How else could it happen? Was there any other way? You tell me.' He spread out his arms.

'You ambushed me,' Nila whispered. 'It was an ambush case, and I—'

Pulis threw up a hand. 'I haven't finished. There's one other thing that P finds out which you couldn't possibly have known. Jagat's consent to taking responsibility for the assassination of Purul *was taken under false assurance.* The Council knew that there had been a breakthrough in mandilicosis II-A cancer research, that in all likelihood a cure would be announced soon. They withheld that fact from Jagat. Had they told him, what might his choice have been?'

Now he did fall silent.

And now Nila finished her unfinished sentence.

'You're lying.'

'Perhaps I am,' the director said. 'But is it *beyond reasonable doubt?'*

Nila stared at him.

'And so, Guardian, you now have two stories about today. What will you do? Should it even matter? Isn't the only thing that matters that you have two stories about what happened, and that one is more likely than the other? But likely or unlikely, as long as there are two stories, doesn't Jagat deserve to live? And are you the one who will deny him life?'

'To bring back Jagat to life, and kill the Commune—that is what you want me to do?'

'How do you know that is what will happen? After all, how did you solve the peacemaker's dilemma, Guardian?'

She felt nausea lick the back of her throat.

Pulis' voice was as quiet as ever. 'Radical uncertainty, remember? We can't know the consequences of our actions. That's why we shouldn't play the gods. And that's also why we shouldn't live with the ghosts that our ancestors made, the ghosts of their cowardice, their venality, their violence. In a few minutes, we're going to walk out of this room, walk down the corridor. I will turn right and you will turn left. Both of us will be going into battle with the ghosts that haunt us, that haunt Peruma still. And so, what will you do, Guardian? Perpetuate the lie, the dishonesty, the violence? Keep Peruma frozen forever in the illusion of what happened that day a hundred years ago, so that we can never move on? Send Jagat to a permanent death, an unjust death? What is the lesson of *No More Regrets*, that story you love so much?' He looked at her pendant, and she knew what the next words would be.

'*No judgement of the past*,' said Pulis calmly. '*No weight of the future*. Remember?'

'You've manipulated me,' she said. 'You've choreographed my every step. All this while, I've had no agency over any of this. Until now. Until this moment.'

'Let's say I have,' Pulis said. 'Should Jagat pay the price for that? Is the justice you want to serve to me—and through me, to the Council—the justice that calls upon you to preserve the Commune, to preserve the myth of Jagat's martyrdom? Will you weigh that in the balance, Guardian, against one human life? And when you do, which will be the heavier?'

They heard footsteps approaching.

Pulis nodded towards the door. 'I think it's time.'

She stood, in a daze, and backed away from him. The door opened, and the rest of the Council entered, fanning around Pulis. She caught sight of Maiyam. For the briefest of moments, their eyes locked. Then Maiyam dropped her gaze and looked away.

'Thank you for coming this morning, Guardian,' said Pulis. 'I wish you well in your arguments. I hope that … justice will be done.'

He left the second half of the sentence hanging between them, a thread that stretched—and snapped as Nila backed away further, until she was out of the room, and into the corridor. People were milling about excitedly. Many were proceeding gradually to the left, where in the Grand Chamber, *Council vs Commune* was due to be heard. There were a few who were moving to the right, to Tribunal Chamber II.

'Nila …'

Maru's voice in her earpiece. They'd both forgotten to disable it.

'You heard that?'

'Every word.'

'What do I do?'

There was a long silence. Finally, Maru said the dreaded words.

'I don't know.'

'Dammit,' she whispered into the earpiece. 'Just tell me what to do, Maru!'

'I can't! I don't know!'

'Look,' said Nila, 'Look. I am a guardian, aren't I? I have to make the best possible case for my client. That's my *literal* job, isn't it?'

'Even in an ambush case?'

But it wasn't Jagat who ambushed me, she almost cried out. Mechanically, attuned to a sense of time, she was walking down the passageway, shifting towards the right, towards Tribunal Chamber II. People passed her by, wishing her good luck or, among the closer of her friends, thumping her on the back. She did not notice.

'You can't say it's your job, Nila,' Maru said softly. 'We are not spared the responsibility of … of …'

'… of the consequences of our actions,' Nila gritted her teeth. 'I know. And what are these consequences? Can we work through them together?'

'Nila, I was thinking,' said Maru. 'On historical inevitability and moral luck. If the world that was born that day was really born of an illusion—'

His voice cut off.

'Dammit!' Nila exploded, remembering too late that, much like the Directorate, the jammers began to operate as you got close to the tribunal chambers. 'What were you going to tell me, Maru?'

Now she was truly alone.

She was just about to step over the threshold into Chamber II when she felt a hand on her shoulder.

'Guardian Nila, where are you going?'

She turned. It was Shurat, one of the senior guardians.

'My—my case,' she stammered, 'It's here—'

'Didn't they tell you?' he said. 'You've been reassigned. You're arguing in Grand Chamber now.' He pointed towards the left, towards the huge baize doors through which people were still pouring in, into the amphitheatre-shaped hall beyond.

'What?'

'We received more than five thousand applications for access yesterday. There was no choice but to switch.' He nudged her gently. 'Go well, Guardian. Good luck.'

Nila gulped. The throng parted for her as she walked, suddenly hushed, so that she heard her own footsteps upon the floor.

'Nila!'

A known, familiar voice. She turned. It was Ghorge.

'Good luck,' said Ghorge. 'I'm rooting for you. We all are.'

'Guardian!' There was something at the back of her mind, a thought clamouring to be shaped into words, something she had to ask *now*, or it would be too late. She stepped towards him, her voice low. 'Guardian, I have a question.'

Ghorge raised an eyebrow. 'What is it?'

'You remember our conversation that evening about moral luck?'

'Yes, of course.'

'Tell me, Guardian. What were you actually supposed to *do* if you got … morally unlucky? According to the philosophers.'

'Well,' said Ghorge, 'that was the point. If you were unlucky enough to be in that situation, it didn't really matter anymore what you did. The only question was whether you could use bad luck to absolve yourself of being judged for what you'd done. The Old Empire decided that it could. For the rest of us … I guess we cannot know until our moment comes.'

'Ah.'

Ghorge looked as if he was about to ask something more, but then only nodded. 'Good luck, Nila,' he said again softly.

She nodded back at him, and walked on until she was at the door. She stepped over the threshold, and into the amphitheatre of the Grand Chamber, just in time to see the prosecutor, and Subba from the Executive Committee, the presiding arbitrator, enter behind her.

'You ready, Guardian Nila?' The prosecutor said, encouragingly. She'd always been a good woman, Nila remembered. Encouraging to juniors.

'I am.'

Automatically, she smoothed her uniform and followed them down the aisle. There was the speaking rostrum, nestled in the little cavity below. At a slightly elevated level, there was the semi-circular table where the arbitrators sat. And facing them, at a level higher still, there were the rows and rows of seats where the people sat, waiting.

As she headed to the end of the aisle and turned left from the rostrum, to the defence counsel's seat, she saw Maru, who'd just entered at the back, watching her, now no longer able to speak.

Their eyes met.

He nodded, just once. *Whatever you decide, I'll be with you.*

She sat. The amphitheatre was at capacity. She scanned the crowd. Ambassadors of the five independent cities were seated at the front. Behind them, the amphitheatre was split down the middle: High Town on the right, Commune on the left. On the High Town side, she saw Director Pulis sitting up ahead, in close conversation with Maiyam, who was next to him. Nila clenched her teeth. Her eyes travelled left. At the back, high above, she saw Anam and Asana, leaning forward, looking at her. She cast her gaze down. Vani was at the front.

Waves of guilt washed over her. Three nights ago, the administrator had tried to get her to understand this. Nila, obsessed with the prospect of failure, had thought she had taken the logic to its conclusion, seeing the set-up for what it was—before her own arrogance had stopped her from *truly* taking the logic to its conclusion, and realising that the set-up was not to make her lose, but to make her win.

She tore her gaze away from Vani's quiet expression, and stared resolutely in front of her, focusing on one protruding wood shaving from the rostrum, making it the centre of her world. Eternities passed. She felt eyes upon her, thousands of eyes. Sweat began to bead at the base of her scalp and trickle down her neck. She ignored it.

'Silence, please.' The voice sounded all around the amphitheatre.

Slowly, the buzz quietened.

Nila risked a glance up. Everything was set. The Grand Chamber was full. Five thousand were in their seats. The prosecutor across from her. The three arbitrators on the bench, in their place, the copies of her files and documents on the table. The great banners of Council, of Commune and of the Confederation, streamed behind them, all the way up to the domed roof.

'We will now commence the live stream,' the tribunal master said, from the side.

With a click, the screens came on, and the broadcast began across all the cities of the subcontinent.

Her hands began to tremble violently. She hid them underneath her desk.

'*Jagat R. vs Directorate,* application for review and retrial, set down for hearing,' Subba spoke from the bench. 'We will first take up the application for stay of execution, for consideration and decision in chambers.'

Fuck, that procedural application! To put this case into the hands of the Commune. She'd forgotten it entirely. If it succeeded, there would be no further argument. Hope began to flutter in her heart, beating wildly against the bars.

She looked up at Maru again. His fingers were locked into each other.

'I will now pronounce the order, on behalf of the tribunal.

'This application asks us to grant a stay upon the deactivation of the applicant's cryobox, in accordance with the automatic operation of law. Section 43(d)(5) of the Peruma criminal code stipulates that a sleep of death sentence is to last for a period of one hundred years, on the expiry of which the concerned cryobox shall be deactivated. Applicant argues that, in light of the pending case of *Council of Peruma vs Commune of Peruma: Regarding Certain Questions of Great Public Importance Concerning the Interpretation of the Charter of Peace and Unity*, this tribunal order that the final execution of the sentence stand suspended until further notice.

'Applicant bases this argument on the "non-trivial possibility" that, should the Commune of Peruma prevail in the aforementioned case, the sleep of death sentence shall be excised from the criminal code in the subsequent renegotiation of the Charter, with retrospective effect. Counsel argues that in light of the irreversibility of cryobox deactivation—in other words, death—all the requirements of a stay are fulfilled.'

Hope rose. *This is a political case. The tribunal doesn't like political cases. Easier to evade than to decide, to send the ball back into the court of Commune and Council.*

'We have carefully considered the argument. We are impressed by its originality and its ingenuity. However, in our mind, it must fail, for the simple reason that *this* tribunal is barred from taking cognisance of parallel, pending proceedings before another tribunal, and whatever consequences that might flow therefrom, and of whatever nature they might be.

This application, therefore, deserves to be dismissed, and is accordingly dismissed.'

Nila closed her eyes.

Live by procedure, die by procedure.

When she opened them again, Maru had his head in his hands.

'We will, therefore, move to a hearing of the main application,' Subba said. 'That is, the application for review and reversal of the judgement and sentence in *Directorate vs*

Jagat R. and the revival of the applicant from the sentence of cryosleep.'

Near the ceiling, she saw the large screens capturing the rostrum and the bench.

Through Council and Commune, from Dominion Hill, to the river and down to the sea.

They would be watching.

The moment she had been waiting for.

The headlines that would write themselves.

Out of the corner of her eye, she saw her mother enter the chamber and take the last vacant seat.

The prosecutor looked at her and nodded.

'Is Guardian Nila ready to present her case?'

Nila stood. She walked forward to the rostrum. She stood there, her back to the crowd, her face to the arbitrators. They were opening the first of her documents, perusing her index, their brows furrowed.

In her mind's eye, one last time, the cryochamber appeared. Within it lay the man who seemed as if he were merely asleep, *ernian* on his still features. Nila blinked it away.

She placed both her hands, palms down, on the rostrum. The world seemed to slow down. The swirling in her head turned into a roar, blotting out everything, and as she opened her mouth to speak, all thought flashed away.

Epilogue

THE BLUE-CRESTED CORMORANT PERCHED momentarily upon the balcony that extended from the Hedgehog's Needle. She darted her neck from side to side, her silhouette framed against the declining day. Then she plunged into space, dropping sharply to skim above the ash-grey Urai.

'*The birds fly in Peruma's sky*,' said Nila softly. '*The everyday river/unmoved by human acts/flows on*.'

They watched the flight of the cormorant eastwards along the water, past the empty Unity Bridge, and into the oncoming night. A few lights glimmered in the crystalline fastnesses of High Town. The skylanes were empty. South of the river, the Commune's weave was still. It was as if the two halves of Peruma were gathering their breath.

'It's so quiet,' said Nila.

'Well, you silenced two cities today,' Maru said.

'The silence before the storm,' said Nila.

Over the western horizon, a skimmer approached them, gradually acquiring form and shape.

'Oh, right on time,' said Nila. 'Before the world begins again tomorrow—without me.'

Maru looked at the skimmer, and then at her. 'There's no changing your mind, then?'

'This is the only other decision,' said Nila, 'that I have *ever* been sure about.'

'Nila,' said Maru, 'this morning before the tribunal, you did what you believed was the right thing. The consequences are not of your making—'

'Maru,' she held up a hand, and he subsided. 'We've grown too old over the last week for false comfort. I made my choice thinking *only* of the consequences. And now the future will decide whether to absolve me. Moral luck, remember?'

'Going into exile will not write you out of the story.'

'No, but it will take me off the stage. I am all emptied, Maru. I need to go somewhere far—out of this future that I've made, for my own sake, until it is resolved—one way or another. Being here, every single moment will remind me—'

'You didn't choose this.'

Nila smiled faintly. 'Every act leading up to that moment was a choice, no matter how illusory, until there weren't any left anymore.'

The skimmer came to float by the balcony. It was not quite the sleek model that Ani had given her, but it was bigger, equipped for longer journeys. On its side, white paint bore the words: CHEMUR SKIMMER RENTALS.

'Give me a hand with this, will you,' said Nila, bending down to her rucksack. Maru helped her pick it up. '*Whew.* What have you got in here, bricks?'

'Well, I don't know how long I'll be away.' They heaved it into the skimmer. 'But let me unburden it of some heaviness.' She fished around at the top, and took out two thin envelopes. Maru raised an eyebrow.

'His wristheld has been dead since morning,' said Nila. 'I don't think he wants to talk to me, after what happened. Probably nobody in the Commune does, to be honest. But will you pass him these letters instead?'

'Of course.' Maru took them from her. 'Any message?'

'He can open the first whenever he wishes to. It is an apology. The second, six months from now; it is my account of the events of last week. The third letter, to be opened a year later, is a justification of my choice, if he needs one. After *that*, if he still wants to, he can come and find me.'

'Where are you going to go?' said Maru.

'Chemur first, it's just an overnight journey. Stop there, take stock. And from there, whichever city has some use for a guardian with a flair for procedural tricks, I guess,' Nila chuckled. 'It's not that they won't know who I am, after today. Don't worry, Maru, I won't do our skylane trip to the white cliffs and the temple spires without you—but it may just be a little delayed.' She turned to him and unclasped the pendant from her neck. She placed it in his palm, and closed his fingers around it.

'What do you want me to do with this?' said Maru.

'Hold on to it as long as the future is in balance,' said Nila. 'If it looks like I'm going to get morally lucky, keep it—I'll be back. But if this world actually burns because of my decision …' she looked over the balcony, to the river far below.

'Understood,' said Maru.

'And write to me,' said Nila. 'I'll be following what happens from afar, but I need your voice to assess it for me.

I know it's too much to hope for an ending, but maybe I can find some closure.'

'I'll write to you,' said Maru, 'until you feel you can return.'

'That is no longer in my hands,' said Nila. 'After everything was.'

They hugged each other. Nila turned and boarded the skimmer. It rose gently in the air. She turned it south. The skylane to Chemur would take her over the Commune, the Commune whose fate she had changed with a few irrevocable words that morning, spoken before a tribunal, before the eyes of a whole subcontinent.

There were still no lights in that weave. The Commune was silent. For the moment, it had nothing to say to her. The future would decide if it would.

'Goodbye, Maru.'

'Go well, Nila.'

He watched her disappear into the Peruman night.

Appendix

MORE INSPIRATIONS THAN I CAN REMEMBER have constituted the melange from which this story eventually emerged. This appendix is a brief and incomplete tribute, with apologies for the inevitable omissions.

Events

The assassination of Chancellor Purul, with which the story begins, is loosely modelled on the assassination of Tsar Alexander II in 1881, by the Russian Narodniks. To know more about the circumstances of the assassination, and the life and times of the revolutionary men and women who planned and executed it, interested readers can take a look at Yuri Trifonov's beautiful novel, *The Impatient Ones* (1973).

The central inspiration for the story is the Paris Commune of 1871. The ascent—and destruction—of the Paris Commune has left us with one of the biggest 'what ifs' of modern history: *what if* the Commune had survived? This is not, of course, an alternate history novel, but I did let my imagination run free a bit with the 'what if' question. There is a lot of literature about the Paris Commune (never enough!); the works I've found most compelling are Prosper-Olivier Lissagaray's *The History of the Paris Commune of 1871*, Karl Marx's *The Civil War in France* and the graphic novel *The Red Virgin and the Vision of Utopia.*

In a smaller way, another inspiration is the lesser-known Guangzhou Commune of 1927, another short-lived attempt at a 'workers' republic' established at the peak of the Chinese revolution. Interested readers can consult Nym Wales's lyric biography of the Korean Revolutionary leader Kim San, called *The Song of Arirang*, for a feel of what the Guangzhou Commune was like.

The Great French Revolution also forms one of the historical backdrops to the story. The first few years of republican Peruma—set out in the chronology, and alluded to by Meera—very loosely track the fate of the French revolution before Napoleon effectively finished it off. The exchange between High Town and Low Town at the beginning of Chapter Two—'Is this a revolt?'; 'No, this is a revolution'—is riffed off Hannah Arendt's account of the French revolution.

The peacemaker's dilemma is not based on one particular historical event, but it draws from post-conflict pacts that were made in certain Latin American countries, where the price of peace after a long civil war was (controversially) a general amnesty for past atrocities, and where societies had to grapple with the kinds of questions about justice and peace that are raised in this novel. One of the most famous instances of this was the peace agreement between the Colombian government and the FARC rebels, where the Colombian Constitutional Court struck down parts of the agreement; so, there is some precedent for Nila's resolution of the peacemaker's dilemma! The form of the peacemaker's dilemma itself is not related to an actual, historical event, but readers would have spotted the similarities with Star Trek's famous Kobayashi Maru, another seemingly 'unsolvable' test with an ethical conflict at its core.

The occasionally mentioned 'Pact of Forgetting' is a nod to the controversial *Pacto del Olvido* in Spain, where all sides of the political spectrum agreed to avoid discussing the legacy of the dictator, Franco, after his death in 1975.

The central debate in the *Council vs Commune* case echoes debates about how—and to what extent—foundational Charters or constitutions can be altered by later generations. The term I use—'the basic structure'—is borrowed from that world of constitutional law, but it felt quite at home in the language of a speculative fiction novel. Some of the arguments that Nila rehearses with her colleagues broadly echo the arguments for and against the basic structure, which have been made before constitutional courts across the world.

There are, of course, many little easter eggs that have to do with contemporary Indian politics and law scattered throughout the book, which I'll leave for readers to discover for themselves.

Concepts

The concept of moral luck—a foundational pillar of the story—was first articulated in a debate between the philosophers Bernard Williams and Thomas Nagel, in the pages of the *Aristotelian Society* journal, in 1976. It has been debated at great length over the last half-century, and interested leaders can consult the very accessible entry on the topic in *The Stanford Encyclopaedia of Philosophy*, freely available online.

The argument that President Mehmandost Naram makes to Maru in his chamber is a microcosm of Nila's own explanation of how she solves the peacemaker's dilemma to Director Pulis, and goes back to a way of thinking about laws and rules that we find in the work of the philosophers John Rawls and Joseph Raz. In an essay called 'Two Concepts of Rules', for example, Rawls argues that the essence of a rule is that the reasons for and against an action have already been weighed up in the formulation of the rule, and that the essence of following a rule is that it spares us from having to redo that calculation in deciding how to act in a particular situation.

The skimmer-for-hire rule is a riff off the lawyer's most prized shibboleth—the 'cab rank rule'—which (to put it simply) forbids lawyers from declining to take a case just because they might not agree with the position their client wants them to advocate.

Anarchism

In a novel where anarchists play a prominent role, references drawn from the history of anarchism are scattered through the pages.

'There is no such thing as harmless power' refers to a quote made famous by the great Ukrainian anarchist, Nestor Makhno. For readers interested in knowing further, Charlie Allison's *No Harmless Power: The Life and Times of the Ukrainian Anarchist Nestor Makhno* is a fantastic book, and its observations about heroes, martyrs and revolution have informed several themes in this story. 'Heroes betray us, and we betray ourselves by having them' is a tribute to Michael Moorcock, one of the very few fantasy writers who took anarchism seriously in his novels. The original quote is from his essay titled 'Starship Stormtroopers', which explores the presence of fascistic and authoritarian themes in science fiction: 'Heroes betray us. By having them, in real life, we betray ourselves.' The Commune's slogan—'Building the new in the ruins of the old'—refers to the idea of prefiguration, one of the sub-currents of anarchist thought. It broadly refers to the fostering of anarchist practices and ways of being *within* existing economic and social structures.

The Commune's street names are the names of some of the poems of Rimbaud, who was intimately involved with the Paris Commune. Readers interested in the intersection of poetry and urban space in the Paris Commune can consult Kristin Ross' fantastic book, *The Emergency of Social Space: Rimbaud and the Paris Commune.*

Of course, the influence of anarchism upon this novel goes beyond literary tributes. The Commune's architecture is modelled upon anarchist philosophies of urban planning (interested readers can consult Paul Dobraszczyk's *Architecture and Anarchism: Building without Authority*, for a flavour). The Commune's governing and administrative structure is likewise inspired by anarchist blueprints. And the Commune's own internal debates mirror debates around power and authority in anarchist history, as well as certain disputes in the history of Council communism. Some of the specifics—that existence is resistance, or the need to decentralise the mind—echo some of the testimonies of surviving communards, recorded in Mitchell Abidor's *Voices of the Paris Commune*.

Intertextuality

Unclean Hands—the play that finally gets Nila to understand what has been happening—is a tribute to Jean-Paul Sartre's famous play, *Dirty Hands* (1948). The two are thematically similar, but I depart in some respects from the script of Sartre's play. Of course, the actual B.V. Karanth (1929–2002)—the famous Kannada playwright—had nothing to do with either play, although he wrote a lot of brilliant theatre himself. Nor, to the best of my knowledge, has *Dirty Hands* ever been performed at Bangalore's Rangashankara theatre.

The theory of the inflection points of history, and the passage from *The Great Unravelling* that both Pulis and Vani cite to Nila about historical determinism, are informed by Bini Adamczak's *Yesterday's Tomorrow: On the Loneliness of Communist Specters and the Reconstruction of the Future*. *Yesterday's Tomorrow* traces its own 'inflection points' of twentieth-century left-wing history, the choices faced, and imagines the impossible futures that might have been. I read the book just before editing the manuscript, and it helped me give more concrete words to the intuitions behind these two ideas.

Sanya's lament for Purul follows the form and structure of W.H. Auden's *In Memory of W.B. Yeats*. Mehmandost Naram's sarcastic jibe at Nila's desire to right unrightable wrongs is a tribute to *The Impossible Dream* song from *The Man of La Mancha*. Chancellor Purul's self-chosen epitaph—'What I shall leave will not be worth a tragedy'—is the last line of Zbigniew Herbert's 'Elegy of Fortinbras', in which a dying Fortinbras reflects upon how, after all the heroes (such as Hamlet) have had their tragic ends, it has fallen to him to clean up the mess, live an ordinary life, and die an ordinary death.

I learned about the etymology of the word 'martyr' from Sofia Samatar's *The White Mosque*. The description of the Commune from across Unity Bridge also owes something to Samatar's description of the city of Bukhara, in the same book.

Nila's image of cupping the world in her hands is a tribute to the great Palestinian writer, Ghassan Kanafani, who has one of his characters talk about the need to make the world smaller, and to fit it within one's hands, in order to go on living.

Nila's description of her mother—that she always knows, with certainty, what the fight is about, and who she's fighting about—echoes Yasmin el-Rifae's account of the early days of the 2011 Egyptian Revolution in *Radius: A Story of Feminist Revolution*. So do the observations about the weight of the revolution, and how it impacts personal relationships.

Anam's plea to Nila—*don't let him die*—echoes a similar plea made by Chinua Achebe in reference to the Nigerian revolutionary poet, Christopher Okigbo, referenced in Obi Nwakanma's beautiful biography, *Thirsting for Sunlight*.

Maru's misdirection to President Mehmandost Naram in order to make him yield up the cryochamber order is very loosely inspired from a particularly dramatic scene in the *Wuxia* television show, *Nirvana in Fire*. *Nirvana in Fire* sets up a deliciously thrilling tension through a series of traps and counter-traps that play out as a clock ticks away, and I wanted to try and replicate a hint of that through this scene.

The name of Purul's samadhi—*Forever Undecided*—is a tribute to Raymond Smullyan's puzzle book about Kurt Godel's incompleteness theorem, which carries the same name. I've always been fascinated by the idea that there might be truths that it is simply impossible to prove—a theme that runs through this novel as well.

'Rise and be born again with me' is a line from Ariel Dorfman's *Heading North, Looking South*, and a reference to Salvador Allende's peaceful Chilean revolution. Staying with Latin America, 'I will return, and I will be millions' ('Volveré y Seré Millones') is a phrase originally attributed to Túpac Amaru II, the Peruvian indigenous leader who led a rebellion against the Spanish, and was executed. It is one of the more recognisable revolutionary invocations in the continent today.

'Defence counsel for the damned' riffs off John A. Farrell's biography of Clarence Darrow, *Attorney for the Damned*. In some ways, Nila is a Darrow-esque figure: insisting that she is only doing her job, while nonetheless grappling with the ethical questions at the heart of wielding a weapon like the law.

Towards the end, Pulis asking Nila to weigh the Commune's potential destruction against the value of one human life is a tribute to the ending of the original anarchist SF novel, Ursula Le Guin's *The Dispossessed*.

And finally, it's always fun to indulge in a self-referential easter egg. *Waiting for the Witnesses* is a story that I wrote for the July 2024 issue of *Grimdark Magazine*, which is available online. Nila has slightly imperfect recall about the story's details, but she remembers the core of it accurately!

Others

The architecture of the Tribunal Grand Chamber is loosely inspired by the South African Constitutional Court, where audience seats dip towards the rostrum, and the judges' seats are just below the level of the street: an architectural reminder that justice ought to serve the people.

There actually does exist a 'Party of the Institutional Revolution' and it was the governing party in Mexico for many years.

'Between equal right, force will decide' paraphrases a line from Karl Marx's *Capital*, referring to the struggle between capitalists and workers over the length of the working day. It is used in a similar sense, although in a different context, in Naina L.'s open letter. Speaking of Naina, her 'appeal to the intelligence of a future day' is a line used by a tradition of dissenting judges in significant cases, tracing its lineage back to the US Supreme Court Justice Charles Evan Hughes.

The briefly-referenced 'Zutiste Collective' that is responsible for the Commune's street art, is a tip of the hat to the anarchic collective of French poets, painters and musicians that met in Paris soon after the fall of the Paris Commune, who referred to themselves as the Zutistes.

The Levellers were a seventeenth-century movement in England which advocated for radical egalitarianism, much, much ahead of their time. The classic work about them probably remains Christopher Hill's *The World Turned Upside Down* (1972).

Acknowledgements

IT ALWAYS TAKES A VILLAGE TO MAKE A BOOK. More people than I can count read some or many of the multiple drafts that this novel went through, in whole or in fragments. Thank you to Gauri, Sanya, Neeraja, Asawari, Pranavi, Essa, Prashanth, Pritesh, Amal, Krittika, Vinita, Rahul, Narayani, Madhubala (thanks also for *Yesterday's Tomorrow!*), Nishi, Tania, Samit—and to anyone whom I've forgotten, I promise to make it up to you.

Thank you to the *Writing Musketeers* WhatsApp group for helping to maintain sanity despite the writing industry trying every moment to deprive you of it; to the Delhi Science Fiction Reading Circle for our monthly meetings; and to my extended family at *Strange Horizons* for everything.

I could not have asked for better, or more caring treatment for the book than what Westland gave it. Thank you to Karthika and Ajitha for believing in it from the beginning; to Sanjana for such a thorough editing job and for the good humour in puzzling through the various anarchist side quests that the manuscript kept going down; to Mukul for doing a fantastic job with the typesetting and layout of the text; to Saurabh for the cover, to Shivani for the wonderful and creative marketing ideas; and to all the staff at Westland. Thank you also to the printers and the distributors who make the existence of this book, and all books, possible.

And to all the anarchists—some remembered, many forgotten—who've struggled to 'build the new in the ruins of the old' and left us a language and a legacy that we can now draw upon in our stories: thank you.

INTRODUCING IF, A HOME FOR SPECULATIVE FICTION BOOKS. OUR LOGO INCORPORATES MANY OF OUR HOPES FOR THESE BOOKS. THE OPENING OF DOORS TO OTHER WORLDS. MULTIVERSES. PLANETS. TRAVELS. LIGHT AND DARK. OTHER LIVES, MULTITUDES, DIVERSITY. QUESTS AND QUESTIONS. ROOTS SEARCHING THE EARTH AND PARTICLES SHOOTING THROUGH THE STARS.